L.A. Rimer is a pseudonym for an attorney
who lives and works in Chicago, Illinois.

To my family…

L.A. Rimer

# CHASING AFTER THE WIND

AUSTIN MACAULEY PUBLISHERS™

LONDON * CAMBRIDGE * NEW YORK * SHARJAH

**Ordering Information**
Quantity sales: Special discounts are available on quantity purchases by corporations, associations, and others. For details, contact the publisher at the address below.

**Publisher's Cataloging-in-Publication data**
Rimer, L.A.
Chasing After the Wind

ISBN 9781649790415 (Paperback)
ISBN 9781649790422 (ePub e-book)

Library of Congress Control Number: 2022918998

www.austinmacauley.com/us

First Published 2022
Austin Macauley Publishers LLC
40 Wall Street,33rd Floor, Suite 3302
New York, NY 10005
USA

mail-usa@austinmacauley.com
+1 (646) 5125767

# Ecclesiastes 4:4 (NIV)

"And I saw that all toil and all achievement spring from one person's envy of another. This too is meaningless, a chasing after the wind."

# One

After 22 years of marriage, Isabelle Owen's stomach still tensed when she heard the front door open and her husband, Clem, enter their dilapidated house that set on a muddy lot behind their one pump gas station.

Clem tromped through the house, tracking snow and mud across Isabelle's clean floors. He tossed his filthy snow-covered coat across the back of a kitchen chair, grabbed a beer out of the refrigerator, and walked into their small living room. Still wearing his oily coverall, he flopped down on the sagging couch and propped his feet on the coffee table. After a couple long pulls on his beer, Clem turned on the television to watch the local news and weather. He particularly liked the curvy, young, weather gal, Dewy Raines. With her cantaloupe sized breasts, tiny waist, and rounded bottom, Clem was often too distracted ogling her to listen to the weather report.

Clem didn't care for sports, which followed the weather report, so he turned the television off and finished his beer. He belched loudly, scratched his crotch, farted twice, and headed into the kitchen.

Isabelle busied herself at the stove with turning the pork chops and stirring the gravy. She hated her life and she hated Clem. Clem came up behind Isabelle and he roughly grabbed her bottom with both his huge hands. Isabelle reached for the gravy bowl and freed herself from him, but she knew what his next move would lead to, so she quickly side-stepped him and began to set table for dinner. Clem's mood quickly soured at Isabelle's rebuff. He walked over to her and as she set the last plate on the table, he shoved her and she fell backward over one of the chairs.

Isabelle knew Clem would hit her harder if she got up, so she laid on the floor, watching his evil grin. Their son, Rick, came into the room and he saw his mother on the floor and his father standing over her. This was an all too familiar scene for Clem and Isabelle's three kids. Rick, who now stood as tall and was as strong as his father, stepped around his father and he helped his mother to her feet.

"Nice going, Dad," Rick said sourly.

Clem laughed and he left the room.

The next morning Clem woke with his usual thundering erection which he took care of by humping his wife's limp body. As he rolled off her he wondered why he couldn't get Isabelle pregnant again. He didn't really want any more kids, but he wanted to keep her tied to him. What Clem didn't know was after the birth of their last child Isabelle had gone to the free medical clinic in town and had asked for birth control pills. To keep Clem from finding them she hid underneath the silverware drawer in the kitchen. She knew that was a safe place to hide them, since Clem only used silverware when they were set next to his plate on the table where he ate.

Clem lumbered off the bed, and Isabelle laid on her back staring blankly at the ceiling. Clem headed into the tiny bathroom to, in his words, shit, shave, and shower. He stood over the stool and peed all over the seat, laughing to himself because he knew how angry his crass actions made his wife,

When Clem came into the kitchen later, Isabelle, wearing her thick blue robe, stirred the gravy on the kitchen stove and tried to ignore Clem. She hated him, and she hated her life. Despite having been reared by decent, well-educated parents in an upper middle-class suburb, Isabelle knew how she'd wound up married to Clem and living in the poorest section of Maramount, Illinois, known as South Trekkin.

Although Isabelle was pretty, petite, and a smart teenager, she wasn't popular. Therefore, she was often overlooked by the celebrated and attractive boys in her class. A few times, she had been asked out by Clem Owens, but she had no desire to date the class bully. She broke her own rule in her senior year when prom came and no one asked her to go. The day before the dance, Clem asked her, and against her parents' wishes and her own good sense, she accepted his invitation. Much to her chagrin, Clem picked her up in his dad's filthy, gas-station pick-up truck. He wore a rumpled brown suit with thick, brown, leather patches on the elbows, a western shirt, and dusty boots. Isabelle miserably gathered up into her hands the bottom of her beautiful, white, beaded gown, climbed into the truck, and sat close to the door.

At the dance, Clem pawed and bumped her with his hips and held her too close to him. Not being able to stand another minute, she asked him to take her home. On the ride back, he swung the steering wheel sharply off-road, drove to a secluded spot out by the lake, and raped her. After Clem finally rolled off of her, Isabelle sat in his truck and sobbed uncontrollably. Although Isabelle was disheveled, battered, bruised, and in a state of shock, Clem dropped her off at her house. Isabelle stumbled up the flower-lined sidewalk to her glossy, white, front porch, but she couldn't go inside. She huddled on the porch swing where she lay for most of the night. At the break of dawn, she sneaked into the house.

She was too embarrassed to tell her parents what Clem had done to her. Her parents knew something was wrong and they worried about how quiet she had become. They chose not to ask any questions, fearing the worst. A few weeks later, she missed her period. When she missed another period, she went to Clem and told him she was pregnant. He married her. And seven months later, their son, Rick, was born.

Her parents never spoke to their daughter about their shame, but Isabelle knew they were both heartsick over the sad fate of their only child. On the few occasions when her parents had dropped by to see Isabelle and the children, Clem had made them so uncomfortable, they often cut their visit short. On those rare occasions Clem allowed Isabelle to go to her parent's house, he sat in their driveway in his gas-station tow truck and leaned on the horn.

Isabelle's parents dreaded ever venturing into South Trekkin. In getting there, they had to pass by a dismal line of empty warehouses and a deserted strip mall. Past the ruins, they drove over four sets of railroad tracks which led them down a bumpy, graveled road faced with dilapidated houses and sagging porches. Commonplace were cigarette butts, beer cans, used syringes, and overflowing-rank garbage cans. Half-starved dogs were tied to sparse trees. The dogs that were left to roam the streets often became roadkill when they attempted to cross the busy intersections. Angry gangs of young thugs armed with hidden guns and knives patrolled the area. Throngs of homeless people lay in doorways, drug deals took place out in the open, and very young girls with swollen bellies solicited passing cars. With the bad economy and the skyrocketing unemployment rate, South Trekkin had exponentially grown in the last few years.

The summer months provided a dismal scene of its own. Idle men and obese women sat on their front porches next to dusty, oscillating fans that moved the humid air over their sweaty, unwashed bodies.

Those persons in South Trekkin who attended church on Sunday morning were mainly there for the air conditioning. But the free coffee and donuts were also a draw.

"It's time for dinner," Isabelle said softly.

Clem got up, and he turned off the television. He walked into the small hallway that led to the two small bedrooms and yelled, "Hey, three stooges! Get your asses in here! It's time for dinner!"

The bedroom at the end of the hallway opened, and ten-year-old Abby and 17-year-old Eden walked quietly past their father and into the kitchen.

Isabelle spooned the steaming meat and potatoes into a bowl. She glanced up and saw her lackluster reflection in the darkened kitchen window. *Why did I waste the pretty on Clem,* she thought and she slowly lowered her gaze.

Clem came up behind her and grabbed her by her arm. "Didn't you hear me, woman?" he asked through clenched teeth. "I asked you where Rick is."

"He's probably with Gina Patterson," Isabelle said tiredly.

"I hate that girl!" Clem raved.

Isabelle set the plastic bowls of food on the table in front of Clem. Abby and Eden, seated across from their father, watched as he heaped food onto his plate. Isabelle looked sadly at her two beautiful daughters. When they were in the company of their dad, the girls often looked fearful and ever on the alert, much like those poor dogs whose owners kept them on a short leash tied to the tree. The dogs were just far enough away so they couldn't reach their food or water bowl, if even they existed.

"Eat, you two!" Clem said to his daughters, and he slammed his fist down on the table, startling the water glasses and making Eden and Abby jump.

The girls dipped small portions onto their plate and silently ate the food.

"This beef's tough!" Clem snapped.

"I had to buy the sale beef this week, Clem," Isabelle said softly.

"Why's these potatoes have black spots in them?"

"That's pepper," she said, wishing she could add, 'you idiot!'

He took a generous helping of bread pudding. "This slop looks like it's a week old," he said, stabbing his fork through the pudding. "Where's the raisins?"

"I used the last of the raisins this week in Abby's school lunch."

Abby lowered her gaze, fearing what came next.

"Hope you enjoyed them raisins, kid," Clem groused.

"I did, Daddy," Abby said timidly.

Clem devoured the bread pudding, making noises that sounded like a hog when he ate. When he'd finished eating, he leaned back in his chair and put his hands behind his head. Isabelle breathed a sigh of relief. At least one of his voracious appetites had temporarily been satisfied.

"How'd your teacher like that science project I helped you with, Squirt?" Clem asked to Abby. He diminished his children's morale by never calling any of them by their proper names.

"She said it was good," Abby said.

"Did she like the part of the Solar System that I built?" he baited.

Isabelle held her breath, as did Eden.

"Teacher said you put Jupiter in the wrong place," Abby said innocently.

Clem's face burned red. "What's the matter with that fool woman, anyway? I've half a mind to go see your teacher and give her a good talking to."

"Don't do that, Daddy, please," Abby cried.

"Then you'd better tell your teacher tomorrow that the mistake was yours," Clem said.

Abby burst into tears, and she ran from the table. Isabelle started after Abby, but Clem grabbed her wrist and forced her to sit down. Eden excused herself and quietly followed her sister to their shared bedroom.

Clem laughed maliciously. He enjoyed nothing more than inflicting pain on an innocent victim.

Eden sat down at the small desk in their shared bedroom to do her homework. Abby lay on the lower bunk bed, hugging her ragdoll and crying.

"Abby, you know what a jerk he is," Eden said.

"But," she sobbed, "he's going to see my teacher (sob), and he'll be mean to her (sob), and then she won't like me anymore."

"He's not going anywhere, Abby, so settle down. He accomplished what he wanted to. He got you upset."

"You promise he won't go, Eden?"

"I promise, sweetheart."

Eden started her homework, but she found it difficult to concentrate. In six weeks, she would graduate from high school. A few days earlier, she nervously asked her dad if he'd set aside any money for her for college. Clem laughed at her and walked out of the room. Eden was crushed. All her hard work, maintaining honor-roll grades and working the late shift at McDonald's meant nothing to him.

Isabelle opened the girls' bedroom door. "He's gone bowling," she said. "You girls want to come in the kitchen and visit with me while I clean up?"

Isabelle knew the girls were miserable living with their dad, but she couldn't help them. Her own mother outlived her father, and the last of their money was spent trying to help her mom deal with fourth-stage breast cancer. After the hospital took their house for past due medical bills, her mother's heart broke. Isabelle was convinced it was the hospital that killed her mom with a broken heart. The day the hospital got the court order to possess her parent's house, Isabelle's mom died. There was barely enough in her savings account to get her mom in the ground, let alone give her a gravestone. Clem said he'd bury Isabelle alive next to her mom's unmarked grave if he found out she'd spent a dime of his money.

When it came to Clem's wrath and his vile temper, the only one of them who didn't back down was Rick. Isabelle had often thought of running away with the girls and never coming back. But all the money she made cleaning the houses of the four wealthiest families in Maramount went toward food, clothing, and the household bills.

"Sure, Momma," Eden said, and she closed her math book. She took Abby's hand, and they followed their mother down the short hallway.

Eden, dressed in an old t-shirt and baggy sweatpants, picked up a dishtowel and started drying the dishes.

"You had such a pretty dress on when you went to school today, Eden," Abby said.

"That's what Katelyn Edwards said. Then she told all of her snobby friends that the dress I had on used to be hers," Eden said bitterly.

Isabelle didn't know what to say, so she changed the subject, "You girls didn't eat much tonight."

"I wasn't hungry."

"Besides his usual snide comments, did your father say something to upset you too, Eden?" Isabelle asked softly.

"I don't want to talk about it, Momma."

Eden loved her mother deeply, but she vowed she would never end up like her—uneducated, married to a brutal man she despised, and working as a maid.

Isabelle hoped Eden's intelligence, her determination, and her beauty would prove to be her ticket out of the slums.

Abby, a talkative, effervescent charmer with blonde hair that hung in ringlets, had porcelain skin, sky-blue eyes, an infectious smile, and a bubbly laugh. She was studious and affectionate, which made her an absolute delight to her teachers.

"Have you finished your homework, Eden?" her mother asked as Eden finished putting the last of the clean dishes in the cabinet.

"Yes, Momma."

"I have a lot of homework tonight, Momma," Abby said, much more animated now that Clem was gone. "We learned today that Yugoslavia broke into seven other countries, and they named all the places with a 'Stan' at the end. Isn't that funny? I bet that's where Frankenstan got his name," Abby said, and she roared with laughter.

"You're being silly, Abby," Eden said affectionately.

"I'm just funny," Abby said, and she jumped to her feet and ran from the room, giggling and saying, "See ya, Eden, but wouldn't want to be ya!"

Isabelle smiled at Abby's enthusiastic banter. She wanted her daughters to become self-sufficient. She so didn't want them to be like her. She knew things and money couldn't make you happy, but they sure could make you more comfortable in your misery. She learned what misery looked like, having firsthand knowledge of the private lives of Judge Caulder's family, the Edward's family, and the Atler's family. Her knowledge of the Pearson family was limited, as they lived most of the year in Hawaii.

Isabelle worried about Rick. He had quit high school in his junior year and had gone to work for his dad at the gas station. Working in close proximity with his brutish father, Rick had developed a few of his father's worst traits. But despite his rough exterior and foul language, Isabelle knew Rick loved her and his two sisters.

She thought Rick would eventually marry Gina Patterson. She hoped Gina would adjust to Rick being a slob and his refusal to be governed by any rules. As it was, Isabelle still cleaned Rick's room, throwing out old pizza boxes, crushed beer cans, and ashtrays overflowing with cigarette butts, and transforming his dirty piles of clothing into neat, clean stacks that she placed on his freshly made bed.

# Two

Although she was a gifted student, Eden didn't really like school except for her fifth-period gifted creative writing which proved a godsend for her. Each day, she looked forward to the class and even found herself writing extra assignments on the weekend. She could lose herself in poetry, short stories, or any of the other homework her teacher, Mrs. Omaha, assigned. Eden adored Mrs. Omaha, and she appreciated her calm demeanor.

Mr. Tomkins, on the other hand, her biology teacher, was often in a foul mood. When he assigned homework, he would say sternly, "Homework not turned in on time is late. And late equals detention!" Clearly Mr. Tomkins took biology very seriously.

This morning, thanks to Abby's dawdling, Eden was late for school. When she finally got to school, she ran to her locker and dropped off her backpack. She grabbed one pencil, which was the only item a student could bring to Mr. Tomkins class when a test was given, hurried to his class, and sat down at her assigned seat, sitting her pencil to the top left of her desk so Mr. Tomkins could inspect it before the testing began.

Mr. Tomkins had enacted his pencil rule years ago after he caught a kid had written notes on his pencil in mnemonics.

"Good morning, Eden," Katelyn Edwards said, blocking Eden's path. "I see you're not wearing any of my discarded clothing today."

Eden thought of a dozen nasty things she could say to Katelyn. *Like, I see bulimia is agreeing with you. And, Botox has certainly improved those ugly creases on your forehead and that slash above your pointed chin. And, your breast implants look so heavy, you might fall face forward and break your new nose.*

Eden didn't respond. She stepped around Katelyn and her friends and walked calmly to her creative-writing class. Eden was anxious to share with her beloved teacher the poem she'd written for class. She was, however, concerned about sharing her inner most feelings with her classmates. Her poem didn't speak of her hopes for a college education, a good job, and a loving marriage. It was a loving poem to be read to her much-anticipated children as she tucked them into bed at night.

When Eden walked into Mrs. Omaha's creative-writing class, she felt like she was floating on air. She carried her poem and her private journal which she always kept close by so that she could often write about her most intimate thoughts and dreams. She tried not to dwell on her many disappointments. As Eden walked past Mrs. Omaha's desk, her teacher gave her a reassuring smile.

Katelyn and her group arrived and took their seats. Katelyn tried to stare Eden down, but Eden decided to ignore Katelyn's meanness. Eden remembered the noted South African anti-apartheid leader, Steven Bantu Biko's quote, 'The most potent weapon in the hands of the oppressor is the mind of the oppressed.' Eden couldn't stop Katelyn's vile behavior, but she could control her reaction to it. That thought gave her hope.

"Eden," Mrs. Omaha said. "Please share your poem with us."

Eden rose shyly to her feet, and she walked nervously to the front of the classroom. When she turned to face her classmates, butterflies filled her stomach. She made it a point not to look directly at anyone. She concentrated on a robust-looking philodendron that spilled out of a porcelain pot which set on a small table at the back of the room.

"I wrote a poem to the children I hope to have when I am happily married," Eden said in a shy, soft voice.

"You'll have to get a date first!" Katelyn shouted.

"Quiet down, Katelyn!" Mrs. Omaha ordered. "You may proceed, Eden," she said gently.

When the laughter died down, Eden cleared her throat and began. "My poem is titled…

### It's That Time of Night

*It's that time of evening that we call night,*
*The time to tuck you in and kiss you so tight.*
*The time you ask questions, answers so hard to say,*
*Or we debate about time, you wanting more time to play.*

*Momma, why is the sky blue at day and black in the eve?*
*Or why is God something I have to believe?*
*Momma, why do spiders have eight legs,*
*and snakes don't have none?*
*Why do men have two legs and a centipede a ton!?*

*Momma, I'm thirsty right now and I have to pee,*
*It's not time for bed, can't you just see!?*
*Can we read a book...how 'bout that long one, oh yes!*
*Momma, we have to say our prayers and tell God we're blessed.*

*So we play a quick game of hide and go seek,*
*I turn down the lights and you take a peek.*
*I giggle out loud and let you find me so fast.*
*You don't understand...I want this moment to last!*

*Today, you are young...loving and kissing me a ton,*
*I'll treasure these moments with you, my fair ones.*
*I'll cherish in my heart the days that have passed,*
*You have given me memories, forever to last!*

*In a few years you'll be gone, and I'll be waiting so near,*
*With understanding and patience, all you need me to hear.*
*No matter where we go or when I may pass,*
*Know the love I have for you, it always will last!"*

Spontaneous applause filled the room, and many of the students stood to their feet.

"Thank you," Eden said and tears welled in her eyes as she lowered her papers and returned to her seat. A few moments later, the classroom quietened down.

"Eden, your poem is lovely," Mrs. Omaha said.

Mrs. Omaha cleared her throat, and she pushed up the sleeves of her cream, cashmere sweater ensemble in preparation for the next reader.

"Riker, would you care to share your poem with the class?" she asked to the burly line-backer of the football team.

Riker came forward, holding what looked like a postcard in his huge hand.

Katelyn whispered to Amanda Bleir who was seated across the aisle from her, "This will be interesting!"

Riker positioned his thick, squat body in front of Mrs. Omaha.

"My poem is called **Riker at the Miker**," Riker said in his dullard voice.

> *"Pro teams want me bad*
> *because I can always get the ball.*
> *I have the best ability in the nation*
> *to shout an aubi-ball—"*

Mrs. Omaha interrupted, "Riker, isn't it aud-i-bull, not aud-i-ball?"

"Sure thing, Mrs. Omaha. Am I done now?"

"No, no, please continue."

"Do you want me to start from the beginning? If you do, my poem is called **Riker at the Miker**."

"Just pick it up where you left off," she said, feeling frustrated.

> *"The audience lives for my touchdowns,*
> *I get back Riker, Riker in unison sound.*
> *I have a perfect image,*
> *'Cause I'm the best in the scrimmage."*

Riker turned the script over.

> *"The world puts the most in me, that is the stock.*
> *I also have the muscles to make a perfect block.*
> *When I yell at my loudest, they know I can shout.*
> *The coach may then accuse another for a time-out.*
> *If I was on the NASDAQ, I'd have the bestest stock,*
> *'Cause I'm a jock who can always beat the clock.*
> *When I get so famous, all know the name of Riker,*
> *I'll be on ESPN, calling the plays on the Miker."*

"What do ya think, Mrs. Omaha?" Riker asked, snickering.

"You have a unique talent, Riker," Mrs. Omaha said.

"We have time for one more," Mrs. Omaha said. "Does anyone have a short poem?"

"I have a really short one, Mrs. Omaha," Tinley Cooper said.

Tinley Cooper and Riker Overall were not academically qualified to be in the gifted honors classes, but their football skills excused their lack of scholastic abilities.

Tinley wore a wrinkled t-shirt, jeans with holes in the knees, and dirty sneakers. Tinley had a good heart. He regularly attended church with his family, and when he was around other kids, bullying was forbidden. Tinley once saw a video showing animals being butchered in a slaughterhouse and the sight made him sick to his stomach. He decided to become a vegetarian. That lasted until the school had a cookout and then he stuffed himself with hotdogs and hamburgers. Tinley immediately felt guilty. To ease his tortured conscience, Tinley ate lifeless meat bought at the supermarket. He also found peace of mind in volunteering at the local animal shelter. To date, he had successfully found loving homes for many animals who were due to be euthanized.

Tinley went to the front of the class; he turned and smiled. "Riddley, riddley, ree, I see something you don't see and it starts with a P."

"That isn't a poem, Tinley," Mrs. Omaha chided. "It's a game I played when I was a girl and my parents took my siblings and me on road trips."

"This was all I could think of and it stuck in my head," Tinley said, describing the brain worm he suffered with because of his O.C.D. Tinley washed his hands so many times a day, they were often chapped and dry. He listened to jazz on the radio because it was the only music that didn't repeat in his head for hours. He obsessively checked the doors at home several times at night to make sure they were locked. He counted objects in his head. He talked to himself. He had a favorite bowl he ate his cereal in. He had all his electronic equipment arranged and squared off neatly on his desk. And even though he was a nice guy, he contradicted everything another person said.

"You may sit down now, Tinley," Mrs. Omaha said. "Now, class, we will discuss tomorrow's assignment and one last thing. Please leave your journals on my desk before you leave this afternoon."

The bell rang, and the students rushed forward and laid their journals on the teacher's desk as they scrambled out the door.

Eden waited until everybody else had gone. She didn't want to leave her journal for Mrs. Omaha to see. It contained many of her secrets and her fears.

"Did you want to speak to me about something, Eden?" Mrs. Omaha asked, noticing.

Eden had stayed behind the other students.

"Mrs. Omaha, I'd rather not hand in my journal, if you don't mind."

"But, Eden, the journal will reflect on your grade."

"I know. But I've written private thoughts in the journal and I'd rather not share them with anyone."

"You needn't worry about me disclosing any of your secrets, Eden."

Eden deliberated over receiving a lower grade or sharing her secrets with Mrs. Omaha. The threat of a lower grade finally won out. She reluctantly placed her journal on her teacher's desk.

Mrs. Omaha smiled and she said, "I will read your journal first, and, tomorrow, I will return it to you."

"Thank you, Mrs. Omaha," Eden said. Instead of leaving then, Eden broke down in tears.

Mrs. Omaha wanted to rush to Eden and put her arms comfortingly around her, but she knew the rules about teachers touching their students. She sat stoically behind her desk and she said, "What's wrong, Eden?"

"I won't be going to college this fall, Mrs. Omaha," Eden sobbed.

"I'm so sorry to hear that, Eden," Mrs. Omaha said, reaching for a tissue and handing it to Eden. "I thought you told me once that you applied for scholarships at several different colleges."

"Yes, ma'am, I did. All of my applications were declined."

"That is sad news indeed," Mrs. Omaha said sympathetically. "I wish I could help you, Eden."

"It's not your responsibility, Mrs. Omaha," Eden sniffled. "Thank you for being so understanding," she said, and she picked up her backpack and left.

Mrs. Omaha ached for Eden. Like Eden, Mrs. Omaha loved poetry and had, in fact, once dreamed of becoming a poet. But her dreams were banished when she discovered she was pregnant with twin boys. Now, she taught creative writing in a small high school in Maramount. She had a sweet husband, Hank, a computer analyst, and four-year-old twin boys, Max and Dan. She hoped Eden could achieve the dream she had let slip by her.

Mrs. Omaha sighed deeply. Then her curiosity to discover Eden's deep, dark, inner thoughts compelled her to open Eden's journal and read for the next hour. Mrs. Omaha slowly closed the journal. She folded her hands on her desk in front of her, and she thought about Eden's vivid description of her family's plight.

When Rick attended Maramount High, Mrs. Omaha thought, *I saw Mrs. Owens at all the P.T.A. meetings and the school's social functions. I never once saw Mr. Owens take an interest in any of his son's academic or sports activities. Mrs. Owens impressed me as a lovely lady who cares deeply for her children. For my taste, she dresses a little dowdy, and she is certainly too skinny, but I believe she is a devoted mother to her three children. I had no idea she had suffered such abuse at the hands of Eden's father, Clem. I remember Rick Owens as a rebellious, angry, young man who constantly defied authority. After reading Eden's description of her miserable home life, I now understand Rick's angst,* she thought. Mrs. Omaha was impressed with Eden's description of her sister, Abby. Perhaps Abby's innocence will not be as adversely affected by her environment as Rick's, Eden's, and Isabelle's have been.

Mrs. Omaha put Eden's journal aside. She read a few more of the student's comments, laughing at their selfish hopes and dreams.

Riker Danver's dream list consisted of a Harley Davidson SuperLow 1200T motorcycle that he wanted to ride on a trip to Las Vegas. *A cute girlfriend would be nice. And a backyard swimming pool would be fab. Duh!* Mrs. Omaha thought.

Allison James, Dr. Milton James's daughter, wanted diamond earrings. She'd like to live abroad in England as an exchange student. And she DESPERATELY wanted to meet Ross Farrelly, the lead singer with the boy band, The Strypes, from Cavan, Ireland. *Grow up!* Mrs. Omaha thought.

Tinley Cooper wanted the persistent voices in his head to stop. He also hoped his scattered thoughts wouldn't whirl with repetitive information, and he wished he could listen to pop music without it driving him crazy. He wished his little sister wouldn't mess with his WIFI, and he hoped the meds his doctor was giving him would finally ease his brain. "Poor Tinley!" Mrs. Omaha said aloud.

Katelyn Edwards desired to be Miss Universe. She wanted a new BMW with licenses plates that read GILTED. She wanted another pair of sparkly

Manalo Blahnik high heels. And she wanted to marry Prince Harry. *Such an arrogant, spoiled brat!* Mrs. Omaha thought.

Eden Owens's wish list included a college education for herself and her sister, Abby. She wanted her mother to be happy and safe. And she hoped Rick would get a good job and settle down with a respectable girl. *Poor child,* Mrs. Omaha thought. *Eden is capable of achieving great things. If only she had the opportunity.* An idea struck her like a thunderbolt. She pulled out her cellphone, and she made a call to a Professor Altgeld at the University of Illinois.

# Three

The attraction for small town living, like that in Maramount, had diminished over the years, resulting in a sharp downturn in jobs. Many of the prosperous factories that had once been located in Maramount called it quits and relocated overseas or to other cities where they weren't forced to fight a laborer's union. The exception to this rule was Edward's Furniture Manufacturers which still maintained its largest factory, warehouse, and corporate-office building on the 20-acre lot the company owned.

Very few young people returned to Maramount after graduating from college. Of those 20 something who did stay, they either worked at Kubey's department store or they found minimum wage jobs at fast-food restaurants and local motels. Presently, the population in Maramount stood at 13-thousand people.

The one-way street that ran through the center of town, commonly referred to as 'downtown,' hosted a post office, Maramount Public Library, Maramount State Bank, First National Bank, The Mercury Movie Theater, the three-story Brick Courthouse, Barley's Furniture Store, Decker's Hardware Store, and the Applewood Diner. Broadrick's Drive-In Theater, McDonald's, and Walmart were located a mile out of town on Route 136.

As is true in most cities, class distinction boundaries existed. Such was true in Maramount. The very poor lived in South Trekkin. The four richest families in Maramount lived in a secluded area called Kingston Bay Estates. They were the Edwards family, who owned Edward's Furniture, Judge Maxwell Caulder, a family law judge and his family, the Atlers, owners of a nationwide chain of organic supermarket, and the Kubeys who owned a chain of upscale department stores.

Isabelle reached over and shut off the alarm on the pressed wooden nightstand before it rang insistently at 4 a.m. She had slept fitfully the night before, dreading the long and tedious work day ahead. After the ice storm began brewing last night, Isabelle called Judge Caulder, expecting that she didn't have to work the next day. Instead, when she called, Judge Caulder stated that he had heard Monday's weather forecast would be milder. He insisted that she be at his house at her usual 6 a.m.

As is true of Illinois weather in April, one day produced snow and ice, the next day turned warm and balmy. The latter proved to be the case. Isabelle carefully rolled the blankets off of her and crept out of bed. She tried to be as quiet as she could, hoping not to rouse Clem and his insatiable libido. She picked up her clean underwear and the dress she intended to put on after her shower and sneaked out of the bedroom, down the hallway, toward the bathroom.

20 minutes later, she emerged from the steamy bathroom, dressed and clean. She went to the kitchen and started a pot of coffee. She washed up the sink full of dishes from Clem and Rick's late-night snacks, and she organized the bowl, spoon, and sugar on the table for Abby's breakfast. Looking at Eden's empty chair, Isabelle hoped that both of her girls could get away from this hellhole. She prayed that Eden and Abby would not let their father's brutality and his disinterest in them influence their choice of a boyfriend and husband.

Isabelle carried the trash can into the living room and set it next to the loaded coffee table. She threw away crumpled newspapers, empty beer cans, candy wrappers, and a potato-chip bag. She emptied her favorite candy dish of crushed cigarettes. She straightened the braided rug in front of the television table and the beige blanket she used as a sofa slipcover. Back in the kitchen, she slipped on a jacket and her rubber gardening boots and took the stuffed trash container to the curb to be emptied later by Maramount Sanitation Service.

Isabelle turned on the hallway light and quietly entered Rick's darkened room. She saw her handsome son lying on his naked back in his rumpled bed and snoring softly. She wrinkled her nose at the unpleasant smell as she gathered up the dirty shirts, socks, and jeans that he had strewn across his floor. She looked closer at Rick's chest, and she was saddened by the content of his ugly tattoos. His gift of beauty came from God, she thought sadly. Too bad he had to disfigure himself with those vile ink images.

Isabelle laid Rick's dirty clothing in a pile in the hallway and softly closed his bedroom door. She opened Abby's bedroom door and walked quietly inside. She saw her sweet-smelling daughter sound asleep next to Eden in Eden's bed. While her daughters slept in silence, Isabelle picked up Abby's neatly folded clothes from the day before and placed them on her bed. Her favorite stuffed animal, a gold-colored seal she called Sunshine, had fallen to the floor. Isabelle picked it up and laid the toy on the bed beside her sleeping daughter. She so wanted to gather Abby into her arms and hold her tightly. Instead, she left and closed the bedroom door.

After placing the dirty clothes in the wash basket, Isabelle made the despised trip back into the room she shared with Clem. She saw he hadn't moved since she had crawled out of the bed. The odor of his body turned her stomach. He lay sleeping on his side, his hairy, barrel chest and stomach bulged in the blanket, and drool ran in a small stream down his cheek and soaked into his rumpled pillow case. His thick hair hadn't been cut in two months, and even in the darkened room, she saw the protruding nose and ear hair he refused to trim. His fingernails were black-rimmed from grease and long enough to be labeled effeminate. She didn't bother picking up his dirty clothes. He wore the same underwear, shirt, jeans, and socks all week long.

"Clem," she said softly from the foot of the bed. He snored on. "Clem!" she said more sharply.

Like a beached whale, he rolled over on his side. "Yeah?" he grunted.

"It's 5:15. I have to go to work now."

He opened his sleep-filled eyes and looked at her. He slowly sat up and hacked a wad into a chipped cup on the night stand. He threw the blankets off of him and sat on the side of the bed.

She saw his morning erection and she said quickly, "Do you want me to get you a cup of coffee to take along on the drive?"

"Yeah," he said, and he stood up and reached for his shirt and jeans. Isabelle hurried out of the room. Within five minutes, Clem came into the kitchen with his wet hair slicked back.

Isabelle waited at the backdoor with a steaming cup of coffee in her hand. Clem pulled on his heavy boots, yanked his ball hat down on his head, and rammed his thick arms into the sleeves of his tattered denim jacket.

"Whose house you cleaning today?" he asked, taking the coffee.

"The Caulder's."

"I hate that guy," Clem said and poured a slug of the hot coffee down his throat. He used the back of his hand to wipe the stream flowing down his chin.

"I think a lot of people feel that way about Judge Caulder," Isabelle said, reaching for her purse.

Outside, the ice had disappeared, and the breeze combing through the budding trees felt balmy. They walked across the sodden yard and got into the tow truck. Clem started laughing.

"What's so funny?" Isabelle asked.

"I was just thinking about all those stupid yokels I pulled out of the icy ditches yesterday. They got a big towing bill coming to them today. And now it's warm and the sun is shining! Damn bunch of morons. Oh well. Their loss is my gain," he said, and he switched on the truck's ignition and the diesel engine thundered.

They drove through town and passed by Sinclair Dental Clinic. Isabelle said cautiously, "Abby has a visible cavity in one of her back teeth."

Clem stiffened. "So what?" he asked, and he took a drink of his coffee.

"After you collect the money from the towing jobs, we could maybe get Abby's tooth fixed?"

Clem tromped the accelerator and the truck raced over the bumpy street. "Not that it's any of your business," he snarled, "but I already got plans for that money."

Isabelle knew she was treading on dangerous ground, but she also knew Abby's tooth would soon be causing her real pain.

"I believe if I explained our financial difficulties to Dr. Sinclair, he might go ahead and fix Abby's tooth now. We could pay for it later."

Clem threw his empty coffee cup on the floor, grabbed Isabelle's wrist, and savagely twisted it. "You keep your mouth shut about our finances," he seethed. "You got that?"

"I got it," Isabelle said, and she struggled to free her wrist from his powerful grip.

They pulled up to the wide wrought-iron gates leading into Kingston Bay Estates.

Jasper Carney, a skinny, gap-toothed youth wearing a khaki uniform and a matching hat, manned the gatehouse.

"Morning, Clem, and Mrs. Owens," he said from inside the gatehouse.

"That's Mr. Owens to you, boy," Clem said nastily.

"Sorry about that, Clem, I mean, Mr. Owens."

"How's Rick doing these days, Mrs. Owens?" Jasper asked as he pushed the button and the gates opened.

"Rick is…" Isabelle tried to answer, but Clem rolled up the window and drove off.

They rode silently up the long asphalt driveway, and Clem stopped the truck in front of the sprawling mansion. Isabelle picked up her purse and hurried to get out of the truck, but Clem grabbed her arm. "What's your hurry?" he asked.

"Judge Caulder said the tow truck leaks oil on his driveway."

"Now ain't that a damn shame."

"I can't lose this job, Clem," Isabelle said urgently.

"This won't take a minute," he said, and he deliberately revved the motor.

"I'll be an hour late picking you up tonight."

"Why?"

"I'm driving to Champaign this afternoon to buy a new hunting rifle." Now she understood where the money from the towing jobs was going. She took a deep breath and let it out slowly.

"Okay," she said, and she dropped down out of the truck. He stopped her when he said, almost apologetically, "They passed a stupid law this year that says if you buy a private firearm, it has to be okayed by the state police. Then they got to check my FOID card to see if it's all right. After that, I've gotta wait for an approval number which takes another 24 hours. I can't believe they put me through all this shit just to buy a new hunting rifle."

Isabelle silently glared at him. In an uncharacteristic move, she slammed the truck door shut and walked up the long, bluestone sidewalk.

# Four

A severe ice storm with 40-mile-an-hour winds that had downed several power lines. All morning long, the local radio station broadcast the state police warnings, telling people to stay off the roads and inside their homes. But a few foolhardy motorists decided to throw caution to the wind. At 3 a.m., the state police had called and asked Clem to bring his tow truck and assist in removing several vehicles that had skidded off the icy road and into the ditches.

It was 7 a.m., and Isabelle was humming a tune, something she never did when Clem was at home. This morning, she prepared a hearty breakfast of bacon, eggs, and hash browns for her daughters to eat. She was looking forward to her day. Church services had been cancelled, and Clem would most likely be gone for most of the day, thank goodness.

Six days a week, Isabelle's work day began at 4 a.m. On those days, she served Eden and Abby steel-cut oats that she let soften overnight on the stovetop. She didn't make breakfast for Clem or Rick. Clem ate breakfast each morning at McDonald's with his hunting buddies. Rick skipped breakfast so he could sleep longer.

On weekdays, Eden and Abby reluctantly ate the free lunches at school provided by the state. Clem didn't mind that his girls were often taunted by their classmates for being poor. But for himself, he had an odd sense of pride. He wouldn't think of going to a food pantry and standing in line with some of his neighbors for a free bag of groceries. But while he waited a block away in the tow truck, he forced Isabelle to go. Humiliated, Isabelle would lower her gaze and rush through the line as quickly as she could.

Tired of listening to the state police's warnings about the inclement weather, Isabelle switched the radio to a gospel music station. Dressed in her bunny-rabbit pajamas and rubbing her sleepy eyes, Abby walked into the kitchen. "Something smells so good!" Abby said. "What are you cooking, Momma?"

"I made bacon, eggs, and hash browns for you and Eden," Isabelle said, dipping a generous helping of each onto two plates.

"Smells yummy," Eden said, walking in behind Abby. Eden wore a pair of jeans and a heavy, red sweatshirt. Isabelle hummed as she set the hot plates of food on the table in front of her daughters.

Eden noticed her freshly showered mother wore light makeup and lip gloss, she had her clean hair pulled up in a bun, and she wore a pretty flowered duster and furry house slippers. It was not the kind of attire her mother would be wearing if Eden's lecherous dad was at home.

Abby filled her mouth with hash browns. "What are you humming, Momma?" she mumbled.

"It's 'How Great is Our God.'" Isabelle said, watching Eden salt her eggs.

"Does Taylor Swift or Rihanna or Katy Perry sing it?" Abby asked, and she heaved scrambled eggs into her mouth.

"It's a band called Casting Crowns," Isabelle said. "And stop talking with your mouth full, dear."

Isabelle often listened to gospel music on the radio to aid her faith and to keep her spirit refreshed. On days when Clem's violence and bad temper needled her frustration, she abated her despair and her hopelessness by cranking up the volume on the radio and dancing wildly to Miranda Lambert's 'Momma's Broken Heart.'

Eden and Abby loved to have their mother all to themselves. Eden enjoyed her mother's gentle, poetic, and thoughtful side. Abby loved her mother's playful, childlike curiosity.

"I'm sure glad you didn't have to go to work this morning," Abby said, excitedly eating her crunchy bacon.

"This is great, Momma," Eden said.

Isabelle poured herself a cup of coffee, and she joined her daughters at the table.

With her mouth full again, Abby said, "Yesterday in class, the teacher told Bobby Sanders that he needed to work harder on his math skills." Abby took another big bite of scrambled eggs and she mumbled, "Bobby said he could add, subtract, divide, and do his multiplication. He said he didn't think knowing any more math than that was important."

Abby picked up another crisp strip of bacon and took a bite. "Teacher said, 'Okay, Bobby. I have a math problem you might consider. There are two cars on the road, and they are driving in the same lane toward each other. One car is going 30 miles per hour, the other car is going 60 miles per hour. When they collide, the car going 30 miles per hour is pushed back at a rate of 60 miles per hour, and the car that was going 60 miles per hour is pushed back to 30 miles per hour. How does that happen?'"

"What did Bobby say then?" Isabelle asked, fearing Abby would ask her for the answer.

"He said math had nothing to do with the wreck. He said the people in the cars were stupid for driving in the same lane."

Isabelle and Eden laughed.

Eden empathized with Bobby Sanders because she too disliked math. It was her hardest subject. Not because she didn't understand it; she made very good grades in math. She just didn't care for it. She loved her gifted-writing class. It was the one place where she felt comfortable and able to express herself.

Depending on her mood, Eden often wrote her poems with different colored pencils. Mrs. Omaha learned to read Eden's frame of mind by the color of pencil Eden used. Blue words translated into sadness and purity. Yellow words spoke of God's love, His caring, His understanding, His warmth, and His peace. Black words brought darkness and fear. Brown words trembled the Earth. They spoke of winter's dead foliage and of the misery of lost dreams. Startling red words spoke of passionate love, unbridled sensuality, and of traveling to a balmy fragrant island with a lover. Green words portrayed freshly cut grass, spring's blossoming trees, and warm summer breezes. Orange words created heat and uncomfortable situations. Purple, Eden's favorite color for a poem, was regal, courteous, majestic, imposing, aristocratic, sublime, resplendent, capricious, and fanciful.

Mrs. Omaha, herself, a 40-year-old frustrated poet with a degree in English Literature, anxiously anticipated the poems she now labeled, 'Eden's Purple Poetry.' Through Eden's works of literary art, Mrs. Omaha was able to live vicariously.

Eden admired her mother's faith. However, Eden's faith was greatly tested when she found out college was out of the question for her. Hoping to earn enough money to pay the application fee for the A.C.T., Eden had saved every cent she earned babysitting for the Grobans's impossible seven-year-old twin boys. She simply hadn't earned enough money. The idea of taking her A.C.T., applying for scholarships, and going to college were out of her grasp. Her dreams were crushed.

To drown out the sadness of her lost dreams, Eden spent her days in the public library, studying books on poetry. With college an unattainable dream, Eden decided to pursue a career as an author of poetry. She often tried to share her plans with Abby, but Abby usually was too busy listening to the second-hand IPOD from Disc Replay that she and Eden shared, or she preferred to read her 'Tell Me Why' books which filled her curious mind with many unique facts.

When Clem and Rick weren't dominating the television set watching World Wide Wrestling, Eden loved to watch the National Geographic Channel. She also loved 'Through the Wormhole,' narrated by Morgan Freeman on the Science Channel. She found the different cultures, habitats, jobs, living conditions, religions, foods, and topography fascinating. Sometimes, she watched a program where a chef traveled the world and ate bizarre foods like fried tarantulas, animal testicles and intestines.

Isabelle once caught Eden and Abby watching Naked and Afraid, a show about two people, one man and one woman, who had to use their own skills and ingenious to survive on a remote tropical island. Isabelle rushed the girls out of the room and quickly turned off the show.

# Five

"Seniors," Vice Principal Adam Parsons said, speaking to the class as they sat in the gymnasium for assembly. "Remember to turn in your permission slips for our annual college tour of the University of Illinois."

Eden hadn't bothered to have her mother sign her permission slip. Why should she? They didn't have the required 20 dollars to pay for her trip. Tears welled up in her eyes when she thought about being excluded from the college tour that her classmates would be enjoying. She wouldn't be there to see the short video. She wouldn't get to participate in the exciting Q and A session. She would miss the long walk around the quad, and there would be no lunch for her at the Illini Union.

The school bell rang. Eden got up and walked out of the gymnasium with her head down. Mrs. Omaha saw Eden heading out of the gymnasium and she ran to catch up with her.

"Eden!" she called through the noisy, crowded hall. Eden didn't hear Mrs. Omaha over the noise of the fast-moving crowd. Tinley Cooper closed his locker and he joined the melee. At six-foot four-inches tall, he could see over most of his classmates' heads. Mrs. Omaha saw Tinley, and she called, "Tinley, stop Eden Owens!"

Tinley looked around. "I don't see her, Mrs. Omaha," Tinley shouted.

Mrs. Omaha gestured by flapping her hand in Eden's direction. Tinley turned and he saw Eden's back.

"HEY, EDEN!" Tinley shouted.

Eden turned around, and she looked at Tinley who pointed at Mrs. Omaha. Eden stopped, and she waited for Mrs. Omaha to catch up with her.

*Did I write something in my journal that offended Mrs. Omaha?* Eden thought in a panic. *Maybe my poems are really no good? Did I say something in class that she found objectionable?* Her head reeled with doomed possibilities.

Breathless, Mrs. Omaha caught up with Eden. "Eden, I need to speak to you about an important matter," she said. She looked at her wristwatch. "But I don't have time right now. Please come to my classroom after school and we'll talk then."

"Did I do something wrong, Mrs. Omaha?" Eden asked nervously.

"I'll tell you when I see you," Mrs. Omaha said, and she rushed away.

Eden sat through her history class, but she couldn't concentrate. She remembered she had to go to Maramount Elementary after school and walk Abby home. She had to call Momma and ask her to get Abby, because she didn't know how long she'd be with Mrs. Omaha. She tried to ease her fevered mind with the assurance it wasn't detention her teacher wanted to see her about. Or was it?

After school, Eden knocked on Mrs. Omaha's open door. Mrs. Omaha ushered Eden in. Eden stepped into the classroom and said, "Mrs. Omaha, may I call my mother and tell her I won't be able to pick up my little sister, Abby, from school today?"

"Certainly, Eden. I'll wait here for you."

Eden laid her books and P.E. uniform on a front-row desk and walked back into the hall. In the school office, she used the telephone to call home. The phone on the Owens kitchen wall persistently rang. Isabelle dropped her floor-scrubbing rag into the bucket of hot soapy water and stood up. She wiped her itchy, red hands on a towel and walked over to the telephone.

"Hello," she answered after the fifth ring.

"Hi, Momma."

"Is everything okay, dear?"

"Mrs. Omaha asked me to stay after school because she wants to talk to me about something. Don't worry. I'm not in trouble or anything. At least I don't think I am. Can you please pick up Abby from school?"

Isabelle sneezed three times in a row, a symptom of breathing powerful ammonia.

"Yes, dear, I can," she said, and she sneezed again.

"Are you catching a cold, Momma?"

"No, sweetie. I was mopping this wasted, old linoleum with ammonia when you called."

34

Eden pictured her mother on her hands and knees, cleaning for their family and others. She had so hoped she could get a good education and free her mother from her life of drudgery.

"Why don't you rest now, Momma? I'll finish mopping the floors when I get home."

"I'm almost finished. Besides, you will be buried in homework. I hope Mrs. Omaha has something nice to say about your poetry. I know how important writing is to you."

"I love you, Momma," Eden said tenderly.

"I love you more," her mother said, and they both hung up.

When Eden walked back into Mrs. Omaha's class, she noticed her teacher was reading through some of the class journals. Mrs. Omaha closed the journal and said, "Were you able to reach your mother, Eden?"

"Yes, ma'am."

"Good. Please take a seat." Eden sat down at the desk where she had laid her things before. Mrs. Omaha laced her fingers together and laid her hands on her desk. "Did you turn in your permission slip for the class fieldtrip next Friday to the University of Illinois?"

"No, ma'am. I won't be going."

Mrs. Omaha could see Eden's disappointment and shame.

"As you know, the University of Illinois is my alma mater. I graduated from there 20 years ago with a degree in English Literature."

"Yes, ma'am, I know," Eden said timidly.

"You also know I studied poetry. In fact, it was my goal to someday become a poet laureate."

Eden nodded.

"But you know the old saying. You plan, God laughs. Must be true because my dreams were never realized."

Eden lowered her gaze, thinking her plans too would never become a reality.

"The thing is, Eden, I now believe God had a greater plan in mind for me."

Eden looked up.

"Not all of us are destined for greatness. I have accepted that. So, I became a teacher of creative writing. All these years, I have waited for a special student, someone who loved poetry as much as I do. And I have found that person in you."

Eden moved anxiously to the edge of her seat.

"You will go to the University of Illinois on Friday as my guest. We will tour the campus, eat lunch at a special place on campus, and later that afternoon, I have a former professor of mine that I want you to meet."

"Really?!" Eden squealed. She had to hold herself back from jumping up and hugging Mrs. Omaha. Eden had never traveled from Maramount. This was a dream come true. She could pretend for one day the University of Illinois was going to be her alma mater!

"Thank you, Mrs. Omaha, for everything!"

"You're so welcome, Eden."

Eden thought she saw Mrs. Omaha discreetly wipe a tear from her eye.

Eden stood up and she gathered her belongings. "May I go now? I need to have Momma sign the permission slip as soon as I get home!"

"Don't forget. Your assignment for Friday is to revise a Dr. Seuss poem."

"I've finished that poem," Eden said, and she headed for the door.

"Why am I not surprised?" Mrs. Omaha asked pleasantly.

Eden turned around, her face flushed with excitement, and she said, "Thank you, thank you, thank you, Mrs. Omaha! Boy! I won't sleep a wink tonight!"

Mrs. Omaha smiled broadly.

When Eden arrived home, her mother was checking the meat and potatoes in the large pot on top of the stove. The smell of the boiling cabbage filled the air. Eden dumped her books and jacket on the crude wooden bench next to the door.

"I'm going on the class trip!" she gushed, waving the permission slip in her hand.

"That's wonderful, sweetheart," Isabelle said, washing her hands at the sink.

"Where did you get the money?"

"Mrs. Omaha is going to give it to me."

A troubled look crossed Isabelle's face. "Do you think that's wise, Eden?"

"I don't know, Momma. I just want so much to go and there's no way we can afford the trip."

"Mrs. Omaha is kind to include you."

"Yes, Momma, she is."

Isabelle signed the permission slip. As she stirred the food in the pot, she thought about Mrs. Omaha's motives in helping Eden. The teacher's avid attention toward her daughter bothered Isabelle. She wanted to find something devious or self-serving in her intentions. But in her heart, Isabelle knew she was just envious.

# Six

When Eden woke up on Friday morning, she noticed Momma had hung Katelyn's dress on the bedroom door for her to wear on the trip to the University of Illinois. Eden's heart fell two notches. She couldn't wear that dress on a confined bus trip. It would be too hard to ignore Katelyn and her friend's whispers, their glares, and snarky comments. Instead, Eden chose her own khaki, corduroy slacks and a cream, cotton sweater. Her dress shoes were beat up, but a little shoe polish improved her only option.

"Get up, Abby," Eden said, shaking Abby's thin shoulder. "I can't be late for school. I'm going on the bus trip today and we're leaving at 8:30!"

"I'm tired, Eden," Abby groused, and she pulled the blankets over her head.

"Then you can walk to school this morning by yourself. But you better watch out for old Mr. Barnett."

Abby threw the blankets off of her. She scrambled to her feet and ran for the bathroom. 15 minutes later, dressed and clean, she met Eden in the kitchen. Eden spread white toast with peanut butter and handed a piece to Abby. Abby took a bite and swallowed hard. "I need something to drink," she said, nearly choking.

"There's no time," Eden said, and she grabbed her backpack. She helped Abby on with her flowered, waist-length jacket, grabbed Abby's books, and they hurried out the door.

"Slow down!" Abby puffed as she tried to keep up with her big sister.

Distracted, Eden stepped off the curb and a big truck roared by with the horn blaring through the next block.

"Don't you tell Momma about this," Eden threatened, and she grabbed Abby's hand and quickly marched them down Porter Street toward Abby's school.

Eden wasn't angry at Abby, even though, at the moment, it appeared she was. Her day had started off badly when she woke up and saw Katelyn Edward's dress hanging on her bedroom door. It proved to be an ominous omen. They were out of shampoo when she showered. Her ancient blow dryer abruptly stopped working halfway through drying her hair. And she discovered a dime-sized hole in the heel of her only good pair of socks.

The girls passed by an old, two-story house with a sagging porch that was crisscrossed with dead vines. Abby saw a tattered curtain at the front window flutter, and she imagined old Mr. Barnett sitting behind the curtain, watching her.

"Why does Mr. Barnett like looking at kids?" Abby asked, huffing and puffing to keep up with Eden.

"He's a perv," Eden said, stopping at the curb for Mr. Ames, the elementary school janitor and crossing guard, to let them cross the street.

"What's a perv, Eden?" Abby asked breathlessly.

"It's short for pervert."

"What's a pervert?" Abby asked innocently.

"It's a dirty old man who would like to do bad things to little girls," Eden said impatiently.

Abby started to wail. She pulled her hand out of Eden's hand and ran and hid in a clump of bushes.

"Get out of there, Abby!" Eden snapped.

"You scared me, Eden," Abby cried.

Eden took a deep breath and let it out slowly. She knew she had no right to take her frustration out on her little sister. Eden bent down and she said, "I'm sorry, Abby, for being so mean."

Abby sniffed, then she smiled pathetically at Eden.

"It's okay," Abby said.

"Thanks for forgiving me," Eden said, and she took hold of Abby's hand and helped her out of the bush.

Standing at the entrance of Maramount Elementary, Eden kissed Abby and told her to have a good day.

"I love you, Eden," Abby said as she skipped inside her school.

For the rest of her walk to school, Eden felt miserable for treating Abby so badly. A momentary thought made her wonder if she had inherited some of her father's meanness. She quickly banished the idea. For penance, she vowed to never act impatient or surly toward anyone again. And she swore she would help her mother more around the house and spend more quality time with her little sister.

When Eden arrived at school, 130 members of her class were restlessly gathered on the school lawn, waiting to board the line of idling school buses.

"Listen up, everybody!" Principal Dean McMurphy shouted through a megaphone. "You will be seated on the buses in alphabetical order. A through E, you're on bus number one. F through J, you're on bus number two. K through O, you're on bus number three. P through Z, you're on bus number four."

Eden breathed a sigh of relief. The three people she disliked most in her class would all be riding together on another bus. The one downside, she would be on the same bus as Riker Overall. But the bonus was Mrs. Omaha would be riding on the bus with Eden.

With the buses filled, the first bus took off, followed by the other three buses. Eden felt adventurous on the ride from Maramount to Champaign, Illinois, home of the University of Illinois. As the bus ventured down the interstate, Eden marveled at how flat Illinois was and at the copious amount of corn, soybean, hay, and wheat fields that lined the road.

"What you gonna be studying at the U of I, Eden?" Riker asked as he unwrapped a Snickers bar.

"If I ever get to go there, I would like to study writing," she said softly.

"What would you write about?" he asked, and he took a large bite of the candy bar.

"Everything. Well, maybe not sports."

"If you don't include sports, then it sounds boring to me," he said through his chocolate-covered teeth.

"What do you want to be, Riker?"

Eloise Ornsby turned around in her seat and she said smartly, "Riker aspires to be a buffoon."

Everybody around them laughed, including Riker.

When the laughter died down, Riker whispered to Eden, "What's a buffoon?"

Eden knew how it felt to be bullied and taunted. She felt sorry for Riker. Eden whispered, "I think she meant you want to be in a platoon."

"That's got something to do with being a soldier, right?"

"That's right."

Riker seemed satisfied with Eden's small fib.

The University of Illinois signs appeared more frequently. Going under the final overpass, Eden's heart sped up when she saw the blue and orange U of I logo with the date '1867' stamped in the middle.

*How many people have graduated from this fine school in 150 years,* she thought. Her emotions fluctuated between intense fear and overwhelming excitement.

As they approached the university, she was struck by the massive size of the campus. Several stately buildings were situated around what was called the Quad. Eden silently read a few of the names on the buildings as they drove by—Foellinger Auditorium, Lincoln Hall, Smith Hall, and Harker Hall which was built in 1878 and was the campus's oldest classroom building.

The buses pulled up in the parking lot next to the Illini Union. Several of the students seated on the right side of the bus saw a mishmash of ebullient students pour out of the union. A tall, good-looking, young man with curly, dark hair, wearing jeans and an orange-and-blue University of Illinois sweatshirt came over to the buses and smiled broadly.

"I believe our tour guide has arrived," Mr. Tomkins said from his seat behind the bus driver. Seated across the aisle from Mr. Tomkins, Mrs. Omaha turned and looked out the window at the young man. Mr. Tomkins, a biology teacher, was the acting bus supervisor. Mrs. Omaha was designated as a chaperone.

Mr. Tomkins gathered his papers together and stood up at the front of the bus.

He said, "When the bus comes to a complete stop, everyone stand and form a single file and quietly exit the bus. Now, remember. There are many high schools on tour here today, so follow the rules and stay with the class. Enjoy your day!"

It took several minutes for all the students to evacuate the buses. When the accompanying faculty and the students were gathered in front of the union, the young man said exuberantly, "Good morning, Maramount High School faculty and senior class!"

"Good morning," the crowd responded in unison.

"My name is Jordan Hendrickson. I am a senior here at the university and I will serve as your tour guide today. Let me start by telling you a few interesting facts about our fine college. On March 2, 1868, the Illinois Industrial University started classes here for the first time. The school had an enrollment of 77 students with only two members of faculty. Imagine, ladies and gentlemen of the faculty, if you had to teach 77 students university courses with just two teachers. Sounds daunting, doesn't it?"

Several of the teachers nodded. Jordan continued, "In 1885, the Illinois Industrial University officially became the University of Illinois.

"The center of the university is composed of four quadrangles, arranged from north to south. The university incorporates 17 colleges in this complex, offering over 150 programs of study. The campus boasts 647 buildings situated on 4,552 acres. Currently, we estimate there are 30,366 undergraduates attending the university. There are 36 sororities with approximately 3,463 members and 59 fraternities that have an estimated 3,674 memberships. The Greek system is self-governed.

"As of this year, the university dauntingly claims of its faculty and alumni 21 persons who are Nobel Laureates and 20 who have won a Pulitzer Prize. The University of Illinois was one of 37 land grants signed into law by President Abraham Lincoln. When we visit Lincoln Hall today, you will see the bronze bust of President Lincoln. Pay close attention to the statue's shiny, bronze nose. Unlike the rest of the statute whose bronze has naturally tarnished darker over time, the nose remains shiny bronze as the superstition amongst students is if you rub the nose prior to a test, you are sure to have great luck.

"Let's begin the tour!" Jordan said.

Mrs. Omaha pushed through the crowd toward Eden. When she caught up with Eden, she said, "I told the other supervisors that we will be gone for a few hours. Are you ready to go?"

"Yes, but where are we going, Mrs. Omaha?"

"First, we're going to get something to eat. I know it's only 10:30, but does Italian food sound good to you?" Mrs. Omaha asked.

"Yes, ma'am."

Eden loved walking around the Quad. She envisioned herself with a backpack full of books, going to a poetry class. She longed to be sitting on one of the benches outside, studying her college homework.

"We're going to Follett's," Mrs. Omaha said. "In my opinion, they have the best Italian food on campus. And you'll love looking at the walls. They display a lot of U of I memorabilia."

When they entered the restaurant, Eden's stomach grumbled from the tantalizing aromas of freshly baked bread, spaghetti, and pizza. She noticed a plaque hanging above the entrance that said, 'If a child cannot learn the way we teach, maybe we need to teach the way that they learn.' The quote was not attributed to an author.

Noticing a few empty seats, Mrs. Omaha said, "Looks like we beat the lunch crowd."

Eden noticed a slender, elderly man with thinning, iron-gray hair sitting in graffiti-etched booth at the back of the restaurant. He wore a rumpled, brown, corduroy, sports coat with frayed leather patches on the elbows, khaki-colored double-knit slacks, a rumpled shirt that had once been white but was now a yellowing gray, and a knit tie with colors of purple, green, black, and orange, one that looked like a schematic in a psychiatric hospital, which a seriously disturbed person might be expected to analyze. He seemed absorbed in reading a newspaper through a pair of small, round spectacles perched on the end of his nose. Eden thought he looked familiar. She studied his face and racked her brain to discover how she knew him. And then it hit her. *That's Professor Samuel Altgeld, the poet laureate,* she thought and she nearly screamed with joy. Eden thought she might faint when Mrs. Omaha led her over to the professor's booth.

"Good morning, Professor Altgeld," Mrs. Omaha said.

The old professor looked up at her, taking a moment to identify who she was.

"Annie!" he exclaimed. "It's so nice to see you."

"Professor, you haven't changed in 20 years," Mrs. Omaha said.

The professor looked at Eden and he said, "Annie always was a schmoozer."

Mrs. Omaha smiled at her old mentor. "This is Eden Owens, Professor. She's the girl I told you about."

The professor studied Eden's expressive face for a full minute. He looked at her trembling hand. His rheumy eyes slipped down the length of her shifting body.

"It's nice to meet you, Miss Owens," he said in his deep, professorial voice.

"I'm so delighted to meet you, Professor Altgeld!" Eden said enthusiastically.

"Please join me," the professor said. Mrs. Omaha motioned Eden into the booth. She followed.

An attractive brunette dressed in a black-and-white waitress's uniform approached their booth. She laid menus in front of Eden and Mrs. Omaha.

"Will you be having your usual today, Professor?" she asked, and she smiled.

"I will indeed, Gladys," Professor Altgeld answered.

"Are you two ladies ready to order?" she asked with her pencil poised over the order pad.

"You order first, Eden," Mrs. Omaha said, studying all the appetizing choices.

Eden looked at the food prices on the menu, trying to select the least expensive item.

"I'll have the small plate of spaghetti and a glass of water," she said shyly.

The waitress looked at Mrs. Omaha. "And what would you like?" she asked.

"I'll have a bowl of minestrone soup, a glass of iced tea with lemon, and a large vegetarian pizza which I intend to share with you, Eden," Mrs. Omaha said, and she handed her menu back to the waitress.

Mrs. Omaha folded her hands in her lap and said, "What did you think of this young lady's writing, Professor?"

"I'm impressed with her grasp of the poetic phrase," Altgeld said.

Eden was thrilled to hear this renowned literary genius praise her work. She was familiar with Samuel Altgeld's poems. He wrote about tropical forests, sunburst skies, red moons, rare flowers, the turbulent and unpredictable seas. His fascination with human subjects caused him to question a person's quest for greatness and how depraved they became to achieve their selfish dreams.

Eden stirred her water with the straw, thinking, *I'm sitting across from this illustrious poet laureate who expresses his feelings in such prolific prose. What can he see in my poems? I write about myself, my strife, my life. Boring! I'm truly embarrassed.*

"Are you still with us?" Professor Altgeld called, trying to break through her self-doubt and harsh self-criticism which he clearly recognized.

"I'm sorry, sir. Did you say something to me?"

"I believe in you," he said.

Tears welled in Eden's eyes, and she looked away.

The old professor reached across the table, and he patted the table near Eden's hand. "Now, now. Life seems so complicated when we are young. But when you reach my age, you will see that the things you deemed so important in your youth suddenly have no relevance at all."

Eden's chin trembled as she tried to smile at him.

"Your beaming smile brings light to this room. I see you someday sitting on a tropical island with a pen and paper on your lap, writing about the gentle waves sweeping across a lapis lazuli ocean and telling of the colorful birds that fly overhead which are framed by a smoky-blue sky."

"Thank you, Professor Altgeld," Eden said.

"You are most welcome, my dear," the professor said, patting the table near her hand again.

The waitress reappeared, carrying a tray filled with mouthwatering food. She served the professor a baked potato with extra butter and extra sour cream, a bowl of rigatoni with red-meat sauce, warm buttery garlic bread, and an iced tea. Then Mrs. Omaha and Eden received their orders.

Following the professor's lead, the ladies ate with gusto.

When they had finished eating, the waitress took their empty dishes away.

"I feel like a snake that swallowed a rabbit!" Professor Altgeld said, rubbing his distended stomach.

"Did you enjoy the veggie pizza, Eden?" Mrs. Omaha asked.

"Oh, yes, ma'am! I believe it was the best pizza I have ever eaten." Technically, Eden was not lying, as it was the only time she had ever eaten a pizza. Snacks at their house consisted of chips, pretzels, and popcorn. Eden knew that Rick often went out with his friends for pizza. But he had his own money.

The waitress made a tour of the restaurant, refilling glasses with iced tea. Professor Altgeld took a drink of the refreshed iced tea and said, "Eden, you are the first writer I have seen, besides myself of course," he chuckled, "who uses a color system to express yourself. It's genius, if I say so myself. Which college will you be attending this fall?"

"I won't be going to college this fall, Professor."

The professor shot a quick look at Mrs. Omaha. He knew the score, having gotten the lowdown from Annie Omaha earlier that week.

"As it happens, I am affiliated with a program called Semester Abroad which, as the name implies, is a semester of college studies on a ship that travels to many exotic places. Each year, the board of directors sponsors a few gifted students with a scholarship. That much being said, I want to endorse you, Eden, as one of the honored students who may receive our all-inclusive scholarship. The scholarship hasn't been given to anyone as of yet because the board will only give it to one they deem worthy. Last year, it wasn't given out at all."

"Thank you, Professor Altgeld!" Eden said, and she jumped out of the booth and hugged the skinny professor. The professor winked at a beaming Mrs. Omaha. He steadied his wobbly iced-tea glass and graciously accepted Eden's heartfelt gratitude.

# Seven

Isabelle stood over the ironing board, pressing Eden and Abby's worn-out clothes. Her children might not have the best wardrobe to wear, but Isabelle was determined to make them look as nice as she could. She picked up the spray bottle filled with water, squirted a pair of Eden's wrinkled jeans, and pushed the hot, black iron back and forth across the damp, faded fabric.

The door opened and Eden burst into the room. "Momma!" she shouted, "I met Poet Laureate Samuel Altgeld today!"

"That's nice, dear," Isabelle said, selecting a blue blouse from the wicker-clothes basket. Isabelle had no idea who Samuel Altgeld was. Poetry didn't interest her.

Isabelle propped the iron up. She went over to the stove and poured boiling water in a cup over her used teabag.

"Aren't you excited for me, Momma?" Eden asked, her disappointment chastising her mother.

Isabelle stirred sugar and milk in her tea. "I'm sorry, Eden, but I have no idea who…what's his name is."

"His name is Samuel Altgeld. And he's a poet, Momma," Eden said, frustrated.

"No, he's more than that. He's a philosopher. He's a professor. He's a writer. He's won the Nobel Prize and the Pulitzer Prize. He's a genius!"

Isabelle went back to her ironing. She sprayed the blouse with water and pushed the hot iron across it. "Was Mr. Adler a guest speaker at the university today?"

"His name is Altgeld, Momma. No, he didn't give a speech at the university. Mrs. Omaha arranged for us to join the professor for lunch. It was a complete surprise to me. Momma, Professor Altgeld was so nice to me. He's read some of my poems and he said I am a good writer. He thinks I could

47

someday be published. Oh, Momma, I had the best time I have ever had in my life!"

"How did he read your poems, Eden? Did you take a few of them with you?"

"Mrs. Omaha sent some of my poems to Professor Altgeld. She told me he mentored her when she was in college."

*Mrs. Omaha to the rescue, again,* Isabelle thought bitterly.

"I have more exciting news!"

Isabelle finished the last piece of ironing. She hung the pressed blouse on a wire hanger, folded up the ironing board, and put it away behind the pantry door. Eden didn't understand her mother's indifference.

"Aren't you interested to know what else happened today, Momma?"

When Clem had driven Isabelle to work that morning, he started his usual tirade about still having to feed and clothe Eden. He thought, he said, it was time to push her out of the nest. She could find a husband to take care of her. Isabelle hadn't responded to Clem. Nothing she ever said made an impression on him.

Exhausted, Isabelle sat down on the kitchen chair. She took a deep breath and let it out slowly.

"Yes, Eden, I am interested in hearing about your day," she said wearily.

Eden's enthusiasm quickly faded. She sat down in the chair next to her mother, reached across the table, and put her hand lovingly on her mother's slender arm.

"I'm sorry I'm so chatty today, Momma. I'm almost as bad as Abby."

Isabelle's gaze remained lowered.

"I wish I had been able to provide all my children with a better life," she said sadly.

"Oh, Momma. You did the best you could do. Your life certainly hasn't been easy. I'm sorry for that. But I have big plans. I don't know exactly how I will accomplish it, but I promise you, I will find a way for you and Abby and me to have a new life."

Isabelle looked up at her pretty daughter. "Abby and I are not your responsibility, Eden. Just find a better way for yourself," she said sorrowfully.

"I would like to show you something on the computer," Eden said, referring to their outdated computer which was big as their old box television.

48

When the towing business slowed down, for extra cash, Clem let people trash their old computers in a metal bin behind the gas station. It was illegal to throw computers in the trash in Illinois. Eden had been able to salvage one computer which proved to be a slow-working word processor, and if Clem's monthly internet-sports bill was paid, she and Abby could use the internet.

Clem ordered Eden and Abby to leave the computer unplugged when not in use. He also restricted their internet usage. He said he didn't want to pay a higher electricity bill.

Eden went into the bedroom she shared with Abby and plugged in the computer.

It took several minutes for it to boot up. When the homepage finally filled the screen, Eden went to Google search engine and typed in 'Studies Abroad.'

"Come and look at this, Momma," Eden called.

Isabelle walked slowly into the room. Eden pulled out her desk chair and asked her mother to sit down. When Isabelle was seated, Eden read the document as she scrolled down.

"Studies Abroad is a spring and fall, semester program. The Fall 2020 program will begin on August 15th and end on December 15th," she said. "For 123 days, students will be expected to maintain a rigorous study curriculum. There will be plenty of time to enjoy all the ship's extracurricular activities, such as watching current movies, dancing to a live band, rock climbing, table tennis, inline skating, miniature golf, working out in a fully equipped fitness center, swimming, or watching movies in our newest addition, the fabulous theater with heated and air-conditioned seats. The voyage will take our guests to an exciting 16 foreign countries. Five of the cities on the tour are designated as overland ports, which indicates the ship will dock and stay in port for several days so our guests may leisurely enjoy such things as shopping and sightseeing. Among those exotic, fun-filled ports of call are Shanghai, Taipei, Hong Kong, and Singapore."

"That sounds fine, Eden. But what does it have to do with you?"

"Professor Altgeld is on the board of directors for the Studies Abroad program, Momma. He told me today that he is going to recommend me for the all-inclusive scholarship."

"I'm very happy for you, dear," Isabelle said, and she hugged Eden. "Is Mrs. Omaha going too?"

Eden looked at her mother oddly. "No, Momma. This is a trip for students." Eden saw the relief on Isabelle's face.

"Momma, why are you crying?"

"It's tears of joy," Isabelle said, wiping her tears on the hem of her dress. Isabelle's tears were also filled with pain. She knew that, before long, both her girls would be leaving home.

"Did the professor tell you how to apply for the trip and what you need to do?" Isabelle asked.

"No, he didn't. Mrs. Omaha said the professor would email her the application and she'd help me with it."

Abby came bouncing into the room. "What's going on?" she asked, seeing the computer turned on. "Momma, are you crying?"

Isabelle pulled her two daughters into her arms and she said, "I love you two girls so much, all the way to the moon and the stars. I want you both to know that I will always love you, support you, and I'll be your biggest cheerleader. No matter where you two are in this great big world, know that I will be waiting for you with my arms open wide. Remember what we used to say when I would tuck you two into bed at night?"

"Our love will go on forever and ever and ever," Eden and Abby said in unison.

"Okay," Isabelle said as she stood up. "Better turn off the computer and get your homework done. And I have to go finish up dinner."

As Isabelle put dinner on the table, Clem stormed into the house. "Where's Rick?" he shouted.

"I assume he's working at the gas station," Isabelle said, setting a piping hot bowl of spaghetti and meatballs on the table.

"Well, he's not at the gas station. You know what that kid did?" Clem screamed.

"I have no idea."

"He let Joe Fenkster borrow the tow truck so he could pull out some old evergreens in his yard!"

"What's wrong with that?"

"The truck ain't Rick's to loan out!" Clem exploded.

"I'm sure Joe Fenkster won't hurt the truck, if that's what you're worried about."

"That's not the point! Rick should have asked me first."

"What's wrong?" Eden asked, alarmed.

"It's that damn brother of yours!" Clem said.

"What did Rick do now?" Eden asked, and she moved a few steps back from her explosive father.

"He loaned the tow truck to Joe Fenkster and he didn't ask me."

"Joe's a nice guy, Dad."

"That's not the point! You and that mother of yours are both hit in the head with the same damn hammer!"

Abby came rushing into the room. "Did Eden tell you she's going on a cruise, Daddy? Is that why you're mad?"

"What the f—" shouted Clem, but Isabelle cut him off, "Please don't use that filthy word in front of the girls, Clem."

"Like they haven't heard me use them before," Clem said bitterly. He looked at Eden. "What's this about a cruise?"

"I'm not going for sure on a study cruise," she said, and she saw the threatening look on her father's face. "I'm applying for a scholarship."

"The whole thing will be paid for?"

"Yes, Dad. If I'm granted the scholarship, it's all inclusive."

"What the hell does that mean?"

"It means everything is paid for," Eden said, and she wanted to add 'Duh!'

Rick walked through the backdoor, and Clem whirled around and headed for him. Isabelle ran toward Rick, and she positioned herself between the two men.

"Cool down, Clem," she pleaded.

Rick held his dad's angry stare. "I can handle this, Mom," he said, and he gently pushed Isabelle out of the way. Standing face to face with his livid father, Rick said, "I guess your mad-on is about me letting Joe borrow the tow truck?"

"You're damn right I am. Who do you think you are? You got no business loaning out my property without getting my permission first."

"You weren't around when Joe came to the station and asked if he could borrow the truck. Besides, I thought he'd return it before you got back."

"So now you're trying to sneak around behind my back?"

"I would have told you, Dad. After all, we all know how you get when you think someone got the upper hand over you."

Clem clenched his fist and he raised it close to Rick's face. "You're a real smartass, ain't ya, boy?"

"You know what they say. The apple doesn't fall from the tree," Rick said, and he shot his unshaved chin out and grinned daringly at his father.

There was a time Clem would have beaten Rick to a bloody pulp for a crack like that. But at 55 years of age, with his once-bulging muscles softened and his biceps hanging loosely, he cautiously watched his much-younger and much-stronger son. Clem backed off.

From across the room, he said, "That tow truck better be back in the garage by six o'clock tonight."

"It will be," Rick said, and, inwardly, he was relieved he didn't have to defend himself against his father.

Eden busied herself setting the table. Clem passed by her without speaking another word. Isabelle poured tap water into five glasses and set them on the table. "Let's not say any more about Studies Abroad tonight, Eden," she whispered. Eden nodded.

When all five of the Owens were seated around the table, eating their spaghetti, Abby said brightly, "Eden's going on a cruise ship, Rick!"

Isabelle's cheeks puffed with exasperation, and she blew the air out slowly.

"Really?" Rick asked, swirling spaghetti around the tines of his fork. "Is that true, Eden?"

"Maybe," Eden answered shyly.

"Who's paying for that?" Rick asked, and he filled his mouth with spaghetti.

"I applied for a scholarship."

"From Maramount High?"

"No, Silly. It's through a program called Studies Abroad."

"I could get into that. I like to study abroad. In fact, I'd like to study two at a time if I could get a couple to agree," Rick chuckled.

Clem, who had been pouting and bulling, huffed a laugh.

"When does this trip start?" Clem asked, his eyes on his plate of food.

"August 15th."

"When does it return?"

"December 15th."

"Hmm," Clem said, and he finished eating, roughly pushed himself from the table, and went into the living room.

52

"Why isn't Dad interested in anything I do?" Eden asked, drying a plate after dinner.

"I'm not sure I know the answer to that, Eden," Isabelle said as she rinsed a large pot and set it in the dish drainer. "You remember Grandpa Owens?" Eden nodded. "He was just as demanding and unreasonable as your father. I once saw him throw a hammer at your dad, narrowly missing his head. I think, if the hammer would have hit Clem, it would have killed him."

"Why was Grandpa like that?"

"Who knows. Maybe he had a bad childhood, or maybe the gas station wasn't doing very well."

"That's no reason to take your anger out on others."

"You're right, Eden."

"I get mad sometimes. But I don't go around screaming and throwing things and slapping people around."

"I'm glad you and Abby aren't like that."

"One of these days, Rick and Dad are really going to get into it, and if I were to bet on the outcome, I'd bet on Rick."

"I fear you are right about your dad and Rick. It seems like the rite of passage for a young man who has been mistreated by his father is to one day show his dad he is no longer afraid of him."

Isabelle turned off the kitchen light. As she passed through the living room on her way to bed, she saw Rick seated in the shabby recliner with his back to his dad and reading an issue of Sports Illustrated. Clem was snoring on the couch as World Wide Wrestling blared from the television.

# Eight

Clayton Caulder walked into his family's kitchen, yawning and scratching his balls. He saw Isabelle hard at work, cleaning the huge, sculpted, steel, convection oven which was self-cleaning but did not meet Mrs. Caulder's rigid idea of spotless. Isabelle finished cleaning the steel side-by-side refrigerator and the shiny metal dishwasher. She had yet to polish the cherry-wood carved cabinets, wash the red-enameled, lava-stone countertops, and mop the black-and-white-checkered, heated, marble floor.

Clayton turned on the indirect lighting in the towering, vaulted ceiling and cast a romantic golden glow on the spacious room. He stepped over Isabelle's bent back and walked over to the refrigerator. He opened the refrigerator door, took out a bottle of orange juice, tipped it up, and drank from the bottle.

"What time did you get in last night?" Judge Caulder asked, seated in the sunlit solarium in a leather wing chair, reading a copy of the New York Times through his square readers. As always, he wore one of his fashionable Brioni suits, a dazzling Giorgio Armani shirt and tie, and his elegant Bertuli dress shoes.

The solarium, a recent addition, had a wall of curved windows, a slate-green floor, and a large indoor water display with a bubbling fountain adorned with fragrant water lilies. Judge Caulder reached for the coffee cup sitting on a marble-topped cherry-wood table, took a sip, and set the cup back on the table.

Clayton, barefoot and dressed in a ragged pair of sweatpants and a dirty sweatshirt, looked like he'd slept under a bridge for two days and was nursing a bad hangover. His boyish face sported a heavy stubble. He had a bushy mop of uncombed blonde hair and a look on his face that warned everyone not to mess with him.

"What time is it now?" Clayton asked, screwing the top back on the orange juice and setting it back inside the refrigerator door.

Judge Caulder looked at his Patek Philippe diamond wristwatch. "It is exactly 6:51."

"In that case, I got in at exactly 5:51 this morning."

"You're going to be late for school again."

"Then maybe you should write me an excuse before you leave for work."

For the first time that morning, Judge Caulder looked at his son, shooting him a warning glare over the top of his square readers. Judge Caulder is a man who affects sensitivity. He demands discipline, order, and control, yet he lacks any form of morality. He believes himself superior to others. He obeys the law and follows the rules of society to hide his true nature which is that of a sociopath. His heart is as cold as ice. He is ruthless. He has a tremendous sense of entitlement and is incapable of love. On the flip side, he can be wonderfully witty and disarmingly charming, but these are the skills he uses to manipulate others.

Clayton laid his upper body over the island countertop and said, "Judge, there's something I want to talk to you about."

"Proceed," Judge Caulder said as he laid his newspaper down on his crossed legs. He blew on his eyeglasses and polished them with his immaculate, monogrammed handkerchief. As put his glasses back, he picked up his newspaper.

Clayton narrowed his eyes and glared at his father. He hated it when his dad treated him like a supplicant. He could not remember one time in his life when his father had called him by his name, which didn't make sense, since Clayton was Judge Caulder's middle name.

Spurred by Clayton's silence, Judge Caulder looked over his newspaper at his angry son. "You're filthy! Go upstairs and take a shower!"

"I want to ask you something first."

"Make it quick. I can smell you from here."

"There's this cruise I heard about the other day at school. It's called Studies Abroad, and me and Ben would like to go on it."

Isabelle's ears perked up.

"Ben and I," Judge Caulder said.

"You wanna go too?" Clayton asked smartly.

"Knock it off," Judge Caulder demanded.

"Will you fix it for us to go?"

"I understand why you two young hooligans might be interested in taking a cruise. I cannot, however, imagine either of you wanting to go on a study cruise. There has to be more to this than meets the eye."

"I think it will improve my grades for college."

"It's too late for that now and you know it."

"Look, Judge. This would mean a lot to me. Just fix it for us. Okay?"

Judge Caulder took a deep breath and let it out slowly. "I've heard of this Studies Abroad program. I believe the trip is for honor students, and neither Ben nor you can claim that lofty title."

"There's talk they might accept some low-life, white trash girl from South Trekkin who's in my class."

Isabelle winced, and she used the steel-wool pad on the oven with a vengeful scrub. Clayton glanced at Isabelle. He knew she was Eden's mother. He liked to rile things up.

"I'll see what I can do," Judge Caulder said, and he stood up and walked out of the solarium's outer door.

Clayton rummaged around in the cabinet where they kept boxes of assorted cereals, looking for something to eat. When he didn't see anything that looked appealing, he looked inside the refrigerator.

"Could you make me some scrambled eggs, bacon, and toast, Mrs. Owens?" Clayton asked.

Isabelle raised up; she looked the haughty young man straight in the eye and said with a sharp boldness that even surprised her, "Mrs. Wilkins will be here to prepare the food at eight. Cooking your breakfast, sir, is not part of my job description."

Clayton smiled crookedly at her. He reached in the cabinet and removed two toaster pastries and headed back upstairs.

Isabelle left the kitchen to polish the mahogany banisters that bordered the carpeted staircase. When she finished with that, she went to the master suite and softly knocked on the carved door.

"Come in," Isabelle heard Rose Caulder say in a soft voice. Isabelle opened the door and walked into the semi-dark room.

Rose Caulder, who was still in her bed at 4:30 in the afternoon, raised up on one elbow and said disagreeably, "What do you want, Isabelle?"

56

"It's 4:30, Mrs. Caulder. I have finished cleaning the house, except for your room."

"Oh, all right," Rose said, and she moved the blankets back and wobbled to her feet.

She wore a black, silk negligee and her bleached blonde hair looked like she'd been electrocuted. Isabelle saw three empty wine bottles laying randomly on their sides on the ornately carved nightstand next to a group of used Baccarat crystal stemware.

As Rose stumbled over a white satin footstool, Isabelle rushed to help her. Rose pushed Isabelle away. "I can manage."

"Yes, ma'am," Isabelle said, and she stripped the bed of the soiled sheets.

"Is Clayton in the house?"

"I don't think so, Mrs. Caulder."

"I need my son!" she said, and she crawled over to the chair and hoisted herself to her feet.

Isabelle knew when Rose Caulder referred to her son, she didn't mean Emile, her special needs son. Emile was kept isolated in a separate wing of the Caulder mansion with his male nurse. The Caulders's only daughter, Barelle Caulder, stayed in college and rarely came home. She had no use for her drunken mother or for her belligerent, indifferent father.

Isabelle heard water running into the copper bathtub in the bathroom. As she cleaned the room, Isabelle found a bottle of wine under the mattress, a second bottle under the bed, and a third bottle was half-hidden in a silk floral arrangement. Isabelle believed Mr. Caulder was partially responsible for his wife's out-of-control drinking, but she also thought Judge Caulder was a dedicated enabler. On many occasions when Isabelle had worked late at the Caulders's home, she saw Judge Caulder arrive home, carrying cases of wine which he usually took upstairs to his wife's bedroom. Isabelle's knew many secrets about her employers, but she never spoke about them to anyone.

As Rose bathed in her copper bathtub, Isabelle tidied the bedroom. She opened the heavy draperies and let in the late afternoon sun. Looking out of the upstairs window, Isabelle saw the gardening team from Garten's Nursery preparing the lawn for spring's arrival. She waved at Bert Talbert from Talbert's Swimming Pools and Spas as he removed the winter cover from the pool.

Rose opened the door of the steamy bathroom. She walked slowly over to the white chaise lounge and sat down. She wore an elegant, mauve, dressing gown and a pair of pink feathery mules on her feet. She pulled her wet hair up in a neat French chignon.

"Are you finished in here, Isabelle?" Rose asked stiffly.

"I have to clean your bathroom, then I'll be done, Mrs. Caulder," Isabelle said. She pushed a button on the vacuum cleaner and the cord disappeared inside.

Rose laid her head on the arm of the chaise lounge and placed the back of her hand on her forehead. "I envy you, Isabelle," she said, and she sighed softly. "Your life is so simple. You don't have to worry about what other people think of you. You don't have to concern yourself with how you look and all those compulsory social obligations one must attend which demand one must be charming, witty, smart, and beautiful. I try so hard to please the judge, but he is always so disapproving of everything I do."

Isabelle wished Rose and a few of the other women she cleaned for in Kingston Bay Estates could walk a mile in her shoes. She looked at her chapped hands and bleeding knuckles. She stretched her aching back and rotated her swollen feet and legs. If all the slave labor she'd done today wasn't enough, now she had to listen to this sad, useless woman moan about her miserable life. She bit her lip and silently straightened the glossy, silk comforter on the bed.

"Did you know Judge Caulder is a teetotaler?"

"No, ma'am, I didn't know that."

"Well, he is. In fact, Judge Caulder hates drunks. In his courtroom, he is known to hand down especially brutal sentences when he finds out the person drinks too much."

Isabelle didn't respond. She just kept unnecessarily tidying the room.

"Do you think it's possible my husband is trying to kill me?"

Yes, Isabelle thought. The drinking had taken a toll on her. She was thin as a rail, and she looked 20 years older than her 50 years of age. Judge Caulder didn't drink, that was true, but Isabelle knew the judge had secrets of his own. On more than one occasion, when she walked into his office to clean, the judge quickly closed down the screen to his laptop computer. She also knew he received thick envelopes once a month with foreign stamps on them.

"Would you like something to eat, Mrs. Caulder?"

"You didn't answer my question, Isabelle. Do you think my husband is trying to kill me?"

"I'm not comfortable talking about this, Mrs. Caulder," Isabelle said, fussing with a stack of books.

"I used to be beautiful," Rose said regretfully.

"I think you still are beautiful, Mrs. Caulder," Isabelle said. She hadn't lied. In a dusky room, Rose still retained the look of faded beauty.

Rose laughed softly.

"Do you know if Clayton spoke to his father about that silly cruise he wants to go on with Ben Atler?"

If Isabelle said she did know, then it would be obvious she had eavesdropped. "A cruise, you say?"

"Yes, a study cruise of some sort. Now that's a laugh."

"Why do you say that, Mrs. Caulder?"

"Clayton is almost flunking out of high school. If it wasn't for his father's influence, Clayton would have been expelled this entire year. How he thinks he will qualify for something as important as a semester studying abroad is beyond me."

"Perhaps, as you say, Judge Caulder can influence the decision," Isabelle said, and she prayed that would not be the case, especially with the ugly things he had said about Eden who may also be on the ship.

# Nine

Through her diligent efforts, Mrs. Omaha had obtained permission from the high school to fund Eden's A.C.T. examination costs. The night before her exam, Eden once again looked over the test-day checklist. She was to report for the test at 8 a.m. She was to bring a printed copy of her ticket and a photo ID. Check. Any prohibited behavior would result in dismissal, and the perpetrator's test would not be scored. Check. A permitted calculator may be used on the mathematics test only. Mrs. Omaha loaned Eden a scientific calculator, which was required, because Eden couldn't afford one. Cellphones and all other electronic devices were strictly prohibited. Check. Students were suggested to bring at least four, sharpened, number-two pencils. Check. There would be a short break after the first two tests. Check. Students taking the A.C.T. should expect to be dismissed by 12:15 p.m. Students taking the A.C.T. Plus Writing would be dismissed at 1 p.m. Check. She looked at the tests on the A.C.T. exam and the time allocated to each subject. Mathematics: 60 questions—60 minutes. English: 75 questions—45 minutes. Science: 40 questions—35 minutes. Reading: 40 questions—35 minutes. Writing: one question—35 minutes.

Friday morning at 7:30 a.m., Eden walked into the gymnasium with dozens of other students. The students formed a line before a panel of testing staff to each have their photo ID and ticket verified. Each student was directed to a seat and given a packet of sealed test material. Eden noticed that Katelyn Edwards, Ben Atler, and Clayton Caulder were nervously looking around. *Normally, being in the same room with my three worst enemies would have been enough to derail me,* Eden thought. *But not today. I am looking forward to taking the A.C.T. My mind is clear. I feel rested. I'm confident that I know the material. Best of all, none of the three evil musketeers are allowed to speak to me.*

At exactly 8 a.m., a member of the test staff said, "You may begin."

Eden opened her packet and whizzed through the English and science exam. After the short break, she breezed through the mathematics test and the reading test, finishing with 15 minutes left to go. At 12:15 p.m., a test staff member announced, "Time is up. Put down your pencils and close your testing material."

Katelyn Edwards walked triumphantly to the front, and, with a flourish, she handed in her test. Ben Atler followed. He looked worn out. Clayton Caulder walked confidently to the front and laid his test on the test staff's table. Eden knew Clayton didn't make good grades because he didn't care to. She also knew he was smart enough to do well on his A.C.T. Eden paused to let the others turn in their test and head out the gymnasium door before she stood up, walked to the front of the room, and handed her test in.

She knew she had done well on her test. With a spring in her step and feeling like she was walking on air, Eden headed home. She was greeted with the delicious aroma of shepherd's pie and the smell of freshly baked bread.

"How did you do on your A.C.T. test?" Isabelle asked, taking the bread out of the oven.

"I believe I aced it."

"That's wonderful, Eden! Did you happen to see Clayton Caulder and Ben Atler there this morning?" Eden thought that was an odd question for her mother to be asking.

"Yes, I saw them."

"I wonder how they scored on the test."

"Ben isn't the sharpest pencil in the box, but I expect he did okay. Clayton is really smart. He probably did great."

"You think they might try to go on the Studies Abroad trip?"

"I hope not! What made you ask about those two?"

"I know they're in your class. And I work for both of their parents. Just curious, I guess."

Eden changed the subject, "What's that on the bread, Momma?"

"That's rosemary, Eden. Mrs. Edwards gave it to me the other day when I cleaned their house," she said, and she brushed oil on top of the bread and sprinkled it with salt.

Eden popped a small piece of carrot into her mouth, and she chewed noisily.

"As I was leaving school today, I ran into Mrs. Omaha. She mentioned the Studies Abroad scholarship doesn't cover the cost of my flight to San Diego."

Isabelle's heart sank. There's always a catch, particularly if something's called 'free.'

"I think I'll need a few more clothes," Eden said, watching her mother's face darken with concern. "But don't worry, Momma. Mrs. Omaha said I can babysit her twin boys to earn some extra money."

"Why is Mrs. Omaha helping you, Eden?"

"She likes me and wants to give me a chance for a better life."

That sounded condescending to Isabelle.

"If something happens and the Studies Abroad program isn't made available to you, what rabbit will Mrs. Omaha pull out of her hat then?"

Eden didn't understand her mother's snarky tone.

"You don't like Mrs. Omaha, do you, Momma?"

Eden called it right. But Isabelle said, "I don't really know her. I just can't imagine why she is taking such an interest in you."

"I don't know the answer to that. I just know I'm grateful to Mrs. Omaha for all the kind things she has done for me. I never would have been able to go with my class the other day to the University of Illinois if not for Mrs. Omaha. She even arranged for me to meet Professor Altgeld! He led me to believe I might be able to participate in the Studies Abroad program. Mrs. Omaha offered me a babysitting job to earn some spending money for the trip which, hopefully, I will get to take. She also arranged for Professor Altgeld to email assignments to me each week this summer so I may gain a better understanding of the creative process needed to write worthwhile poetry. That is, if I get the scholarship, of course. You do understand why I don't want to look a gift horse in the mouth, don't you, Momma?"

"Of course I do, sweetheart. I'll try to be less critical of Mrs. Omaha."

"Thank you, Momma."

"When will you start the babysitting job for her? Oh, my goodness! I just remembered something. I promised Mavis Pollard that you would watch her three kids on the weekends while she works at the I.G.A.," Isabelle said while pulling the steaming casserole out of the oven. "Any chance you will have time to do both babysitting jobs?"

"I don't think so. I feel really bad about this. I owe Mrs. Omaha so much for all she'd done for me. What would I tell her, Momma?"

Rick came strolling in the backdoor. He tossed his grimy denim jacket and soiled hat on the wooden bench as he pulled off his muddy boots.

"Afternoon all," he said, ambling over to the stove and sniffing the casserole. "What's the grass doing on top of the bread?" he asked.

"It's rosemary," Eden snapped.

"Eden, I'll tell Mavis I will be glad to take care of her sons for her."

"I can't ask you to do that, Momma. You're already nearly worked to death."

"It's okay, Eden. I'm the one who obligated you. The scholarship program is far more important."

"You two talking about Mavis Pollard over at the I.G.A.?" Rick asked, flopping down on a kitchen chair. He crossed his right leg over his left leg and picked on the toe of his dirty sock.

"Yes, not that it's any of your business," Eden said.

"I saw her today at the station when she was getting gas in that old beater she drives. I don't think she's gonna be needing a babysitter now."

Eden sat down across from her brother.

"Why won't she need a sitter?"

"She got laid off today," he said. "And you know her man left her a couple months ago. Looks like she'll be moving back in with her folks in their one-bedroom house over on Claremont Street."

"Well, I guess my problem is solved."

"How'd you do on your A.C.T. test today?" Rick asked, moving the salt shaker around the center of the table like a triangle on an Ouija board.

"I think I aced it."

"I'm not surprised. You know. Every time I have to crawl under a rusted-out old beater, I wish I'd taken school more seriously."

This was the first time Isabelle had ever heard Rick voice regret about his lackluster performance at school.

"It's never too late to go back to school, Rick," Isabelle said as she set the table.

"Yeah, it is, Mom," Rick said, and he lined the salt shaker up next to the pepper shaker.

"Mom's right, Rick. I bet Mrs. Omaha would help you get your G.E.D. Then you could take a few local college courses and later go on to a better college."

Isabelle resented the idea of Mrs. Omaha influencing another of her children.

"Rick, you can get a G.E.D. on your own," she said.

"The old man would laugh his head off if I crawled back to school."

"Remember how interested you were in mathematics when you were young, Rick?" Isabelle asked, placing silverware next to the plates.

"Yeah, I do."

"Have you ever considered going to a junior college like Eden suggested and getting a degree in accounting?"

"I've thought of a lot of things. But I don't have the moolah," he said, rubbing his forefinger and thumb together.

Clem came into the kitchen. He'd been asleep on the sofa in the living room. His clothes were rumpled and his hair shot up in oily spikes.

"Supper ready yet?" he asked, stretching and yawning.

Isabelle answered, "Yes, dinner is ready. Call Abby, Eden."

Clem threw his heavy leg across the chair and sat down at the head of the table. Isabelle placed the casserole on a pot holder in the middle of the table, next to the platter of sliced rosemary bread.

"What's that shit on the bread?" Clem roared.

"It's called rosemary, Clem," Isabelle said softly. Clem threw his thick arm out and shoved the platter of bread crashing to the floor.

"Now, get me some real bread," he said.

Isabelle picked the bread up off the floor along with the broken platter, and she threw it all in the wastebasket. She got a loaf of white bread in a plastic wrapper, and she set it on the table in front of Clem. And, once again, the five of them ate their dinner in a disturbed silence.

# Ten

Toward the end of May, Isabelle sat at the laminated kitchen table with a large unopened envelope in her hand. When Eden and Abby came through the door, Isabelle said, "Eden, something came in the mail for you today."

Eden swallowed hard. The only mail she knew she would be receiving was her A.C.T. score. This was an important part of the Studies Abroad scholarship because without a top score, even the best recommendations and her talent weren't enough to give her a 40-thousand-dollar scholarship.

Abby ran and grabbed the envelope. She waved it over her head and ran into the living room. "Eden's got a letter! Eden's got a letter!" Abby chanted as she ran around the sofa and Eden frantically chased her.

"Stop it, Abby, and give the letter to Eden at once!" Isabelle said. But Abby's heady enthusiasm caused her to tear open the letter. "I see a number 32!"

"I'm going to wring your neck!" Eden shouted, jumping over the sofa, her hand just missing Abby. Isabelle intervened, and Abby was caught in her mother's outstretched arms. Eden grabbed the letter out of Abby's hand and analyzed the document.

"I got a perfect score on the English exam! That means I'm still in the race to win the golden ticket to Studies Abroad," she said, referring to the golden ticket in Charlie and the Chocolate Factory that Isabelle read to them over and over as children.

"I'm so happy for you," Isabelle said, and her voice broke with emotion.

"Mrs. Omaha and I were hoping for this, Professor Altgeld too. Isn't this wonderful, Momma?" Eden asked, and she tightly hugged her mother. "I have to take this to school tomorrow and show Mrs. Omaha."

"Make Mrs. Omaha a copy of your test scores, Eden. You need to keep the original."

Eden said she would make a copy at the school library. She didn't fully understand why her mother was so fearful and always on guard. Eden placed the paper back into the thick envelope that she had received them in.

"We have graduation rehearsals at school this afternoon," she said. "They announced earlier in the week that Edie Welcher, our chubby, baby-talking, home-economics teacher, and tough gal Tina Lassiter, the girl's P.E. teacher and former Marine, are conducting today's run through. That should be interesting. Those two women are polar opposites. We had a short run through yesterday, with Ms. Lassiter telling us to, 'Concentrate and focus!' She said the graduation program will be recorded on a D.V.D. so none of us better goof off. We were warned to, 'Make the school and your parents proud!'"

"Ms. Lassiter sounds tough," Isabelle said as she washed the last of the breakfast dishes.

Isabelle didn't have to work at the Kubey's today. They had out-of-town guests staying the weekend at their house.

"What did Mrs. Welcher advise your class to do?"

"She wished us good luck, and she said she knew we would do our best."

"Mrs. Welcher sounds nice. Ms. Lassiter, well… I guess you can take the soldier out of the marines, but not the marine out of the soldier."

Eden looked at the clock on the kitchen wall. "I have to go," she said.

"When you get home, we'll go to Goodwill and look for a nice dress for you to wear to your graduation," Isabelle said.

Internally, Eden cringed.

After the short graduation rehearsal, the students were dismissed from school for the rest of the day. Eden needed to get her jacket out of her locker. She turned her combination lock and opened the door. Taped to the inside of her locker, she saw a photo-shopped picture of herself sitting naked on a metal chair with her hands and feet tied and duct tape stretched over her mouth. She heard laughing. She turned and saw Clayton Caulder and Ben Atler with their thumbs raised and pointing their index fingers like a gun at Eden. Trembling, Eden ripped the picture down, wadded it up, stuffed it in the pocket of her jeans, and quickly left the school.

"Hi, Eden!" Abby yelled, standing outside her elementary school as she skipped toward her sister. Abby didn't notice Eden's preoccupied, disturbed state of mind. Eden and Abby usually raced each other home. But this time when Abby said, "Ready, set, go!" Eden kept on walking. Abby didn't question her big sister's change of routine. Instead, she walked alongside Eden.

"Today is Vanessa Donnelley's birthday," Abby chatted excitedly. "Her momma brought our entire class some pretty, pink, iced cupcakes, juice boxes, and presents for all of us! I got some Bubblicious gum. Want some?" Abby asked, holding a piece of gum up to Eden.

"No, thank you," Eden said quietly.

"You better take some gum while you can," Abby taunted. "Or, I'll have it all chewed up by tonight."

Eden kept walking; her troubled gaze focused straight ahead.

"What's wrong, Eden?" Abby asked, stuffing her mouth with the piece of bubble gum she'd offered Eden. Eden never spoke the rest of the way home. When the girls arrived home, Isabelle was busy peeling potatoes, paying close attention to the rank-smelling black spots. Eden took off her shoes at the door and walked quietly to her room.

"What's wrong with Eden?" Isabelle asked Abby.

"I don't know, Momma," Abby said, dropping her backpack on the floor. She had so much gum in her mouth, she looked like a blow fish. Isabelle dried her hands on a towel that hung over her left shoulder. She went to Eden and Abby's bedroom. She opened the creaky bedroom door and saw Eden sitting on her desk chair with her back to the door, looking out the window.

"Are you all right, honey?" she asked.

"I'm fine, Momma," Eden said quietly. Isabelle came into the room. She sat down on Abby's bed and laid her cool hand on Eden's bare arm.

"I can see something is bothering you, Eden. Please tell me what it is."

Eden couldn't tell her mother about the incident with Clayton and Ben. What could her mother do about it, anyway? Instead, she said, "I guess I'm a little nervous about all the changes going on right now… Graduation, maybe Studies Abroad, hopefully college."

"I imagine all the things happening to you right now seem overwhelming. But sometimes God changes things because He's preparing you for something much better."

Eden turned her tear-streaked face to her mother and said, "Thank you, Momma, for always knowing the right thing to say to make me feel better."

Isabelle hugged her daughter tightly. "I love you, Eden," she said.

"I love you too, Momma."

"Okay. Can you take out the trash for me? Some of those potatoes smell awful."

"Sure, Momma," Eden said, smiling weakly.

For the rest of the evening, Isabelle surreptitiously watched Eden. She wondered if Studies Abroad would be too big a change for her. She knew Eden wasn't entirely prepared for what may come if she gets the scholarship. She also knew the scholarship might prove to be Eden's one-way ticket out of Maramount.

When Eden returned from taking out the garbage, Isabelle said excitedly, "I have great news! Judge Caulder just called, and he said if I want to work a few extra evenings, he will pay me twice what I'm making now."

"Oh, no, Momma. Don't take the job. Please don't take it."

"Don't be silly, Eden. We need the money to pay the bills."

"If you insist on taking the job, promise me you won't ever take Abby to the Caulder's."

"Why would you want me to promise that, Eden?"

"Abby is so young and impressionable. I don't think it's good for her to see how poor we are compared to the very rich Caulder's."

The truth was, Eden's concern was that Abby might meet Clayton and Ben.

"If it means that much to you, then I won't take Abby there."

"Thank you, Momma." Eden said. For the umpteenth time that night, Eden wept.

# Eleven

It was the Tuesday before the Friday graduation day. Eden worked hard on the poetry assignments Professor Altgeld sent to her. Eden was falling in love with the potential of her future. She never in her entire life had felt so elated, curious, magical, and optimistic. She sent a copy of her poem to Professor Altgeld and Mrs. Omaha via email. Both responses came back enthusiastic and delighted with her work.

Eden sat in the gymnasium with the rest of the graduating class, listening again to the dictatorial instructions coming from Ms. Lassiter. Mrs. Omaha, carrying a large packet in her hand, rushed into the gym and hurried over to Ms. Lassiter.

"Excuse me for interrupting, Ms. Lassiter, but I have an urgent message for Eden Owens."

Eden heard her name and something about an urgent message. Her mind flew in a hundred different directions, picturing many dreadful scenarios. Maybe Abby was hurt. What if Momma got run over by a car? Maybe their house burned down.

"Eden Owens, front and center!" Ms. Lassiter barked.

Eden sat in the front row in the middle of the other honor students. The rest of the class was seated behind the first row in alphabetical order. As she stood, Eden saw Clayton Caulder three rows back, intently watching her. Her stomach flipped with nervousness. She walked quickly to the podium. Mrs. Omaha and Eden quickly left the stage and stood behind the scene, away from the prying eyes of Eden's classmates.

"I apologize for the dramatics, Eden," Mrs. Omaha said, "but I have just received a package for you."

Eden stared nervously at the envelope in Mrs. Omaha's quivering hand.

"Open it, Eden. This may very well determine your future."

Eden placed the thick envelope next to her heart and she prayed, "Please, dear Lord, let it be the scholarship."

Eden slowly opened the envelope and read...

*"Dear Ms. Owens: We are honored to inform you of your admission to the Fall Studies Abroad program. We commend you on your scholastic and personal accomplishments. Furthermore, you will be pleased to know we are awarding to you a full scholarship which shall cover all costs associated with the trip and the onboard study program. Best wishes for your continued success."*

Eden looked through the accompanying papers and she saw the glowing recommendations written on her behalf by Professor Altgeld, Mrs. Omaha, and her mother, Isabelle Owens.

Eden started to cry. "My mother wrote a letter of recommendation for me?"

"Yes, Eden, she did. Your mother came to see me after our trip to the University of Illinois. She said she wanted to thank me for arranging for you to go to the university. We talked for quite a while. I could see how much your mother loves you and admires your talents. I asked her if she would be interested in writing a letter on your family's behalf."

The thought of her mother reaching out to Mrs. Omaha humbled and surprised Eden.

Eden wiped her teary face on her sleeve and continued to read the attached pages.

*"Please confirm your acceptance by having your parent or guardian sign the attached documents. Your signature is also required. When you have completed the material, forward them back to my attention. For your convenience, we have enclosed a self-addressed stamped envelope."*

The letter continued, *"After we have received the signed documentation, we will send to you the entire package of instructions and details. In addition, you will need to complete the enclosed summer reading list prior to the voyage.*

*"We look forward to you experiencing an exciting shipboard education and exotic world travel. Bon Voyage! Signed Will Gertz, President and C.E.O., Studies Abroad."*

Mrs. Omaha said tearfully, "I think this is what is referred to as living vicariously through someone else."

She gave Eden a big hug.

"I want to tell my exciting news to Momma, Mrs. Omaha. May I please be excused?"

"Certainly, Eden. You have a lot of work ahead of you this summer. Are you still intending to babysit my boys?"

Eden nodded.

"Good. It is imperative you get your summer reading and poetry studies done before the trip. OMG! This is the most amazing opportunity!" Mrs. Omaha said, sounding like an exuberant school girl herself.

Eden ditched the rest of the graduation rehearsal. Like a gazelle, she ran home.

She burst through the kitchen door, calling, "MOMMA! COME QUICK!"

"What's wrong?!" Isabelle said as she rushed into the kitchen, still dripping wet from the shower and with a large bath towel wrapped around her thin body.

"Read this!" Eden said, and she handed her mother the envelope.

Isabelle read the contents... *"Signed Will Gertz, President and C.E.O. of Studies Abroad."*

"Oh, Eden! God has answered my prayers for your future." The clock on the kitchen wall struck 4 p.m. Isabelle looked around, and she didn't see Abby.

"Where is Abby?" she asked.

"Oh my goodness! I was so excited to tell you about the scholarship that I forgot to pick her up from school."

"Let me get dressed and we'll both go," Isabelle said, and she hurried to her bedroom and threw on some clothes.

Dashing out the door, Isabelle said, "We'll take the tow truck. Do you have your driver's license with you?"

"They're in my backpack."

Isabelle didn't drive or have a driver's license. Clem liked it that way. It kept her dependent.

When the tow truck arrived at the school, Isabelle and Eden saw Abby eating an apple and sitting with her pretty, young teacher, Miss Favershaf, in the deserted playground on a stone bench. Miss Favershaf stood up and met Eden and Isabelle as they hurried across the freshly mowed grass toward the playground.

Miss Favershaf said, "When Eden didn't come for Abby, as she usually does, I called your house, Mrs. Owens, but there was no answer. Then I called

71

your husband at work. I explained to him that Abby had not been picked up by Eden. I asked him if he would like to come to the school and get Abby. He suggested Abby walk home alone. I waited here because I felt sure you or Eden would eventually show up and accompany Abby home."

"Thank you, Miss Favershaf, for staying with Abby until we got here. Oh my goodness! I left supper cooking on the stove. We have to get home. Come on, Eden and Abby," Isabelle said, panicked, and she hustled her daughters toward the dusty tow truck.

Eden drove the truck too fast, as she could see how upset her mother was. In the distance, they saw smoke behind the gas station. As they got close enough to see the house, they saw a fire truck with flashing lights parked in front and its long hose wound up the porch and into the front door.

"Oh no!" Isabelle said. Eden pulled the tow truck close to a gas pump under the worn awning and shut off the motor. They saw two firemen exit the house and speak to Clem who stood back from the smoke-filled house. As Isabelle, Eden, and Abby approached, they heard one of the firemen say a pot on the stove had boiled dry and caught fire.

Clem turned and silently accused Isabelle with his bloodshot glare, his flared nostrils, and his twisted, rageful sneer. Isabelle silently warned the girls not to get involved.

"Clem, I'm sorry. I had to go pick up Abby up from school. I know I should have turned the stove off but I forgot."

Eden heard her mother take the blame and she lowered her gaze.

"Maybe this will help your memory!" Clem barked, and he slapped her across her face, knocking her across the yard. He stood threateningly over Isabelle's body.

"Get up you fucking pea-brained idiot!"

Three firefighters rushed forward and they grabbed Clem and threw him to the ground. "Call the police!" the driver of the fire truck yelled from the cab.

"Let me up!" Clem yelled, viciously fighting off the one that seemed to be in charge. Sirens could be heard in the distance. Within a very short time, two police cars came to a screeching halt behind the fire truck. Four uniformed policemen shoved open the squad car doors and rushed to where two firemen held Clem pinned to the ground.

A burly cop with bulging biceps, knotted thighs, thick, heavily veined forearms, and a military haircut went over to Isabelle and helped her to her feet. His name tag read Jonah Gancey.

"What's the trouble, ma'am?" he asked.

"This guy we're holding hit her," one young fireman said.

"Is he your husband?"

"Yes, sir," Isabelle said softly, trying to rub the sting from her cheek.

"Did he hit you?"

Isabelle knew she couldn't deny the charge because there had been too many witnesses.

She looked at Eden who held Abby tightly in her arms. Both girls looked fearfully for their mother.

Isabelle didn't say a word, and the police officer repeated, "Listen, you can tell me here or you can tell me at the station. Did he hit you?"

Isabelle looked helplessly at her two daughters who were intently watching her.

"Yes, sir."

"Take him to the police station, Ron," the burly cop said to his partner.

"I won't press charges, Officer," Isabelle said, trembling.

The cop looked balefully at Clem who smiled smugly back.

"You're making a mistake letting him get away with this, ma'am," Officer Gancey said.

"You're probably right, Officer," she said as she walked past him and over to her daughters. Isabelle wrapped her arms around the girls and headed into the smoky house.

Clem stood up and rudely brushed through the smoke-filled air. Officer Gancey stepped in front of Clem. He flipped his thumbnail against the steel baton which hung next to the metal handcuffs looped through his belt loops and said, "I'm going to tell you this just once. If we ever get a call regarding this house again concerning domestic violence, you, mister, will answer to me personally."

"Ouch! Such a tough guy," Clem said, and he faked fear.

After the fire truck and the police had gone, Clem opened every window in the house to dissipate the smoke. For dinner that night, they ate bologna sandwiches and potato chips.

Isabelle busied herself, cleaning up the mess in the kitchen which included a soot-soaked floor from the fire hose and the scorched food. Her cheek was bruised and swollen and her jaw ached from Clem's attack.

"I'll go to Sampson's tomorrow and buy a used stove," Clem slurred, downing the last of his six beers. His sour attention suddenly turned on Eden. "Once Eden graduates from high school, she is out of here."

Clem never once insisted Rick move out of the house. But Rick worked like a slave at the gas station.

After dinner, Eden and Abby lay quietly in their separate beds, listening through the thin walls to their parents quarreling.

"Eden is leaving in eight weeks, Clem," Isabelle said flatly.

"Who's the lucky guy?" Clem asked sarcastically.

Isabelle considered making up some male name to satisfy Clem. Instead, she chose the C.E.O. of Studies Abroad and used his name. "Will Gertz," she said, and she physically felt her hatred for Clem grow even more fierce.

"He never asked me for her hand or nothing. What's this Gertz think that he can screw my girl and then walk away?"

Eden cringed. Abby didn't understand the conversation she overheard, but she felt bad for Eden.

"I just may not approve of this Gertz guy," he said, and he belched loudly.

"You stupid moron," Isabelle whispered under her breath. *I already approved Eden's future,* she thought, as she knew the signed permission slip for Studies Abroad was already safely packed in Eden's backpack.

# Twelve

Dressed in their Sunday best, Isabelle and Abby walked into the crowded gymnasium and looked around for a seat in the bleachers. A shapely woman with flaming red hair and dressed in a flamboyant green floral dress stood up and waved her arms at Isabelle.

"Mrs. Rutledge is waving at us, Momma," Abby said, waving back.

"Where is she, Abby?" Isabelle asked, looking in the upper tier of the bleachers.

"She's sitting on the first row. See her there?" Abby asked, pointing.

Isabelle waved and Fanny pointed enthusiastically at the two empty seats next to her.

"I think Fanny saved us a seat, Abby," Isabelle said, and she and Abby hurried across the gym. They climbed the short stairs and sidestepped past the people seated on the first row. Isabelle sat down next to her friend. Abby sat next to Isabelle.

"It was so kind of you to save us seats, Fanny," Isabelle said, smoothing her skirt and adjusting to her seat.

"I figured you and Abby would be here for Eden," Fanny said, rummaging through her huge, gaudy, bejeweled purse. She found her lipstick and applied a heavy red coat to her collagen-injected lips.

Abby looked around her mother and said, "You look pretty, Mrs. Rutledge."

"Thank you, baby cakes," Fanny said, and she smiled, showing her dazzling white caps.

Isabelle watched the heavy gold chain that held Fanny's jeweled eyeglasses move seductively against Fanny's ample cleavage. She wore a mid-length flowered dress, dangling rhinestone earrings, rings on all of her fingers, and a dozen bangle bracelets. Fanny smelled like she had taken a bath in a potent flowery perfume.

"I take it Clem isn't coming to see his daughter graduate?" Fanny asked disapprovingly.

Before Isabelle could answer, Abby said matter-of-factly, "My dad said Eden has to move out of our house right after graduation."

"What?!" Fanny said, and she clucked her tongue disapprovingly.

"That's enough, Abby," Isabelle said threateningly. But Abby was on a roll.

"We had a fire at our house the other day, and my dad got mad at my momma and he hit her. It wasn't the first time. He hits her all the time. My dad drinks a lot of beer too. I know at church the preacher says nobody should drink beer. But Rick drinks beer. Me and Eden and Momma, we don't drink beer. We like root beer, but that don't make you drunk like Daddy's real beer does."

Isabelle was so embarrassed she wanted to run out of the gymnasium and hide. She felt like everyone seated around them was now engrossed in Abby's tales. She turned to Abby and she pleaded, "Abby, please be quiet!"

"Oh, Momma," Abby said innocently. "I've seen my dad walking around our house naked."

"One more word, Abby, and you and I are leaving!" Isabelle said. Abby looked bewildered at her mother. The stories she'd told were everyday occurrences at their house. She didn't know why her mother was making such a big deal about it.

When Abby finally settled down, Isabelle said, "I apologize, Fanny, for Abby's outburst."

"Oh, that's all right, honey," Fanny said, and she patted Isabelle's cool arm with her hand which was adorned with long, acrylic fingernails painted bright fuchsia. On her fingers, she wore 16 assorted rings.

"I feel bad that Harry's dad can't see our son graduate tonight," Fanny said.

Isabelle thought Fanny talked about her late husband like he was working or playing golf.

"You know, when that delivery truck ran over my Bert and killed him, I thought it was the end of the world. But as it turned out, Harry and I got a ginormous big settlement from the trucking company, and, now, we're set for the rest of our lives."

76

Isabelle thought, *When Bert was alive, Fanny and I worked together as maids at Traveler's Inn. Fanny also worked nights as a bartender at Elmer's Hideaway. Now, she lives in a lovely home and she drives a new Cadillac.* Isabelle felt a pang of jealousy. *I wish a truck would run over Clem,* she thought. *Maybe then the kids and I could get a settlement like Fanny did and live happily ever after.*

Isabelle immediately realized her wish for Clem's death was a sin. Silently, she asked for God's forgiveness for her evil thoughts. But for a few seconds more, she entertained the financial and emotional benefits of his demise. She even considered his funeral. She would ask Mr. Cleary, the funeral director, to put Clem in the casket face down. That way, when Satan came to collect Clem's miserable soul, Clem could look his creator in the eye.

Estelle Kampner awaited her cue from the principal to start the Graduation March.

An elderly lady sat at the organ and began playing Pomp and Circumstance.

"Estelle's big ass looks like a massive pink candle that's melted on the piano bench," Fanny whispered to Isabelle. Isabelle lips twisted in mild disapproval.

When the music started, the students formed a double line and walked side by side down the center aisle between the rows of metal chairs set on the gymnasium floor. The honor students, dressed in white gowns and white mortarboards, were the first in line.

"There's Eden, Momma!" Abby said, and she stood up and hung over the steel banister, waving at her big sister.

Eden saw Abby and her mother and smiled briefly. Harry Rutledge, also an honor student, walked alongside Eden.

Fanny put her forefingers in the sides of her mouth and whistled hard and loud at her son, Harry. Harry looked over at his bawdy mother and his pale face blushed bright red.

"Harry looks like a beet," Abby said.

Fanny winked at Abby.

The graduation ceremony lasted two hours. When it ended, Fanny said, "Would you and the girls like a ride home?"

"Thanks for the offer, Fanny, but Rick is supposed to pick us up."

"It is sure good to see you again, Isabelle," Fanny said, and she hugged her friend tightly. "And the same goes for you too, Pumpkin," Fanny said, and she pulled Abby into a bear hug.

"I thought you liked to call me Baby cakes," Abby mumbled, her face smashed between Fanny's breast implants.

"This is one precocious kid you got here, Isabelle."

"What's precocious mean?" Abby asked.

"It means you're full of yourself, sweetie," Fanny answered affectionately.

Abby pulled away, and she put her small hands on her hips. "Now you're calling me another name!"

"Don't be rude to Mrs. Rutledge, Abby," Isabelle said.

"It's okay. She didn't mean nothing by it," Fanny said, and she ruffled Abby's curly, blonde hair.

Fanny looked up and saw Harry walking across the gym toward her. "Isn't he handsome?" she asked tenderly.

"Yes, Fanny, he is," Isabelle agreed.

"Well, he ought to be. His dad was a real looker."

Isabelle remembered Bert Rutledge as a man who stood five-feet five-inches tall and weighed 200 pounds. He had large moles sprouting on his face and a thick neck. Because he was severely nearsighted, he wore thick lens eyeglasses that made his eyes look tiny enough to fit into a shrunken head.

Fanny got a sassy gleam in her eyes. "You probably guessed Bert wasn't Harry's biological father."

Isabelle didn't ask any questions. She didn't have to. Fanny was an older version of Abby. She would tell you everything about herself, given the chance.

"You remember that tall, good-looking salesman from Chicago that sometimes stayed at Traveler's Inn when we worked there?"

"You mean the guy that sold pharmaceuticals to the doctors?"

"That's him. Well, one night, I worked late. I don't remember where you were. Probably got a night off. Anyway, after work, he invited me out for a drink. And one thing led to another. And nine months later…my Harry was born. I never saw the guy much after that night. When my pregnancy began to show, I guess he figured he might have trouble, so he found another place to stay when he was on the road.

"Bert probably guessed Harry wasn't his, but he never once let on. I'm thankful to him for that. He was a good dad to my Harry."

Without hesitation, Fanny said, "Gotta go, kiddo. Don't be a stranger," and she walked away, leaving behind a fog of perfume.

Isabelle and Abby stood near the exit door, waiting for Eden. Isabelle envied the happy families she saw grouped together in their secure cliques. Most were talking, laughing, and taking pictures of family and friends with their expensive filming equipment. Isabelle held Abby's hand and the two of them stood apart from the crowd. She worried Eden would be embarrassed by her small family gathering, not to mention their old Polaroid camera.

Eden threaded her way through the crowd, looking for her mother and Abby. She saw them standing alone, next to the door that led to the lobby. Eden thought her mother looked so pretty in her pale-blue dress that perfectly matched the shade of her beautiful eyes. And delightful little Abby, with her rosy cheeks and curly, shoulder-length hair, dressed in a lacy pink dress and white, patent, leather shoes with a satin bow on top. Eden thought she resembled a porcelain doll.

Isabelle saw Eden coming and her face lit up like a beam of sunshine. Isabelle thought, *this closes one chapter of Eden's life and makes way for a positive new one to begin. This summer, Eden will work for Mrs. Omaha and write poems for Professor Altgeld's approval. And best of all, she has the magical trip, Studies Abroad, awaiting her.*

Isabelle thought back to when Eden, Abby, and she had watched Titanic at the movies. She loved the shipboard romance between the penniless artist and the rich girl. Isabelle prayed that Eden and Abby would someday find men who loved them that much.

"I'm so glad to see you both!" Eden said, gathering her small family in her arms.

"You look so pretty," Abby said.

"You mean right now?" Eden asked, leaning down to eye level with her little sister.

Abby shrugged her thin shoulders. "I just mean you look pretty all the time!"

Eden looked up and saw Clayton Caulder and Ben Atler pass by them. She quickly diverted her eyes. She couldn't wait to get away from those two guys. *Bullies always need a victim,* she thought. *At least it won't be me anymore.* She thought about the day she saw Ben and Clayton bullying Brent Tiddley, their class valedictorian.

Brent was small in stature. His height hadn't even reached five-feet five, and his physique made him appear more like a middle-school student than a high-school student. He didn't appear to have reached puberty yet, as his legs and his chest were hairless. He wore khaki shorts and socks up to his knees, pressed shirts, and wire-rimmed glasses. He looked like Forrest Gump.

"I told Rick to pick us up at ten sharp at the Dairy Queen," Isabelle said.

"If we hurry, we can walk the two blocks there and still have time for a banana split."

"Oh goodie, goodie, goodie!" Abby said, rubbing her hand together.

Eden turned in her cap and gown. With the crowd dispersing, a long line of cars were leaving the school parking lot. As they stepped off the curb to cross the street, Isabelle recognized Clayton Caulder's sleek, silver, BMW sports car as it raced toward them. She grabbed her daughters by their arms and hauled them back.

Clayton and Ben waved cockily at them as they sped by.

Shaken, Isabelle said, "That boy deserves a good thrashing!"

A gust of wind from a passing car stirred Abby's hair. "What's a biological father, Momma?" Abby asked.

Isabelle knew Abby had again heard too much. "Do you want one dip or two of ice cream in your banana split, Abby?" Isabelle asked, deftly changing the subject.

"I want two, Momma!"

Early the next morning, Isabelle roused her tired body from the dilapidated recliner next to the bed that she usually shared with Clem. She woke her as she heard the kitchen door softly close and assumed Eden had gone to babysit for Mrs. Omaha. She dropped the blanket on the floor, stood up, and wrapped her threadbare chenille robe around her.

She glanced at Clem, asleep in the double bed she no longer shared with him, and fought hard to still the revulsion she felt for him. She quietly opened their bedroom door and headed down the hall toward the bathroom.

She emerged from the bathroom showered and dressed. She walked down the stairs to the kitchen. She saw a folded note lying on the kitchen table. She opened it and read, "*Momma, I'll be babysitting for Mrs. Omaha at her house until three this afternoon. I hope I have time to do some homework. If not, I'm going to the library after. See you later. I love you. Eden."*

Isabelle prepared the coffee pot for Clem. She preferred the taste of tea. She ran cold water into the silver pot, added a filter and some coffee, set the pot on the stove, turned on the flame, and let the coffee percolate.

Clem lumbered into the kitchen, wearing his heavy boots, old jeans, a t-shirt, and his hunting jacket. He went to the hallway and yelled, "Rick, get your ass in here. You got a six o'clock appointment at the shop for an oil change."

Isabelle heard angry noises coming from Rick's room. Rick stumbled over something and she heard some bad cursing.

Isabelle filled a huge cup with scalding coffee and set it on the kitchen table in front of Clem. She dipped the steel-cut oats into a large bowl, grabbed the sugar bowl and milk, and set those in front of Clem. Clem dumped three teaspoons of sugar in his coffee and three in his oats and added milk to both. He gobbled the food, but his manner was resentful.

Isabelle quietly exited the kitchen and went into Abby's room. She saw Abby awake but still in bed. "I have to leave for work now, Abby. I'll be at the Caulder's again all day. Breakfast is on the stove. I packed your lunch and it's on the counter. It's cold out this morning. Don't forget your jacket."

"Give me a kiss, Momma, before you leave."

Isabelle bent down into Abby's open arms and kissed her daughter's rosy cheek. "I love you, Abby."

"I love you too, Momma," Abby said as she pulled the covers up over her head.

In the kitchen, Isabelle slipped her jacket on and grabbed her sack lunch, a cold meatloaf sandwich.

Rick wandered into the kitchen, bleary eyed and his hair in total disarray. He reeked like a man who'd spent a week sleeping under a bridge. He wore a filthy t-shirt and oil-stained jeans.

Rick poured a cup of coffee into a traveler's mug, kissed his mother's cheek in passing, and headed out the door.

As Clem drove Isabelle to work, they passed by Abby's elementary school. She saw the empty schoolyard and knew, in a few hours, when the neighborhood children woke for the day, they would be romping around the playground. She didn't look forward to the day Abby would discover how poor they were and that a lot of other kids her age lived so much better than they did. Bullies, she knew, exist in every classroom and in every school of life.

Clem drove Isabelle to the Caulder's estate. When she got out of the truck, Clem tromped the accelerator, leaving a black cloud of acrid smoke behind. She walked to the back of the house and rang the doorbell, announcing her arrival in a glorious melody of chimes. She raised her gaze to the overhead camera and wanly smiled.

Judge Caulder opened the door. He wore a sharply pressed pin-striped suit, a blazing white shirt, a navy silk tie, blue suspenders with gold buckles stretched over his expanding girth, and black shoes so shiny, Isabelle saw her reflection in them.

"Weren't you here yesterday?" he asked in his official voice.

"Yes, sir. Mrs. Caulder asked me to return today and wash the upstairs windows."

"I see. Well, Rose is not home this morning. I believe she has gone to her Monday morning yoga class. Proceed with her instructions."

"I assume, as usual, Clayton's room is off limits?"

"If that is the rule Rose has imposed, then stick to it."

He opened the door wider, let Isabelle in, and walked past her out the door.

Eden spent the morning at Mrs. Omaha's playing with the rowdy twins. Eden made the twins some toasted cheese sandwiches and chicken-noodle soup. She washed the dishes. She picked up the scattered toys all through the house. Her study time was disturbed when the twins made a unified decision, they would not take a nap that afternoon. Eden had no choice but to postpone her assignments until later.

Earlier in the week, Professor Altgeld had sent Eden, via email, a series of eight poetry lessons to complete during the summer. Mrs. Omaha was to oversee the lessons. But the professor stated he alone would critique Eden's work. Altgeld assigned poetry from—Robert Frost, Keats, Shakespeare, Tennyson, Whitman, Woodsworth, and Yeats. *"On the other hand,"* he wrote, *"If you prefer a list of female poets, that I myself enjoy, Maya Angelou, Emily Bronte, Emily Dickinson, Rita Frances Dove, and Nikki Langston.*

*"I have alphabetized the names of the poets I wish you to study, simply because I do not wish to grant superiority to one poet over another."*

On Eden's first day of work at Mrs. Omaha's stylish ranch-style house, she saw a small library filled with books of poetry. Mrs. Omaha suggested Eden borrow her books. Eden agreed to borrow the books, and she silently vowed to take particular care of her teacher's literary treasures.

Carrying an armload of books, Eden arrived home at 7 p.m. that evening.

"I expected you home at five o'clock, Eden," Isabelle said. "Did you have to work late for Mrs. Omaha?"

"No, Momma," she said, carefully setting the books on the kitchen counter.

"Are you hungry? I have some leftover spaghetti. I can reheat it for you."

"I ate dinner at Mrs. Omaha's house. She suggested it might be best for me to have dinner with them through the week, since I will be there so late watching the twins. Besides, Dad will be relieved to hear he won't be feeding me."

Isabelle felt terrible. She dreaded the day her children would leave home permanently. She knew she would miss them terribly.

# Thirteen

Eden's departure date finally arrived. Clem left early that morning for a tow-truck job and didn't bother to say goodbye to his daughter. Eden was accustomed to her father's lack of concern, but his indifference on such an important day really stung. She assumed he ignored her because he didn't want to show his eagerness to see her gone.

Rick never came home last night, so he wouldn't be there to say goodbye to Eden either.

"Mrs. Omaha is going to be here in ten minutes, Eden," Isabelle said, helping Eden pack. The battered suitcase Eden had her clothes in was old, but the clothes inside were all new. Eden had earned enough money over the summer to buy herself the first new clothes she had ever owned.

"It's kind of Mrs. Omaha to fly to San Diego with you and see that you get on the ship safely."

Isabelle's mood turned melancholy. "I don't think I can stand to be away from you for a whole semester," she said, and she brushed away a tear with the back of her hand.

"Don't cry, Momma. Now, look. Abby's crying too. Think of it like this. When I return home, I'll have lots of exciting adventures to share with you both. And you, Abby, will have our room all to yourself."

"I don't want the whole room to myself. I'll be lonely without you, Eden," Abby said as her lower lip quivered.

"You'll adjust quicker than you think," Eden said tenderly. She picked up her little sister and hugged her like a panda bear hugs a bamboo tree.

"I promise to send you an email every chance I get. And I'll send you postcards from all over the world. You can start a stamp collection."

"Oh, boy! Can I use your pencil box to put them in?" Abby asked.

"I need my pencil box for my colored pencils because I am taking them with me on the voyage."

*Voyage?* Eden thought, delighted. *Yes. I'm going on a voyage!*

The doorbell rang, and Isabelle hurried to answer it. It was Mrs. Omaha. Isabelle invited her into their humble house. Mrs. Omaha casually looked around at the squalor. Isabelle watched her closely, and she was pleased to see that in Mrs. Omaha's keen observation, she didn't seem to pass judgment or condemn the way they lived.

"Good morning, Mrs. Omaha," Eden said, coming into the living room, carrying her beat-up old suitcase. Eden wore a new pair of jeans from J.C. Penney, a new beaded white shirt from the super-sale rack at the Gap, and a new pair of sneakers from Payless Shoe Source.

"Good morning, Eden. Are you ready to go?"

"Yes, ma'am, I am!"

Mrs. Omaha turned to Isabelle and she said, "My husband, Hank, and our twin boys are driving us to Chicago, Mrs. Owens. Hank has taken a few days off work to watch our boys while I'm chaperoning Eden."

"I cannot thank you enough for all you have done for Eden."

"It was a team effort, I assure you, Mrs. Owens," Mrs. Omaha said.

Isabelle assumed Mrs. Omaha was referring to the time when Isabelle had drafted the letter on Eden's behalf to present to the board of Studies Abroad. After Mrs. Omaha read Isabelle's letter, she asked very kindly if Isabelle would like for her to correct any grammatical errors Isabelle might have made. Isabelle graciously accepted Mrs. Omaha's offer.

"I pray for you and your family every day," Isabelle said. "I believe God will reward you for all your kindnesses."

"Thank you for your prayers, Mrs. Owens. God already has blessed me with a fine husband and two healthy boys."

They heard a friendly toot from Hank's car horn, saying it was time to leave.

"Have a wonderful time, sweetheart," Isabelle said, hugging Eden tightly. She pressed two 100-dollar bills in Eden's hand. "In case of an emergency," she whispered.

"Oh, Momma, thank you so much!" Eden cried, and she clung to her mother, knowing her mother had to sneak away each dollar she could to give this to her.

Eden said a tearful goodbye to Abby, then she and Mrs. Omaha left. The house seemed so empty after Eden had gone. Isabelle wished she and Abby could have gone with Eden. She thought about taking Abby and leaving for good. She did have 800 more dollars hidden under the silverware tray in the kitchen next to her birth-control bills. But how long would that last? She didn't fear Clem would ever find the money. He made her prepare all the food, including his sandwiches and his snacks. She'd become his slave in that regard too.

"Abby, I have to leave in a few minutes and go clean Judge Caulder's house. Do you want to come with me? You can bring your coloring books and crayons, but you will have to stay out of sight and be as quiet as a mouse."

"Yes, Momma. I would like to go with you," Abby said, clapping her hands in delight.

Isabelle immediately regretted her impulsive decision to ask Abby to accompany her when she went to work. She blamed her lonely surroundings and her miserable life for prompting her outburst. She hoped Judge Caulder wouldn't object to Abby coming with her. She knew Mrs. Caulder wouldn't be there to protest. Monday mornings, Rose went to her yoga class. *Apparently, one can do yoga with a raging hangover,* Isabelle thought. And in the afternoon, Rose enjoyed a spa day.

"Gather your things, and we'll leave in a few minutes," Isabelle said tensely. Clem returned in time to take Isabelle to work. When Abby climbed into the truck, he growled, "Where do you think you're going, young lady?"

"I'm going with Momma to work," Abby said confidently.

"Since when?" Clem asked Isabelle.

"It's just for today."

"Does 'His Honor' know about this?" Clem asked sarcastically.

"No, he doesn't."

"Maybe I better wait around when we get there just in case I have to bring the brat home."

"Don't call Abby a brat, Clem."

"Yeah, Daddy. That's not nice," Abby said, seated between her parents.

When they crossed over the railroad tracks, Isabelle saw Abby's reaction to the privileged world that existed beyond South Trekkin.

"Look at all the pretty houses, Momma," Abby said wide eyed. "Why is their grass so green? Did you ever see so many pretty flowers? Look at all the kids in that backyard swimming pool. See those two girls sitting on the porch of that fancy tree house? They're sure lucky, aren't they, Momma? Why are those boys chasing each other around that huge swing set? See that chubby boy on the long, shiny slide? Why don't we have pretty streetlights in South Trekkin? If we followed this long stretch of black top road, would it lead to a castle and a wizard, like the yellow brick road in the Wizard of Oz?"

"SHUT UP FOR ONE DAMN MINUTE!" Clem yelled. Abby dropped her head and her bottom lip stuck out. She began to whimper.

Isabelle put her arm around Abby and scooted her closer. She straightened her daughter's plain dress and smoothed her hair. She looked at the coloring book and the box of crayons Abby held onto so tightly.

"The answer to all your questions is those children have well-to-do parents, sweetheart, and you don't," Isabelle said tenderly.

"Stop filling her head with shit like that!" Clem roared.

When they pulled onto Caulder's long, shaded driveway, Isabelle knew Abby must be internally bursting with questions, but, to her credit, she silently looked around with big-eyed wonder.

Clem dropped them off next to the bluestone sidewalk. Isabelle got out of the truck and helped Abby down. Clem laid his heavy left arm across the top of the steering wheel and turned to look at Isabelle. "You want me to wait?"

"No," Isabelle said defiantly. "If Judge Caulder tells me Abby can't stay, then I will quit my job."

"That better not happen!" Clem shouted. He reached over and closed the truck door, slammed his big-booted foot on the accelerator, and drove off, leaving Isabelle and Abby standing in a fog of exhaust.

Isabelle took Abby's hand and they walked up the bluestone pathway, past the columned porch and around to the back of the house. Isabelle let Abby ring the ornate doorbell. Abby was amazed when she heard the melodic bells announce their arrival. Isabelle held Abby's hand, and, together, they stood, looking at the ornate door like two beggars.

The door swung open and Judge Caulder looked from one tattered female to the other. He was immaculately dressed in a white, designer, golf shirt with a fancy logo stitched on the breast pocket, a pair of pressed, pleated, khaki slacks, and elegant golf shoes. Next to the door stood his gold-and-platinum, custom-made golf clubs in a hand-tooled leather golf bag.

"Good morning, Your Honor," Isabelle said nervously.

"Good morning," Judge Caulder said as he looked down at Abby. "And who do we have here?" he asked, examining Abby like she was an interesting specimen on a petri dish.

"This is my daughter, Abby. I hope you don't mind that I brought her to work with me this morning. I didn't want to leave her home alone."

"I have no objection to your daughter accompanying you today. However, I suggest, in the future, you arrange daycare for her."

"Thank you, Your Honor," Isabelle said humbly.

The judge slipped the leather golf bag strap over his thick shoulder. "Clean Clayton's room today. He will be gone for a few months."

Judge Caulder pushed past Isabelle and Abby. He walked across the patio and headed toward the six-car garage. As Isabelle situated Abby on a footstool in the solarium, Judge Caulder roared down the driveway in his brand-new black Bentley.

Isabelle put fabric booties over her shoes and Abby's.

"Why do I have to wear socks over my tennies, Momma?"

"Because the Caulders don't want us to wear our street shoes inside their house."

"Judge Caulder had his shoes on. I saw them on his feet."

"That's different, Abby."

"I don't understand."

"I'm not sure I do either, sweetheart."

Isabelle went to the pantry and gathered her cleaning supplies that were situated neatly on a slotted metal tray. Consumed by curiosity, she decided to clean Clayton's room first. This would be the first time she had ever been allowed to enter his private domain. Before going upstairs, she checked on Abby who sat on the kitchen floor, coloring in her book. Isabelle went to the kitchen cabinet where she knew the Caulders kept snacks. She found a box of pretzels that had already been opened. She ripped off a paper towel and put a handful of pretzels on it.

"Here, honey," she said, handing the pretzels to Abby. "Try to eat them over the paper towel."

"I will. Thank you, Momma. I won't make a mess. I promise."

"Wait here for me. I'll be back as soon as I can."

"Okay," Abby said, and she greedily bit into a pretzel.

Isabelle filled a bucket with hot water at the kitchen sink. One last look at Abby and she headed into the main foyer. She walked carefully up the spiral, marble staircase. When she reached the second floor, she headed toward the east wing of the house.

A tall mahogany door sealed Clayton's bedroom. Expecting to see something resembling Rick's filthy bedroom, Isabelle opened the door and stepped inside the dark room. When she flipped on the overhead brass chandelier, what she saw shocked her.

Everything looked so obsessively neat, clean, and organized. A magnetic bed that didn't require chains, straps, or wires to keep it afloat hung in midair in the center of the huge room. A 98-inch, curved, flat-screen television dominated one wall. A state-of-the-art audio system that no doubt had the power to rock the whole house, occupied a long table directly under the television. Surround sound speakers were built into the walls. An elaborate computer system with three oversized screens and a curved main monitor hung on a massive built-in desk. Isabelle looked inside the walk-in closet, saw color-coordinated clothing hung neatly on wooden hangars and exactly spaced racks of expensive shoes. A door at the back of the closet led to a windowless room that displayed a collection of video games that would rival those sold at Game Stop.

It was when she turned to leave that she noticed the picture of Eden taped to the back of the closet door. Tears flowed down her cheeks when she saw Eden naked with her mouth taped shut and tied to a chair. Isabelle didn't know about photo-shopping a picture. She was sure this horrid thing had happened to her sweet Eden and Eden hadn't shared this tragedy with her. *Was Eden raped by Clayton Caulder and Ben Atler?* she thought, horrified. *When did it happen?* Her mind raced frantically.

She set her cleaning supplies down and carefully searched the room for more clues. She looked through Clayton's collection of games and his D.V.D.s. In his walk-in closet, she anxiously searched his clothing and his chest of drawers.

In his bedroom, she looked behind the television, around the bank of computers, and under the magnetic bed. Nothing. She went over to the desk. The first two drawers held neatly placed paper, pencils, and several books about computers. When she opened the third drawer, her heart missed a beat. She saw a packet marked Studies Abroad. She opened the envelope and read the first page. On the Studies Abroad letterhead, it was the same welcome letter from Will Gertz, the president of Studies Abroad, welcoming Clayton to the nautical study program.

With a heavy heart, Isabelle put the packet back exactly as she had found it. She assumed Ben Atler had also received a similar notice. She wished there was some way she could warn Eden. But even if she could warn her, Isabelle didn't think Eden would relinquish the trip.

A tall, thin boy intensely locked his gaze on Abby who was eating her pretzels and looking at her coloring book. He walked stealthily across the kitchen toward her. Abby dropped her red crayon on the floor. When she reached down to pick it up, a pair of long legs and tennis shoes stepped in front of her. She raised up and said to the pale, auburn-haired boy, "Who are you?"

The boy cocked his head to one side, and he looked quizzically at Abby.

"Who are you?" he asked in return.

"My name is Abby. What's your name?"

"I am Emile Alexander Caulder."

"I'm with my momma. She's upstairs, cleaning."

"Is your momma Isabelle?"

"Yes, that's her name."

"Oh," he said, and his attention suddenly turned to her coloring book. "I have lots of those books in my room. You want to come and see them?"

Abby hesitated. Momma had taught Eden and Abby never to talk to strangers. But, hey, this boy was a Caulder and that meant he lived here. Since Momma was in the house, Abby didn't think she would mind her going to his room to see his coloring books.

Abby stood up. She laid her book and crayons on the leather barstool and followed Emile. Like a pied piper, Emile led Abby through the massive marble foyer and up the spiral staircase. On the second floor, they turned a sharp left and walked down a long-carpeted hallway.

Emile opened the door to his bedroom. He walked in, and Abby followed him into fairyland. Fluffy white clouds were painted on the sky-blue ceiling and rolling waves decorated the light-blue walls. An elaborate built-in fish aquarium filled with tropical fish of all shapes and sizes dominated one wall, creating an oceanic scene. On the other side of the room, a large aviary held assorted birds.

Awestruck, Abby stood next to the aviary and watched the birds. Emile joined her. He rotated his pointed forefinger as he spoke, "That's a cardinal. That's a robin. That's a wren. That's a raven. That's a martin. That's a mockingbird. Those are parakeets. That's a dove. Those are sandpipers. That's a sparrow. That's a red-headed woodpecker.

"That bird over there is called a kingfisher," he said, pointing to a teal, white, and orange bird. "The bird on the perch is a painted bunting. The bird grooming himself is a scarlet macaw. And that black-and-orange bird is a Baltimore oriole. I want a lorikeet; it's a tree parrot that lives in Asia. My dad said he will get it for me," he said, and he nonchalantly walked away.

He pulled out a drawer in the built-in desk and lifted out a stack of coloring books and two boxes of new crayons. He dropped them on the floor next to Abby.

He started to walk away, and Abby said, "Aren't you going to color with me?"

"I don't think so," he said, and he went over and sat down on a padded bench next to a bay window and sleepily gazed at the cloudy ceiling.

Abby didn't think she wanted to color anymore either. She sat down on the hardwood floor and watched the birds.

Emile's eyes grew heavy, and he quickly fell asleep. Abby didn't understand why he didn't take a nap on his nice bed.

"There you are!" Isabelle said, rushing into the bedroom. "I have looked all over this house for you, young lady."

"I been here with Emile, Momma," Abby said innocently.

Isabelle saw Emile sleeping. "Where is his nurse?" she whispered.

"I never saw a nurse. Why does he need a nurse, anyway?"

"He takes care of Emile, Abby."

"Well, I don't think he's doing a very good job!"

At that moment, a heavy-set male nurse with a shaved head came sauntering into the room, carrying a tray of food.

"What's going on?" he asked, setting the tray on the desk.

"My daughter and Emile were visiting," Isabelle said.

"Are you finished here today, Mrs. Owens?" he asked sternly.

"Yes, I am."

"If you will excuse me, I need to feed Emile now."

"Why can't Emile feed himself?" Abby asked. Isabelle took Abby's hand and dragged her impulsively inquisitive daughter out of the room.

# Fourteen

Isabelle and Abby stood at the end of Judge Caulder's long bluestone sidewalk, waiting for Clem to pick them up. Isabelle thought about Clem's tow truck arriving at the scene of an accident or a tragedy and hauling away the mangled wreckage—*that's an apt description of my life with Clem. I wish I could live my life over again. My regrets increase daily, and, nightly, I am tormented with bitter memories.*

"Momma, why doesn't Emile go outside?" Abby asked.

It took Isabelle a moment to respond, as the demon lament pestered her once again. "What makes you think he doesn't go outdoors, Abby?"

"He's pale, like he's never been in the sun."

"You're very observant, Abby. Emile has Asperger Syndrome."

"Is that like the measles?"

"No, dear. Do you remember Joey Sterling? He used to go to our church."

"I remember him. He was weird. He used to sit at the back of the church and talk to himself. And he wouldn't play with any of us kids. One time, Mrs. Peterson took our Sunday school class to the park and Joey started running in circles and screaming because he said the sun was too bright and the kids were loud."

"Joey acted the way he did because he too has Asperger Syndrome."

"Emile's not weird like Joey, Momma. He talked to me about his birds. And he got his coloring books and crayons out for us to color together."

"When no one else is in the room with Emile, he talks to himself about his birds, Abby. You told me he wouldn't color with you. Like Joey, Emile has a difficult time communicating with other children."

"Have they got a shot they can give Emile for Aspirin Syllable?"

Isabelle laughed softly. "No, sweetheart, they don't have a shot that will cure Emile."

"Even if Emile is weird like Joey, I like him, Momma. Can I come with you next time you work here?"

"We'll see, sweetheart."

A warm breeze swept over them, lifting their hair and brushing their flushed cheeks. Isabelle shook all over.

"I think Eden has arrived in Chicago, Abby. Let's wish her a safe trip, shall we?"

"Have a safe trip, Eden," they said in unison. "We love you."

Awestruck and inspired, Eden gazed at the towering skyscrapers that lined Chicago's skyline as they sped along amidst the fast-moving traffic. A fancy billboard caught her eye, but her attention was diverted by the quarreling twins who were fighting this time over a videogame. She had waited her whole life for a trip like this, and the obnoxious Omaha twins had ruined most of her adventure with their spoiled behavior. She would be glad to get out of the backseat of the car and even happier that she wouldn't have to spend any more time with Pete and Repeat, the silent nicknames she gave the twins because whatever rotten thing one of them did, the other followed suit.

Mrs. Omaha looked back at her boys as they struggled, spat, and slapped one another.

"Boys, stop fighting this instant or I will take the videogame away from both of you!"

The boys stopped temporarily. But the minute Mrs. Omaha turned her back, Pete put his forefinger and his thumb together and pinched Repeat hard on the inside of his leg.

"Ouch!" Repeat screamed.

"That's enough, boys," Hank Omaha said patiently.

*One trip with my dad and these two brats wouldn't be able to walk into the house,* Eden thought.

"O'Hare is straight ahead and to the left a bit," Hank Omaha said, turning the blue Hyundai into the left lane of traffic.

"I have to potty, Daddy!" Repeat yelled.

"You can potty when we get to the airport," Hank said, exasperated.

"But I have to go now!"

Mrs. Omaha turned around and glared at her son. "I told you to go potty before we left McDonald's."

94

"I didn't have to go then," he said, and he stuck his lip out in typical five-year-old fashion.

Mrs. Omaha looked at Eden and she said, "I'll bet, after this trip, you won't want to babysit the boys again for us."

Eden smiled. "I really appreciate you and Mr. Omaha driving me to Chicago." She didn't say anything about babysitting the boys again. She had been taught not to lie.

When they arrived at O'Hare Airport, there were so many fascinating things Eden wanted to see. But dragging the twins through the terminal proved to be as daunting as the ride from Maramount. Mrs. Omaha said she and Hank would check in and take care of the luggage. Eden was told to take the twins to the family restroom.

Eden grabbed the boys by their arms and hauled them through the terminal, looking for the family restroom. She finally found one. Both boys pottied and everything went fine until a woman and her small daughter came into the restroom. Pete told the girl she wasn't allowed in a boy's restroom, and Repeat agreed with his brother. Eden tried to explain what a family restroom was, but the boys ran out the door. Eden chased the two little monsters across the vast airport, fearing they would separate and run in different directions. If that happened, how could she find them in this enormous complex?

When they were ready to board the plane, Mrs. Omaha kissed her husband and boys goodbye. Eden bid Mr. Omaha a fond farewell and thanked him again for driving her to Chicago. Eden bent down to say goodbye to the twins, and Pete pulled her nose and Repeat kicked her shin.

They boarded the plane for San Diego and Eden breathed a giant sigh of relief. Mrs. Omaha instructed Eden to place her backpack, which contained her pencil box and her money, in the overhead compartment. Eden sat down in her assigned seat next to the window. She buckled her seatbelt and looked out of the window as the luggage was being boarded, silently acknowledging her one suitcase was the worst of the lot.

"Isn't this exciting, Eden?" Mrs. Omaha asked, settling into her seat next to Eden.

"Yes, it is."

"I hope the boys sleep on the way home. It will make the drive easier for Hank."

Eden nodded. Her unpleasant experience with the Omaha twins had diminished her desire to have children of her own.

When the last of the passengers were seated on the plane, the jetway rumbled back and the male flight-attendant closed and locked the door. The plane slowly backed up, turned, and taxied to the runway. Positioned at the end of the long runway, the jet gained speed, lifted off the tarmac, and slowly ascended into the sky.

Adrenaline shot through Eden's blood, giving her a high like she had never experienced before. She wanted to laugh and cry and run happily through the aisle. She said a giddy silent goodbye to O'Hare Airport, vowing to someday return and really see it.

The flight attendant, a tall, handsome, young man with curly black hair and brilliant white teeth, recited the safety precautions. Eden only half listened; her attention was on the patchwork of land below. She saw huge lakes and acres and acres of squared-off crops.

Small towns flew by and larger cities lingered. An occasional bridge dotted a river, and lots of green landscape filled in the spaces. Slowly, the plane ambled up over the clouds and the glowing, white, cotton balls occupied the space below.

An hour-and-a-half into the flight, a voice came over the intercom, "Ladies and gentlemen, this is Captain Michael Radner. We are flying over Kansas City, Missouri, famously named The City of Fountains. In 1904, the Humane Society of Kansas City erected many fountains as a hopeful reminder to prevent cruelty to women, children, and animals."

Eden watched with bated breath. "I think I see the city through the clouds, Mrs. Omaha!" she said.

Mrs. Omaha sleepily doubted Eden's claim at this altitude. But she did peer over Eden's shoulder and saw what she believed was sunshine focused on a large body of water.

Captain Radner continued, "In approximately one hour, we will fly over the Grand Canyon, one of the Seven Natural Wonders of the World. The canyon is 277 miles long, 18 miles wide, with a depth of 5,000 feet. The Colorado Plateau at its highest point rises 9,000 feet above sea level.

"Further on is The Grand Canyon National Park, located in Grand Canyon, Arizona. This beautiful park encompasses 1,218,375 acres, is 4,000 feet deep, and lies on the Colorado Plateau. Thank you for choosing Trans Allied

Airlines. We hope you enjoy your trip with us. Please consider us for all your travel needs."

A male voice behind the two women said, "What's the captain rambling on for?"

A female flight attendant came down the aisle, pushing a cart filled with soft drinks, packaged nuts, crackers, and assorted candies. "Would you ladies care for some refreshments?" she asked.

Mrs. Omaha chose a Coke and a bag of M&M's which cost her $9.50. The price was too high for Eden to indulge herself.

An hour later, Eden saw the Grand Canyon below. "From up here, it looks like God ran an orange crayon zigzag through the earth."

"Professor Altgeld would applaud your description, Eden," Mrs. Omaha replied.

Two hours passed, and the plane landed smoothly at San Diego International Airport. As they were taxing to the gangway, Eden and Mrs. Omaha noticed on the north side of the airport a large building with a rounded bow and squared-off stern. It resembled a dry-docked ship.

"Excuse me," Mrs. Omaha said to the stewardess as she walked by, collecting trash before landing. "What is that building over there?"

"That's the new Rental Car Center," she answered.

"It resembles a ship at port."

"It was meant to," the stewardess said pleasantly.

The airplane finally came to a complete stop. The passengers stood and pulled their belongings out of the overhead storage bins. The male flight attendant opened the door. People slowly made their way off the plane.

Standing next to the circling luggage carousel, Eden saw her battered suitcase among many designer bags; she quickly pulled it off and set it down behind her. The small angel-shaped nametag that her mother bought for her had come off in her hand. Her emotions bubbled up inside of her as she thought of Momma and Abby. Without any warning, she felt faint and her stomach fluttered like she'd swallowed a hundred butterflies.

"Let's eat lunch here at the airport," Mrs. Omaha said, placing her hand on Eden's arm to steady her.

"Thank you," Eden said weakly.

They found a clean restaurant with a forgettable name and sat in a booth next to a window.

Eden felt completely revived after she had eaten. "I am so looking forward to this trip. I wish you could come with me."

Mrs. Omaha gazed wistfully at Eden. "No offense to Hank and the boys, but I wish I could accompany you too, Eden."

Eden left a two-dollar tip, all in quarters, for the smiling waitress. The two women headed for the taxicab stand outside the baggage-claim area. A stocky man with a toothpick in the side of his mouth watched them as he leaned against a yellow-and-black-checkered taxi. He hurried over to them.

"You ladies need a ride?" he asked, reeking of garlic and speaking with a foreign accent.

"We're going to The San Diego B Street Cruise Ship Terminal," Mrs. Omaha said.

"I can take you there," he said, grasping their luggage and placing it in the trunk of his taxi.

Eden and Mrs. Omaha settled into the worn backseat of his taxicab. Mrs. Omaha took her right forefinger and thumb and pinched her nose. "It stinks in here," Mrs. Omaha mouthed to Eden and they both rolled down their windows.

Riding with the traffic on San Park Pacific Highway, the driver looked in his rearview mirror. "Did you ladies have a nice flight?"

"Yes, we did," Mrs. Omaha said.

"B Street Terminal is ten minutes from the airport," he said. "Have either of you ladies ever taken a cruise before?"

"No," they replied in unison.

"It will take several hours to get checked in."

"Why does it take so long?" Eden asked.

"The terminal is usually loaded with travelers, and each person has to show their ID, passenger ticket, passport, and birth certificate. Before they board the ship, the officials will again want to see a picture ID and security card."

"My goodness!" Mrs. Omaha said. "Eden, did you bring all of that with you?"

"Yes. I looked the boarding rules up on the internet before we left Maramount. Momma took me to the post office to get a passport."

"I always said you are a smart girl."

At the pier, the taxicab stopped by two armed guards wearing United States Coast Guard uniforms. One of the guards, a short, heavily muscled young man with a crew cut, called the taxi driver by his name, Eli. Then, he turned his attention to Mrs. Omaha and Eden. He asked for their IDs and tickets. Mrs. Omaha explained she was accompanying Eden to the terminal, but she wouldn't be going on the ship.

When the women walked into the busy terminal, they saw long lines of people waiting for the 20 or so agents working behind a long counter to perform the final check in.

Eli led the way through the crowd, to a small dining area near a coke-dispensing machine. "There's a lot of people in here," he said.

"There are indeed," Mrs. Omaha agreed.

Eli set Eden's suitcase down. He put two one-dollar bills in the soda machine and pushed the coke button. With his icy drink in hand, he said to Mrs. Omaha, "I'll wait for you outside, ma'am." Then he turned to Eden. "Have a safe trip, miss," he said. He took a long drink of his soda, discreetly belched, and side stepped his way through the crowd and out of the terminal.

"I wonder how many people are going on Studies Abroad," Mrs. Omaha said.

"They expect 720 students, plus teachers and their staff, and the ship's crew, will make approximately two-thousand people on the ship."

"Are you anxious to meet your new roommate, Eden?"

"Yes and no. I sometimes feel nervous around strangers. But having a roommate doesn't bother me. Abby and I have shared a bedroom for our whole lives."

"You'd better get in line now, Eden."

"Thanks again for everything, Mrs. Omaha," Eden said, and she quickly hugged her favorite teacher, grabbed her suitcase, and ran across the terminal. Eden took her place in line, and a group of students quickly lined up behind her.

Finally passing the last rigid inspection, Eden headed toward the entrance that led to the ship, paused, and waved back to Mrs. Omaha. Mrs. Omaha tearfully waved in return.

On the dock, hundreds of people were heading anxiously to various ships. Eden followed a group of students up the gangway to a gleaming four-tiered ship. They were met by a young man dressed in all white who introduced himself as David Franklin, the assistant ship's purser. He directed all passengers to the main deck.

Watching the wandering crowd from his lofty position on a high platform on the main deck was a tall, distinguished-looking man. He was dressed in an all-white short-sleeved suit, with fancy black-and-gold epaulettes on his shoulders and gold leaf on the black bill of his captain's hat. Standing alongside him were his equally impressive crew. He picked up a microphone and his pleasant voice broadcast over the P.A. system.

After all of the passengers were onboard, the captain began, "Good morning, ladies, gentlemen, and faculty. I am Captain Robert Evert. Welcome to Studies Abroad. I would like to introduce my staff. To my right is First Mate Thomas Kinley."

Kinley's lapels did not bear the same ornaments as the captain's. Kinley stood about six-feet four, and his belted waist proved he was an avid weightlifter. His blonde hair was slicked back with a gel that was as stiff as the starch on his outfit. His shoulder epaulettes showed three, horizontal, gold stripes enclosing a diamond. As uniformly as he moved forward to silently greet the audience, he stepped back as the captain continued, "Kinley is second in charge of the ship.

"Next is Second Mate Frank Rosen." Frank was a heavy-set man with a pock-marked face.

"Rosen is in charge of all navigational and communications equipment. In addition, Rosen is in charge when neither Kinley nor I are navigating. His typical shift is from zero to 400 and from 12 to 1600."

Frank Rosen, like the captain and Kinley, sported a short-cropped military haircut. His brown hair was streaked with sunlight, and it was clear by the dark tan he sported that he was a sun worshiper. His shoulder epaulettes bore two gold stripes enclosing a single diamond. He wore his white socks clear up to his knees as his legs were considerably thinner than both Kinley's and the captain's. On his wrist, he sported an expensive Russian Raketa watch which allowed the hand of the watch to spin in 24-hour segments as used on the ship.

At that moment, the P.A. system screeched loudly.

"Better fix that, Frank!" a male voice in the back of the crowd yelled, and everyone laughed.

"Our chief engineer is Amal Nagesh. Nagesh is responsible for the overall care and maintenance of the electrical and mechanical divisions on the ship."

Nagesh's epaulette showed a purple inlay between four, horizontal, gold stripes enclosing a single diamond. Nagesh appeared to be of Indian descent, as his hair was the deepest shade of black and his skin was noticeably darker in tone. He moved in unison as did all of the members.

"Then we have our purser, John Cleaver. He is in charge of the crew's payroll."

Several members of the crew loudly clapped.

A young man who looked like a student himself moved forward as the captain announced, "Assistant purser, David Franklin, welcomes passengers aboard the ship, exchanges currency, and attempts to solve our guest's smaller problems."

"To my left is Dr. Ansel Robbins. And his nurse is Miss Olga Portinski."

Eden noted the nurse seemed less formal than the rest of the crew and easily approachable. Her shoulder epaulettes were adorned in red and gold. Her hair was a muddy brown and her body was of healthy proportions. One could assume when she was not on duty, she was likely in the main dining hall. The doctor too was short and fat.

"Summer Wind has a James Beard award-winning Master Chef. Let me introduce you to Carl Siciliani."

Siciliani was a short man with a shiny bald head. He wore a white chef's frock with his last name on the right breast area and simple black pants. On his feet, he wore orange Crocs. Around his bulbous neck, he had tied a red silk scarf. He definitely looked like a man who enjoyed tasting his own creations.

"Mr. Siciliani comes to us from Chicago, Illinois, where he has collected numerous awards for his Italian fusion gourmet meals. He also has been a private chef for several celebrities. He will oversee all of our meals in the main dining hall, including those meals for those of you with special dietary restrictions. I am pleased to bring Siciliani onboard.

"Last, but certainly not least, is our cruise director, Miss Sandreen Gavel."

Sandreen stepped out from behind the rest of the crew. She wore a plain ship's uniform with a golden badge sporting her name in gold block letters. Even though the day was wearing to a close, she was beautifully flawless. She waved a friendly wave to the crowd and dropped her eyes in a subtle yet sexy manner.

The male students hooted and wolf-whistled for the exotic beauty with the stunning figure and long, black hair. The captain silenced them by pushing his elevated hand down.

Inside the packet Eden had received from Studies Abroad was a stateroom number, a key, and a short bio of the girl who would be her roommate. She looked the crowd over for an Asian girl she thought could be from California. *Wong is an Asian name, right?* she thought. Then again, she'd gone to school with David Wu and he was a full-blooded Caucasian who had been adopted by the Wu family. She looked for someone small, tanned, sexy, and probably anorexic, which she imagined fitted the description of a California girl.

Eden's heart sank. *What are those two doing here?* she thought in panic. Ben Atler lowered his gaze and looked straight at Eden. Clayton Caulder saw Eden too. He raised his right hand and moved his middle finger up and down on his forehead.

Captain Evert finished his speech, but Eden was too distracted by her tormentors to hear what he had to say.

The students were directed to their staterooms by Assistant Purser Franklin as he said, "All students who are in a single stateroom, you will be on the first tier of the ship. If you have one roommate, you will be on the second tier. Three roommates to a stateroom will be on the third tier. And four roommates will be on the fourth tier."

"Duh!" some smart aleck yelled from the back of the crowd and several people laughed.

They were dismissed by the captain. Eden headed for the staircase that led downstairs to tier two. Once there, she paced the narrow hallway, looking for her room number. Sandreen Geval, the cruise director, happened to be walking along that tier of the ship. She noticed Eden and asked, "Do you need help finding your room? What room were you assigned?"

"Room 304."

*Up close, she is even more beautiful,* Eden thought, admiring Sandreen's olive skin, shiny black hair, and full lips, coated with deep red lipstick. Her green-and-gold-flecked eyes were accentuated with black eyeliner which gave her the appearance of an Egyptian princess. Eden guessed that Sandreen might be from India. She had an accent, but given Eden's lack of exposure to different ethnicities, her knowledge of one's native tongue was limited.

Sandreen said in a sultry voice, "You are on the second deck. Take the lift up to the second level. Your room is three doors down from the elevator."

Eden thanked her as she headed for the elevator. When the elevator doors opened, Clayton Caulder, Ben Atler, and several other students stood inside.

Eden pressed the second-floor button and stood with her back toward Clayton and Ben. She wished she'd taken the stairs. The elevator headed up to the second floor. She got off the elevator along with several other students and went in search of her stateroom.

Clayton and Ben followed closely behind her.

"Looks like we're going to be neighbors, huh, Scribbler?" Ben said.

Eden ignored the two of them. She quickly found her room which was exactly where Sandreen Gavel said it would be. Eden noticed that Clayton and Ben's stateroom was two doors past hers. She unlocked the door and walked inside. She chose the bed on the left side of the room because it was on the same side of the bedroom that she shared with Abby at home. A nostalgic feeling swept over her. She missed her little sister and her mother.

On the wall, she saw a map of the world titled 'Fall in Love with Your Campus: The World.' She set her suitcase on the bed and opened it. She pulled out the drawer beneath the bed and began placing her clothes inside. When she finished emptying its contents, she went to the port window and looked out at the ocean. The bright sun and blue sky glistened on the undulating water.

Eden drank the orange juice and ate the bagel that she had purchased earlier at the airport. She saved the apple for later.

She noticed a plugin for a laptop, iPhone, and an IPOD, however, she didn't own any of those. She thought, *I am here and that's all that matters. I'll use one of the computers in the ship's study hall to email my poems and completed assignments to Professor Altgeld. I won't forget to cc Mrs. Omaha.*

*According to the brochure, it takes 24 hours to send and receive emails,* she remembered. *One nice thing is the University of Illinois, University of Wisconsin, Stanford, Harvard, Pepperdine, and U.C.L.A.'s entire library system is on the Studies Abroad hard drive and available to all the students at the touch of a button.*

Eden heard a key turn in the door. A small, tanned, sexy, and somewhat-emaciated-looking Asian girl came bounding into the room, carrying Louis Vuitton luggage and a matching Vuitton computer case. She carelessly dropped her things on the floor.

"You must be Eden," she said. "Glad to meet ya!"

"Nice to meet you too," Eden said shyly.

Regan pulled out her computer equipment and plugged them into the servers and outlets.

Eden was glad Regan showed up. She didn't feel completely on her own now.

Regan snapped off her Burberry tummy purse around her tiny waist. She mussed her black hair, slipped on stylish Tom Ford sunglasses, and fell back on her bed.

"I've been on lots of cruises with my mom and with my dad," she said matter-of-factly. "They're divorced which isn't so bad. When you're a kid with two wealthy parents who hate each other, money and vacations become the bargaining chip they use to buy the kid's love. As I always say, it sucks to be them, but it's sure good to be me.

"I'm going to U.C.L.A.," Regan continued. "Well, maybe I am, if I can get my Algebra II grade up from last semester. My mom wants me to go to U.C.L.A. because it's close to her house. My dad wants me to go to Stanford for the same reason. All they do is argue. Right now, they're in court, fighting for custody of my ten-year-old brother, Timmie. I turned 18 a month ago and I'm now officially 'emancipated.' That means, technically, they can't boss me around anymore, but that doesn't hold much sway when I'm still dependent on the money they give me. My goal here is to have a blast and pass Algebra II in the interim. What's your story?" Regan asked.

"My life is not as eventful as yours. I'm from Maramount, Illinois. My mom and dad have been married 22 years. Momma works as a housekeeper for some rich people in our town. Dad owns a gas station, and my older brother, Rick, works for him. My little sister, Abby, is eight years old, and she is in elementary school. I love to write poetry, and, with the help of my English teacher and Professor Altgeld, I got a scholarship at Studies Abroad."

"I've never heard of Maramount, Illinois. Is that a suburb of Chicago?" Regan asked.

"No. It's a small town about four hours south of Chicago."

"Cool. Sounds like your family is ideal. Mine are freaks," she said.

"Not really. We're just different," Eden said, wanting to change the subject.

"Besides Algebra, what else are you going to study?"

"Law. I'd like to be a lawyer. That way, if some jerk cheats on me, like my dad cheated on my mom, I'll bankrupt him and throw his sorry ass out on the street."

"That sounds like you hate men," Eden said.

"I don't hate men at all. But what makes me think I won't attract a jerk like my mom did? Currently, the divorce rate in this country is over 50 percent. I intend to be prepared to take care of myself."

"I see what you mean. My plans don't sound as lofty as yours. I want to study and write poetry. But if I ever marry a 'jerk,' I will be sure to look you up."

"You do that, kid," Regan said.

The two new friends left their cabin to attend the orientation in the auditorium. As they walked down the hallway, Clayton opened his stateroom door.

"Hello there, Beautiful!" Clayton said to Regan.

"Hello yourself, Handsome," she cooed.

"I'll go on ahead," Eden said, and she quickly walked away.

In the elevator, Eden thought, *Regan talks a good line, but she sure didn't recognize that Clayton is one of the jerks she's so afraid of attracting. She may need a law license after all.*

# Fifteen

On the morning of their first day at sea, the students filed in through the two main doors of the auditorium. They were handed a brochure by First Mate Thomas Kinley. Seats weren't assigned.

Regan eyed two seats in the middle row, close to the podium's huge video screen.

"Follow me," she said to Eden.

Eden replied with a smile and followed close behind her roommate.

When seated, Regan and Eden concentrated on the brochure which contained a map of the ship. The map showed different highlighted and labeled areas—the dining hall, the library, the classrooms, common restrooms, the internet room, the snack room, the gift shop, and the medical triage. It also designated the student's staterooms.

When the last of the students were seated in the auditorium, Captain Evert, dressed in his crisp, white, captain's outfit, stepped up to the podium. His presence silenced the audience. He adjusted the microphone.

"Good morning. I hope your first night aboard Summer Wind has been pleasurable."

Clayton Caulder, sitting on an aisle seat at the back of the room, thought about his friend, Ben, who was presently in their shared stateroom, throwing up after suffering with the galloping trots. Clayton suspected Ben's affliction might be seasickness. He enjoyed the irony of Goliath being felled by Neptune's undulating sea.

Captain Evert continued, "Before we begin the academic portion of this program, I want to take this time to familiarize you with our fine ship." He dipped his head toward Second Mate Rosen who started an informational video about the Summer Wind ship.

The deep melodic voice on the screen boomed with accompanying visuals, "The Summer Wind is 825 feet long. Its beam is 95 feet wide and its height is 155 feet. The ship's weight is 112,407 G.T., and it travels at the speed of 21.6 knots. There are seven decks. Sleeping accommodations are on the first, second, third, and fourth decks."

The video illuminated each deck on the ship as the voice spoke. "On the fifth deck is the main dining hall. All classrooms are on the sixth deck. On the upper deck is an Olympic-size swimming pool, a health club, a sunbathing area, shuffleboard, and a movie theatre."

Regan whispered to Eden, "Now aren't you glad you didn't have to shell out some bucks for that video. It was pretty rudimentary if you ask me."

The lights came on and Captain Evert continued, "When you boarded the ship earlier, you were given a list of your study schedules. Classes will begin tomorrow at 8 a.m. and tardiness will not be excused. In four days' time, we will arrive in Honolulu, Hawaii. After our sojourn there, we will be traveling to the Orient. When we are in port and you do not have on-land class assignments, you may leave the ship for sightseeing trips and shopping excursions. There is a curfew that remains in effect at all times, which, prior to boarding the ship, each of you have acknowledged by signature. I want to remind you, if you break curfew, you will be sent home at the next port if Summer Wind is at sea or the current port if on land. Best of luck to you all." Captain Evert gallantly walked off the stage.

The auditorium began to slowly clear. Many of the students headed for dinner in the main dining room. Clayton Caulder went to his stateroom to check on Ben. When Clayton opened the stateroom door, the blast of fecal odor nearly overpowered him. Ben, wearing a pair of stained boxer shorts, laid pale and gasping across his unmade bed. Clayton walked over, opened the porthole, and took a deep breath of fresh air.

"This room reeks like an open sewer!" he complained.

"I'm sorry, man," Ben said weakly.

"You haven't eaten anything in 24 hours. Get up and take a shower. We need to get some food in you."

Ben moaned at the mention of food; he jumped to his feet and ran to the bathroom, held his head over the toilet, and dry heaved. For several minutes, he gagged and tried to vomit, but nothing happened. He crawled back to his bed and fell spread-eagle across it.

"I'm going to go get the doctor," Clayton said, and he gladly left the room.

20 minutes later, Clayton returned to the stateroom with Dr. Robbins.

"I hear you're not feeling too well," Dr. Robbins said, opening his bag on the bed next to Ben. Ben moaned his answer. Dr. Robbins pulled out a stethoscope and laid the cold instrument on Ben's naked chest. Ben jumped violently.

"I apologize for my cold instrument."

Clayton thought he could have used that excuse many times in the past with some of the fast girls he'd been with.

Dr. Robbins took Ben's temperature, checked his blood pressure, used a tongue depressor to look at his throat, then leaned down and sniffed the acetone smell on Ben's breath. "Have you eaten anything in the last 24 hours?"

Ben weakly shook his head.

"Have you experienced severe nausea, dizziness, and repeated bouts of vomiting and diarrhea?"

Ben nodded weakly.

"I believe you have a case of seasickness, Mr. Atler. Now, there are a couple of things I can give you to make you feel better. The first is a rectal suppository which will take some time to abate your unpleasant symptoms. Then there is a much faster intramuscular injection of promethazine I can give you. The downside to promethazine is you will notice a painful sore spot at the site of the injection and you will be very sleepy, which is a good thing. Plenty of rest and the suppository or injection will have you on your feet much quicker. So, which would you like? The suppository or the injection?"

Ben looked at Clayton like a scared, brown-eyed puppy. Clayton quickly responded, "The Hulk here is afraid of needles, Doc."

"I understand," Dr. Robbins said gently. "Would it make it better if I whistled a tune and asked you to guess the name of the song while I gave you the injection?"

Ben nodded like a timid child. As Dr. Robbins prepared the injection, he whistled an old tune hoping that would keep Ben guessing and his mind off the shot. When the needle went into Ben's arm, he barely flinched. Dr. Robbins continued to whistle as he disposed of the used needle and syringe. He put a colorful Pokémon Band Aid on Ben's arm. "Did you guess the name of the song?" he asked.

The shot did the trick and Ben felt much better. "No, I don't know the song," he said, pulling himself up and sitting with his bare back pressed against the white headboard.

"I know the answer," Clayton said. "It's the theme song from the movie 'Bridge on the River Kwai.' That's my dad's favorite movie."

"It's mine too," Dr. Robbins said as he closed his bag and turned to Ben.

"There are a few precautions I can give you to help in case the seasickness returns. One is, when you are well enough, learn to ride the waves. By that, I mean anticipate the motion of the waves and adjust your body's rhythm to the sea's movement. Avoid alcohol. Now I know you are probably too young to legally drink, but I am a practical man. Eat moderately. Such things as crackers and hard candy may be helpful. Electrolytes are also important after prolonged periods of vomiting. If you are able to stand, go to the top deck and sit in a deck chair. The fresh air will make you feel better. If all these precautions fail to prevent your seasickness from returning, there is an adhesive patch you can wear behind your ear that will continuously administer a dose of scopolamine for three days. Is there anything else I can help you with, Mr. Atler?"

"Nothing I can think of, Dr. Robbins," Ben said, and his voice was stronger.

"You sound like you feel better already," Dr. Robbins said. "If I can be of further assistance to you, feel free to call upon me," he said, and he bid both young men a good day as he left their stateroom.

Clayton sat down on his bed across from Ben's. "You need a shower," he said, wrinkling his nose.

"I know," Ben said sleepily, and he opened his mouth for a prolonged yawn. His eyes grew heavy, he yawned again, snuggled down in his bed, pulled a blanket up over him, and fell into a deep sleep.

Clayton wordlessly left the stateroom.

In the main dining hall, Eden and Regan grabbed a food tray and joined the long line of hungry people filing past the buffet. Like a deprived child at Christmas who unexpectedly sees a beautiful tree with dozens of pretty presents underneath, Eden looked with amazement at the loaded food bar. She saw an assortment of soups. The bread list included white bread, French bread, whole wheat bread, biscuits, scones, cornbread, bagels, and English muffins. Steak, fried, broiled, and baked chicken, pork chops, and hamburgers were piled high on large platters. A seafood bar displayed lobster, shrimp, and clams on the half shell. Hot baked potatoes were dressed with many delicious toppings. Eden passed by the Mexican food, the kosher food, a Thai section, gluten free, and sugar-free foods. She ignored the Ramen noodles. At the Italian bar, she loaded her plate with spaghetti and pizza. Then she went to the soda bar and got a glass of coke. She avoided the standard meat and potatoes that she ate regularly at home.

When she sat down at the table she shared with her roommate, Regan looked at Eden's plate and she said, "Pizza and pasta? That is so passé. Try this," she said, and she laid a crispy fried something on Eden's plate.

"What is it?" Eden asked, suspiciously eyeing the foreign object.

"It's a piece of fried apple."

Eden picked up the foreign object, sniffed it, and looked it over carefully. She glanced at Regan who picked up a similar piece of food and popped it in her mouth. Eden slowly raised the object to her mouth and bit off the tiniest piece and chewed it. She was pleasantly surprised at how tasty it was. She ate the rest in one bite.

"Did you like the fried grasshopper?" Regan asked, and she roared with laughter.

"You've got to be kidding me!" Eden said, and she quickly drank her entire glass of coke.

Regan took a hefty bite of the Phat Thai Kung which resembled a plate of combined leftovers like the ones Eden often fed to their neighbor's dog.

"Some resident Thai people eat deep fried crickets, bee larvae, ant eggs, termites, and the giant water bugs are eaten like chips with a chili dip."

Eden thought about the damage the termites had done to their house with their voracious appetite for wood. They had eaten through many of the supports under their floors, causing sagging and creaking boards, and, in some places, the floors were too soft to walk on. She lost her appetite and pushed her plate away.

Regan went to get another soda. Eden saw Regan approach some well-dressed girls. She envied her roommate's magnetic personality and her ease when meeting new people. When Regan returned to the table, she sat down and ate her sticky rice and mango. When she finished her meal, she said, "The girls I was chatting up asked me if I'd like to join them at the pool and get some rays. Want to come along?"

Eden didn't own a swimming suit, and she also didn't know how to swim.

"I didn't bring a swimsuit," she said shyly.

"No worries, girlfriend. I'll loan you my turquoise-string bikini with the gold ties. It'll look smashing on you with that brunette hair of yours."

Regan pulled her phone from her fanny pack and texted. "Okay, I have us on a group text with our new friends. What's your number so I can add it to the group?"

"I don't have a phone," Eden said and her face flushed.

"You don't have a phone?" Regan asked incredulously. "That's simply amazing. How many people live in Maramount?" she teased.

"Plenty of people in Maramount have iPhones, Regan," Eden answered defensively. "It's a luxury I cannot afford."

Regan was dumbfounded that one could exist without a phone and text. She simply never heard of it.

"Okay," Eden said, feeling awkward. "Wanna go?"

The girls went back to their stateroom. Regan rifled through her luggage and pulled out the cutest and skimpiest swimsuit Eden had ever seen with the price tag still attached. Next came a pair of Chanel sunglasses. At Regan's encouragement, Eden took the swimsuit and the sunglasses into the bathroom. Before she undressed, Eden glanced at the price tag on the top which read $275.00. She didn't recognize the designer label. She quickly slipped out of her clothes and put on the swimsuit. When she looked at herself in the large mirror that hung on the wall over the double-sink vanity, she got the shock of her life. She filled the swimsuit out in all the right places and it still protected her modesty. Satisfied with what she saw, she pulled her thick auburn hair up in a ponytail, slipped on the Chanel sunglasses, and walked confidently out of the bathroom.

Regan's delighted reaction pleased Eden enormously. "WOW!" Regan said, and she turned Eden around and looked her over head to toe. "That swimsuit fits like it was made for you, girlfriend. Tell you what. You can have it."

Regan bit off the tag on the back of Eden's top. "Voila."

"Are you sure, Regan?" Eden asked, and her excitement blushed her cheeks.

"I'm sure, Pussycat."

Regan wore a skimpy, white, bikini top with a silver O in the center which provided a peek at her enhanced cleavage. On the tiny bikini bottom were silver O's on either side of her waist.

Regan put on a pair of stylish Armani sunglasses, grabbed some coconut oil, and headed for the door.

Eden picked up a room towel which Regan quickly grabbed out of her hand.

"Don't kill your dramatic entrance by wearing a bed sheet, girlfriend."

The two beautiful women walked out of their stateroom and headed for the pool. They got on the elevator with a group of other students and several of the guys wolf-whistled at them. Regan took the male approval with her usual aplomb, but Eden basked in their wolfish attention.

Seated on a deck chair beside the pool with the sun shining on her body, Eden warmed up her limbs and felt herself relaxing. She watched Regan glide across the sparkling water like a mermaid. She took a sip of her iced tea, removed her sunglasses and laid them on the small glass table next to her. She laid her head back and closed her eyes, taking in the sun's warmth.

"How's it going, Scribbler?"

Eden opened her eyes and saw Clayton Caulder seating himself next to her. He wore a tight, black Speedo and a pair of Nike flip-flops. She started to get up, but he put his hand on her arm and stopped her.

"Wait a minute. I want to talk to you," he said.

Eden wrenched her arm free, jumped up, and hurried away. After Eden had gone, Clayton reached over and took the Chanel sunglasses. He stuck one of the long earpieces down the front of his Speedo's, leaving the glasses looped over his bulging crotch and reflecting the sunlight.

From the other side of the pool, Regan had watched the fascinating scene take place between Clayton and Eden.

Regan's intense gaze locked with Clayton's nonchalant glance, and he smiled that crooked smirk that made him so maddeningly attractive.

\* \* \* \* \*

At 3 a.m. the next morning, Eden lay awake in her bed, watching the shimmering moonlight of the sea dance around the darkened room through the porthole. Regan had not returned to the stateroom. Eden was worried about her.

Where was she, and what was she doing? Eden decided to go in search of her. She got up, dressed, and headed for the door. Just as she reached for doorknob, she heard whispering outside in the hallway. Listening more closely, she recognized Regan's soft whisper and her husky, ribald, intimate laughter. The next voice she heard sent chills down her spine.

"Sleep tight, baby," Clayton Caulder said softly.

"You too, lover," Regan whispered sexily.

Eden hurried back across the room. She tore her pants off and jumped into bed.

The lock softly turned and Regan opened the door just enough to slide her rail-thin body inside. She crept over to Eden's bed and made sure her roommate was fast asleep. Regan softly padded into the bathroom, ran some water, and flushed the toilet. Regan opened the bathroom door, wearing her baby-doll pajamas, climbed into her bed, and fell instantly to sleep.

*So Crafty Clayton has won Regan's heart,* Eden thought. *Now I will have to be careful of her too.*

# Sixteen

Eden's class schedule included Women and Creative Writing, Literature of the World, Comparative Literature, Modern Fiction, Mediterranean Noir, and The Literature of Travel. For the three days she had been at sea, she had diligently attended all her classes, completed her assignments, and her writing schedule was up-to-date and emailed to Mrs. Omaha and Professor Altgeld.

Regan's classes contained general studies and Algebra II. To date, Regan attended her classes, but due to lack of sleep and her preoccupation with Clayton Caulder, she had fallen behind in her assignments.

Clayton occasionally attended his classes, and his assignments were presently up-to-date thanks to brainy Amy Wadkins, a heavy-set girl with an obnoxious overbite and thick eyeglasses. Clayton was a consummate user, and since Amy had a mad crush on him, the situation worked out perfectly. For the homework Amy couldn't handle, Clayton and Ben compensated Steele Elliott, a boy-genius from Detroit, Michigan, to complete their assignments.

Clayton's innate ability to ferret out debauchery had not been wasted on the three days he spent at sea. He learned enough dirty secrets about a few corrupt crew members to keep his room happily supplied with booze, contraband Cuban cigars, and cocaine. He had also recently discovered a new vice. A guy named Juan who cleaned the staterooms once gave Clayton some funky monkey incense to smoke.

He and Juan had a standing 3 a.m. appointment to meet in a shadowy part of the ship's upper deck so Clayton could purchase the new stimulant. On one of those clandestine meetings with Juan, Clayton saw Sandreen Gavel, dressed in a see-through white negligee, sneak across the moonlit upper deck. He asked Juan where she was going. Juan said she was headed to Captain Evert's stateroom.

114

Clayton's opinion of her fell a few notches. He had tried to woo her with his masculine charm, but she sharply rebuffed his overtures and spoke to him like a prepubescent school boy which made him even more determined to break through her unapproachable facade and penetrate her arrogance.

Ben Atler liked his classes and handed his assignments in on time. He wore a scopolamine patch behind his right ear for the seasickness which had returned with a vengeance. Clayton suggested Ben wear the patch over his eye to add some mystery and enhance his sexuality. Ben said he was too smart to fall for that. Clayton doubted that statement.

Eden sat by herself in the dining room, eating her lunch, just as she so often had done in high school. Not to appear pitifully alone, she read her Comparative Literature homework for her next class.

Regan bounded over to the table, carrying a tray of exotic food, and sat down next to Eden. "You put the rest of us to shame," Regan said.

"How's that?" Eden asked, looking warily up at her roommate.

"I never see you study except in here; must be nice to be so smart."

"I study a lot," Eden said defensively. "You're not in our stateroom enough to know what I do."

Regan giggled. "You do have a point. Lately, I have been busy doing other things."

Eden guessed Regan referred to the nights she and Clayton spent having sex in the lifeboat. Regan also spent her afternoons lolling in the sun and hanging out with her new friends.

Eden noticed Steele Elliott sitting by himself at a table next to the exit door. She knew that he too usually ate his meals alone. They once shared a table in the crowded library. Steele had introduced himself. During their brief conversation, Steele said he had been given a scholarship for the trip and that he hoped to finish his thesis on Aberrant Social Behavior. His superior intellect astounded Eden. But Eden could not help but notice that Steele seemed awkward around people and socially inept. She felt sorry for him. It appeared he couldn't escape his genius.

"We will arrive in Honolulu, Hawaii, in approximately one hour," a voice announced over the P.A. system.

Excitement pulsed in the dining room, and the students quickly finished their meals.

"I'll catch up with you later," Regan said as she stood up, leaving her tray filled with half-eaten food on the table. Eden gathered up her homework and placed it in her folder. She picked up both Regan's and her tray and neatly stacked them before she left.

Right on schedule, the ship arrived at the Port of Honolulu. As the students left the ship, they were greeted by women dressed in tropical-patterned, ankle-length muumuus. The brightly dressed women draped a lei made of fragrant Prumeria around each student's neck. Every student carried a map of the island that gave directions to the many fascinating places to explore. A series of field trips, labs, and cultural experiences were also listed as part of their four-day Hawaiian-study curriculum.

Eden's wish to experience a luau and hear some of the local music came true as the students gathered together in a verdant garden, teeming with flowering plants, palm trees, and a waterfall. Exotic fragrances blending with a balmy breeze created a botanical paradise.

A portly, dark-skinned, Polynesian man dressed in a bright yellow-and-red Hawaiian shirt, loose-fitting white, cotton slacks, and sandals walked to the stone podium.

"Welcome to Hawaii!" he said. "My name is Tandoor Kalani. I am the Mayor of Honolulu."

A tropical breeze fanned his head of white hair and ruffled the legs of his cotton slacks.

"My staff has planned a tradition Polynesian luau for you today. The word luau in English means party. I'm sure that is a term many of you young people are familiar with."

Laughter came back in answer.

"In past centuries, women were not allowed to eat with the men at luau, nor could they taste the food they had prepared." Regan led a group of her new friends in booing that idea. Mayor Kalani smiled. "So right you are, ladies."

Eden thought about Momma who was allowed to eat with her dad but that was so she could put food on his plate.

Mayor Kalani continued, "In 1819, King Kamehameha abolished that law. From then on, the women were allowed to attend and enjoy the luaus. I suppose you could say that was a first in Hawaiian women's emancipation.

"In the early days, Hawaiian women wore coconut bras, grass skirts, lei wreaths around their necks, and colorful feathers in their hair. When they danced the hula for their suitors, husbands, or visiting dignitaries, the accompanying music was played on a Pahu drum. Please be seated, and we will start the entertainment."

The students sat down on the thick grass mats. Eden looked around at some of her peers. She didn't see any friendly faces smiling back at her, which made her feel more alone than ever.

Mayor Kalani placed a thick, deep-green cushion on the ground and sat down on it. When he crossed his arms over his chest, bent his knees, and tucked in his legs, he looked like an Indian Guru.

As trays of food arrived, Eden was reminded of Jesus when he sat five-thousand people down on the ground, blessed two small fish and five loaves of bread and fed the entire mass.

A half-naked young man carrying a lighted fire stick burst onto the scene. He wore a lush, green, leafy wreath on his head, one around his neck, two flaps of yellow cloth covered the back and front of his skimpy yellow Speedo. He was joined by two men dressed in similar outfits. One man carried a set of Pahu drums made from a coconut tree and dried sharkskin. The other man carried an Ipu, a hollow gourd played by striking it with the fingers and palms.

As the music started, the dancer gave a primal yell, swung around wildly, and twirled the fire stick above his head with such speed that the light formed a fiery halo. "I dance for your pleasure and your delight," he shouted in a Polynesian accent. The music increased in tempo, and the young man danced more provocatively, spreading his toned legs and thrusting his hips.

The nearly naked young man's fiery, wild dancing reminded Eden of what a satanic ritual might look like. She said a silent prayer to ward off any evil spirits.

Much to Eden's relief, the entertainment portion of the program ended.

"May I join you?" Steele Elliott asked, standing over Eden.

"Sure," she said, and he sat down on the thick grass mat next to her.

"Did you enjoy the dance?" he asked.

"I wouldn't say I enjoyed it. I found it interesting."

"That's one way to put it," he said, and he shyly smiled at her.

Traditionally dressed Hawaiian women began distributing food throughout the crowd.

"This is poi served with unleavened bread," a woman said, setting identical trays of food on the ground in front of Steele and Eden. Then she walked away and served others from the five-tier cart she pulled behind her. Steele dipped the bread into the poi and ate it.

"Is it good?" Eden asked softly.

"It tastes like Elmer's glue."

"I think I'll skip it."

"Don't do that. You should try everything at least once. When in Rome…" he said, and he dipped a corner of bread into the poi and handed it to Eden. She tasted a small bite to appease him. She laid the rest back on the tray, thinking his Elmer's glue description was apt.

Both Eden and Steele enjoyed the next course of Lomilomi salmon with tomatoes and onions, as well as the third course of Kalua pork and purple sweet potatoes. Neither of them cared for the pork or the raw fish marinated in lemon juice with coconut cream. But they both savored the charred pineapple spears and the watermelon. For their parting gift, the students were given Pipi, a seasoned beef rope that tastes like beef jerky.

After the luau, the students were dismissed for the rest of the afternoon to go exploring.

"Mind if I hang out with you?" Steele asked.

"I'd welcome your company," Eden said, and, now, instead of dreading another day alone, she looked forward to spending the day sightseeing with her new friend.

The two of them took out the previously distributed map and arranged the places they wanted to see in alphabetical order. First was Diamond Head Crater. The downside was they didn't have a lot of time, so they would need to rent a car. They checked with three or four discount car-rental agencies and the least expensive place still wanted 250 dollars for four hours. They decided they would rent a motorcycle. They scouted around and found one for 200 dollars for four hours. Steele suggested to take it down another notch and rent a moped. They found a place that would rent them a moped for 65 dollars for six hours. They counted the money they had between them and they both paid 32.50. Eden filled out the paperwork, the man handed the keys to Steele, and Steele handed them to Eden.

"Don't you want to drive?" she asked.

"I can't. I don't have a driver's license."

"Did you get a ticket?"

"No. I'm only 15."

Eden's jaw dropped. "But you said you're starting your sophomore year in college this fall!"

"I am, Eden. I was allowed to jump a few grades in school."

Eden reluctantly took the keys. Bravely, she threw her leg over the yellow-and-turquoise moped and patted the seat behind her. Steele climbed on.

"I've never driven one of these before, so hang on!" she said, and she slipped the key in and the motor came to life. Their initial takeoff proved jerky, but, soon, Eden found her groove as they sailed along Kamehameha Highway.

Steele wrapped his arms around her waist, and he laid his head on her back. He knew at that moment that he loved her. Not the love he would someday feel for a lover. This felt like safe love. He believed he could count on Eden not to let him down. She would be a true friend, much like an adoring sister, a faithful and honest companion.

Since they had chosen the sightseeing ventures in alphabetical order, Eden and Steele had a friendly windblown disagreement on which came first. Would it be Diamond Head, or the U.S.S. Arizona? Eden said Diamond Head came first because it started with a D. Steele said U.S.S. Arizona because Arizona started with an A and the U.S.S. wasn't relevant. Eden said the U.S.S. was very relevant. That it stood for United States Ship, and his disparaging the title was like saying 'the land of the free and the home of the brave' wasn't relevant. Steele agreed with Eden's passionate statement, and he relented.

First, they visited Diamond Head Crater. On the two-and-a-half-hour tour, they walked up to the 763-foot summit and saw a breathtaking view of the greenish-blue Pacific Ocean and a 360-degree panoramic site of Waikiki. Hanauma Bay came next. They agreed that before they left Hawaii, they would go scuba diving and snorkeling in the beautiful embayment formed within a turf ring.

As they flew down Kamehameha Highway, Eden checked the odometer and it read 42 miles. The man at the rental center told them the moped could safely handle a 70-mile distance before it ran out of electric power. They had intended to go see the Polynesian Cultural Center, but the map said it was on Oahu's north shore in the town of Laie and that was 32 miles from Honolulu. The other deterrent was the 45-dollar per person admission fee. They decided instead to stop for a banana-mango smoothie and sit on the beach outside the Surfrider Hotel.

119

Eden and Steele sat on the beach in the gathering twilight, watching the last of the swimmers head to shore.

"This has been the best day of my life," Eden said, squishing her toes in the warm sand.

"Mine too," Steele said, and he reached over and took Eden's hand.

Eden turned and she smiled at him.

"I love you, Eden," he said, and tears slipped down his wind-burned cheeks.

"I know. I love you too, Steele. I wish I could take you back home with me. I would love to have a little brother. My brother, Rick, isn't nearly as sweet as you."

"I don't want to go back home. My parents are divorced. I see my dad and his icky new wife every other weekend. My mom is alone and always depressed. I wish we could stay here forever," he said, and he laid his head in her lap.

Eden stroked his hair, and she hummed a song that Abby and she sung with their momma. Steele's eyes grew heavy and he fell asleep. Eden sat wide awake, taking in every sound, movement, and smell. She didn't want to miss a moment of the experience. An hour later, Eden woke him, and they rode the moped back to the rental agency, walked back to the ship, and made curfew with 30 minutes to spare.

On the upper deck, Steele and Eden said goodnight. He hugged her and she hugged him back.

"Save me a seat in the dining room tomorrow," Steele called to her as he walked away.

"Will do," Eden said, and she headed down to her stateroom.

She unlocked the door and stepped into the dark room. When she flipped the light on, she saw Regan's empty, unmade bed. She went into the bathroom and washed her face and brushed her teeth. She sat down on her bed and read her assignments for the next day. She didn't notice the slight rippling movement under the blankets. She laid her homework folder on the nightstand and pulled back the blankets. She threw her hand over her mouth to stifle her terrified scream. Lying on the white sheet, a large, hairy, zebra-striped spider fought its agonizing, imminent demise against the number-two pencil that pierced its bulbous middle body.

Eden found a large brown envelope and she carefully levered the flap under the twisting spider. When the suffering creature was inside, she quickly closed the envelope and opened the porthole and threw the envelope out on the sea. She took the sheets off her bed, and after a thorough inspection of the mattress and under the bed, she laid down on the blanket and covered herself with the bedspread.

She laid with the lights on and her troubling thoughts turned to the tormented, drowned spider. She felt as sorry for the innocent spider as she did for herself. *Who would do such a cruel thing? Clayton? Ben? Regan? Or were all three of them in on it?*

A key turned in the lock, and Regan walked in. She saw Eden was awake; she slammed the door, threw herself across her bed, and started to cry.

Eden lay perfectly still, listening to her roommate sobbing. A few minutes later, Regan said, "You'll be pleased to know Clayton dumped me tonight."

Eden didn't respond; she just continued staring at the moonlight's reflection dancing around the room.

"Aren't you going to say anything?" Regan asked angrily.

"There's nothing to say," Eden said softly.

"Don't you want to know what happened?!"

"Not particularly."

Regan jumped on Eden's bed and straddled her body. Eden looked up at her. "Get off me," she said coldly.

The anger drained out of Regan, and she collapsed on top of Eden. Eden refused to give her any pity. She pushed Regan off her and stood up.

"If you're going to sleep in my bed, then I will use yours," she said, and she turned off the overhead light, threw the blankets back on Regan's bed, and crawled in.

The silence in the room became unbearable for Regan.

"I'm sorry, Eden, for being such a bad roommate."

Eden's resolve eased. "I warned you about Clayton."

"You did. But I thought I could recognize a scumbag when I saw one."

"I assume he is with another girl now and he threw it in your face. Rest assured. You're not the first girl he's done this to."

"I'm sure that's true. Tell me something, Eden. Why do Clayton and Ben hate you so much?"

"I really don't know."

"Today, the three of us went to an upscale pet store on Ala Moana Boulevard and Clayton bought the most obnoxious-looking, striped spider. I asked him what he wanted with it. He said he bought it for a friend of his. That was the creepiest spider I ever saw," Regan said, and she yawned loudly.

"Goodnight, Eden," she said, and she turned over and quickly fell asleep.

Eden lay awake for a long time, thinking.

# Seventeen

Eden and Steele formed a permanent bond of friendship. They spent all their free time enjoying each other's company. They ate their meals together, enjoyed an occasional movie, and Steele taught Eden to swim. They joined forces on their homework and, given Steele's superior tutelage, Eden excelled in all her classes.

Steele's unselfish and adoring attention also helped Eden to forget the horror of the striped spider. Even Clayton and Ben soon became inconsequential. On starry nights, the two of them would sit on the moonlit upper deck and Steele would point out the constellations and tell Eden made-up stories about their travels to different galaxies and visits with alien creatures. They told each other things about themselves that neither one had ever shared with another person. Steele was genuinely interested in Eden's poetry. She read him her poems, sharing her most intimate secrets with him. They often had heated yet friendly discussions on controversial topics such as religion, politics, and abortion. But they both agreed that domestic violence, child abuse, and harming and killing animals for sport, should be abolished.

Steele told Eden he had been bullied at school. Eden said she was bullied too. She didn't disclose to him that her two worst antagonists were Clayton and Ben. Steele had confided in her about the monetary arrangement he had with them to complete their homework, and she didn't want to interfere. Steele said he didn't understand why he was picked on. Eden said the same.

One day, after her last class, Eden waited for Steele at their favorite spot on the upper deck. She stood at the railing, gazing at the soft blue sky, thick white clouds, and enjoyed the balmy breeze and the glistening sea. Steele walked up beside her and looked out at the sea. Eden noticed he was unusually quiet and seemed troubled.

"Is something wrong, Steele?"

"I'm not feeling so good."

"Did you eat something that made you sick?"

"I don't think so. You're not sick and we ate the same food."

Eden had noticed lately that whatever food she chose, Steele chose the same. At first, she took it as a compliment, but lately she worried that he might have developed an unhealthy obsession with her. She felt certain his interest in her wasn't of a sexual nature. More like a big sister or a mother figure. But either of those scenarios could prove troubling.

"Maybe you should go see the doctor."

"I don't want to do that yet. Could we sit down? I feel a little nauseated."

They sat down next to each other on the deck lounge-chairs. Eden saw Steele wince when he scooted back in the chair.

"Are you in pain?"

"My side hurts," he said, and he gently rubbed his right side.

"I wrote a new poem last night," she said, hoping to take his mind off his discomfort. "Want to hear it?"

"Sure," he said softly.

She took a sheet of paper out of her homework folder. "I titled my poem…

### *LIFE IN TECHNICOLOR*

*When a person's feeling overwhelmed,*
*And life is out of hand,*
*Sometimes she may realize,*
*It's because someone took away hiser stand.*


*Everyone needs a purpose,*
*A reason to believe,*
*It can be something simple,*
*A dream that brings one ease.*


*Life can be so harsh at times,*
*Harsh when critics are too much.*
*They take away one's rhymes,*
*Adding their own privy touch.*

124

*Creativity is so personal,*
*It's something that gives great pride.*
*It makes a dreamer's life have color,*
*It brings a skip into one's stride.*

*To kill a person's spirit,*
*Is to abolish her right to see.*
*The world from her own perspective,*
*The right to simple glee.*

*A crushed spirit should be a crime,*
*Particularly when one's a poet.*
*She lives to make her world a rhyme,*
*To have others see it as she knows it.*

*But a poet has another day,*
*To move forward yet to view.*
*She can choose to listen to what a judge may say;*
*She can start each day anew.*

*Because a poet has a special talent,*
*One the rest of the world may envy.*
*She sees the world in Technicolor,*
*While others live a monotonous frenzy."*

Eden, dressed in denim shorts and a white t-shirt, laid the paper on her bare legs. "Did you like my poem, Steele?"

"It's nice. But do you really believe someone has the power to 'take your stand' away from you?"

"Yes, I believe it is possible for someone to kill a dream you have."

"I don't agree. I believe with enough faith, perseverance, and hard work, you alone have the power to achieve your dreams. I also believe a strong, determined person will work their way to success."

Eden thought about that. "You do have a point."

"When a person blames others for their personal shortfalls, it's counterproductive and a total waste of time. We all could wallow in our

125

disappointments. The true winner is one who grabs the bull by the horns and never stops trying."

Eden wadded up her paper. "You have profound insight, Steele."

Steele said, "Don't destroy your poem. It's excellent."

Eden smoothed out the paper and she said, "Do you really think so?"

"I absolutely do. I just wanted to point out another perspective."

"And you did. Thank you, Steele."

"Thank you, dear friend," Steele said. He moved his leg and it felt like a red-hot poker stabbed his side.

"You're going to see the doctor," Eden said, and she stood up and reached for Steele's hand. He let her help him to his feet, but he fell down on the deck, moaning with pain.

Eden caught two guys as they walked by and asked them to help her get Steele to the doctor.

When they lifted Steele in their strong arms, he screamed with pain. As quickly as they could, they carried Steele down to the doctor's office.

Eden paced the waiting room, praying for her friend. Half an hour later, Dr. Robbins came out of the examining room.

"Your friend needs to have his appendix removed. I gave him a shot to ease his pain. My nurse called the Coast Guard and they are sending a Medi-Evac helicopter to pick him up. Good thing we are close to the next port. The chopper should arrive in half an hour. For the time being, you can go inside and be with him. But try to keep him calm."

"Where are they taking him?" Eden asked.

"To Kadena Air Base in Okinawa, Japan."

"Is that one of our military bases?"

"Yes, it is. The 'Keystone of the Pacific,' as it is sometimes called, is the largest air-force installation out here."

"It's good to know Steele will be in good hands."

"Yes, indeed."

Steele lay under a dim light on a stretcher, covered with a clean, white sheet. He looked frail, ghostly, and sleepy.

"How are you doing?" Eden asked softly.

"Better, I think," he mumbled. "They're going to remove my appendix."

"I know. The doctor told me."

"I hate this because I have to leave you."

"I hate this for you too. But you'll be back before you know it."

"I won't be coming back, Eden."

"You mean to the ship?"

"I mean I am going to die."

"Don't be silly. This is a routine surgery. They'll have you back on your feet in no time."

Steele opened his icy-blue eyes and he looked at her. "I know these things," he said firmly.

His intense gaze and his being so positive of the outcome of his illness spooked Eden. She took his hand in hers and she said, "I can't lose you now. I won't let you die."

He smiled that endearing, crooked smile that melted her heart. "You are the best thing that ever happened to me in my whole miserable life," he said, and he raised her hand and kissed it.

Eden laid her head on his thin shoulder. "I feel the same about you, sweet, dear friend."

Steele closed his eyes. "Tell me a story," he said, sounding like a five-year-old she had just tucked into bed.

She pulled a stool up next to the stretcher and she sat down. As the ship gently rocked on the waves and the sunlight stayed at bay outside the porthole, Eden told Steele a story about a poor girl from a small Midwestern town who had great aspirations of becoming a poet. In the interim, she had gone on a study cruise and she had met a wonderful, smart, kind, and decent young boy who stole her heart.

The door opened and two muscular E.M.T.s came into the room, toting a red basket stretcher. Eden moved away from Steele so the medics could do their job. One man took hold of the bottom sheet by Steele's feet and the other man took hold of the sheet corners at Steele's head. On the count of three, they picked Steele up in the sheet and gently placed him in the red basket stretcher. They strapped him in and covered him with a thin white blanket. The men positioned themselves on either side of the stretcher and they lifted Steele. Eden walked a few paces behind the medics as they headed for the elevator.

A crowd had gathered on the upper deck, forming a semi-circle around the helicopter. A man dressed in a coast-guard uniform opened a path through the crowd so the medics could get through. The helicopter's whirling overhead blades worried Eden for the tall men who walked upright beneath them. The medics started to put Steele in the helicopter, but Steele said something to them and they set the stretcher down on the deck. One of the men, a tall young man with dreadlocks and chiseled cheeks, turned around and motioned for Eden. Eden went quickly across the deck.

"He wants to say goodbye to you," the young man shouted above the helicopter's roar.

With tears streaming down her face, Eden bent down and she placed her ear close to Steele's lips.

"You know I said I love you like a sister?" he asked. Eden nodded. "It's not true. I love you more than my life, more than my soul, more than my spirit, with every beat of my heart."

Eden started sobbing, and she laid her head on his chest. "I love you too," she said, and she tenderly kissed his trembling lips.

The medics picked up the stretcher and placed it inside the helicopter. Just before they closed the door, Steele looked at her one last time with tear-filled eyes. He weakly waved goodbye. Eden was told by the pilot to move back and stand with the crowd.

Sobbing, she walked away. She stood apart from the crowd and watched the helicopter blades gain speed. The great bird lifted off the platform, turned sharply, and, in a minute, it was gone from sight.

Sandreen Gavel, the cruise director, put her arm around Eden's shoulders and led her away from the subdued crowd. Silently, the two women walked to Sandreen's stateroom. Sandreen opened the door to her apartment and led Eden inside. She motioned for Eden to sit on a small, white sofa. Sandreen sat on a large, white ottoman facing Eden.

"Would you like to talk?" Sandreen asked softly.

Staring at the teak floor, Eden slowly shook her head no.

Sandreen went into a small kitchenette and made hot tea. She brought the tea service on a silver tray and placed it on the ottoman. She poured a cup of tea, added a generous spoonful of sugar, and handed the cup to Eden. Eden held the warm cup in her hands, but she didn't drink the tea.

Sandreen softly walked over to a chair and sat quietly. The afternoon slowly passed outside the porthole. Twilight changed the hue in the room to a soft blue. With the darkness came Eden's heartbroken tears.

When Eden's tears finally stopped, she sat motionless on the sofa and stared into the darkness. Sandreen went over and took the cup of tea out of

Eden's hands. She gently laid Eden down on the sofa and went into her bedroom. She returned with a blanket which she spread over Eden. Sandreen entered her bedroom and quietly closed the door.

The next morning, Eden woke up in the strange room. Bewildered, she looked around at the pretty furnishings. Then she remembered Steele. She bolted to her feet and rushed out of the stateroom.

Eden burst into Dr. Robbins's waiting room, and she asked the nurse about Steele's condition. The nurse called for Dr. Robbins. When he came out of his office, in his kindest voice, he told Eden that Steele's appendix had burst on the way to the hospital and he had died.

That night, Eden went to the upper deck and she sat beside an empty chair. She poured her heart out to God, mourning, crying, and saying silent prayers to Him for her dear friend. She knew in her heart she would never recover from the loss of Steele. But she vowed to go forward with her life and try to make Steele proud of her.

The following morning, Eden sat at a table by herself in the dining room, poking at her cold breakfast. A few passing people offered quick condolences to her for the loss of her friend. Marvin Howard, Steele's former roommate, came into the dining room, looking for Eden.

"May I sit down?" he asked Eden.

"I guess so."

He pulled a chair out and sat down across from her. He said, "When I was packing Steele's things yesterday to send to his mother, I found a book he had with your name in it."

"I don't remember giving Steele a book."

"Here," he said, and he laid a leather-bound book on the table in front of her. The title read, 'The Book of Job.' Marvin stood up. "If you don't want it, I'll send it along with his things to his family."

After he had gone, Eden looked inside the book and she saw a sheet of folded paper. She opened it and she read…

*Dear Eden,*

*I never had much interest in poetry until I met you. And when it came to accepting your idea of a higher power, as you well know, I often scoffed at the idea. For years, I have considered myself to be, at best, agnostic. But you changed my mind about many things.*

*I bought this book the day we went to Diamond Head. Remember when you left me alone so you could go sit on the cliff overlooking the bay and write your poem? Well, I went to the gift shop and I found this book. The flyleaf at the beginning of the book says that many world scholars consider the Book of Job to be the greatest poem in literature. I read this book and I agree with their assessment. I hope you read it and find as much pleasure in it as I will have in giving it to you.*

*With all my love,*
*Steele*

Eden closed the book and pressed it against her heart.

# Eighteen

The Heisenberg Uncertainty Principal states that to observe something without changing it is impossible. Steele taught Eden the principle by example. He had a simple appendicitis, but he foretold his death. And, sadly, his altered state of consciousness fulfilled his prophecy.

Eden stood on the crowded upper deck, watching seagulls swoop and dive toward the choppy water as the ship moved at a steady 25 knots across the ocean. As she had done so many times in the last few days, she thought of Steele and all the plans they'd made for sightseeing in Yokohama. *This will be a bittersweet visit to Japan without him,* she thought. Hoping the seagulls meant that land was near, Eden put her hand up to shade her eyes and she looked into the distance. All she saw was a tiny island. She wondered how the birds survived with so little land at their disposal.

Mourning and celebrating her dear friend came in waves. Like the sailors who fell in love with the mythological sirens, an ambient melody evoked passionate feelings in her. Other times, she would recall Steele's hilarious sense of humor and she would laugh out loud as she remembered one of his zany observations. But her strongest emotions surfaced when she was wrapped in her dark-gray, wool blanket, seated on a lounge chair on the upper deck, listening to the ocean's haunting melody. A day such as this had provoked her to write a poem about her cherished friend.

### *A HAUNTING MELODY*

*I met you on a college cruise,*
*Searching for my destiny.*
*I came from little, with nothing to lose,*
*Seeking to live successfully.*

*But I met you, Steele, a kindred heart,*
*With wisdom, love, and adventure.*
*Your laugh and smarts way off the chart,*
*To a starved girl, you were a quencher.*

*You're younger than me, that is true,*
*But there was wisdom in your manner.*
*Inside me...you sure saw right through,*
*Instinctively, you waved your banner.*

*The ocean sings a lullaby,*
*To send Steele off to sleep.*
*I do not have an alibi,*
*My loss is far too deep.*

*We shared laughter, dreams, a painful past,*
*We got each other as we stood.*
*We knew our friendship, always would last,*
*All promises would be made good.*

*But God's decision about your life,*
*Said your purpose here was fulfilled.*
*Maybe he bore you for easing my strife,*
*I cry out, God, why was he killed!?*

*God, Oh, God, the Maker of all,*
*My loss is far too deep.*
*Couldn't you have chosen someone else?*
*Because I mourn and cry and weep.*

*The ocean sings a lullaby,*
*To send Steele off to sleep.*
*I do not have an alibi.*
*My loss is far too deep.*

*Some people are irreplaceable,*
*Life put our paths to meet.*
*Steele, you made me know I'm special as is,*
*Being without you feels like a cheat.*

*As I mourn your loss, I feel quite sad,*
*Because I cry for my own pain, you see.*
*Maybe you're at rest and finally glad,*
*God knew where you needed to be.*

*The ship's deck is too quiet now, I know,*
*I hope you will round the corner.*
*Your life's end makes me spin at the bow,*
*In my pain, I'm a silent mourner.*

*The ocean sings a lullaby,*
*To send Steele off to sleep.*
*I do not have an alibi,*
*My loss is far too deep.*

*It's rare in life to meet a soul,*
*A smart, bright, and kindred spirit.*
*Your absence is sharply taking a toll,*
*I ache for your smile to be near it.*

*I thank you, dear friend, for giving me hope,*
*That someday I'll meet my dreams.*
*And when that happens, I will not mope,*
*Because your smile will always beam.*

*The ocean sings a lullaby,*
*To send Steele off to sleep.*
*I do not have an alibi,*
*My loss is far too deep.*

Eden folded the poem and she placed it inside the Book of Job which Steele had given her.

A loud howl, a playful scream, and a thundering splash of water caused Eden to turn her face toward the crowded swimming pool. She saw Sandreen Gavel, wearing a skimpy lavender bikini and fashionable sunglasses, sitting in the lifeguard tower overlooking the swimmers. On the few occasions Eden had run into Sandreen following Steele's death, Sandreen's furtive glance and aloof attitude warned her to stay away.

Eden thought Sandreen's avoidance of her might have something to do with an unpleasant scene Eden had witnessed. Two nights earlier, Eden saw Clayton shove Sandreen against the bulkhead and hold her there with his strong arms. Eden could see they were engaged in a heated argument. She moved into the shadows and eavesdropped on their conversation.

"Let me pass, Mr. Caulder," Sandreen said sharply.

"We know each other well enough for you to call me Clayton," he said lustily.

"I'm late for work!"

Clayton moved his face closer to hers. "A few minutes one way or another won't make any difference."

Sandreen put her hands on Clayton's hard chest and tried to push him away, but she didn't succeed in freeing herself. Her rejection infuriated him.

"You won't have this job very long if I go to the captain and tell him what a tease you are."

Sandreen laughed in his face. "You might get an unpleasant surprise if you try that," she said, and the breeze whipped her luxurious, dark hair across her face.

"You'll give me what I want or I'll make your life very difficult."

"There are a hundred gorgeous girls on this ship who are dying to spend time with you. Why don't you choose one of them and leave me alone?"

"I'm not interested in any of the *girls* on this ship. I want you."

"Only because you know I don't want you."

"You're not like other women I have been with."

"How do you know what I'm like?"

Clayton pulled her closer. "You are beautiful and sexy," he moaned.

"You act like a spoiled adolescent!" she said, and she shoved his arms aside and walked away.

As Sandreen passed by Eden's hiding place, she said to Eden, "Did you enjoy the show?"

Eden thought about that night as she headed back to her stateroom. She figured her promiscuous roommate was with her newest conquest, a handsome but morally deficient member of the crew. Regan once confided in Eden about Seaman Second Class Rowdy Raine's emotional and physical shortcomings. Eden had listened to Regan's explicit description of Rowdy's less-than-perfect sexual prowess with her usual, silent yawn. Eden and Regan were close friends now. They had renewed their friendship after Regan's relationship with Clayton ended.

Later that day, Eden went to her Modern Fiction class. She tried to concentrate on what the professor was saying, but her mind kept drifting to the scene on the deck between Sandreen and Clayton. Sandreen had it right when she called Clayton a spoiled adolescent. *He's used to getting his way, and he's never been held accountable for any of the rotten things he's done.* Judge Caulder's wealth and position managed to protect Clayton from anything unpleasant.

After class, Eden went to the library and emailed her poetry assignments to Professor Altgeld. She cc-ed Mrs. Omaha. Eden went back to the stateroom to gather her colored pencils, notepaper, and backpack. Regan came out of the bathroom, wearing a thick, white, bath towel around her middle and another towel on her wet hair.

"Long time no see," Regan said, fluffing her long, black hair with the towel. "Better take your shower now or we'll be late for the Masquerade Ball." She saw the puzzled look on Eden's face and she said, "Did you forget the ball is tonight?"

"No, I didn't forget. I'm not going."

"Why?"

"Do you really have to ask?"

"Is it because you don't have anything to wear?"

*Regan, you are so insensitive sometimes,* Eden thought. "I just lost my best friend. Remember?"

"Life goes on, girlfriend," Regan said. She went to her closet and pulled out a glittering gold, Zuhair Murad form-fitting gown with tiny petal sleeves. Regan turned the silk hangar around and Eden saw a wide band of Swarovski crystals formed a sparkling choker at the neckline.

"Is that what you're going to wear?" Eden asked, trying to keep the envy out of her voice.

"No, Silly. This is what you're going to wear." Regan handed the dress to Eden. "Now, go shower and blow-dry your hair. When you're finished, I'll style your hair and do your makeup."

Eden tried to cool her excitement about attending the ball. After all, her best friend had just died and she wanted and needed to mourn his loss. But going to the ball won over her indecision. To assuage some of her guilt, she silently promised herself she would make sure she didn't have a good time.

After her shower, Eden joined Regan. They both wore a thick white towel wrapped around them and tucked in at their breasts. Regan sat down on the ottoman and opened her fancy makeup case. She pulled out a dozen bottles of OPI nail polish.

"How sizzling do you want to look?" Regan asked.

Eden looked over the beautiful selection. "The Devil Wears Red looks good," she said shyly.

"Excellent choice. Now sit down on the sofa," Regan said, and she placed a towel on her lap and picked up Eden's hand and set it on the towel. "I'll give you a mani first, then a pedi. I'm going to paint your fingernails red. Then I'll stripe them with glittery-gold nail polish. That's the new look."

An hour later, Eden stared at her beautifully shaped and painted nails. "Thank you, Regan. My hands look so beautiful."

"You're welcome. And thanks for the compliment. That's high praise for a spoiled brat."

Staying true to her gothic style, Regan painted her fingernails and toenails with OPI Black Vixen. Then she added an opaque white stripe.

Regan went to her closet and pulled out her large Louis Vuitton trunk.

"I thought we were limited to one backpack and one duffle bag," Eden said.

"You know the old saying… 'Money will buy…'"

Regan dialed the combination for the lock and the lid popped open. Several cocktail dresses were neatly aligned on padded hangers. Regan chose a stunning gown made of white silk with a wide V that ended below the navel and a long slit up the side to the waist.

"How do you think I'll look in this?" Regan asked, holding the size-zero dress up for Eden's approval.

"It is perfect for you!"

136

"Okay. Now we need some shoes. What size do you wear?"

"I wear a five-and-a-half."

"Really? I thought your feet look bigger than mine." Regan handed Eden a pair of Jimmy Choo four-inch strappy sandals. For herself, she chose a pair of Christian Louboutin crystal glimmers.

"Put this rose oil on your legs to give them a hint of fragrance and a beautiful glow."

"Shouldn't we put on our underwear first?"

"You can if you want to, but you'll have to take it off when you get dressed."

"You're kidding!"

"Look at these dresses, Eden. Underwear would show right through them."

Eden didn't put on her underwear, but she felt self-conscience and a little naughty. Regan expertly applied makeup to Eden's unblemished face. She used her Nars cosmetics, and when she announced the name of the product she was using, 'Orgasm,' Eden blushed.

Regan laughed at Eden's discomfiture. "You think that's risqué? Check out these other names. I have Threesome, Foreplay, Inner Glow, After Hours, and, my favorite, Pussy Galore. My dad balked at the notion of buying makeup for me with such provocative names. I finally got my mom to buy it for me. But I think she did it to provoke my dad. Such is my life with antagonistic, divorced parents.

"Now for your hair. How about I fix it like Kate Middleton's? I think you can pull off the long, luscious-curls look."

"But I'm not a princess."

"Neither is she. Her official title is Catherine, Duchess of Cambridge."

Eden appreciated Regan's worldly knowledge. She looked forward to going to the masquerade ball with her sophisticated and unpredictable roommate.

Regan styled Eden's hair in an upswept mass of curls, crowning her bouffant with a diamond tiara. Regan twisted her hair into an ebony knot and pinned it close to her head. She grabbed a platinum, blonde, pixie-cut wig and positioned it on her head. She put her hair in two ponytails that looked like a bear's ears. Then she painted her mouth with bright-red lipstick. Both girls slipped into their gowns.

Standing side by side in front of the mirror, Eden said, "Who am I pretending to be?"

"Audrey Hepburn."

"And you're Miley Cyrus?"

Regan raised her black eyebrows and said, "Good guess, girlfriend."

Regan handed Eden a jewel-encrusted white mask. For herself, she chose a black lace mask with glittering gold accents. Eden was loaned a studded Judith Lieber clutch. Regan carried a white-beaded Chanel bag.

"You want some Xanax? It'll keep the nerves at bay."

"No, thank you."

"It's a great mixer with a glass of champagne." When Eden didn't take the pill, Regan popped it into her mouth and swallowed.

In the elevator, Regan said, "You can dance, right, Roomie?"

"I've tried a couple of times with my sister, Abby. But I've never danced with a boy."

In the hallway heading for the ballroom, Regan said, "If you can't dance, twerk!" And she thrust and ground her hips which provoked sexy whistles from a crowd of guys congregated in the hallway. "Loosen up, girlfriend. You look fab, absolutely gorgeous, delish, ahhh-mazing!"

"With a lot of help from my friend," Eden said, remembering an old Beatle's song that her mom used to sing in the kitchen while mopping the floors.

# Nineteen

Eden and Regan arrived fashionably late to the masquerade ball. The double doors on opposite sides of the dimly lighted ballroom stood wide open, allowing the cool ocean breeze to pass through. Rihanna and Calvin Harris's song 'This is What You Came For' accompanied the crowd of masked couples dancing on the parquet floor.

Jeweled masks decorated white linen tablecloths set with fragrant floral arrangements. Glittery streamers hung from the vaulted ceiling and swayed gently with the cool electric air. A line of costumed couples moved to the beat.

A slender guy dressed in a tight, black leotard mimicked Justin Timberlake's moves to 'Can't Stop This Feeling.' And an androgynous male performed his perfect rendition of Michael Jackson's moonwalk.

D.J. Bobby Headstrong, also known as Seaman Second Class Bobby Conrad, a tall, muscular guy with spiked, platinum hair, stood on a platform above the brawl, searching through his mp3 files for current songs. When he found a song he liked, he pushed select, ramped up the beat, twisted a couple of knobs, and pushed a button.

"Let's go have some fun!" Regan shouted.

Regan left Eden standing alone in the doorway while she joined the crowd on the dance floor. Regan's twerking attracted several males who were dancing with female partners. When Regan saw a guy she liked, she stepped between the guy and his date and would rotate her bottom against his crotch until the helpless guy made a fool of himself. She bored easily. So, her attention didn't last long.

Clayton, seated at a table set for four couples, watched Regan. He had experienced her tantalizing sexual favors, but, like her, he had a problem with boredom. He slipped his Don Juan mask off and laid it on the table. Ben sat across from Clayton, wearing a Jolly Green Giant costume. By the time he and

Clayton had gone to the ship's costume department, the only outfit left that fitted Big Ben was the silly one he now wore.

Dressed in a Zorro outfit, Captain Evert sat with six members of his staff at the long, rectangular table at the head of the ballroom. His attention was directed to Sandreen who sat next to him.

Sandreen's replication of a scene from Marie Antoinette's glamour years was a sparkling white gown with a plunging neckline overlaid with strips of 18-carat gold. On her head, she wore a towering blonde wig. She wore an oversized citrine necklace with matching earring and large, black, diamond ring.

Captain Evert whispered something into Sandreen's shell-shaped ear and she smiled at him.

Clayton didn't miss the coy smile that Sandreen gave to the captain and he burned with envy.

Eden sat down at an unoccupied table and self-consciously envied the masked couples.

Having had enough of Sandmen's casual flirting with the captain, Clayton put his mask back on, stood up, and walked over to the captain's table. "May I have this dance?" he asked, holding his hand out to Sandreen. Sandreen hesitated, but she decided not to make a scene. She put her bejeweled hand into his and Clayton led her to the dance floor.

He gently wrapped his arm around Sandreen's waist and pulled her closer to him. Joe Cocker sang 'You Are So Beautiful to Me' as Clayton deftly led Sandreen across the floor.

"You look beautiful tonight," he said softly.

"Thank you," Sandreen said, and she glanced at Captain Evert who was intently watching the two of them. Sandreen had told her lover about her unpleasant encounter with Clayton. Since then, Captain Evert had kept a close eye on his privileged young rival.

Captain Evert stood to his feet and crossed the crowded dance floor. He tapped Clayton on the back and said, "I'd like to cut in, if you don't mind." Clayton glared at the captain and angrily walked away toward Ben who tried to fist-bump him.

Sandreen moved into Captain Evert's waiting arms. Sandreen and Captain Evert moved gracefully across the floor. Their familiarity with one another led them to sway in perfect unison. This was their fourth voyage together.

The captain had made up his mind to ask his wife of 20 years for a divorce when he returned home. He justified his decision by thinking she had gained a significant amount of weight with her pregnancies. The fact that she refused to keep their house clean and, in immaculate order, infuriated him. He knew Sandreen's expensive taste in jewelry and clothing wouldn't be cheap. Therefore, he made plans to financially ruin his wife. He considered the devastating effect a divorce and a lack of financial support would have on his two small sons but justified it as something his lazy-ass wife had caused. He smugly reasoned his actions by thinking he was the only one in the marriage who had contributed to the financial part of their partnership. Forget his wife and sons. Sandreen was his priority now.

When the song ended, Captain Evert and Sandreen headed back to their table. The captain stepped to the microphone and said, "Ladies and gentlemen, please be seated for dinner."

The couples wandered around the room, looking for their assigned tables. When all the guests were seated, a dozen waiters dressed in black slacks, shiny black shoes, and a white chef's jacket served butter lettuce topped with candied walnuts, goat cheese, and golden raisins overlaid with sweet-reduced balsamic-vinegar dressing. The guests passed around the crusty warm bread and chilled butter plates.

Eden and Regan sat at a table with a fat Cleopatra and a pimply girl who was trying to mimic J-Lo by adding a small pillow tucked in the back of her skintight leopard tights. A Mark Antony impersonator sat next to J-Lo. Eden thought that the mock Leonardo DiCaprio looked like a girl in drag, the Bruno Mars parody was adorable, and Jaden Smith's dreadlocked mocker was gorgeous.

"I'm Susie Hensley and I'm from Atlanta, Georgia," Cleopatra said to Eden in a heavy, southern drawl. Susie was fat. Her ash-blonde hair hung limply on her heavy shoulders, and her face sported a bad case of acne. The dark-green dress and black eye-shadow she was wearing made her look dramatically unappealing.

"I'm Eden Owens from Maramount, Illinois."

"Is that near Chicago?" the girl asked.

"Not every city in Illinois needs to be located close to Chicago to be considered important," Regan snarked.

"I guess you're right. I love your dress and makeup."

Regan started to respond. Then she noticed Susie was talking to Eden.

"Thank you," Eden said. She thought to admit the dress belonged to Regan, but she decided to keep quiet. Regan winked at her. Eden noticed a young man seated at the next table was avidly watching her. He looked familiar. He smiled shyly at Eden, and she quickly looked down at her empty plate. Eventually, she sneaked a peek at him, letting her eyes drift over his boyishly handsome face, his broad shoulders, and his strong, elegant hands. He wore a black tuxedo and a white French cuff shirt. He seemed engaged in an absorbing conversation with the young woman seated next to him. At one point, he reached into his inside suit pocket, took out a pair of glasses and put them on. *That's Alan Honnecut,* she thought. *He's in my Creative Writing class.*

The entree of steak and lobster with garlic mashed potatoes and green beans almondine was served. Some guests were served salmon. When the main course was finished, the guests helped themselves at the bubbling chocolate-dessert fountain.

During the final hour of the dance, at exactly 2300 hours, the ship arrived at Osanbashi Pier, Yokohama, Japan. The music blared and several of the guests remained on the dance floor. Clayton wandered over to Eden's table and sat down in an unoccupied chair.

"Would you like to dance?" he asked. Clayton loved to see Eden squirm.

"No, thank you," she said, and she stood up to leave.

Clayton stood up and he rounded the table. "Don't make such a big deal out of it," he said, and he grabbed her hand and dragged her onto the crowded dance floor. He held her tightly against his body, delighting in his slow torment of this very shy girl.

Eden awkwardly tried to stumble through the song while Clayton tortuously smiled at her.

A sharp tap on Clayton's shoulder caused him to turn and look at the perpetrator. Alan Honnecut said firmly, "I'm cutting in, if the lady will allow it."

Eden nodded frantically and she nearly ran into Alan's arms. Clayton held up his hands in mock surrender and walked away with a satisfied smirk on his face.

The D.J. played 'Turn Up the Party!' The music pounded and Regan took center stage. She yanked off the blonde wig and seductively flipped her long hair. At one point, she opened her mouth and flicked her tattooed tongue at her applauding audience. Be it good attention or bad, Regan had captivated the interest of everyone in the room.

"Could we get a breath of fresh air?" Alan asked loudly to Eden.

"I was thinking the same thing."

They pushed their way through the mesmerized throng. Standing next to the door, Clayton and Ben watched Regan's raunchy performance. As Eden and Alan passed by them, Clayton said to Eden, "I'd give a hundred dollars to see you do a dance like that one."

"Watch your mouth," Alan threatened, and he and Eden headed for the promenade deck.

Clayton saw Sandreen standing in a shadowy corner of the room. She was talking intently to a tall man dressed like The Phantom of The Opera. He noticed Captain Evert's gaze sweep the room, trying to locate his paramour. But the man standing in front of Sandreen kept her hidden from his view.

"What are you doing here, Erik?" Sandreen asked.

"Jax sent me around the world looking for you. It's a quirk that I finally found you here tonight."

"Is Jax in Yokohama now?"

"He is. His new yacht is moored at Pier 23."

"His new yacht?"

"That's right. A billionaire can afford to indulge his whims."

"What does Jax want to see me about?"

"If I knew the answer to that question, I wouldn't answer it. Can I tell him you'll be at the yacht at midnight?"

Sandreen peered around Erik's side; she saw Captain Evert desperately looking for her.

"It won't be easy, but I'll be there."

Erik turned to leave and she said, "How did you find me?"

"Jax has a person on every ship, every plane, in every hotel, and at every tropical resort on the lookout for you."

"Which snitch on this ship turned me in?"

"Why does it matter?"

"I like to know who my enemies are."

"I guess Jax won't care if I tell you. His name is Rowdy Raines."

Sandreen glanced at Regan who tirelessly dirty-danced her way through another blaring song. She knew Rowdy and Regan were sexually involved.

"Tell Jax I'll see him at midnight," she said, and she turned and walked away.

* * *

"Mind if I join you?" Alan asked, trying to keep pace with Eden. "It's a balmy night, and there's a blood moon tonight. They only come once every 33 years. Could we slow down and enjoy the moment?"

Eden became aware of her fast pace. "I'm sorry. I didn't realize I was walking so fast." She took a deep breath and let it out slowly.

"If we take the north stairs, we'll be closest to the bow and can see the moon in full view."

*He's chosen a romantic place, close to the bow,* she thought. She suddenly felt nervous.

"You're in my Creative Writing class, and you sit in the back. I didn't realize who you were until you put on your glasses."

"Your name is Eden Owens and you are from Maramount, Illinois, right?"

"I'm impressed," she said, blushing.

"I didn't mean to embarrass you."

"You didn't embarrass me. I'm flattered that you were interested enough to learn a few things about me. I'll fill you in on the rest. I am presently wearing my roommate's dress, she applied my makeup and fixed my hair, the tiara is hers, and so are the shoes and the purse. I guess you could say I don't feel like myself tonight."

He laughed. "I like your sense of humor."

"After that fiasco on the dance floor with Clayton Caulder, I don't feel like I have much of a sense of humor left."

"What's up with that guy?"

"It's a long story. And definitely not something I want to talk about."

"I'd like you to tell me sometime when you feel like it."

Eden liked the sound of that. "You're taking a Creative Writing course. Are you interested in writing?"

"I think I am. Currently, I find myself interested in poetry," he teased as they walked slowly toward the bow.

"Have you ever heard of the poet laureate, Professor Samuel Altgeld?"

"Did he write, 'Third Story Widow'?"

"Yes, he did!"

"Do I sense a connection between Professor Altgeld and you?"

"I met Professor Altgeld through my favorite teacher, Mrs. Omaha."

"You have a teacher named Mrs. Omaha? Man! How easy is it to refer to her as Mrs. Obama by mistake?"

Eden laughed. "It has happened to me occasionally."

"So what part does Professor Altgeld play in your life?"

"He is directly responsible for my receiving a full scholarship to pay for the Study Abroad program."

"Then I owe the professor a big thank you."

"What for?"

"For making it possible for me to meet you."

Eden liked Alan more by the moment. She felt almost as comfortable with him as she had with Steele. Her mood suddenly saddened.

"Are you thinking about your friend who passed?"

His intuition astounded her. "Yes, I am."

"I was standing with the crowd when the helicopter took him away. I feel really bad for you. I could see how much you cared for him."

"Steele was very special."

Standing at the bow in the redness of the moon, Alan said, "Were you in love with him?"

"I don't think so. But he meant a lot to me."

"Can I share a Walt Whitman quote with you?"

"I'd love that."

"He said, 'The future is no more uncertain than the present.'"

"I know that one."

"Another of his that's a favorite of mine is, 'I no doubt believe I deserve my enemies, but I don't believe I deserve my friends.'"

"Do you really think that statement is true?" Eden asked, thinking of her situation with Clayton.

"It certainly gives a person pause for thought."

Alan rested his arms on the brass railing, and they both peered out at the Yokohama skyline illuminated in the redness of the moon which shone in red ripples on the seawater below.

"The moon is spectacular," Eden paused. "Red is my favorite color." *It means passion and love,* she thought.

"It's spectacular for sure," Alan said. "Next time we may witness this, we'll be middle-aged, well on with our lives, and maybe explaining this phenomena to our children."

Eden blushed. She fancied for a split second if Alan meant collectively or independently 'our' children.

They looked at the outline of skyscrapers and the sea of dazzling lights. "It must be wonderful to write a story or a poem," he said. "Think of the insight a writer must possess. The ability to create interesting characters and bring them to life on a page is truly a God-given talent."

"Henry David Thoreau said, 'If a man does not keep pace with his companions, perhaps it is because he hears a different drummer. Let him step to the music which he hears, however measured or far away.' That's one of my favorite quotes, probably because I've always felt so misunderstood."

"Me too," he said quietly. "Now, you want to hear my story?"

She turned her full attention to him.

"New York Senator Michael Honnecut is my father. If you don't know of him, he is considered a major powerhouse. This year, when it came time for me to apply for college, Dad tried to force me to go to his alma mater, Stanford University. I explained to him that my grades aren't up to Stanford's high standards, but Dad felt certain he could bypass the usual channels and get me admitted to the college anyway."

"My roommate, Regan, told me a similar story about her parents and their expectations. But she's okay with breaking rules to get what she wants."

"I noticed that," he continued.

Alan put his hands on the railing and looked thoughtfully out at the ocean. He seemed to be deep in thought for a moment, as if he was reflecting on a great sadness.

He turned toward Eden. "My whole life, Dad has pushed me toward a degree in law. I think it was his intention to build a Kennedy-esque family dynasty. The problem is, I never had any interest in following in his footsteps. My mom, Honey Honnecut, well, Honey is her nickname. Her real name is Susanna. Mom got her nickname because she is the sweetest woman you could ever meet. She is labeled a New York socialite by the fan mags and the newspapers. She actually spends the bulk of her time doing charitable work to raise money for underprivileged children."

"What do you want to be?"

"I want to teach secondary education. I like biology. It's certainly not my dad's dream for me. But I know my mom will support my decision. I heard the University of Kentucky has a pretty good program."

*Despite his wealth and social status, Alan seems so normal,* Eden thought.

"Curfew is over!" a male crew member called from the bridge.

"Can I walk you back to your stateroom?" Alan asked.

"Sure."

They both paused with a small crowd to gaze up one last time at the glowing scarlet moon. Alan took out his iPhone and caught a picture.

"Do you mind if I take a picture of you?"

Eden blushed. "What for?"

"The moon has cast a beautiful rose hue on your smile. Or maybe you have cast a beautiful rose hue on the moon. Either way, I'd like to save the memory if you don't mind."

"Okay." She smiled and tilted her head slightly to the right and gazed toward his phone.

When they reached her stateroom, Alan said, "Talk about a coincidence. My room is at the end of this hallway."

"Is that a good thing?" Eden asked coquettishly.

"It's a very good thing. Before you go in, can I share my favorite song with you?"

"I would love that."

He pulled his iPod out of his inner breast pocket. He put one earplug in his ear, the other he gently handed to Eden who placed in her ear. The song he shared with her is Passenger's 'Let Her Go.' By the second verse, he had taken her hands into his. On the last verse, he held. When the song ended, he placed his lips on hers and kissed her.

"I hope you will let me spend more time with you," he whispered. Eden smiled and she said she hoped that too.

# Twenty

Eden and Alan spent every free moment together. Eden remained silent about her struggles with Clayton and Ben. She also didn't yet have the nerve to tell Alan about her life in South Trekkin. She feared if he knew her past that it would discourage his interest in her. She wouldn't risk that happening. She felt understood. She felt cared for. She knew Momma and Abby loved her. Rick, well, maybe he loved her too. But Daddy wanted a quick marriage for her and to get her out of his house. That's not love. She feared for Abby's future as well.

English Literature classes became more enjoyable for Alan and Eden now that they could share a smile, a wink, or an intimate nod. They shared handwritten copies of their weekly schedule. During their private moments, Alan shared his dreams of becoming a teacher, and Eden read her poetry to him. Their mutual trust and affection formed a strong bond. Every day, they ate lunch together as they had similar lunch periods.

Alan quickly discovered Eden's untrained eye when it came to food, architecture, travel, and a few social situations. In his gentle manner, he took it upon himself to educate her about such things. In doing so, he helped to build her confidence and self-esteem. Acting as a mentor of sorts, it made him feel even closer to Eden. In turn, Eden taught Alan about books and poetry. She also told him how to change a tire and replace the oil in his car. Alan said he didn't have a clue about those things. As it turned out, they became a perfect complement to each other.

Alan loved seafood, Thai food, and Mexican entrees. Eden loved fried potatoes, fried chicken, and homemade bread. Alan's fair skin easily sunburned. Eden was born to be outdoors. Alan liked to sit quietly in a comfortable library chair and read. Eden also loved to read, so they often shared in this quiet past time. The one thing they had the most in common was they loved spending time together, especially at night on the upper deck of the ship.

After 12 days at sea, Alan and Eden both were anxious to enjoy the scenery of Yokohama, Japan. They had a two-day layover in Yokohama. Then the ship would depart on the third day for Kobe.

They studied the maps of the city and both agreed they first wanted to visit the historic Yokohama Red Brick Warehouse. Eden pulled her hair back in a ponytail. Alan loaned her a New York Yankees baseball hat to protect her face from the scorching sun. Alan wore a pair of Izod pleated cargo shorts, a white knit Thomas Pink shirt, a pair of leather back-strap sandals, a three-thousand-dollar Tag Heuer wristwatch, and around his neck was an eight-thousand-dollar Nikon D3X camera. Eden wore a pair of ragged-leg denim cutoffs, a white t-shirt, and her five-dollar flip-flops. She placed her two-dollar notebook and three-dollar colored pencils in Rick's old hand-me-down backpack.

"Since our time in Yokohama is limited, I suggest we take the three-hour sightseeing taxi," Alan said as he read the Yokohama sightseeing brochure.

"Won't it be terribly expensive to take a taxi to all the places we want to go?"

"Don't worry about that."

"That's easy for you to say. I do worry about not having enough money, Alan."

"I will take care of all our expenses."

"I tell you what. For the next two days, let's see how much fun we can have without spending much money."

"I don't know if I can do that, Eden."

"Are you chicken?" she asked playfully.

He smiled. "Okay. But let's give pauperism a try for just one day."

"Agreed," she said, and she stuck her hand out to shake his hand. He reached for her hand and kissed it.

"You humble me. I realize I have just scratched the surface to discovering the true person you are inside," Alan said.

"I hope when you reach the deepest part of my being that I don't disappoint you."

He cupped her smooth chin in his elegant hand and said, "I can't think of anything you could ever do to disappoint me. You challenge me every day with your insightful words and deep thoughts. I find ease in your profound kindness

149

and your love of life. One thing is for sure. If I am lucky enough to know you for the rest of my life, I most certainly will never be bored!"

Eden giggled. She threw her arms around him and hugged him.

Eden talked Alan into renting a moped, just as she had done with Steele when they were in Hawaii. They found a bike-rental shop right off port. When the vendor asked for 30-thousand yen for a motorcycle for the day, which translated into 350 dollars in U.S. currency, she told Alan no way because she reminded him of their 'going cheap' agreement. Alan explained that he was too tall to ride around on a smaller cycle. They finally compromised. The owner of Rental Cycles suggested they rent his G.P.S. self-guided tour apparatus. Eden baulked at this suggestion. She said unless he threw the G.P.S. in at no charge, they would go look elsewhere to rent. The tiny Japanese man bowed, literally, to her demands.

As they waited on the curb for the motorcycle to be delivered to them, Alan said, "Remind me to take you with me next time I buy a car." Eden playfully punched him on his shoulder.

They rode to the Red Brick Warehouse which, much to Eden's surprise, actually ended up being two separate buildings. Alan and Eden read a plaque on the side of the building that said that during World War II, American troops took over the buildings and occupied them from 1945 to 1956. The literature stated that due to the high probability of earthquakes in the area, those two buildings were considered at the time to be the safest place for the troops to be in due to the reinforced steel beams that concreted the buildings to the foundation.

Eden wasn't too interested in building number two, which looked like any average American shopping mall, as it was laden with jeans stores and fast-food joints. Building number one, however, she found to be of great interest. It held film festivals, plays, cultural events, art exhibitions, and music competitions.

They spent an hour looking at all the posters of the famous performers who had appeared there. When Alan and Eden peeked into the theater, they saw a large, seated audience quietly watching the empty stage. A Japanese man, dressed in black, silk, Hakama pants, a white, silk, Haori jacket with a gold, silk, haori-hima cord tied around his narrow waist, walked onto the stage. He greeted the audience in Japanese. He spoke for a few minutes longer. Then he said in perfect English, "Tonight is our amateur-talent night. We have several performers backstage waiting to display their talents to this most gracious audience. Our first performer is no stranger to this stage. He has been playing the cello since he was the tender age of four years old. This remarkable young man deems it an honor to play once again for you, our most kind patrons. Please warmly welcome back to the stage, Kazuhiko Nakamuca!"

Thunderous applause accompanied a slender, young, Japanese man carrying a cello as he walked onto the stage. He sat down and placed the cello between his legs. The audience stilled. The young man drew his bow across the cello and rapturous music filled the air.

"Do you mind if I buy a couple of tickets?" Alan asked. "We'll grab seats and listen to the music."

"I'd like that very much," Eden said, thinking she had just broken her 'going cheap' rule. She remembered she had saved Alan money on the G.P.S. That eased her conscience.

Alan returned with two tickets which he handed to the usher as they entered the theater. They spotted two seats in the middle section, edged their way past a row of avid listeners, and sat down.

The young man played Brahms Cello Concerto in C Minor. As Eden listened to the haunting music, she felt new life stir inside her. Alan sat mesmerized. It felt to the two young lovers as if the music was meant for them alone. The world around them faded and only they existed in the moment.

Alan reached for Eden's hand. She saw he had tears in his eyes.

"This is a perfect day," he whispered.

She smiled and squeezed his hand. The concert ended and the audience rose to their feet, cheering and clapping for the young man's performance. The pair stood up and quietly slipped out when a sumo wrestler/singer warbled his off-key rendition of 'A Rainy Night in Georgia.'

After they visited a few souvenir shops and got tired of taking selfies, Alan asked a young Japanese girl to take a picture of them at a distance. She agreed she would. The girl stood with her back to a massive flowing fountain. Eden and Alan sat down next to each other on a stone bench under a flowering arch. The girl took their picture and set the camera down on the ledge of the fountain. Still having the young woman's attention, Alan held up four fingers. The girl picked up the camera and took four more pictures. Then she returned Alan's camera.

Alan thanked her and he handed her a fragrant Camellia which he had swiped from the arbor over their heads.

"I'm starving," he said to Eden. "Let's go to Chinatown."

"But I brought some protein bars with me," Eden protested.

"Tell you what, I'll eat one of those later, after I get some real food."

"You would have a difficult time living on a budget."

"You got that right!"

It took five minutes to walk from the Red Brick Warehouse to Chinatown. Four ornate gates served as the entrance to Chinatown. Inside the gates stood the large, boldly mesmerizing temple, Kanteibyo, which the Chinese built in 1873 and dedicated to the god of good business and prosperity. Eden and Alan entered through the East Gate.

The narrow streets teemed with tourists, local residents, and laborers. The pungent odors of incense, oil, and food permeated the area. Pagoda-style architecture, bright colors, and Oriental lanterns welcomed the hungry travelers.

Alan read from the brochure, "It says that Yokohama's Chinatown is the oldest of its kind in all of Asia. There are 250 stores in this complex and probably at least that many restaurants."

"Any restaurant you choose is fine with me."

"Have you ever eaten Szechuan food?"

"I don't know. I ate a grasshopper once on the ship."

Alan laughed until tears ran down his face. When he recovered, he said, "You are hilarious!"

"I didn't think it was too funny at the time."

"I assume Regan is behind this duplicitous act?"

"Yes, she was."

They found a small restaurant with an English-speaking staff. They were seated in a cozy booth, surrounded by Japanese people who chattered happily to their companions. A pretty Asian girl dressed in a green, silk kimono brought them menus.

Alan ordered xiaolongbao for both of them. When the food arrived, it turned out to be dumplings filled with meat and soup. Eden breathed a sigh of relief. On a small television screen hanging from the ceiling, a video demonstrated how to correctly eat the dumplings. The customer was to open the dumpling and take a spoonful of soup and throw it at their friends. To be sociable, Eden and Alan threw a tiny bit of soup at each other.

"What a mess!" he exclaimed as he slurped the rest of his soup. "But the dumplings were delicious."

The locals glanced at the couple as they walked through the street, laughing at each other's humorous observations. One older Japanese man said, "*Mei guo de!*" and he pointed sternly at the two of them.

Alan pulled out his iPod and he looked up the word. "You know what that old man said?"

"I don't have a clue."

"He said, 'Americans!'"

"I suspect the Japanese people consider Americans rude. I hope they didn't video us eating the dumplings. If they did, we'll be on the Japanese version of the blooper show."

When the bill came, Eden dug deep into her backpack and took out the 200 dollars that Momma had given her.

"What are you doing?" Alan asked.

"I want to pay my part of the bill."

"I may be lacking in some areas, Eden, but I'm still a gentleman. I asked you out on a date and I expect to pay for it."

"This is a date?" she asked shyly.

"I thought it was."

"In that case, thank you for lunch, Alan."

"You are very welcome. Would you like to stay in town and watch the sunset at Yokohama Bay?"

"I would love that. Will it be another blood moon?"

"No," he added. "Unfortunately, that was a one-night show. It doesn't come back for standing ovations, just hibernates until it's time to show up again," he explained.

Eden smiled at Alan's poetic words.

They walked in a leisurely manner, hand-in-hand through the crowded streets. Alan saw a small jewelry shop. "Let's go in there," he said, leading them in the direction of the store.

Inside the fashionable shop, Alan approached the Japanese merchant and asked, "Do you speak English?"

"Yes," the man said. He wore a traditional Chinese long gown made of royal-blue silk decorated with golden dragons. On his head, he wore a black brimmed hat made of bright-red silk topped with a gold knob. His hair was fashioned in a long, black braid that lay in the center of his back.

"How may I be of service?"

"Do you have a necklace with the Chinese character for love?"

"I do," the man said. He opened the glass-jewelry case and pulled out a black velvet box that displayed a fine gold necklace with the Chinese 愛 character dangling from it.

"This symbol means 'love with all my heart,'" he said.

"How much is it?"

"300 American dollars."

"I'll take it," Alan said. He pulled out his cash and paid the merchant.

"Would you like me to wrap it for you, sir?"

"No, thank you. It's for my lady here."

"I don't want you to spend your money on me, Alan," Eden said, and she backed away as he tried to place the necklace around her neck.

"I'm not spending my money, Eden. I'm spending my dad's money. And believe me, he can afford it."

Alan turned to the merchant and he said, "Have you ever seen a girl turn down such a gift as this?"

"I have not. But I think this young lady cares more for you than she does for a piece of expensive jewelry. You are a fortunate man."

Alan moved behind Eden. He dropped the necklace over her head and fastened it.

"I want you to wear this always. Then, on those days when I cannot be with you, I hope that I will at least be in your heart."

Eden stroked the symbol of love with her fingertips. "Thank you, Alan," she said softly. He tenderly kissed her on the back of her neck.

At dusk, the paper lanterns glowed more brightly. The sun breathed its last breath of the day and melted into the earth in a fiery glow. Lights in buildings flashed on like fireflies igniting against a midnight sky.

"We'd better head back to the ship," Alan said.

"Okay. What do you want to do tomorrow?"

"Let's go to the Curry Museum in the morning. We can grab a bite to eat there. And, later, we'll go visit the quiet, serene beauty of the Sankei-en Japanese garden."

"That's an odd way to describe a garden you've never seen before."

"I have seen it before, Eden. My parents and I vacationed in this beautiful city my sophomore year in high school."

"You sly devil! And all this time I thought you were a virgin to this city, like me."

"I am a virgin, Eden, in more ways than one."

Eden blushed. Alan took her into his arms and he passionately kissed her trembling lips. A tear slipped down Eden's face. He picked up the symbol of love and he caressed it. He whispered, "As this symbol promises, 'love with all my heart.'"

# Twenty-One

Alan waited for Eden at the entrance to the dining room. When he saw her, he smiled broadly and said, "Good morning, Beautiful!" and he kissed her rosy cheek.

"Good morning to you too."

Neither of them had slept very much the night before, each thinking about their exciting new romance.

"I see you're wearing your necklace this morning."

"I will never take it off. I would be devastated if I lost it."

"That makes two of us. You hungry?"

"Not very."

"Want to head into Yokohama then?"

"I have to email my completed poetry assignment to Professor Altgeld and Mrs. Omaha. I also want to send my love to my family and let them know how well I'm doing. And you know how long the lines are to use the library computers this time of the morning."

Alan pulled out his iPhone. "You can call your family to save time. Use this," he said.

"Thank you, Alan. I'll call my family later." Eden sat at an unoccupied table and logged onto the computer with her student ID. She sent her homework assignments to the Professor and Mrs. Omaha and wrote Abby and her mother a short email. She told them about the wonderful time she was having, about her classes, how much she loved Hawaii, and now Yokohama. She didn't want to jinx her new relationship with Alan, so she didn't mention him yet. She let the image of Steele remain her private memory.

Regan walked into the library. She saw Eden with Alan sat down across from them. "Wow! That's some iPhone you got there," she said, noticing the gold case.

156

"It's Alan's."

"Of course it is," she said, and she glanced at Alan. He returned her gaze with a cool stare.

"Where you two off to?" Regan asked, rubbing her bloodshot eyes.

"We're going to the Curry Museum and the Sankeien Japanese Garden."

"I don't have a thing planned for today. Mind if I tag along with you two?"

Eden looked at Alan and she read the unmistakable refusal on his face.

"Alan rented a motorcycle for us to use today and, unfortunately, there isn't a sidecar."

"Well, that's the shits! I guess I'll go swimming. You two have a nice day. Do everything that I would and it's sure to be exciting," she chirped on her way out.

Eden handed Alan his phone. "I feel guilty excluding Regan. For the most part, she's been a good friend to me. She even loaned me her clothes."

"Don't feel bad for her, Eden. Regan is a self-centered slut."

"That's pretty harsh, Alan."

"I'm sorry if I offended you. It's just that I've known girls like her before."

"Known them how?"

"I haven't slept with any of them, if that's what you're asking. You wouldn't believe the disgusting things women are willing to do to get close to a United States senator. I've even had a few of them proposition me to try to meet my dad."

"I'm glad you didn't fall for their feminine charms."

"On a few occasions, I have to tell you, it took all my willpower to say no."

"I'm sure it did."

"Are there any guys in your past you would like to tell me about?"

"I haven't dated a lot, Alan." She considered telling him about her trouble with Clayton and Ben. But the notion quickly passed.

As Eden and Alan left the ship, Clayton and Ben sat in deck chairs near the pool, watching half-naked girls lounge in the sun. Ben pulled out his phone and browsed through the pictures and videos he'd taken.

"Look at this," Ben said, turning the screen toward Clayton.

Clayton saw a picture of Sandreen and him dancing at the masquerade ball. Clayton studied the exotic beauty he held in his arms. He looked away and generously applied coconut oil to his tan legs.

"Would you do me a favor, Ben?" Clayton asked.

"Depends on what it is."

"I want a couple hours alone with the cruise director. Think you can help me with that?"

"I've never seen her give you a second glance."

"She's just playing hard to get."

"I don't think so. She's totally disgusted with your bad behavior. Besides, she's too old for you."

"I dream about sex with her."

"Every female gives you wet dreams."

"Will you work with me or not?"

"I don't want to get involved in that."

"Then take some pictures of her for me."

"Now you want me to stalk her and take some pictures of her so you can look at them while you beat off. Buy a smut magazine, man, and leave me out of it. You know. You scare me sometimes."

"I would do it for you because you're my friend."

"And what if I get caught? Where will you be then? I'll tell you. You'll be on the sidelines, laughing your fool head off at my stupidity for listening to you."

*I've underestimated him,* Clayton thought. To punish Ben, Clayton turned his back on him and ignored him. A few anxious minutes of silence later, Ben said, "I'll take some pictures of her."

"That's Yokohama Bay Bridge," Alan shouted over his shoulder to Eden as they whizzed through Yokohama Harbor. Eden lovingly tightened her arms around his waist.

"We could park and walk to the museum, if you'd like to."

"I'd like that," she yelled, getting stung by her windblown hair.

Alan parked the cycle in a city parking-lot. Alan and Eden eased their way into the crowd of people bustling along the city streets.

"I've never seen this many people in my whole life," Eden said.

Alan pulled out his iPhone and he read the entry on Wikipedia, "Yokohama is the second largest city in Japan with a population of nearly four-million people."

"Is Yokohama larger than New York City?"

"No. New York City has over eight-million residents."

Alan asked Eden to sit on the bench in a city park so he could take a picture of her.

"You're taking too many pictures of me."

"That's not possible."

He took another picture of her at the entrance to the Yokohama Curry Museum, beneath the two cute images of baby elephants, one yellow, the other pink, holding spoons and smiling at each other. He read from a plaque on the wall, "It says the museum is in the city district known as Isezakichō."

Eden's stomach growled loudly. "Ooops," she said.

"Sounds like you're hungry. There's a restaurant straight ahead. According to the picture out front, they serve curry. Want to eat there?"

"Isn't curry just a spice?"

"It is. But when mixed with other spices, it creates a pungent mixture used in 'wet' and 'dry' curries. The 'wet' curries are made with poultry or seafood and lots of liquid, like coconut milk, chicken, or vegetable stock, and yogurt, which turns it into gravy. The 'dry' curries are made with meat and vegetables, which are coated with a generous amount of spices and a small amount of liquid. The dry curries only use a small amount of liquid. If you've never eaten curry, I would recommend you try the spicy chicken and whole potatoes. It's delicious."

Alan enjoyed enlightening Eden with his worldly knowledge. It made him feel more connected to her.

"When I'm home, my dad and I often drive to Midtown East and there's a place there called Amma. They serve the best curry you will ever eat. I hope you get to visit New York City soon. It's a foodie's heaven." Talking about food made Alan's stomach growl as well. The both laughed at that.

At the picturesque restaurant, the walls were decorated with large, Oriental fans, bright tapestries imprinted with images of geisha, rainbow paper-lanterns, and the three-panel Shoji screen depicted a serene, Oriental landscape. The two were seated by an American male waiter wearing black, duck slacks, a white long-sleeve shirt, white tabi socks, and a pair of wooden geta sandals. He clomped over to a table and seated them.

"You two want menus?" he asked in a Bronx accent.

"You have butter-chicken curry and pork vindaloo for two?" Alan asked.

"Sure we do. Hey. Where you two from?"

"I'm from New York."

"I'm from Illinois."

"Mr. New York here, I recognize his accent. But, honey, you sound like you're from Tennessee."

"I've been told that a couple of times lately," Eden said pleasantly.

"What are you doing working in Yokohama?" Alan asked the waiter.

"It involves a girl who left me, then I lost my job, and to top off my good times, my dog ran off. You know. You've probably heard a version of my story before.

"So, what do you folks want to drink? Before you answer that, I highly recommend you try a Pocari Sweat. I know, I know. The name sounds disgusting. It's actually a non-carbonated grapefruit drink."

"I'm game if you are, Eden."

"As you always say, 'When in Rome.'" Alan looked oddly at her, and she realized her mistake. Alan didn't use the phrase. Steele was the one who used to say that to Eden.

When their waiter, brought the curries, Eden was relieved to see that he laid a fork and spoon next to their steaming plates of food. After one brave taste, Eden discovered she loved curry. The Pocari Sweat tasted like bubbly Gatorade. For dessert, Alan ordered Matcha cake with red-bean icing. The waiter brought them a thick slice of bright-green cake with red-brown icing.

Alan took a bite and declared it delicious.

Eden poked at her dessert with a fork, lifting edges of it off the plate and inspecting it for bugs, legs, and bulging insect eyes.

The waiter said, "The cake is made with green tea, thus the hue. And the icing is mashed red beans and confectioner's sugar." Eden took a bite and she gave it a thumbs up. Alan paid their bill and added a generous tip.

They passed by an Asian street vendor peddling gaudy Japanese souvenirs. She wore a long purple wig parted on the side, a skintight leopard-print leotard, and a pair of nine-inch, high-platform, silver-tone strap shoes.

"You a fan of Lady Gaga?" Alan asked Eden.

"I love her song 'Born This Way.'"

"Me too. I believe she is one of the most vigorous advocates against any form of bullying."

"I admire her for that. When someone is bullied, it's devastating." Eden recalled her many painful experiences with Clayton and Ben.

Changing the subject, Eden said, "You want to go to the Sankeien Japanese Garden now?"

"Perfect timing, as always," he said, and he gently placed his hand in hers.

"We'll take the bus to Honmoku Sankeien Mae Station. From there, we'll catch another bus to the park."

"What about the motorcycle?"

"We'll pick it up later. If we take the bus, I can hold your hand the whole time."

She liked the sound of that.

When the rumbling rust-bucket arrived, Alan had second thoughts about getting onboard. It appeared all the seats were occupied and the windows were open to let some of the oppressive heat escape. Considering their time in Yokohama was limited, Alan made a quick decision to bite the bullet and take the bus. He read the charge and held out yen to the driver. The driver looked at the money in Alan's hand and he vigorously shook his head.

Alan said, "Do you speak English?"

"Yes," the driver said, smiling and displaying his mouth full of bad teeth.

"You pay yen at end."

"When will we arrive at Honmoku Sankeien Mae station?"

"35 minute. Sir!"

They saw a gap on the long seat at the back of the crowded bus between an ancient Asian man and a young woman who held a nursing baby. The oppressive heat combined with the smell of unwashed bodies assailed their senses as they made their way through the filthy aisle to the back of the bus.

Alan squeezed in next to the old man. Eden pressed against Alan, trying to distance herself from the woman with the sucking infant. Eden said, "I think it's risky trusting all of us to pay at the end of this trip."

"I can't imagine that ever happening in New York."

The scenic backdrop became a pleasant distraction to balance the unpleasant drive to the park. For several miles, a young Japanese boy in front of them hung his head over the back of his seat while he made hideous faces. Tiring of the obnoxious child's antics, Alan made a scary face of his own and the child wailed and dropped into his mother's lap.

"Good going there, Frankenstein," Eden said.

The two were relieved when they saw the sign that read, 'Honmoku Sankeien Station.' The driver yelled, "Americans, off!"

Taking their cue, Alan and Eden walked to the front of the bus. Alan handed the driver the appropriate amount of yen. He exited the bus first, followed by Eden. The screeching bus door closed, the driver hit the accelerator, and the tailpipe shot out a thick cloud of bluish smoke as the bus rolled away.

"May I keep the receipts, brochures, and pictures of all the places we've been?" Eden asked. "I'd like to include them in my journal. When I look at it later, we will enjoy reliving all the fun things we've done."

"You mean when we look at it later, don't you?"

A crowd of people waiting at the Sankeien Mae station boarded the new, air-conditioned bus. Alan and Eden got on and sat behind the driver and across the aisle from an elderly Australian couple.

The bus took off. And the man across the aisle said, "Lovely day, Mate, isn't it?"

He wore a Hawaiian print shirt, khaki slacks, a pair of leather sandals, and white hair showed around the edges of his Boston Red Socks ball hat. A Rolex watch and a thin, gold, wedding band completed his outfit. The woman seated next to him was heavy-set, wearing a leaf-print dress, a straw hat with a wide pink band, and a large diamond ring. She peered around the man at Eden and Alan.

"It is a lovely day indeed," Alan said.

"Is this your first trip to the Sankeien Garden?" the woman asked.

"I have been to the garden before," Alan said.

"It's my first time," Eden said, and she smiled at the grandmotherly woman.

"This is our fourth visit to the garden," the woman said. "The last time we were here was on our 50th wedding anniversary."

The man smiled. "My wife and I made it a point to—" His wife interrupted him, "You two must see the elegant pagoda built by the late silk baron, Tomitaro Hara, and the tea houses are so authentic, one might expect to see a geisha kneeled on the floor serving tea." The woman cooed. "The small lake has the most panoramic view, and the bridge that crosses over the colorful koi pond is the perfect place to take pictures. Don't miss the fragrant lush paths, and the—"

"Whoa!" the husband said as he flagged his hands at his wife.

He addressed his next remark to Alan and Eden, "My wife is concerned you might overlook a beautiful feature of the landscape during your visit to the garden."

His wife furrowed her brow at her husband. "I can speak for myself, Charles," she snapped.

The man lifted his hands palms up, admitting his defeat.

Embarrassed, Alan and Eden lowered their gaze and pretended to read the brochure.

For the rest of the trip, the man sat with his hands in his lap and he stared straight ahead. The woman turned her back on her husband and stared out the window.

Finally, the bus stopped at Sankeien Garden. Alan and Eden gathered their things and quickly exited. Eden looked back at the elderly couple. The man looked around like he was lost. The woman ignored him and walked on ahead.

Alan and Eden crossed the beautiful bridge over the koi pond. They removed their shoes at the entrance of the elegant, three-tiered pagoda and set them neatly on a straw mat next to the door.

"Are all Japanese houses this impersonal and minimalistic?" Eden asked.

"I believe most are."

"Can you imagine their reaction to the T.V. show 'Hoarders'?"

Alan laughed. "I adore you," he said, and he hugged her. "It does appear we Americans buy too much stuff in an attempt to bypass our peers."

"It's easy not to be envious of others when you have more than you need."

"You're probably right."

Eden and Alan meandered through the gardens and found themselves on a fragrant, leafy trail. Alan looked around and saw that they were alone. He took his glasses off and put them in his breast pocket. He pulled Eden into his arms and he said, "God made you so perfect. You're just right for me."

"I'm so happy you think so. Do I look better up close without your glasses?"

"I would know you are beautiful if I was blind. I am nearsighted. Without my glasses, I can focus on you and you alone."

They spent some time getting to know each other better in what Alan called, 'their tiny Garden of Eden.' After breathing in the rich scents of the garden and filling his heart with happiness, Alan put his glasses on and they walked on to explore.

As the day moved into afternoon and their curiosity was fully satiated, Eden and Alan boarded the bus that would take them back to Sankeien Mae Station.

"I don't see the old couple, do you?" Eden asked softly.

Alan looked around the bus. "I don't see them either."

"I wonder if she abandoned the poor old man in the woods."

"She probably shoved him into the lake and fed him to the hungry carp," Alan said, and Eden playfully shot her elbow into his ribs.

"You'll be a great teacher, Alan."

"If I can have a positive influence on just one person's life, I will consider myself a success."

"Then you have already achieved your dream, Mr. Honnecut, because you have certainly made a profound difference in my life."

# Twenty-Two

Alan and Eden walked dreamily back to the ship. But Eden's love-struck spell evaporated when she saw Ben walking toward them with his iPhone in his hand.

"Let's go this other way," Eden said, and she pulled on Alan's arm.

"This way is closer to our staterooms."

Ben walked past Eden and Alan and said cheerfully, "Hey, Eden!"

"Hi, Ben," Eden replied. She looked around for Clayton, but he was nowhere in sight.

After Ben had passed, Alan said in a jealous tone, "Who's he?"

"His name is Ben Atler. We went to high school together."

"Is he a friend of yours?"

"I wouldn't exactly say we're friends. Maramount is a small town with one high school. We all know each other."

"His loss is my gain."

"I'm not sure Ben would agree with that statement."

They paused at the bow and gazed at the inky, black water.

"When we lived in our Fifth Avenue apartment, my sister, Peeney, and I attended Marymount School," Alan said. "My parents decided private school would provide a better education for us. Besides, it's hard to make friends in a public school with 700 kids."

He didn't mention when he and his sister walked to school, they were accompanied by their bodyguard and often hounded by hordes of paparazzi. They usually saw at least one celebrity taking their child or children to the same school he and his sister attended.

"Is Peeney your sister's first name?"

"No, her name is Penelope. But I couldn't pronounce Penelope when I was little. So I called her Peeney. The nickname stuck."

"Do you have a nickname?"

"I do. But it's not one I'm thrilled with."

"Awww, tell me. Pretty please with sugar on top?"

"A few of my classmates call me China White."

"That's a nice nickname. Why don't you like it?"

He envied Eden's innocence.

"China White is the street name for heroin, Eden."

"Oh my goodness! Why would anyone call you that?"

"I called the cops on two really bad guys in my class for using and selling drugs. When they were charged, found guilty, and hauled off to jail, some of my classmates started calling me China White."

"You were really brave to do what you did."

"I don't think so. I had a personal vendetta to settle."

"I don't understand, Alan."

Alan pulled out his wallet and he showed Eden a picture of a very pretty girl.

"Who is she?" Eden asked nervously.

"Her name is Amanda Barrow."

"I guess she's special to you, huh?"

"Yes, she was very special to me."

"Was?"

"She's dead, Eden."

"I am so sorry, Alan. I know how painful it is to lose a good friend."

"I loved her, Eden," Alan said, and tears filled his eyes.

Eden fought down the envy looming inside her. She had hoped he'd never loved anyone before her.

"What happened to her?"

"She was given an overdose of heroin by one of the guys I turned in to the police."

"Oh my goodness!"

"Now you understand why I did what I did?"

"Was she your girlfriend, Alan?" Eden tried to ask the question discreetly, but she couldn't keep the pain out of her voice.

"No, Eden. Amanda and I were cousins."

Eden felt guilty for being so relieved, considering the girl in question was dead and just a cousin to Alan.

166

"She would have been so proud of you for sending her killer to prison."

"I'd like to believe that's true, but Mandy had a history of dating really bad men. Technically, they didn't kill her. She killed herself. They preyed on her addiction."

Standing outside Eden's door, Alan said, "I hope my dirty little secret didn't change your opinion of me."

"I think you are a dear, sweet, young man," she said, and a tiny voice inside her made her fear his opinion of her when he learned all her family's shameful history.

Alan kissed her. He thanked her for the lovely day. Eden responded in kind. She unlocked her stateroom door and walked into the dark room.

"You can turn the light on," Regan said from the shadows. Eden flipped the light switch on and saw Regan sitting on the small sofa with her feet tucked under her. She wore the same clothes she had on that morning. Only, now, they were torn and dirty and her face had a nasty purple bruise starting on her left cheekbone.

"What happened to you?" Eden asked, rushing over and sitting down next to Regan.

"Rowdy and I got into a fight," Regan said, and she lightly dabbed her swollen lip with her finger.

Eden thought about what Alan had said about his cousin always choosing really bad men. The same could be said for Regan.

"We should go to the captain and tell him Rowdy beat you up."

"I'm not going to do that, Eden."

"Why not?"

"You haven't seen Rowdy," she said, and the evil gleam in Regan's eye relayed the extent of Rowdy's injuries. "He got the worse end of the stick."

Eden went into the bathroom and ran cold water over a clean washcloth. She handed the cloth to Regan who pressed the cloth against her jaw.

"What were you two fighting about?"

"The usual. He's got the hots for another girl on the ship."

"Do you know who she is?"

"Oh, yeah. Sandreen Gavel."

"Is Sandreen interested in Rowdy?"

"Of course not, but that won't stop him, or half the men on this ship from trying to…" Eden saw Regan bite down on her lower lip to form the f word, and she said quickly, "Make love to her."

"Whatever! Where did you say you're from?" Regan asked smartly.

"Maramount."

"Is that like… Amish country?"

Eden ignored Regan's snarkiness. "Can I get you anything before I go to bed?"

"No," Regan said, and she scooted down on the sofa and closed her eyes. Eden took a blanket off Regan's bed and spread it over her battered friend.

"You are so lucky to have a guy like Alan Honnecut interested in you," Regan said, sobbing softly.

At midnight, Ben took the last picture he intended to take of Sandreen as she came out of the captain's stateroom. That made 35 pictures in all. Surely that number would satisfy Clayton. Ben went back to his stateroom. Clayton sat on his bed, reading something on his iPad.

"I got the pictures you wanted," Ben said.

Clayton laid his book down and he said, "Show me." Ben handed his phone to Clayton. Clayton flipped through the pictures.

"She's doing ordinary things," Clayton said. "I wanted to see some skin, like naked, you know?"

"This is the best I can do. I don't have time to do your dirty work. I'm failing a couple of my classes because you've had me running around like some demented stalker."

"Do you have any better ideas?"

"As a matter of fact, I do. I thought I would approach Sandreen and ask her if I can make a video of her boasting about how great Studies Abroad is. I'd have her wear a tiny bikini and high heels and really pack on the makeup. We could add some music and make it like one of those M.T.V. extravaganzas."

"Now who's having a wet dream?"

"You don't think she'd go for it?"

"I think she'd have you arrested."

"You got any better ideas?"

"Not at the moment. But I'll get my chance. You'll see."

Over their lunch period, Eden and Alan read about Kobe, Japan, where the ship was scheduled to arrive the following morning at 0800 hours.

"Check out the Naka Pier Cruise Terminal," Alan said. "Those boarding bridges are spectacular."

"It says here the downtown area is within walking distance from the port. And they have those neat bullet trains!" Eden read.

"The longest suspension bridge on Earth, the Akashi-Kaikya Bridge, is 3,911 meters long and joins Kobe to the Awaji and Shikoku Islands. The Festival of Ages takes place tomorrow in Kobe."

"What does the festival celebrate?"

"It's the anniversary of the founding of Kyoko. It says the people dress up in historic costumes and they have a parade that starts at the Imperial Palace and ends at the Heian Shrine. Does that sound like something we would be interested in seeing?"

"You bet."

Alan closed the brochure. "Enough of the travel guide. How's your journal coming along?"

"Great. I put the menu in it from yesterday's lunch."

"You are the best!" he said with a great big grin.

"I'm so glad you think so. Alan, I'm concerned about the money you're spending on our excursions. I have 200 dollars I'd like to contribute."

"Keep your money, Eden. If I get in a jam, I'll accept your contribution then."

"I love my necklace," Eden said, rubbing the gold-necklace medallion with her fingertip.

"Perhaps we can find a pair of earrings in Kobe that match your necklace."

"I adore you," she said.

"The feeling is mutual, I assure you."

"Great! Are you ready to head back to class?"

"Ready as I'll ever be," she said. She grabbed her backpack, took Alan's hand in hers, and they walked out of the dining room.

# Twenty-Three

Eden and Alan were grouped among the early morning throng waiting on the ship's main deck to disembark at the Port of Kobe Terminal. Alan had taken many pictures of Eden on this bright, sunshiny morning and most of those photos had been taken of her in a flattering pose. But when Eden saw the Rokko mountain range for the first time, her mouth dropped open in awe of the magnificent green hills. Alan quickly snapped a picture of her startled expression. When he reviewed the photo, he decided it would be best to keep that picture of her to himself.

"Until I saw Mount Rokko, I never realized how flat Illinois is," Eden said.

She turned to Alan and she said, "If it's okay with you, I'd like to ride the bullet train first."

"It's fine with me. I'm looking forward to that ride myself."

The crowd rushed forward to disembark and Alan and Eden had to hold onto each other just to stay together. At the end of the gangplank, the two of them split off from the others and headed for the boring process of passing through customs and immigration. After an hour in processing, they walked to the taxi stand outside the terminal.

Alan flagged down a taxi. The taxi driver pulled up, stopped, and rolled his window down, freeing the rank odor inside. Alan held his breath and stepped back.

"Do you speak English?" he asked the driver.

"Yes, very well," the driver said.

"Can you take us to the Sannomiya Train Station?"

"Yes, I can. Please get in."

Alan opened the door and Eden scooted across the torn leather seat. Alan climbed in behind her. Before they could buckle their seatbelts, the taxi lurched forward and sped down the twisting road. At the end of the boulevard, the driver floored the gas pedal and the taxi shot into the teeming highway traffic.

"Have you ever ridden on a train before?" Alan asked, holding on for dear life to the back of the driver's seat.

"No. Riding on a bullet train is something I am really looking forward to."

"We'll see how you feel when the landscape zooms by at 200 miles an hour."

Alan glanced out the window and saw their taxi was weaving through the traffic at an aggressive speed.

"Driver, could you slow down please?" Alan asked.

"Sure thing," the driver said and his foot eased up on the accelerator.

Alan sat back in the seat. "When I was in middle school, my family and I took a trip on the Orient Express. That was one of the best vacations. Another time, Dad booked a trip on India's Palace on Wheels. You should see that train, Eden. It truly is a palace. On that trip, we saw the Taj Mahal and Old and New Delhi. We rode bareback elephants and traveled to Varanasi by boat. After those adventures, we flew to Kathmandu. Our whole family had a great time."

Alan spoke so casually about his privileged life that it made Eden feel like she was a poor kid standing outside in the freezing cold with her nose pressed to the window of a warm, beautiful castle.

Alan and Eden arrived at the train station a little worse for wear. He paid the taxi driver and the pair went to the ticket window. Alan asked for two round-trip tickets on the Shinkansen bullet train. Alan counted out a stack of money and laid it on the counter. Alarmed by all the money Alan was spending, Eden looked away. The ticket master counted the yen and handed Alan two tickets.

Alan put the train tickets in his jeans pocket. "We don't have much time to waste," he said to Eden. "Follow me."

He quickly crossed the lobby of the train station, with Eden scrambling to keep pace. They hurried into the food court and Alan grabbed two bento boxes, a pink one with pictures of happy Japanese children for Eden, and a blue one with a picture of the bullet train for himself. Alan quickly selected plastic-eating utensils and wrapped them in a stack of paper napkins.

He handed Eden her bento box and said, "Fill this at the buffet."

Eden followed behind Alan and watched him fill his bento box with chicken and pepper rice, 'ants on a log' or celery filled with peanut butter and topped with raisins and 'rainbow bento' or, in other words, mixed vegetables, sushi, and watermelon.

When it came to her turn to select her food, Eden nervously studied the many items on the buffet.

"Hold my box," Alan said. He took Eden's box and quickly filled it with sweet-potato latkes, turkey roll-ups, caprese, and sweet watermelon. He grabbed two cokes and paid the cashier. They ran back to the waiting room.

Breathless and excited, Eden surveyed her wondrous surroundings. She turned her attention to Alan. She gazed lovingly at his aristocratic profile and said a silent prayer: *Thank you, God, for bringing this extraordinary young man into my life. I promise, if you let me keep him, I will always love and cherish him.*

Alan turned his head toward her and he said, "What are you thinking about?"

"I'm thinking I'm the luckiest girl in the whole world to have you here with me."

He stroked her chin. "I think you are lucky to have me too."

"Oh, you!" she said and she playfully bumped him with her hip.

What looked like a sleek aerodynamic platypus with a very long tail appeared in the distance.

"Is that our train?" Eden asked.

"No, our train is after this one. See the long line of uniformed people over there?" he asked with a nod of his head toward a group of people wearing dark-blue twill pants, light-blue cotton shirts, and dark-blue hats.

"Who are they?" Eden asked.

"They're the clean-up crew for the bullet trains. Each bullet train remains in the station for 12 minutes. It takes five minutes for the passengers to disembark. That leaves seven minutes for the clean-up crew to thoroughly clean the train."

"That's not possible!" Eden said. "A team of a hundred people couldn't get that train clean in seven minutes."

"Want to bet?"

"Sure, I'll bet you. What do you want to wager?"

Alan thought for a minute. His hooded ice-blue gaze held her innocent stare. He smiled that crooked sneer that sent her heart into orbit and he said, "I would like to consummate our relationship. If you lose the bet, we do it."

"If I lose the bet, we stay the same as we are. Agreed?"

Eden's devastation showed on her face. His wager had taken her completely by surprise.

"I can't make that promise to you right now, Alan," she said sadly.

He pulled her into his arms and he said, "Nor would I ask you to."

Relief swept over Eden.

The bullet train glided into the station.

"Watch the clean-up crew," Alan said.

The group of uniformed workers rushed to their stations next to the train doors. They each opened a garbage sack and held it out to the passengers as they disembarked, bowing and thanking each person for depositing their trash in the garbage sacks. When the passengers departed, the clean-up crew quickly boarded the train. Three crew persons per car gathered all the trash, wiped down all the food trays, swept the seats and the floor, cleaned the restroom, and made a flying trip down the immaculate aisle, making sure each seat was upright. New head cloths were placed on the back of the headrest. With all that done, they grabbed the trash sack and their cleaning supplies and hurried off the train. Once again, they formed a long line and bowed in unison.

Alan's watch alarm went off. "That took exactly six minutes and 54 seconds."

"I wouldn't have believed it if I hadn't seen it with my own eyes," Eden said.

A group of passengers boarded the train, and as soon as the train doors were closed, the train pulled out as smoothly and quietly as it pulled in.

Their train arrived three minutes later. The cleaning crew repeated their seven-minute magical act.

Alan and Eden were amazed to see the immaculate condition of their first-class railcar when they boarded the train.

"You can have the window seat," Alan said.

They sat down next to each other on plush, purple, velvet seats. Draped over the headrest of each seat hung a clean, white cloth. On the back of the seat was a fold-down food tray and a black, net, magazine holder which held the latest copy of several of Tokyo's popular magazines—the Tokyo Journal featured articles on current art exhibits, entertainment, music, film, and Japanese sports; the Japanese Echo detailed the latest news; Nikkei Business spoke for itself; Outdoor Japan was a tourist's delight. Both Eden and Alan rested their feet on the two grooved pedals on the floor in front of their seats.

The attractive female staff wore dark-blue jackets with gleaming gold buttons, starched-white blouses with bright scarves tied around their slender necks, a dark-blue pencil skirt, and a dark-blue hat with a rolled brim and a centered gold medallion. Each woman had a gold nametag on the breast pocket of her jacket.

A young, attractive attendant approached Alan and Eden. "Good morning," she said in perfect English. "May I please see your tickets?"

Alan handed her their tickets. She scanned them, handed them back, and was swiftly and gently onto the next passenger.

Eden wouldn't have known the train was moving if she hadn't looked out the window at the blurred landscape.

Alan pulled out their food trays. He set Eden's bento box, eating utensils, a paper napkin, and a coke on her tray. He did the same for himself. He took a generous bite of watermelon and declared, "This is delicious." He turned his head and discreetly spat an unexpected watermelon seed in a paper napkin.

"Every summer, Abby and I go to Mead's Fruit Stand in Maramount and we buy watermelons. But none of the melons we ever got there can compare to this," she said, enjoying another juicy bite.

A young man sitting three seats ahead of them was hassling a distraught attendant.

"I want a hamburger!" he said loudly in a slurred-upper Midwest accent.

"I am sorry, sir, but we do not serve food on this train," the female attendant said politely.

"Then bring me a hotdog."

"Again, sir, we do not serve food on this train."

The man angrily kicked the back of the chair in front of him, jolting the passenger ahead of him into a whiplash and causing her full loaded bento box to crash to the floor. Her food splattered on the shocked attendant. The attendant stooped down to clean up the mess and the inebriated man grabbed her by her arm and threw her across the aisle into the lap of a well-dressed Japanese man.

Alan bolted out of his seat. He ran up the aisle and wrapped his muscular arm around the man's thick neck. Alan said, "You apologize to the lady or I will personally throw you off this train!"

174

The man struggled against Alan's tight grip, but Alan easily restrained him.

The scuffle slightly sobered the guy up. When the man saw he couldn't break Alan's hold on him, he said, "Let me go, man. I won't cause any more trouble."

Alan tightened his grip even more. The man gagged and fought, but Alan held him firmly.

"I said, apologize to the lady," Alan said, and he pressed his thumb against the man's carotid artery.

"I'm sorry, lady!" the man gasped.

Alan released his hold. The man panted and coughed and rubbed his sore neck with his trembling hand.

"Now clean up this mess," Alan said, towering over the man. The man's bulging gaze dropped to the mess on the floor. He looked up at Alan. "I don't have anything to clean it up with."

"Use your shirt," Alan said, tightening his grip. The man struggled out of his shirt. Alan released the man and pointed at the mess on the floor. Alan pointed a warning in the man's face. The man dropped out of his seat onto his knees and cleaned up the messy aisle with his overshirt. Alan walked back to his seat and he sat down.

"You were magnificent!" Eden said.

"I despise rudeness," Alan said sharply. Alan saw the man glance back at him. He returned the oaf's query with an unyielding stare.

Eden quietly finished her food and watched the mesmerizing scenery whiz by. She thought about Momma and wishing someone would stick up for her against Clem's incessant rage and their dilapidated surroundings.

When Eden and Alan arrived at the Shinkaisoku Station and exited the train, a chilly wind swirled around them. Eden's jeans, long-sleeve shirt, and tennis shoes felt good. She slipped on the light jacket which was tied around her waist. Alan did the same with the cable-knit sweater that he had looped around his neck.

A beautiful geisha wearing white tabi socks and eight-inch-high geta sandals made small scooting steps out of the second railcar. She wore a vivid, red, silk kimono adorned with delicate blue-and-yellow flowers and a wide. The yellow obi circled around her tiny waist was fastened behind her back in a fan-shaped knot. She held a white, silk umbrella decorated with pink cherry blossoms and colorful Lorikeets.

Her black eyebrows and vivid red lipstick stood in sharp contrast to her milk-white face. Her shiny, black hair was shaped in three tiers and adorned with multiple bejeweled sticks and elaborate hairpins and combs.

"I didn't know the Japanese still entertained the art of geisha," Alan said.

"What exactly do they do?" Eden asked, watching the delicate-figure baby step toward the boulevard.

"I believe they are entertainers. They sing. They dance. They act. But probably what brings the men back so often is, from what I've read, geishas are very attentive to their male customers and they're good listeners."

"Those are traits most women would like in a man."

"Should I wear a white face and clogs then?" he asked.

Eden giggled. "I wouldn't change a thing about you, Alan."

"The perfect answer, my dear. You would make a fine geisha!"

The geisha stood at the boulevard, peering first one way and then the other down the busy street. She opened her umbrella and held it over her head. It appeared something in the left distance caught her attention.

A long, black limousine pulled up to the curb and stopped next to her. The back car-door opened and a well-dressed, tall, heavy-set man got out. The geisha bowed to the man. He picked up her hand, flipped it over, and kissed her palm.

Even with his back turned to Eden, something about the man's mannerisms seemed familiar to her. She studied him more closely. The geisha spoke to the man with her demure gaze lowered and in a respectful manner. The limo driver stepped out of the car and said something to the man over the hood of the car. The man's shoulders straightened authoritatively and his head lifted arrogantly. Eden knew then exactly who he was.

"Judge Caulder!" she called loudly.

The man whirled around and looked at Eden. Eden waved exuberantly and she started toward him, but he quickly grasped the geisha's elbow and hustled her into the backseat of the limo. Before Eden reached the boulevard, the limo sped away.

"You know that guy?" Alan asked when he caught up with Eden.

"That's Judge Maxwell Caulder. He's from Maramount. His son, Clayton, is on the ship. My mother works for their family. What do you think he is doing in Japan?" Eden knew she sounded like a blathering idiot, but she'd been caught off guard. She instantly regretted mentioning her mother.

176

"I don't suppose the geisha is his wife?"

"Of course she isn't, Alan. We don't have geishas in Maramount."

"Are you sure that was Judge Caulder?"

"I am absolutely positive it was him!"

"I have a funny feeling the judge is up to something," Alan said, and he hailed a taxi.

"What are you doing?"

A dirty taxi pulled up to the curb. Alan was surprised to see the man behind the wheel wearing a dingy, white tank top and a soiled ball hat. "See that black limo about 12 cars ahead?"

"Yeah, I see it."

"I'll double your fee if you can catch that car."

"Get in and hold on!" the driver said.

# Twenty-Four

Alan and Eden scrambled into the backseat of the taxi. It smelled like stale, greasy French fries. The driver glanced in his rearview mirror at the traffic, then tromped the accelerator. Within a few minutes, they were riding behind the limo. Alan laid his arm on the back of the driver's seat and watched as the limo crossed lanes and jumped ahead of traffic.

"So Clayton Caulder is a judge's son?"

"Yes, he is."

"Is he the guy who's always dogging Sandreen Gavel?"

"Yes, that's Clayton. Ben Atler is his sidekick."

"He's the guy you tried to avoid the other night on the ship?"

"Yes, Alan, that is Ben." She should have known Alan was far too smart not to notice her avoidance of Clayton and Ben.

"You said your mother works for the judge. Is she his paralegal, or his secretary?"

"Well… Uhh… Okay. It's like this. Judge Caulder has a son, Emile, and he has Asperger's Syndrome. My mother helps take care of Emile."

"Is your mother a nurse?"

"No, Alan, she isn't." Eden saw her opportunity to change the subject. "The limo turned!"

"They're going to Samilomani Street," the driver said. "Lots of expensive condos there."

The limousine stopped in front of a luxurious, 20-story, brick building. A doorman dressed in a red jacket, black trousers, and matching hat walked to the limousine. He opened the car door and warmly greeted the couple. The judge said something to the geisha; she bowed and followed the doorman into the building. The judge got back into the car and it sped away.

"Where's he going now?" Alan asked.

The taxi discreetly followed behind the speeding limo. Several blocks later, the limousine pulled into a wooded area. A mile back from the road stood a flat-roof building with three swing sets and half a dozen sandboxes in the grassless yard. The limo pulled into the gravel parking-lot and stopped. The judge got out of the car, carrying an armload of gaily wrapped gifts.

A scrawny, weather-worn, Japanese woman opened the bamboo door. She bowed to the judge and stood aside so he could enter the building.

"What is this place?" Alan asked.

"Mayaxim Orphanage," the driver said.

"Judge Caulder is very involved with the foster-care program in Maramount," Eden said. "Maybe he's been doing something along those lines here in Japan?"

"Ha!" the driver snorted.

Alan turned to Eden and he shrugged his shoulders at the driver's outburst. A few minutes later, the judge walked out of the orphanage, holding the hands of two small Japanese girls. One little girl cooperated as the judge lifted her and put her in the back of the limo. The other small girl fought the judge. She kicked him and tried to bite his hand. He grabbed the tiny child and threw her inside the car.

Furious, Eden reached for the door handle. Alan stopped her.

"Let's see where he's taking them," Alan said calmly.

The limo drove away. The taxi maintained a safe distance behind. Without warning, the limo sped out of sight.

"Don't lose them!" Alan shouted.

The driver gave him the universal thumbs up.

A few miles from the orphanage, the limo pulled onto a long, paved driveway that led to a beautiful, four-tier, pagoda-style house, nearly hidden inside a forest of flowering trees and lush, green plants. The taxi idled out of sight. Alan, Eden, and the driver got out of the car and edged their way through the tall brush about 100 feet from the house. They waited for the passengers to exit the limo. Eden noticed the limo was next to a well-maintained koi pond. The driver followed closely behind Eden and Alan. They quietly moved through the brush toward the large arborvitae outlining the house. Hidden inside the bushes, they were able to watch the scene unfold in front of them.

The glass-and-bamboo front doors opened and a short, plump, American male and a beautiful, delicately thin Japanese woman came out onto the porch.

They greeted the judge as he stepped out of the limousine. The man wore jeans, boots, and a leather jacket. The woman wore a cream trouser suit that perfectly fit her slim figure, and on her left lapel was a large sapphire, emerald, and ruby brooch shaped like a hummingbird.

The judge reached his hand inside the car. A small hand went peaceably into his hand. The agreeable child stepped out of the car. The judge took her around and introduced her to the couple. The little girl waited as the judge went back to the car for the other. He tried the same ploy with the second child, but the little one refused to take his hand. He lost his temper. He reached inside the car and caught the child by her arm. Judge Caulder dragged the little one out onto the ground. He attempted to yank her to her feet, but she fought him like an infant tiger.

The beautiful woman came over to the car. She squatted down and spoke softly to the child. The child seemed to respond to whatever it was she heard. The woman held her arms out to the child. The child stared at the woman's arms. Then she looked up at the judge's angry face. She fell into the woman's arms and held onto her. The woman stood up with the small child in her arms and walked into the house.

"What do you make of that?" Alan asked.

"There's a bad vibe coming from that place, Alan," Eden said.

"I think that couple is adopting those children," Alan said.

"Humph!" the driver snorted.

"Look, man, if you have something to say, then let's hear it!" Alan said.

"They heard you, Alan!" Eden said. Alan looked toward the house and he saw the judge and the other man looking in their direction.

"Let's get out of here!" the driver said, and he scrambled toward the waiting taxi. Alan and Eden quickly followed him.

On their way back to the train station, Eden said, "Something is terribly wrong, Alan. Why is Judge Caulder in Japan? I don't think it had anything to do with Clayton. Why was he at the orphanage? Who were those people he left the children with? And why was that little girl so afraid?"

"I don't have the answer to any of your questions, Eden. We may never know what the judge is up to. If he's a good man, well, I mean he's probably an adulterer, but he might have some good traits. Perhaps he is trying to help Japan's forgotten children. At least we can hope that's what he was doing."

When they returned to the train station, Alan gave the taxi driver two, crisp, 100-dollar bills. The driver quickly put the money into his pocket and turned his meter on for the first time that day.

"Are you going to tell Clayton Caulder that you saw his dad today?"

"I wouldn't warn Clayton if an alligator was about to eat him alive!"

"I see," Alan said, and he grinned at her vehemence.

Alan and Eden's once-festive mood had turned introspective and sombre.

"Would you like to go to Tony Roma's and eat some barbequed ribs?" Alan asked.

"No, thanks. I don't have much of an appetite."

"Okay. Want to go to the Cube Food Court and get some sashimi?"

"I don't know what sashimi is. But I'll try it."

They sat down among a crowd of young people.

"You take the first bite," Alan offered. "But be careful. The wasabi is hot."

"Is this raw?" Eden asked.

"Yes, it is. But I promise it is very good."

After Eden took a small bite of the wasabi, she gasped and fanned her mouth. She took a long, hard swallow of cold water and pushed the bento box toward. "You can have the rest."

Two teenage girls sitting in the booth behind them started giggling.

Alan pointed to Eden and he said to the girls, "*Mei guo de.*" He remembered the old man spoke those words to them at the dumpling emporium. Both girls laughed, nodded at Alan, and pointed to Eden.

"I guess I'm the butt of the joke?" Eden asked.

"Depends on how you look at it. I called you an American."

Eden smiled. "It is funny. I'm just not in the mood, I guess."

They tried to gather enthusiasm for their sightseeing venture. Downtown in the Sannomiya area, they passed under the vibrant, red, tori gate that led to the Ikuta Shrine. They were joined by a quiet, respectful crowd of people as they passed through the sacred shrine.

Eden and Alan walked through the verdant, green Ikuta Forest. Eden noticed a man raking the white gravel that covered the temple grounds. He made perfect lines with his rake, meticulously erasing the visitor's footprints.

The troubling events of the day came crashing down on Eden. She felt vulnerable, scared, tearful, reverent, and melancholy.

"Do you believe in God, Alan?" she asked.

"I never gave it much thought," he said, brushing his foot across the gravel to smooth his tracks.

"I believe in God. But I don't understand why He allows such bad things to happen to good people."

"No doubt that's the question most pondered by people with great spiritual intellect. I do believe it's our duty to be kind to one another. For those with great gifts, I think they should share their time, skill, and resources with the less fortunate.

"There are so many 'bibles' in this world. But most of them agree we are to share, care, love, and find peace with our fellow man. Wouldn't it be ironic if we someday discover we all serve the same God, even though we pray to Him in different languages and we call him by other holy titles?"

A soft breeze stirred in the top of the trees. Eden watched a rose-ringed parakeet soar across the clear, blue sky.

"Did you ever notice the most magnificent things on this earth, like the stars, the sun, and the moon, move silently around the world?"

"That's the poet in you speaking. The fact is the stars, the sun, and the moon are prone to violent explosions."

Eden looked at Alan. "You realist, me dreamer?" she asked.

He pulled her into his arms. "I am so in love with you."

# Twenty-Five

Restless and bored, Sandreen paced her stateroom. On her fourth pass across the room, she decided she would quit her job and end her affair with Robert, the captain. The thought of change renewed her spirit.

She placed three suitcases on her freshly made bed. While she emptied her closet, armoire, and dresser drawers, her excitement grew as she planned for the new adventures that lay ahead and the interesting men she would meet. She gathered up her perfumed soaps, expensive makeup, toothbrush, and fancy silver comb and hair-brush set.

The trick, she thought as she set her suitcases next to the door, would be to keep her plans a secret from Robert until it was too late for him to try and change her mind.

She decided she would leave a resignation letter thanking him for all the nice things he'd done for her. She knew Robert was in love with her, but that was his problem. He got what he deserved for being a lying, cheating bastard, she coldly thought.

Sandreen drew her cellphone out of her purse and called a private number. When her party answered, she said, "Good morning, Jax. I'll be in Shanghai this afternoon. Would it be all right if I stop by your place this evening?"

He agreed it would be.

"I'll see you at seven," she said and pushed 'end.' She put her cellphone back in her pocket.

*Back to work for the last time,* Sandreen thought. She took a deep breath and headed out the door.

Jax checked the fuel gauge on his sleek, black Gulfstream G550 jet with the 24-karat gold letters 'Sky Eagle' emblazoned across the side. He radioed the tower and asked for permission to land at the airport. It felt good to be home again, he thought. He longed to have a cup of coffee on the railed balcony of his luxurious home situated in Xintaindi which literally meant 'new heaven and earth.' He had a few changes he wanted to make to his enormous flower garden. He wanted to add more flowering trees, add three more Koi ponds, and replace the marble fountain in the center with one twice as large.

Besides his house in Shanghai, Jax owned a magnificent villa in Rome, a castle in Ireland, a chateau in the south of France, and a manor in Monte Carlo. But it was his historic Shanghai house, known as *shikumen*, or literally 'stone gates,' where he found the peace that generally eluded him.

A restless spirit was one of the many things he and Sandreen shared in common.

Jax Greeley, being a man of diversified tastes, met Sandreen for the first time when she worked as a prostitute at the Baishōfu Brothel in the slums of Shanghai. He knew she was beautiful, but he quickly learned she was also very clever. He had no idea she was only 15 years old.

He learned much later that Sandreen's parents, an Asian mother and a French father, had two things in common. One, they had a daughter that neither of them wanted. And two, they shared an addiction to heroin.

Over the years, the sexual tension between Jax and Sandreen had waned, yet they would remain lifelong friends. With Jax's help, Sandreen left the brothel at age 20. From there, she went to the University of Shanghai where she earned a degree in engineering.

For Sandreen's sake, Jax had hoped she might decide to settle down. However, Sandreen's search for excitement and adventure kept her ever on the move.

Jax knew everything about the few people he allowed into his inner circle, but he kept his past, great wealth, and enormous portfolio as closely guarded secrets. He moved easily through the ranks of the rich and famous and had intimate knowledge of them as well the thugs who could cut a man's throat as easily as he could open a can.

His golden rule was to never overlook a trespass and get even. Jay believed in an eye for an eye. He insisted that those he did business keep their word and if they ever once lied to him or cheated him, the consequences were severe.

Jax lowered his landing gear and slowed the plane. The tires moved smoothly across the runway as he taxied to his private hangar. The large metal door on his state-of-the-art warehouse slid open with great ease, and Jax drove the plane inside.

Jax private hangar housed his collection of luxury airplanes, a custom-made fleet of opulently appointed helicopters, and his impressive collection of cars which included a Lamborghini Veneno, a Ferrari 458 Spider, a Bugatti Type-41 Royale, a Rolls-Royce Ghost, and his newest acquisition, a Koenigsegg CCXR Trevita.

Jax shut down the instrument panel. Upon descending from the airplane stairs, Jax was met by Erik Rivera, Jax's most trusted friend. Erik welcomed his old friend with a hug.

"I like the snazzy outfit," Erik commented, referring to Jax's black leather pants, matching jacket, and chrome Ray Ban aviator sunglasses.

"You think this outfit lends to my mystique?" Jax asked with a grin.

"I wouldn't go that far. Do you have time for a cup of coffee?"

"Sure," Jax said, joining Erik at the small chrome table.

Erik poured fresh black coffee into a stainless-steel mug and handed it to Jax.

"Was your trip to London everything you'd hope it would be?" Erik asked.

"Yes, it was," Jax said, rubbing his tired eyes.

Seeing how tired his friend appeared, Erik said, "I hope you trip wasn't all work-related."

"I did have some downtime. After my business with Count Ramsport concluded, I had dinner at the castle with the Count and Countess. I found the food they served rather interesting. We started the evening with Royal Beluga caviar and a bottle of nice Bordeaux from the Count's vineyard. But new to me, the rare Dodine turkey and Waygu beef heart, which came wrapped in 50-carat gold leaf. Then, for dessert, Densuke watermelon, whipped Kopi Luwak coffee beans, and Amedel premium chocolate.

"And something you'll find amusing, Erik. The Kopi Luwak coffee beans are extracted from the shit of the Asian civet cat."

"That's disgusting!" Erik said, and he curled his nose up.

"Later, we enjoyed a bottle of 1907 Piper-Heidseick Champagne. In my opinion, Piper Heidseick is the holy grail of all champagnes."

"Expensive, I take it?" Erik asked.

"$59,000 dollars a bottle," Jax said flippantly.

"That's too rich for my blood," Erik said, and sensing his good friend's growing restlessness, he got up and went over to the rack that held all of the keys to the vehicles.

"Which car will it be, Jax?" Erik asked.

Jax stood up and stretched his tall, slender body.

"I'll take the Lamborghini."

"I would have guessed the Bugatti," Erik said, and he put the Bugatti keys back on the rack and got the keys for the Lamborghini.

Erik pressed the key fob and the Lamborghini's driver's side door raised to the sky and low, fluorescent, blue lights came on.

Jax lowered his tall body into the luxurious seat and started the engine, admiring the deep bubbling sound of the high-powered motor. He revved the engine, and Erik opened the warehouse door. The Lamborghini shot out of the hangar, sailing like a silver bullet and into the teeming traffic.

Eden and Alan were on their own evening tour, heading toward Xintaindi to find an outdoor café. Both were starving and tired. Wandering around aimlessly, they began to notice their surroundings were turning dingier and darker. The inhabitants staring out them made them feel all the more out of place.

The place reeked of a strong stench of raw sewage. The streets were filled with begging, half-starved children, garbage, and filthy bums. Since they had no idea which direction they had come from, the two huddled close together and walked nervously forward. Eden noticed Alan's hand had become increasing tight around hers. They anxiously watched for any sudden movement coming from the darkening alleys and abandoned storefronts which were graphically adorned with what appeared to be violent Chinese symbols and profanity.

As Eden's fear built, she soothed herself by silently chanting Bible verses that Momma had taught her. "Believe and trust in God; knowing that He is real, even though we cannot see Him." She repeated the mantra over and over in her head. Alan made eye contact with a man, but Eden's mental recitations kept her gaze averted.

The young man took Alan's interested gaze as a challenge and he yelled something at Alan. Alan turned, but he didn't respond. The man clenched his fists and crossed his snake-imprinted arms across his chest.

"Let's go, Alan!" Eden said anxiously, and she pulled on his clenched, sweaty hand and they both started running down the littered street.

When they finally stopped to catch their breath, Alan said, "I am so sorry, Eden. I wanted this to be a romantic evening. Instead, I brought you to this hellhole."

"You had no way of knowing this place even existed," Eden said softly. "Maybe we've accidentally run off the suggested spots on the tourist map."

Alan hugged her to him.

"Eden, getting to know you has been the best part of this whole trip."

"I feel the same way about you, Alan," Eden said, and she hugged him tighter.

Alan cleared his throat self-consciously and took a step back. Eden's nearness was definitely having a strong effect on this young, virgin male.

"Can you call us a taxi and get us back to the ship?" Eden asked innocently.

Alan looked apologetically at Eden and he said, "I feel like an idiot. I left my cellphone in my stateroom so we wouldn't be disturbed today."

Eden patted his arm reassuringly.

A group of young, seedy-looking males came strolling down the street. When a couple of the men looked lustily at Eden, Alan panicked. He looked around quickly and, in the distance, he noticed a small grocery store. And it was open for business!

"Let's go," he said, and he grabbed her arm and they moved to the other side of the street.

From a distance, the grocery store held some promise, but up close, Alan and Eden saw a leaning shed with a pitted tin roof, a sagging porch, and a lop-sided screen door, minus the screen wire. They passed by an outdoor display of rusty tools laid out like instruments of torture, and two, large, wooden barrels overflowing with rancid potatoes and dusty rice. A crude, wooden plaque hammered into the crumbling wood next to the screen door said, 'Ching Wu, Proprietor.'

Alan opened the squealing screen door and they were greeted by a tiny, ancient Chinese man standing on a ladder, placing tins of tobacco on a top shelf. He wore a black silk Hanfu, a knee-length tunic with matching pants, and on his feet, he wore white cotton socks and wooden sandals.

Alan and Eden moved cautiously across the sagging, straw-covered floor, noticing swarming flies feasting on the dead duck carcasses as they hung by their necks over a thin wire. They saw meager amounts of tin cans displayed on the slanting shelves that were labeled in English, Thai, and Cantonese. On a wobbly table near the back of the store sat bags of millet, sorghum, matcha, ginger root, sliced deer antler, bear bile, and black tea, all crowded around a century-old Abacus. Beneath a curtained doorway, a skinny Siamese cat squatted and did his business, then wandered back out of sight.

"This place is scary," Alan whispered to Eden.

Ching Wu welcomed Alan and Eden in Chinese, "*Huānyíng.*"

"Good morning, sir," Alan said. "Do you perhaps have a telephone we could use to call a taxi?"

The tiny man smiled and looked quizzically at Alan.

"I don't think he speaks English," Alan whispered to Eden. For the Chinaman, Alan mimed holding a cellphone and he then placed the imaginary telephone against his ear. The Chinese man leaned his head to the side, like a dog asking a question of his master.

"Perhaps he doesn't know what a cellphone is, Alan," Eden said kindly.

"In this day and age, who doesn't know what a freaking cellphone is?" Alan asked testily.

"Let me try," Eden said, and she mimed an old-fashioned telephone with a rotary dial and held her hand to her ear.

Alan didn't understand Eden's parody. Eden didn't bother telling Alan she and her family still used an old-fashioned rotary telephone at home.

"Ahhhhhh!" the old man said, and he eased himself down the ladder. From a shelf, he pulled down a weathered cardboard box. Opening the box, he brought out a small item and handed it to Alan.

"He gave me earache medicine!" Alan said, and he shook his head no and handed the item back to the old man.

A door in the backroom of the store opened and closed. A trio of tough-looking young thugs walked into the room. The Chinese youth in the center was small, fit, and good-looking. His two companions were built like Sumo wrestlers on steroids. The three were dressed in designer sneakers and loose-fitting running suits.

Eden shyly looked at the cold, detached stares on the three men's faces, realizing theirs were much like the look she often saw on her father's face.

She thought of the famous Italo Svevo quote… 'There are three things I always forget…names, places, and the third I cannot remember.'

Alan watched the fearsome group, expecting at any moment to see one or all of them pull out a lethal weapon. The good-looking man in the center spoke to the old man in Cantonese. The old man nodded and then looked nervously at Alan and Eden. The young man gave a two-word order, and the old man ambled off the ladder and quickly disappeared through the curtained door.

The trio moved in unison toward a nervous Eden and Alan.

"What is it you're looking for?" the good-looking man asked in perfect English.

"A telephone to call a taxi," Alan said, jittery.

"Does this look like a place that would have a public telephone?" the good-looking man asked, laughing so loud his bulky comrades followed suit.

"I guess not," Alan said, and he noticed the cellphones hanging on the waistbands of all three men.

"Sorry we bothered you," Alan said, and he took Eden's hand and they started for the door.

"Wait up, you two," the good-looking man said, moving closer. "Perhaps we can make a deal."

"What kind of deal?" Alan asked, and he gripped Eden's hand tighter.

"You need a phone, and I might have one to sell."

"Okay," Alan said warily.

The good-looking man looked Eden over head to toe, then he did the same with Alan. It became obvious by their clothing which of them carried the money. He spoke to Alan.

"I got an iPhone 4 I'll let you have for two-thousand bucks."

"You've got to be kidding!" Alan said, and he felt Eden squeeze his hand, meaning calm down.

"Take it or leave it, Pal," the good-looking man said, and his comrades crossed their heavy arms over their massive chests.

"Sir, do you have a less-expensive telephone?" Eden asked softly.

The good-looking man liked Eden's respectful tone. He also liked the way the front of her blouse bulged.

"Tell you what, Sugar, how 'bout I let you and your tightwad boyfriend here look at the phones I have for sale."

"Alan?" Eden asked softly, and she gripped Alan's hand.

When Alan hesitated, the two behemoth henchmen moved behind them and blocked their exit.

"Sure," Alan said, and his voice quivered.

Alan and Eden knew to be afraid, but they had no idea that these men, known as Three, and their boss, a vile, murderous woman they called One, composed the worst gang in Shanghai. Together, they ran the largest import-export business in the country; their lucrative black-market business specialized in high-grade cocaine, heroin, opium, and marijuana. But in recent years, they had made a fortune selling stolen iPhones, iPads, weapons, exotic animals, human kidneys, livers, lungs, and hearts.

Alan and Eden, followed closely by the two henchmen, were led through the curtained doorway and into a cluttered backroom.

"Let me see your wallet," the good-looking man said to Alan as he held out his hand.

"Why?" Alan asked. A strong arm behind him gave him a hard shove. Alan got the message. He handed over his wallet.

The good-looking man pulled out Alan's driver's license and his ID, both had Alan's picture on them. He saw a picture of a pretty brunette and read the words, "To Alan, with all my love, Kristy." The good-looking man raised his gaze to Eden, compared her face to the girl in the picture, and with an evil grin, he handed Alan's wallet back to him.

He pointed at Eden's backpack and snapped his fingers. Eden pulled her backpack off her shoulders and handed it to him. He pulled back the flap and rummaged inside the bag, finding a pale-pink lipstick, a comb, a half-empty bottle of tepid water, four packages of peanut butter and cheese crackers, several colored pencils, writing paper, and a small box of tampons. She took particular notice of the scrapbook she was keeping.

He handed the backpack to Eden. He went over to the paneled wall and pushed an invisible button; the wall opened, exposing what looked like a bank vault. He placed his eye against the camera on the front, placed his thumb down on a small, black, electronic pad, and spoke his name, Dhee Ling, into a microphone. A series of clicks sounded, the thick door opened, and a stainless-steel elevator appeared. Eden and Alan hesitated, and the two men behind them shoved them forward. As Alan and Eden stood behind the triple wall of flesh, Eden thought, Ecclesiastes Chapter 4 verse 12… '*A cord of three stands is not quickly broken.*'

The full elevator dropped a long distance. The elevator doors opened inside an enormous state-of-the-art facility. They saw and heard the agitated noises made by the vast collection of exotic animals. On one wall, leopards, cheetahs, orangutans, and spider monkeys roamed restlessly inside steel cages. On the other wall were a white alligator, assorted poisonous snakes, a star tortoise, a glass frog whose organs were visible, and a giant, yellow salamander. An aviary stocked with exotic birds sat next to terrariums holding tarantulas and whistling spiders, both as large as dinner plates. In a cage by itself, a large Southern Cassowary, a flightless bird capable of killing or kicking a person to death, closely watched the spiders. The place was immaculate, and in spite of all of the caged animals, the air smelled clean. The animals appeared to be well-nourished. The overhead lights cast a soft yellow hue among the large room.

"Quite a zoo we got here, huh?" Dhee said.

Alan didn't answer. He had no tolerance for people who thought it was okay to keep exotic animals in cages or zoos. He despised all hunters, particularly canned hunting. Judging by the number of empty cages, Alan assumed the illegal trade in exotic and nearly extinct animals was extremely profitable.

Dhee looked down at the gold Rolex watch on his wrist and he said, "Watch this."

The warehouse brightened and at the same time, several of the big cats moved to the edge of their cages. Water began flowing from the top of each cage, moving the animal's waste toward a small drain where a vacuum of sorts sucked it into a sewage-treatment plant.

"Pretty neat, huh?" Dhee said.

Alan wondered at Dhee's westernized colloquialisms.

A door opened and a team of 20 silent people dressed in similar uniforms entered the room and went about their duties of caring for and feeding the animals.

"See those guys up there in the skybox?" Dhee asked, pointing at the four men operating a group of security cameras. "Everything that happens down here is recorded. Now, you see that small dome over those guys' heads? That is another security camera that keeps an eye on the security team. And so the surveillance goes, on, and on, and on. Until it finally reaches One."

He turned to Alan and Eden. "Thought I'd mention that just in case you two get any ideas."

Trying to break free of this place or to try to overpower the two tough guys was the last thing on Alan's mind.

"What do you mean when you say 'until if finally reaches one'? One what?" Alan asked.

The muscular guard spoke something in Cantonese, and Dhee laughed.

"Chong says you're funny," Dhee translated.

Alan wisely decided to keep quiet.

"Follow me," Dhee said.

As they walked through the long hallway, they passed a pristine, brightly lit room that appeared to be an operating center. Inside, they saw a group of men and women dressed in surgical gear, all wearing facemasks. They appeared to be waiting for someone or something. For a moment, Alan let his mind wonder at the possibility that this was the place where they harvested the human organs. The thought occurred to him that the warm corpses might become dinner for the large cats.

With a shiver, he continued on down the hallway. They entered a cavernous room filled with computers with ever-changing screensavers. Another display boasted Apple's newest and best products. There were racks of handguns, assault rifles, and assorted knives with fearsome blades that could easily be used to dismember an elephant, cut down a tree, or, Alan thought, carve up a human. A tall glass case measuring 50 feet in width and 20 feet in height displayed an assortment of neatly stored, narcotic-prescription drugs and bagged premium heroin, cocaine, opium, and marijuana were lying in selective groups of kind. The drug paraphernalia were displayed on racks of their own. The D.V.D.s of child porn were stacked six-feet tall and covered a section of the warehouse next to the drugs. It was clear by the warehouse that it served the desperately ill, willing to pay anything to obtain an illegal organ, the addicts, the vile, the depraved, the pedophiles, and the sociopaths. Alan couldn't even wrap his head around the clientele that this placed served.

"What do you think?" Dhee asked smugly.

Eden and Alan looked stunned.

"Could you show me the telephone now please?" Alan asked in a state of total shock.

"Get one of those disposable phones," Dhee said, and the behemoth with the devoid expression ambled over to a cardboard box where he got a nondescript cellphone and handed it to Alan.

"What do I owe you?" Alan asked.

"Since I'm suddenly in a generous mood, I'll let you have this exceptional cellphone for a thousand American dollars."

Alan knew approximately what a cheap cellphone like the one in his hand was worth, but he also knew in his present captured position he had no room to argue.

"I don't have that much cash on me," he said miserably.

"Got a credit card?"

"You take credit cards?" Alan asked incredulously.

"Of course we do. Whadda think? You implying we're not a legitimate business?"

"No, no, I didn't mean that," Alan said, and he took his wallet out of his pocket and handed his credit card over. Dhee took the card over to the transaction table and ran it through the credit-card machine.

"Sign here," he said to Alan, and Alan signed his name in the electronic box.

"You probably guessed we don't give any receipts."

Alan tried to turn the cellphone on and nothing happened.

"This phone isn't charged," Alan said politely.

"You want a charger? That'll be another 500."

Defeated, Alan said, "No, thanks."

"Can we leave now?" Eden asked softly.

"Sure, you can," Dhee said. "But we have one more thing we have to do before you two go."

Alan swallowed hard and Eden's insides started to quiver.

With his back turned to the security camera, Dhee said, "Give them the bags, Chong."

Chong reached into his jacket pocket and brought out two taped bags filled with white powder. He handed one each to Eden and Alan.

"Smile for the camera like you mean it," Dhee said under his breath. They smiled weakly. Dhee then led them back through the zoological menagerie and over to the elevator.

Even though Alan and Eden both knew they had been framed, they still breathed a collective sigh of relief when the elevator doors opened and they found themselves once again in the store's cluttered backroom. Chong grabbed the bags of drugs that Alan and Eden held and he put them in his pocket.

"I suppose you mean to blackmail us now?" Alan asked angrily.

"Not at all. We just took out a little insurance. Now, if there is ever any question of us using force to detain you, well, the camera saw how well we all got along. And it also saw you and your girlfriend buying drugs."

"What the camera saw was me buying a cheap cellphone, and if anyone listens to the audio part of that tape, they will know that's all I paid for," Alan said hotly, his anger dampening his fear.

"From the moment we stepped foot into the bunker, the audio part of the tape was turned off. And, no cop I know would ever believe you paid a thousand dollars for a disposable cellphone."

Dhee's tone suddenly turned menacing, "I got our drug deal on tape, and I got your credit-card number, Alan Honnecut. Furthermore, I know where to find you. So, if you and your girlfriend here don't want any trouble, you both better keep your mouths shut about this place."

Eden and Alan indicated they understood the threat.

As they were leaving the store, the old Chinaman bid them farewell as he was filling a grocery sack with cigarettes, beer, and condoms for a group of noisy teenagers.

# Twenty-Six

"We have to get out of here, Eden," Alan said, taking Eden's hands into his.

"I'll go look for a cop, a telephone, or a taxi. But you should hide. If I go alone, it will be safer for both of us."

"I don't want you to leave me here by myself, Alan," Eden pleaded.

"We were very fortunate Dhee and his gang didn't do something much worse to us. This is a rough area, and as far as I'm concerned, we've seen too much already. If I take you with me, you'll be a calling card to every hoodlum who sees us."

Eden agreed with Alan's logic. But she was also terrified to stay behind.

They found what appeared to be an old, abandoned, cat cafe, judging by the dozens of emaciated cats roaming around and through the open storefront. Cats of all colors and sizes lounged on filthy countertops, broken chair seats, and scarred tabletops. One striped cat hung by its front paws from a dusty light fixture.

"I think this place looks fairly safe," Alan said, trying to sound encouraging. "And you'll have the cats to keep you company until I return."

Before he left, Alan took Eden in his arms and he kissed her passionately.

"I love you, Eden Owens," he said, stroking her hair.

"And I love you, Alan Honnecut," Eden said.

Alan paused and looked back at Eden. His heart ached, leaving the love of his life in such desperate circumstances, but he felt Eden would be safer here than on the dangerous streets with him. He raised his hand in a silent goodbye. Eden did the same and crouched down behind the counter.

An orange-and-white kitten came to inspect this new visitor. Eden put her hand out palm side up toward the kitten and the kitten ran to her. The cat's silky fur and contented purring was reassuring. Soon, other cats were begging to be pet too. Eden had always wanted a pet, but the high cost of pet food prevented her family from having any.

Eden's stomach growled. She took a package of peanut butter and cheese crackers out of her backpack, opened them, and ate slowly. She noticed the scrapbook that Alan and she were making. The best time in her life, she thought with tears streaming down her face.

The food brought the cats begging. Eden opened two other packages of crackers and offered small bites to all the cats. After a sip of lukewarm water, she leaned her head back against the wall, and with the contented cats curled up against her side, she fell asleep.

Around midnight, raunchy music brought the crowds of subversive rabble crawling into the darkness and inhabiting the filthy streets, startling Eden awake. A sandpaper-rough tongue licked Eden's hand. Peering into the inky darkness, she wondered how long she had slept. It felt like Alan had been gone for hours.

Eden crept across the room and peeked outside at the street. She saw a few people wandering around. Although she was frightened, she decided it was time for her to go find Alan. Eden walked no more than half a block when, in front of a dingy bar, she saw a crowd of hellish-looking men and their salacious girlfriends gathered around two men viciously fighting each other.

Scooters zoomed by the dark street, and young Asian women, dressed in provocative clothing, congregated together on street corners.

Sandreen Gavel saw the fight in front of the bar, but she wisely took a shortcut to avoid the brawl. She had stopped off in Lowtown to see her old friend, Zhang, and one of her former colleagues at the Baishōfu Brothel. She was on her way to see her friend, Jax, who, like Sandreen, was a night owl.

Sandreen came quickly around the corner and ran smack into Eden.

"You shouldn't be here, Eden," Sandreen scolded.

The sight of a familiar face brought tears to Eden's eyes.

"I am so glad to see you, Sandreen!" Eden said, and she hugged Sandreen tightly.

"Weren't you and the other students warned not to visit this part of Shanghai?" Sandreen chided.

"We got lost, Sandreen," Eden said timidly.

"We?"

"Alan Honnecut and I."

"I see. So, where is Alan now?"

"He went to find someone to take us back to the ship."

"Why didn't you use your cellphone to call for help?"

"Alan left his cellphone on the ship this morning."

"Did you also leave your cellphone behind?"

"I don't have a cellphone, Sandreen," Eden said, and, once again, her family's extreme poverty shamed her.

Sandreen of all people should have recognized what poor looked like.

"Maybe Alan made it back to the ship by now and he has his cellphone on him. I'll call him and tell him where we are."

"Alan didn't make it back to the ship," Eden said miserably, "because if he had, he would have come back for me."

"You trust him so completely?"

"I do."

Sandreen thought to warn this naive young girl about the promises men made while in the throes of passion, but she decided that like most women, Eden would have to learn the brutal rules of sexual posturing on her own.

"Alan should have taken you with him."

"I wish he had too," Sandreen said, dreading returning to the ship.

When Sandreen was leaving the ship for the last time that morning, Captain Evert had caught her. What Sandreen hoped would be a friendly farewell had escalated into an ugly confrontation.

"Stay close to me, Eden, and don't speak to or make eye contact with anyone we happen to pass by."

"Thank you, Sandreen," Eden said weakly, and she started walking briskly behind the cruise director.

"Don't thank me yet," Sandreen said, and Eden and she crossed the street opposite the fight in front of the bar.

The two women were briefly illuminated by the harsh headlight on a passing scooter. One man in the raucous crowd caught a glimpse of them. Standing with the crowd of rowdy revelers, Clayton Caulder let out a roaring cheer and stumbled backward. Ben, who'd designated himself the safe driver, had limited himself to two beers. Ben had seen Clayton drunk many times before, but, tonight, his old friend had really outdone himself.

"We'd better get back to the ship," Ben said, struggling to keep Clayton on his feet.

"Let go of me!" Clayton shouted, and he yanked his arm free, dropping face down on top of the fighting men. The two fighters jumped on Clayton and started beating him with their fists. Ben grabbed Clayton by the back of his sweaty shirt and hauled him out of the fray. He set his drunk friend aside on his ass and tackled the two exhausted fighters. He threw each of them into the street. With his fists knotted, Ben turned and glared at the crowd. Apparently, no one dared the risk of taking on Goliath. The crowd dispersed and headed back inside the bar.

Ben picked Clayton up off the sidewalk and hauled him over to their rental car. With Clayton's limp body draped over his huge arm, Ben opened the car door on the battered Saab and manhandled Clayton inside.

"Man, you are cooked," Ben said.

Clayton gagged. Ben reached for a thermos in the backseat, unscrewed the cap, and poured water into the thermos' cup. He took a packet out of his pocket and put a pill in the water, holding the cup out to Clayton.

"Drink this," Ben said.

"I don't want that," Clayton slurred, and he shoved the cup away with his arm. Ben righted the cup, checking to see if any of the contents had spilled.

"You'll drink this, Clayton, or I'll pour it down your throat!"

Clayton's bleary gaze turned toward Ben. "Don't you tell me what to do," he said.

"Drink it, dammit! It'll sober you up."

"What is it?" Clayton mumbled.

"It's something called D.H.M., don't ask me what that stands for. This stuff is said to sober up drunken rats, and they're supposed to be testing it now on humans."

"You want me to drink some rat drink?" Clayton slurred incredulously.

"I want you to sober up," Ben said, and he held the cup out to Clayton.

Clayton took the cup and he drank it down in one long gulp. Within five minutes, he felt alert.

"Wow! This is great," Clayton said while scratching his beard stubble. "There's finally something that'll let me drink all I want and sober me up quick. That's great news for all us drunks!"

"I don't think it's meant to be used that way, Clayton."

"Probably not, but for me, I shall."

"You're probably right, 'you shall,'" Ben mocked.

"Where did you hear about it?"

"I heard a couple guys on the ship talking about it. I asked them where I could get some. They sent me to this dude, said he worked in a lab where they made this stuff. I bought half a dozen pills for a couple hundred bucks."

"Where was I when you were off sightseeing without me?"

"Passed out in our stateroom."

Clayton laughed.

"How about one more drink for the road?" Clayton asked.

"Forget it, Pal. At this rate, you'll go through all six pills in one night!"

Ben started the grumbling Saab and headed down the street.

"I saw Eden Owens and Sandreen from the ship about 15 minutes ago," Ben said.

"Together?"

"Looked like it to me."

"What were those two doing in this part of town?"

"I have no idea."

"Were they in a car or on foot?"

"When I saw them, they were walking past a bar."

"Which direction did they go in?"

"Same way we're going now."

"Let's try to find them," Clayton said eagerly.

"Why?"

"To have a little fun."

"Eden Owens? Fun? Since when?"

"I'm not interested in her. It's Sandreen I'd like to spend some time with."

"Spend time with or screw?"

"Screw her for sure."

"You'd better leave well enough alone, Clayton."

"There's no fun in that."

Ben didn't like what he was hearing.

Sandreen tried to call Jax to tell him she was running late, but when she looked at her cellphone, she saw that her battery had run out.

"What if Alan has returned and he can't find me?" Eden asked. "Maybe we should go back."

Sandreen stopped suddenly, causing Eden to bump into her. "You really don't have a clue how bad this place is, do you?"

They were in an isolated section of Lowtown where the streets were mostly deserted. Bright headlights suddenly swept the street close to them and Sandreen said, "See that trash container in the alley, Eden?" Eden nodded. "Go hide beside it and keep quiet."

Eden ran as quietly as she could into the alley and crouched beside the stinking garbage container.

"What luck!" Clayton said, eyeing Sandreen up ahead.

The Saab slowed down and stopped, idling next to Sandreen. Clayton rolled the window down. "How's it going, Sandreen?"

Sandreen was in no mood to deal with these two miscreants, but it did occur to her she might ask Clayton and Ben to take Eden back to the ship. Then she remembered an incident on the ship when she saw Clayton and Ben bullying Eden.

"Can we drive you back to the ship, Miss Geval?" Ben asked.

"No, thank you."

"Where's Eden Owens?" Clayton asked sharply.

Eden heard Clayton ask about her and she sat still as a mouse.

"Why would I know that?" Sandreen asked.

"Ben here says he saw the two of you together a little while ago."

"Oh, that. Eden got lost and I showed her the way back to the ship. If you hurry, you might catch up with her."

"Eden can wait," Clayton said, and he got out of the car and walked over to where Sandreen stood.

"What brings you to this part of town?" he asked lustily.

"I took a shortcut," Sandreen said smartly.

"I don't think so," Clayton said, and he moved closer to Sandreen.

Sandreen knew what to expect next. Better to defuse the situation before it got out of control.

Clayton had sobered up enough to see Sandreen was prepared to retaliate.

"Ben, get out of the car," Clayton said.

Reluctantly, Ben followed Clayton's orders.

Standing in the glare of the headlights, Clayton grasped Sandreen's wrist and yanked her against him.

"I'm sick of your high and mighty attitude," he said. "I don't know who you think you are, but what I see before me is a common everyday whore."

"Hey, Clayton, let's go get that drink," Ben said anxiously.

Clayton grabbed Sandreen's breast and Sandreen shouted, "Let go of me, you impotent juvenile!"

Sandreen swung her knee at his crotch. Clayton swerved and grabbed Sandreen by her arm and dragged her by both arms above her head into the alley. In front of the trash container, he threw her down on the ground with such force, the breath was knocked out of her. He straddled her thighs and held his hand against her chest to restrain her which proved unnecessary since Sandreen has suddenly quietened down.

"Smart gal, you've stopped fighting me," Clayton said, and he pulled out his cellphone, made sure he had a good shot of the scene, and pushed record. With both hands, Clayton savagely ripped Sandreen's skirt and underwear off. Terrified, Eden watched as Clayton viciously raped Sandreen. Panting, Clayton rolled off Sandreen's still body and he said, "Your turn, Ben."

Ben moved closer and looked at Sandreen in the dim light.

"She's not moving, man," Ben said in a worrisome tone. "Something's wrong with her."

Clayton rolled over on one elbow and he looked at Sandreen. Her eyes were open and her head hung at an odd angle. He reached over and felt on her broken neck for a pulse. Finding none, he jumped to his feet.

"We gotta get out of here!" Ben said, and he ran toward the car.

"Ben, wait!" Clayton said.

"Wait, for what?" Ben asked nervously.

"Help me get her into the car."

"You got to be kidding!"

Clayton reached down and grabbed Sandreen's legs and started dragging her out of the alley.

"I don't want anything to do with this, Clayton," Ben said, following alongside the body.

"Fine time to go chicken on me, Ben," Clayton grunted.

Ben conceded and he helped Clayton lift Sandreen's body off the ground and carry her to their rental car.

Eden bolted from her hiding place, grabbed Clayton's cellphone, and dashed past Ben and Clayton.

"I'm going after her!" Clayton said, and he dropped Sandreen's body and took off after Eden.

Eden ran like a gazelle toward the red-light district. She heard Clayton's galloping footsteps narrowing the gap between them. Eden slammed into one of the scarred doors with a red light illuminating the pavement below it. She frantically pounded the door with her fists and screamed, "Help me, please, help me!" As Clayton extended out his hand to grab Eden, the door opened and a thick, hairy arm dragged her inside.

# Twenty-Seven

Raymond Austin, Jax Greeley's houseman, finished his coffee, being careful not to spill a drop on his formal attire. He gingerly pushed a handkerchief around the place where his lips touched the porcelain and placed the empty cup and saucer in the stainless-steel dishwasher. He neatly folded the handkerchief along its creases and placed it in his breast pocket.

Raymond surveyed the elegant apartment Mr. Greeley allowed him to occupy. Situated in the opulently appointed subterranean complex beneath Jax's mansion, his apartment was pristine. He made sure that not a single item was left out of place. He glanced at the clock on the wall which read 5:15 a.m. He smoothed his hair and reached for the ornate doorknob. He paused when the intercom, which hung on the wall next to the door, buzzed.

Raymond saw it was Sing Li calling from his post at the gate.

"Good morning, Li," Raymond said, following Jax's example and calling the man by his surname. Jax once stated he couldn't bring himself to call a grown man Sing.

"I'm sorry to call so early, Mr. Austin, but there is a man and a young woman here who are insisting on speaking to Mr. Greeley."

"It's 5:15 a.m., Li. As you are aware, Mr. Greeley maintains very late hours. Please ask them to call for an appointment at a later date."

There was a pause on the line and Raymond could hear excited mumbling in the background.

"The man says his business with Mr. Greeley won't wait," Li said.

"Ask the people to identify themselves, Li."

"The man says his name is Zhang Lui and the girl is Eden Owens."

Raymond knew Zhang, and, knowing his history in the brothel, Raymond felt comfortable addressing Zhang by his given name. But Eden Owens he'd never heard of.

"Li, please put Zhang on the telephone," Raymond said.

"I am so sorry to disturb you, Mr. Austin," Zhang said politely in halting English. "If this was not a matter of a most-urgent nature, I would never bother Mr. Greeley at this early hour."

"Can you tell me what this is about, Zhang, so that I may forward the message to Mr. Greeley?"

"I can't speak about the matter on the telephone, sir, but what I can say is it involves Miss Sandreen."

"I see. Please wait where you are and I will see if Mr. Greeley is available," Raymond said. He disconnected and quickly left his apartment.

Raymond took the service elevator up to the first floor. From there, he passed through the luxurious, marble kitchen, walked the wide, carpeted hallway adorned with priceless works of art, and came into the massive foyer where a magnificent gold-and-crystal chandelier hung from the center of the two-story-high ceiling. He hurriedly climbed the right side of the semi-circular, marble staircase.

At the carved mahogany door leading to the master bedroom, Raymond knocked softly.

"May I come in, sir?" he asked.

Jax awoke instantaneously. By the same token when his head touched the pillow after a long day, he quickly fell into a dreamless sleep. On the few occasions Jax had mentioned his ease of sleep to any of his insomniac friends, he was rewarded with their opinion, "You must have a clear conscience." It never occurred to them that Jax had no conscience at all.

Jax groped toward the nightstand and flipped on the Pink Lotus Tiffany lamp. He then reached for his Patek Philippe Chronograph wristwatch and looked at the time.

"Come in, Raymond," Jax said, annoyed.

Raymond opened the door and his attention went directly to Jax, where he sat with his broad, naked back pressed against the massive, carved headboard on his bed.

"I am sorry to bother you this early, sir, but it seems there is an urgent matter that requires your immediate attention."

Jax yawned. He had been in bed one hour.

"And what might this 'urgent matter' pertain to?" Jax asked, sounding bored.

"I don't know exactly, sir. But when I spoke to Zhang Lui, he did say it has something to do with Miss Sandreen."

Jax yawned again and he stretched his long body.

"Is Sandreen with him now?" Jax asked, thinking Sandreen no doubt drank too much last night and that would explain why she stood him up. *Now Zhang shows up here first thing this morning to drop her off so she can sober up,* he thought.

"No, sir, Miss Gavel is not with him. He is accompanied by Miss Eden Owens."

"Who the devil is Eden Owens?" Jax asked sharply, and he threw the blankets off and stood up.

Raymond quickly averted his gaze to avoid viewing Jax's nakedness.

"Admit them, Raymond, and have them wait for me in the library. I'll be down in a few minutes," he said, and he headed toward the master bathroom.

"Yes, sir," Raymond said, and he hurried away.

Raymond pressed the intercom and said, "Li, allow Zhang and Miss Owens to come up to the house."

"Yes, Mr. Austin," Li said, and he pressed a button and the black, ornate, iron gates soundlessly opened.

With his teeth brushed and his hair combed, Jax returned to his bedroom. He placed his watch on his right wrist. He pulled on the cotton and hemp khakis he'd worn two hours before, buttoned his stylish, white Eton shirt, threaded a 24-carat, gold-studded belt through the belt loops, and slipped his slender feet into a pair of burgundy Berlutti shoes.

When Jax descended the staircase, as per their usual arrangement, Raymond met him with a steaming cup of coffee served on a silver tray.

"Thank you, Raymond," Jax said, accepting the coffee.

"Zhang and Miss Owens are in the library, sir. I offered both a cup of coffee, and both declined. Is there anything else you require at this time?"

"No, Raymond."

Raymond made a slight bow and backed away.

Jax walked across the marble foyer. He sipped on his hot coffee and once again admired the Great Vitrine showcases built of Zitan hardwood, a wood so dense, it sinks in water and is more expensive than gold. The cases held his priceless collections of antique jade vases, ancient Chinese ivory carvings, and priceless porcelain figurines.

Jax opened the door to his library and at first glance, he noticed Zhang pacing in front of the towering, stone fireplace. He saw Eden, looking pale and fearful, seated on the colorful, oriental tapestry loveseat.

"Good morning," Jax said.

Zhang rushed forward, bowed, then quickly said in halting English, "Good morning, Mr. Greeley. I am so sorry to bother you at this hour of the morning, but what I have to tell you is of the upmost urgency."

Jax looked at Eden who, at that moment, was staring at the Persian-style Oriental area rug spread across the empress-green marble floor.

Jax's attention returned to Zhang.

"You told my houseman your visit here this morning has something to do with Sandreen," he said.

"Yes, sir, it does. If I may be so bold, Mr. Greeley, may I ask you to accompany me outside to my car?"

Jax looked at Eden and he saw a distraught, frightened, young woman.

"Miss Owens, is it?" Jax asked. Eden nodded dully. "May I offer you a cup of tea? You look all done in."

"No, thank you," Eden said softly, her eyes never meeting his.

Jax set his coffee cup down on a gold-leaf end table and said, "Why all the intrigue, Zhang?"

"Please, sir, just come with me. Everything will be explained then."

Jax led Zhang out through the opulent foyer. He opened the wide, etched glass doors and walked over to Zhang's shining black Maybach Zeppelin.

Running his hand across the sparkling hood, Jax said, "Snazzy car you have here, Zhang. Business must be good."

Zhang owned the Baishōfu Brothel. He had started there 20 years ago as a bodyguard, hired to protect the prostitutes. Although he was small in stature and did not have the usual appearance of a brawny enforcer, Zhang made up for his deficit by maintaining a fifth-degree black belt in Northland Kenpo Karate.

"Business is very good, Mr. Greeley," Zhang said humbly.

Then, in a moment, Zhang switched tracks.

"Please accept my most sincere condolences, sir," he said.

"Your condolences, Zhang, what are you talking about?"

Zhang opened the backdoor on the driver's side of the car and gestured politely at something in the backseat.

Jax came around and saw what appeared to be a pile of blankets lying on the backseat. Zhang reached down and pulled the top blanket back, exposing Sandreen's bruised face and her dull, lifeless stare. Jax's breath caught in his chest. For a moment, he had to steady himself. He said softly, "What happened to her?"

"I want Miss Owens to tell you that, sir," Zhang said.

"What does Miss Owens have to do with Sandreen, Zhang?" Jax asked, his voice now fueled with rage.

"Please, Mr. Greeley, let her tell you."

"I will do just that," Jax said, and he headed toward the house.

"Mr. Greeley?" Zhang asked. Jax turned and looked at him. "I was wondering, sir, what should I do with Miss Sandreen's remains?"

For a moment, Jax looked nonplussed. Then he cleared his throat loudly and he said, "Call Hui Ting and have him send for her body."

"Should I contact the authorities, sir?"

"No, Zhang. I prefer to handle this matter in my own way. Have I made myself perfectly clear?" Jax asked firmly.

"Indeed, you have, Mr. Greeley," Zhang said, and he bowed formally. Zhang pulled out his cellphone and dialed Hui Ting's Funeral Emporium.

"Tell me about Sandreen's death, Miss Owens," Jax said sharply.

"My name is Eden," she said softly. She handed Clayton's cellphone to Jax and said, "There is a video on this cellphone of Sandreen's rape and murder."

Jax sat down on a Qing Dynasty armchair opposite Eden.

"You were able to film Sandreen being murdered?" Jax asked incredulously. "Dammit! Why didn't you scream or yell for the police or do something to try to prevent it from happening?"

"Sandreen told me to hide and that's what I did," Eden said guiltily. "The cellphone doesn't belong to me, Mr. Greeley. It belongs to Clayton Caulder, and he filmed the video. I wouldn't blame you if you didn't want to see it. It's terrible."

"I want to see it," Jax said, and he watched quietly as his dear friend was raped. The video caught Clayton pushing off Sandmen's lifeless body.

When the video ended, Jax stood up and walked over to his Chinese-style writing desk. He pressed a button.

Eden stood in silence as a few minutes passed. A knock on the library door broke the silence.

"Come in," Jax said. The library door opened and Erik Rivera entered the room.

"Erik, this is Eden Owens," Jax said abruptly. "Eden, this is Erik Rivera."

"It is very nice to meet you, Miss Owens," Erik said politely.

"Please call me Eden."

"Sit down, Erik. I have something I want you to see." Erik sat down in the chair Jax formerly occupied, then Jax handed him Clayton's cellphone and started the video.

When the video ended, Erik lowered the cellphone and slowly lifted his gaze to Jax.

"Make a copy of the video," Jax said.

Erik excused himself and quickly left the room.

Jax judged Eden as timid, intelligent, and kind, but her clothes and her gestures denied any gilded sophistication and moneyed poise. Sandreen and Eden as friends seemed highly unlikely to him.

Jax resumed his seat across from Eden.

"Tell me, Eden. How did you meet Sandreen?"

"I met Sandreen when I boarded the ship for Studies Abroad. She was the cruise director."

So that was where Sandreen had been for the last few months, Jax thought.

"I've heard of the Studies Abroad program," Jax said. "It's very expensive, isn't it?"

"I'm sure it is. Ordinarily, I wouldn't have been able to go on such a trip, but I was given an all-inclusive scholarship."

"I'm sure you earned it. Now, Eden, tell me how you know Clayton Caulder?"

Eden's lip began to tremble.

"Clayton and I are from the same town in Illinois," she said nervously. "We also attended the same high school."

"So, he's your age? Which is, I'm guessing, 18?"

"Clayton is actually 19-and-a-half. He was at one time a year ahead of me in school. But in his sophomore year, he disappeared. I assume he didn't take any classes while he was gone, because when he finally returned, he and I were in the same grade."

"Was he ill?"

"I don't think so. A lot of folks in my hometown, which is Maramount, Illinois, sir, believe Clayton left town after a fight he had with Johnny Bradford. Clayton beat Johnny so badly with a club that Johnny lost the sight in his left eye."

"Do you think he ran away to avoid facing criminal charges?"

"Clayton has no fear of the law, Mr. Greeley. His father is Judge Maxwell Caulder who strikes terror in the heart of nearly everyone who stands before his bench. My brother, Rick, once got a D.U.I., and Judge Caulder sent him to Joliet prison for one year. Clayton, and a few of his friends, had several D.U.I.s, but theirs were all dismissed."

"It sounds to me like Judge Caulder is holding your town hostage."

"My dad says Judge Caulder is a dictator and he should be shot. My mother says Judge Caulder is a man who acquits the guilty for a bribe and denies justice to the innocent."

"Your father sounds impetuous," Jax said. "On the other hand, your mother sounds tolerant and reflective."

"That's my folks all right. The irony is, a few weeks ago, my mother was hired as Judge Caulder's housekeeper."

"Is that something you are okay with?" When she didn't answer, Jax asked, "Have you had problems with Clayton Caulder, Eden?"

Tears welled in Eden's eyes.

"Yes, sir."

"Would you care to talk about it?"

"Not really."

"I understand. Tell me about yourself and your family, Eden."

Apart from Alan, and her private journal that Mrs. Omaha read, Eden had never told anyone about her family. But she found Jax easy to talk to. For the next hour, Eden told Jax about her gentle mother, Isabelle, her sweet sister, Abby, her rebellious, troubled brother. Rick, and her angry, distant father, Clem.

"My father hits my mother," Eden said sadly. Then she quickly defended her father. "But he is always sorry afterward."

"Why do you think your mother stays with a man who hits her?"

"I believe she's scared. She isn't educated and she has nowhere else to go."

"I see."

Erik opened the door and came into the library. He had been standing outside the door for quite some time but knew better than to interrupt Jax when he was talking to Eden. He handed the cellphone to Jax who then handed it back to Eden.

"I don't want this back!" Eden said, looking at the cellphone in her hand like she had just been handed a rattlesnake.

"It will soon dawn on Clayton Caulder that he can contact you via his cellphone," Jax said.

Eden dropped the cellphone and she said, "Please don't make me talk to him!"

Jax ignored her plea.

"I heard a male voice in the background when I watched the video. Was someone with Clayton when he attacked Sandreen?"

"Ben Atler was there," Eden said flatly. "He's Clayton's best friend."

"Sit down, Eden," Jax said kindly.

Eden sat back down and she laid her hands in her lap and twisted them.

Jax reached over and patted her hands.

"You have nothing to be afraid of now," he promised.

As if prompted by a devilish cue, Clayton's cellphone lit up and a rap song howled.

Jax picked up the phone and saw Ben Atler's name and number appear. He held the phone out to Eden and said, "Answer it, Eden. And no matter what he says, stay calm."

Trembling, Eden took the phone.

"Turn on the speakerphone," Jax said softly.

Eden pressed the speakerphone button. She said nervously, "Hello."

"Hello, Eden darling!" Alan said.

"Alan!" Eden said and tears streamed down her face. "Where are you?"

"I'm waiting for you at the cat cafe, sweetheart. I came back for you and you were gone."

"Thank you, Alan, for caring enough to come back for me," Eden said tenderly.

"You mean more to me than words can say," Alan said, his voice filled with love." Where are you, darling? Clayton, Ben and I want to pick you up and take you back to the ship."

"I'm safe, Alan. Just talk to me. Okay?"

"Sure."

Eden wanted to warn Alan to get away from Clayton and Ben, but she feared Alan's reaction to the truth would have disastrous results.

"Ask him why he has Ben Atler's phone," Jax whispered.

"Why are you using Ben Atler's cellphone, Alan?"

"Clayton and Ben caught up with me on the ship. I had gone back there to ask for help. But Clayton intercepted me before I had a chance to get my phone or before I could speak to anyone. He said he and Ben had run into you in Lowtown and they said they offered to take you back to the ship, but you insisted that you wanted to wait where you were until I returned. Seriously, Eden, you should have come back with the two of them. Clayton also said he loaned you his phone. Otherwise, I might never have found you."

"Clever," Jax said softly.

"Eden, did Clayton and Ben tell you what happened to Sandreen Gavel?" Alan asked.

Eden paled and her hands shook and she looked like she might faint.

"What did you say, Alan?" Eden asked, her voice quivering.

"Did Clayton and Ben tell you about Sandreen?"

"I… I don't remember. You tell me, Alan."

"Sandreen has disappeared."

"Oh?"

"Eden, you sound upset. Are you all right?"

"Uh, sure."

"What I'm about to tell you was told to me by your roommate, Regan. So, consider the source. It seems that shortly after you and I left the ship this morning, Sandreen appeared on deck along with a load of suitcases. And just as she was departing the ship, Captain Evert showed up. He begged Sandreen not to leave. According to Regan, the captain and Sandreen were lovers. But rumor has it she quit her job yesterday and also ended her affair with the captain."

"And no one knows where she is now?"

Jax now had the answers to some unasked questions about Sandreen.

Thinking of Sandreen's broken body lying in the dark alley, Eden said sadly, "I'm sorry to hear that."

"Ask to speak to Clayton," Jax whispered. "Tell him you don't want Alan involved in this. Tell him to take Alan back to the ship. Then tell Clayton you'll meet him and Ben at ten o'clock tonight at the cat cafe."

Eden put her finger over the mouthpiece and she said, "That's after dark!"

"Trust me, Eden," Jax said.

Eden took a deep breath and let it out slowly.

"Alan, let me speak to Clayton," she said, sounding more confident than she felt.

"Eden wants to speak to you, Clayton," Alan said, and he handed him the cellphone.

"Hello, Eden," Clayton said, sounding cocky and sure of himself.

"I don't want Alan involved in this, Clayton. Take him back to the ship. I'll meet Ben and you at the cat cafe at ten o'clock tonight and I'll bring your cellphone with me."

Eden could hear Clayton walking across the dead leaves in the cat cafe. In the far distance, she could hear Alan questioning Ben about her odd behavior.

"Can you hear me, Eden?" Clayton spoke softly but firmly.

"Yes."

"If you're planning on calling the police, or if you already have called them, you'd better tell me now. Because if you're thinking about double-crossing me, Ben will see to it that your friend, Alan, dies a slow and painful death."

"Please don't hurt Alan!" Eden cried.

"Remember what I said," Clayton demanded, and he hung up.

Eden turned the cellphone off. She laid her head in her hands and softly wept.

"I'll have Tipay bring you a sandwich and a cup of herbal tea," Jax said. "After you have eaten, I want you to rest for a few hours." He took Eden's trembling hands into his and he said, "I give you my word, Eden, nothing will happen to you or to Alan. Now, try to relax," he said, his voice once again assuming his position of supreme authority.

"Erik, keep Eden company while she eats. Then show her to the guestroom in the east wing. I have a few calls to make. I want to see you in the library in exactly one hour."

Erik sat down across from Eden and he quickly engaged her in conversation about Studies Abroad.

Alone in the massive foyer, Jax dialed a number on his cellphone.

"Good morning, sir," Zhang said.

"I have a job for you, Zhang."

"Of course, Mr. Greeley."

Exactly one hour to the second, Erik joined Jax in the library. Jax handed Erik a stack of folders with different names on the flaps.

"Read these on the plane," Jax said. "If you have any questions, call me later tonight."

"Will do," Erik said, and he turned to leave.

"Be particularly brutal," Jax said.

Erik turned and smiled and he walked out the door.

# Twenty-Eight

A jagged bolt of lightning flashed across the darkening sky. Thunder violently shook the ground, echoing the likeness of wooden barrels filled with bricks rolling down a concrete driveway.

Isabelle pushed her kitchen curtain aside and peered at the angry sky. It had rained for a solid week and everything she saw was saturated with water. She looked at her pitiful vegetable garden which, at the moment, was underwater. *At least my garden will die an honorable death,* she thought, *instead of Clem running over my budding plants with the lawnmower.* She didn't mind the rain as much as she did the snow. On snowy days, Clem shoved her out of bed an hour early so she could shovel a path to the gas station for him.

Isabelle looked at the cat clock with the moving eyes on the wall. Five o'clock. That meant Clem would be coming around the side of the gas station at any minute. She took a deep breath and braced herself for another miserable night.

Clem ambled around the corner of the gas station, carrying a bulky gunny sack over his thick shoulder. He swung the sack off his shoulder and dumped its contents into a large barrel overflowing with discarded oil cans. Then, he rummaged through a pile of used transmission parts. He went back to the front of the gas station and returned carrying two used car tires which he threw on a mountain of old tires. Rubbing his filthy hands on his greasy orange coverall, he wiped his dirty forehead with his torn sleeve. Although the vile, black, sock hat on his head was soaked, Clem would not remove it until bedtime. Isabelle had often tried to wash the hat, but Clem insisted she keep her damn hands off of it.

Clem lumbered toward the house, adding another layer of thick mud to his rubber knee-boots.

As he neared the house, Isabelle stepped away from the window. She heard Clem's heavy steps cross the porch, and she hoped, this time, he would wipe his feet on the straw mat she had recently purchased at the Dollar Store with the money she earned as a housekeeper.

The backdoor opened and Clem came inside, stomping clods of mud across her clean kitchen floor.

As Isabelle watched silently, Clem unzipped his greasy coverall and pulled it down over his muddy boots. Wearing the same plaid shirt and faded jeans that he'd worn all week, Clem hung his coverall on a peg next to the door, ready for use the next day. He sat down on a wooden bench and pulled off his muddy boots and tossed them at the backdoor. He rolled his toes back and forth in his grungy Rockford socks and scratched his balls. Isabelle waited silently for the next stage of his familiar routine.

Clem sniffed the air and his expression turned mean.

"You made meatloaf again?" he asked sourly. "Every time I eat that slop, my piss and shit stinks for two days."

*One down and two to go,* Isabelle thought as she stirred the green beans.

Clem grunted and pulled himself up. With the lumbering gait of a Neanderthal, Clem dragged himself over to their 1980 Montgomery Ward refrigerator and opened the door. He pulled out a beer. Popping the top, he took a long swallow, belched loudly, and said, "This damn refrigerator ain't cooling like it used to."

Isabelle added butter to the mashed potatoes and waited for number three to complete this portion of Clem's latest rant.

Clem finished his beer, crushed the can, and threw it at the plastic trashcan. Missing the can by a good foot, he yelled, "Foul!"

He grabbed the newspaper and headed for the bathroom which was behind the door next to the kitchen.

Isabelle quickly wiped the mud off the floor. She placed the dirty rag on the basement knob. She gathered the table settings. Her heart sank. She missed Eden enormously. She set the plastic plates on the white laminate tabletop, followed by a knife and fork and spoon for Abby, Rick, and herself, but for Clem who ate meat with his hands, she laid out a large serving spoon.

Nearly everything Isabelle and Clem owned, they had inherited from Clem's parents. That included the gas station, the house, the threadbare, sagging furniture, the old-fashioned wringer washer, and a chrome dinette set.

Once, when Isabelle went to the library and borrowed one of their computers, she happened to see a chrome dinette set labeled 'retro' that looked exactly like theirs used to. The $1400 price tag astounded her. Of course, that table didn't have a nasty jagged scratch running across the table top and the vinyl chair seats weren't split open and oozing the stuffing.

The backdoor opened and Rick came inside, carrying his dirty boots in his hand. Isabelle almost ran over and kissed him for being so thoughtful.

"Hi, Mom," Rick said, setting his muddy boots on an old newspaper. He shed his leather coat, placing it on the peg farthest away from Clem's greasy coverall, and laid his cheap knockoff fedora on the wooden bench. Rick fussed with the hat, making sure it held the triangle finger imprints.

Rick, who had watched the 56th Annual Grammy Awards at his girlfriend, Gina's, house, first saw the hat worn by Pharrell Williams when he'd performed at the Grammy's. On Gina's home computer, Rick later Googled Pharrell Williams and saw the handsome young man wearing the enviable Vivienne Westwood Fedora.

Rick peeked under the lids on the simmering pans. "Looks great, Mom," he said, and he kissed her on the cheek.

Isabelle noticed the new tattoo of a skull and crossbones under Rick's left earlobe. And on his forearm, he had added Gina's name to his collection of tattoos. She knew he carried the inked names of two other girls on his body.

Rick walked over to the refrigerator and got a beer. After a swig, he sniffed the air and said, "I can smell Dad's home."

"I can hear you, Smartass," Clem yelled from the bathroom. The toilet flushed and Clem walked out with his pants belted higher on his waist.

"Use the Glade!" Rick said, fanning the air.

Clem walked past him and smacked him on this side of his head. He walked over to the sink and washed his dirty hands in the clean dishwater.

"Rick," Isabelle said softly. "Tell Abby it's time for dinner."

"Time for dinner, Abby!" Rick yelled from his chair.

"Not like that," Isabelle said disapprovingly.

"Might know you'd not do it right enough for Miss Mary Manners here," Clem said.

Rick used his dirty fingernail to dislodge something stuck between his canine and first bicuspid.

"Wash your hands, dear," Isabelle said, "particularly if you're going to put them in your mouth."

"Listen to your mother, Rick," Clem said contemptuously. "Don't forget to wash your hands, sit up straight, brush your teeth, go to bed early, and don't screw bad girls."

Abby came bouncing into the kitchen as Isabelle silently dipped food into serving bowls and set them on the table.

Abby sat down next to Rick and said, "Guess what I learned today, Rick."

"Okay. Can you give me a hint?"

"I learned a German word," Abby said eagerly.

"A German word, huh? Like maybe, Heil Hitler," Rick said smartly.

That got a laugh out of Clem.

"No, Silly, I learned the word for a cute little girl, like me," Abby said sweetly.

"Tell Momma the word," Isabelle said.

Abby turned her cherubic face to her mother and she said proudly, "The word is *Liebchen*, Momma."

"That's a lovely word, sweetheart," Isabelle said as she set the bowls of hot food on the table.

Clem grabbed the bowls and filled his plate. Shoveling the food into his mouth, he said, "I know a couple of German words myself, Abby."

Isabelle cringed, fearing the worst.

"Tell me, Daddy," Abby said excitedly.

"One word is *arschloch*," he said, still chewing, then he grabbed another handful of meatloaf and dumped it on his plate. "And the other word is *vollarsch*."

"What do they mean, Daddy?" Abby asked.

"*Arschloch* means asshole. And *vollarsch* means total asshole!" he said, and he opened his overflowing mouth and roared with laughter.

Rick laughed so hard, he spat his food across the table. But Abby ran to Isabelle and started to cry.

"Momma says we're not supposed to say those bad words," Abby said from the folds of her mother's faded dress.

"Your Momma's got no sense of humor," Clem said, still chewing.

Isabelle patted her sweet daughter on the head and she said, "Sit down, Abby, and finish your dinner."

"Could I take my dinner to my room, Momma?" Abby whined.

"No, you cannot, Young Lady!" Clem roared. "I work hard all day for this family and I am not going to be ignored when I get home. Now, get over here and eat your food!"

Isabelle led Abby back to the table and she sat down next to her daughter to offer her comfort, but Abby's appetite, like her mother's, had fled.

Clem finished his meal and scooted his chair back across the worn places cut into the linoleum. He loosened his belt, belched loudly, and drank the last of his iced tea.

Looking at Abby's untouched plate, Clem said, "If you don't want to eat that's okay by me, but don't think for one minute that your mother is going to sneak food up to you later tonight."

Clem shot Isabelle a warning glare.

"May I be excused, Momma?" Abby asked tearfully.

"Just get up and go!" Clem shouted at Abby, and he knotted his fist and shook it at Isabelle.

When Abby had hurried from the room, Clem turned to Isabelle and he said venomously, "You think you're smarter than me because you've read some books. But you're not! You and your highfalutin' ways have turned them two girls into sniveling crybabies! And you've made them despise their own father."

Clem moved threateningly closer to Isabelle. "I've had it with all your shit and I'm not gonna stand for it any more. I'm layin' down the law right now. You better believe it! The first new rule in this house is you're never again takin' Eden and Abby to that holy roller church of yours. I can see it's had a bad influence on you and them girls."

Rick could see his father's rage building and he knew, any second, Clem would fly out of his chair and start beating his mother.

In many ways, Rick could be as cruel and as heartless as Clem. But when it came to protecting his mother and his two sisters from his vicious father, Rick usually rallied.

"What about me, Dad?" Rick asked, trying to disarm his father's rage.

"What about you, Rick!?" Clem shouted, his eyes were glazed over, his breath pounded in his chest, and he looked about, ready to explode.

"Can I go to Mom's church?" Rick asked innocently.

Nonplussed, Clem stared at his handsome son.

"What the hell are you talking about?" Clem asked.

Rick was pleased to see some of his father's raging torque had eased.

"I asked if I can still go to Mom's church with her."

"When did you get religion?" Clem asked snidely.

"Well, I don't know that I got religion. What I got is the hots for Marianne Beasley who happens to go to Mom's church."

Clem threw his head back and roared with laughter.

Rick looked over at his relieved mother and he winked.

"You're one sneaky son of a bitch," Clem said, and he reached across the table and playfully slapped Rick's face.

"Let's go watch the St. Louis Cardinals, Dad," Rick said, and he and Clem headed for the living room where they watched the baseball game on their 25-inch box television.

Isabelle finished washing the dishes. She locked the backdoor and turned off the kitchen light. Hidden inside a stack of folded towels, Isabelle had a sandwich and a small bottle of homemade chocolate milk for Abby. As she passed through their shabby living room, Clem reached out and he roughly grabbed her arm.

"Put them towels down," Clem said. Isabelle set the towels on a chair, praying Clem wouldn't notice the sandwich and bottle of milk. Clem ran his rough hands up and down her body, paying close attention to her private places which he rubbed a little too hard.

"Just checking to see if you're trying to smuggle food into Abby," he said lustily.

Rick saw an edge of the sandwich peeking out from between the towels. He stood up and picked up the towels and held them tightly against him.

"You look tired, Mom. I'll put these away for you. Besides, I wanted to say goodnight to Abby."

Isabelle looked nervously at her son, and Rick winked at her for the second time tonight.

When Rick left the room, Clem grabbed a handful of Isabelle's crotch.

"I'm comin' to bed shortly," he said greedily.

Repulsed, Isabelle stepped back and Clem's hand dropped to his side. She walked away.

Clem knotted his fists and silently vowed he would once and for all break Isabelle of her haughty ways.

Isabelle opened Abby's bedroom door and, startled, Abby quickly hid her sandwich under her pillow.

"It's just me, sweetheart," Isabelle said.

"I was afraid you were Daddy checking up on me," Abby said nervously.

Isabelle hated the stress and humiliation her children had to endure because of Clem's bad moods and his general meanness.

"Finish your sandwich, darling," Isabelle said, sitting down on Abby's bed next to her.

Abby quickly finished her sandwich and drank her chocolate milk. Wiping her pretty mouth on her pajama sleeve, she said, "Momma, did you know they make chocolate milk that's already mixed up at the grocery store?"

"I did know that, Abby."

"But you always pour brown syrup into my milk. Why don't you buy the other kind?"

"The way I make chocolate milk is cheaper than the store-bought kind, dear."

Abby thought about her mother's answer. Then she said, "Are we poor, Momma?"

"It depends on whose standard you are comparing us to, Abby. In America, I suppose we are considered poor. But in some third-world countries, I am sure there are families who have it much worse than we do."

"Why did Daddy say those bad words tonight at supper?"

How could she explain a crass, ignorant bully to her sweet daughter, and what made it even more difficult was that Clem was Abby's father.

"I don't know how to answer that, Abby," Isabelle said sadly.

"You don't like Daddy much, do you, Momma?"

Isabelle had tried to hide her feelings about Clem from her children, but she'd obviously failed.

"Why do you say that, Abby?"

"Well, I've seen Daddy get real mad and hit you. And I wouldn't like him if he hit me."

Isabelle hugged Abby tightly.

"Do you know how much I love you?" she asked, kissing her daughter's shining, blonde hair.

"A bushel and a peck?" Abby asked, and she giggled.

"A bushel and a peck and a hug around the neck!" Isabelle said, and she laid her daughter back and tickled her tummy.

The door opened and an ominous portent entered with Clem.

"Go to sleep now, Abby," he said.

"Yes, Daddy," Abby said soberly.

Clem stood at the door, staring at Isabelle.

"Goodnight, sweetheart," Isabelle said, and she kissed Abby on her flushed cheek.

Isabelle got up and silently passed by Clem who closed Abby's door behind her. With profound dread, Isabelle walked the 12 steps to the bedroom she shared with Clem.

Clem followed her into the bedroom, shut the door, and locked it. Facing away from him, Isabelle closed her eyes and held her breath. Clem came up behind her and he roughly started removing her clothing. Isabelle gritted her teeth and forced herself not to scream. When he had taken everything off of her except her bra and panties, he picked her up and threw her across the bed. He yanked his clothes off, and, standing naked before her, he pointed to his inflamed erection.

"I can't, Clem," Isabelle said and she started to cry.

Clem's nostrils flared and his eyes narrowed. He reached out and grabbed Isabelle by her hair and he dragged her face down to his foul-smelling crotch.

"Do it!" he ordered, and he pressed Isabelle's closed mouth against his oozing fetid penis.

On a few occasions before when she had refused Clem's demands, he had dragged Abby, Eden, and Rick, when he was younger, into their bedroom and made them watch while their mother begged for his forgiveness on her knees. Isabelle thought of Abby and how frightened she had been of Clem tonight. She couldn't bear to see her precious daughter terrorized by him. With tears streaming down her pale cheeks, Isabelle opened her mouth.

# Twenty-Nine

Heading down Jax's long, winding, asphalt driveway, a silent Chinese man drove a dusty, black-paneled truck carrying Eden. This was the exact place that ten years earlier, Jax had bought four properties on Wukang Road, formerly known as the French Concession. Originally situated on the land were four houses. He had them all torn down and rebuilt into a single palace.

Although he owned a second palatial residence in Shanghai, this home on Wukang Road was his favorite. The black truck passed through the manned, wrought-iron gates, then drove past a row of lovely houses with lush, well-kept lawns which were shaded by beautiful, French Wutong Trees.

Just yesterday, Eden thought tearfully, *I was happier than I have ever been in my life. Alan and I visited the magnificent YuYuan Gardens with The Grand Rickery in the center. We went to The Jade Buddha Temple, and we saw the 19th century White Jade Buddhas. We both loved the cultural walk through the fashionable Xin Tian Di in the heart of the city.*

Straight ahead, Eden saw Shantytown wrought with the crumbling apartment buildings called lilongs. Eden's heart went out to the people whose overwhelming poverty had sentenced them to a life of such despair. Erik had told Eden that Shanghai has a population of 23-million people. As many as eight million of those residents live in Shantytown's deplorable slums. On the few occasions Eden had complained to her mother about their poor living conditions, her mother said, "Be thankful for what we do have, Eden, because there are people in this world so much worse off than we are." Eden never thought her mother's admonishment held much truth. That was until she saw Shantytown.

Trying to distance herself from what lay ahead, Eden thought about Alan's promise to take her today to The Botanical Gardens, The Ocean Aquarium, and Shanghai Tower. The place she most wanted to see, however, was the

Oriental Pearl T.V. Tower with the three metallic spheres. Alan suggested that they'd sing karaoke on the lowest floor of the Oriental Pearl T.V. Tower. Alan wanted to take Eden for dinner at the rotating restaurant called The Jewel. After dinner, he wanted to surprise Eden by going to the top floor so they could stand on the Observation Deck and enjoy the magnificent view of The Bund and the Huangpu River.

Tears filled Eden's eyes. *I am with a man I don't know or trust, driving down a dark street in Shantytown, going to meet Clayton Caulder, a murderer, in a blackened, deserted cat cafe. And there's no one here to protect me,* Eden thought. As they neared their destination, the driver slowed down the truck. The streets were nearly deserted, leaving Eden to surmise that all the really scary people were inside, fulfilling their evil pleasures. Eden saw the battered Saab that Ben had driven the night before parked alongside the curb in front of the dark cat cafe. But nowhere did she see Clayton or Ben.

The driver pulled the truck up behind the Saab and stopped, leaving the engine running. He motioned for Eden to get out, but when she refused to move, he reached over and opened Eden's door and sharply spoke something to her in Chinese.

"Are you sure Mr. Greeley instructed you to leave me here alone?" Eden asked, and her voice quivered. The small man nodded slowly. Fear gave her new resolve.

"I'm not getting out of this truck. You take me back to Mr. Greeley's house this minute!" Eden said, and she folded her arms across her chest and sat, defiantly staring ahead.

The man got out of the truck and went around to the passenger-side door. He opened the back passenger door, dragged Eden out, and dropped her onto the buckled sidewalk. He turned, jumped back into the truck, locked the door, and drove off.

Terrified, Eden jumped up and started to run, but Clayton stepped out of the shadows.

"Long time no see, Scribbler," Clayton said, and he had a cruel look on his face.

Eden looked nervously around for Ben.

"If you're looking for Ben, he's hiding behind that deserted storefront across the street," he pointed, "waiting to see if you brought the cops with you."

"I'm alone," Eden said, instantly regretting her candor.

"Hand over my cellphone," Clayton said, and he held out his large hand.

Sauntering out of the dark, the cat that kept Eden company the night before began rubbing its long body against Clayton's leg. Clayton savagely kicked the cat and sent it flying into the street.

Eden wanted to help the crying cat, but, instead, she stood frozen to the spot, watching Clayton, trying to anticipate his next move.

"Give me my damn phone!" he shouted.

"You killed Sandreen, Clayton," Eden said boldly.

"It was an accident, as you well know!"

"When you raped her, was that an accident too?"

"There's something you don't understand, Eden. Ever since we got on the ship, Sandreen threw herself at me. Then when I made my move, she acted all coy and uninterested."

The cat limped over and, this time, nervously stood next to Eden's leg.

"I don't believe you, Clayton," Eden said.

"You don't have to believe me," he said, moving menacingly closer to her.

The cat hissed and threw its wounded body at Clayton's leg. Clayton viciously kicked the cat again with his booted foot and, this time, the poor thing didn't get up.

"You're the meanest person I know!" Eden said, and, suddenly, she didn't feel as afraid of Clayton because he lacked Ben's hulking support.

Clayton reached for Eden's backpack and Eden ripped her backpack off her shoulders and swung it wildly at Clayton's head, knocking him sideways. Clayton righted himself, and, with a cruel smile, he said, "I like a woman who challenges me. Never thought you had it in you, Scribbler, but this is going to be fun."

Eden held her ground, holding her backpack in front of her like a weapon.

"I'm not done with you yet," Clayton said, and he jumped on Eden and threw her to the ground.

From the back of the dark café, a loud roar erupted and a band of men burst onto the scene. They wore military, tactical, camouflage uniforms, military boots, night-vision goggles, and black, skull-face masks. Each man carried a sheathed machete strapped to his side and an AK-47 assault rifle.

Two men grabbed Clayton and lifted him off Eden. Clayton fought the men, but one man kicked Clayton in the face and that quieted him down.

Two men dragged Ben across the cafe floor, his wrists were bound behind him with zip ties and his legs were held together with heavy leg irons. Around Ben's thick neck, a man behind him tightly held a wire garrote.

A black van came to a screeching halt in front of the cafe. The two holding Clayton picked him up, three men picked up Ben, and, together, they were thrown into the back of the van. After the backdoors of the van were slammed shut and locked, the mercenaries all climbed into the van and the vehicle sped away.

Eden stood whimpering, her eyes wide, her heart hammering, and her whole body shook violently.

Jax walked out of the darkness.

Eden turned to look at him, her eyes as big as saucers.

"Were you here the whole time?" she asked, her voice trembling.

"I was."

Eden's fear turned to fury and she said, "Why did you do this?"

"Tonight, you learned a very valuable lesson, Eden."

Eden picked up her backpack and she strapped it on her shoulders.

"You have been very kind to me, Mr. Greeley, and I wish it was in my power to repay you. But I don't understand why you forced me to meet Clayton here tonight."

"You could have run away, you could have cried, you could have conceded. Instead, you fought. And that makes me very proud of you, Eden. Now, you are free of Clayton Caulder and his kind forever."

For the first time in her life, Eden understood why her mother was still living under the total domination of brutish, cold-blooded Clem. No one had ever made Isabelle believe she could stand on her own two feet.

"Thank you, Mr. Greeley!" Eden said, and she hugged Jax tightly.

Jax held Eden at arm's length and said, "After a hug like that, I think you better call me Jax."

Eden giggled and tears of relief filled her eyes. For the first time since she'd met Jax, Eden considered how good looking he was.

"I'd like to go find Alan now," she said, and her face bloomed with love.

Jax called for his car.

A long, black limousine with darkened windows pulled up and stopped next to the ship's gangplank.

"Thank you, Jax, for everything," Eden said, seated next to Jax in the back of the limousine.

"You're welcome, Eden. Will you continue your studies, or will you return home?"

"I'll continue my studies. I hope I do well, then perhaps I'll be accepted to a fine college."

"Good luck to you."

Eden started to get out of the car, paused, and turned to look at Jax.

"What's going to happen to Clayton and Ben?" she asked.

"Do you really want to know?"

"No, I don't think I do. I'll never see you again, will I, Jax?"

Eden's gaze searched Jax's unexpressive face.

"I will never tell anyone about you and what happened over the last two days."

"You're a smart girl."

"I don't know anything about you. I don't even know if Jax Greeley is your real name. But this much I do know. If I am ever in trouble again, I hope you show up as my knight in shining armor," Eden said, and she hugged Jax and kissed his cheek.

Eden got out of the car, and she stood on the dock and watched until Jax's limousine drove out of sight.

# Thirty

When Eden boarded the ship, she went straight to Alan's room. She anxiously knocked on the door, but no one answered. Although she was embarrassed by her disheveled appearance, she still took the time to search the ship, paying close attention to their special hideaways. He was nowhere to be found.

Eden went to her stateroom. She noticed that Regan was gone. She dumped her backpack on her bed, making sure her scrapbook was still in good condition, and pulled off her soiled clothing. She took a long hot shower in the tiny bathroom. She put on a pair of cutoffs, a gray t-shirt, and a pair of flip-flops.

She brushed her teeth and pulled her clean hair into a clip. She didn't need blusher because her cheeks were already rosy with anticipation of seeing Alan. She put on a light pink gloss that Regan had given to her on the night of the captain's ball.

Regan burst into the room. "Hey, Roomie!" she squealed. "Where the hell have you been?!"

"Alan and I got lost. It took me a while to find my way back here."

"It's always a mistake to take a small town girl and let her run wild in a large city," Regan sniped. She was bursting with nervous energy. "Say, have you heard the news?"

"What news is that?" Eden asked, placing her soiled clothing in a burlap bag. Regan threw herself down on her unmade bed.

"Well, those two guys from your hometown, Ben Atler and Clayton Caulder, called it quits on Studies Abroad. Ali Summers is the one who told me. Remember her? She's such a gossip. She was kind of dating Ben Atler. She said he was a real drag.

"Anyway, she said Clayton called his dad and told him he was ditching the program.

"Ben called his folks and cut out too. It doesn't surprise me Ben followed Clayton. Those two always acted like they were connected at the hip." Regan scooted across her bed and sat with her feet dangling over the side.

"Ali told me something else and it's really juicy," Regan said, lowering her voice like a delighted conspirator. "Sandreen Gavel, the cruise director, quit her job. And, according to Ali, Sandreen and Captain Evert were having an affair!"

Eden felt guilty listening to Regan's tales, knowing Sandreen was dead.

"I'm sorry to hear that," Eden said, and she continued straightening her clothes in her battered suitcase.

"May I borrow your cellphone, Regan?" Eden asked.

"Sure," Regan said, and she handed Eden her smartphone.

Eden dialed Alan's number.

"Hello," he answered.

"Hello, Alan. Where are you?"

"Eden! I am on the ship, waiting for you," Alan said, his voice bursting with excitement.

"I'm on the ship too."

"That's great news. Can you meet me for lunch after classes? I was going to ditch them looking for you! We'll have all afternoon to talk."

"Sounds great," Eden said and put together her backpack for the day's studies, trying to forget the whirlwind of events that led up to this day.

"Thanks," Eden said, and she handed Regan's phone back to her.

"It's a good thing a nice, innocent girl like you met a quiet guy like Alan Honnecut," Regan said. "Otherwise, this would have been the most boring trip of your life!"

Eden smiled. But in her heart, she knew her innocence had been forever shattered.

# Thirty-One

The rented, white Lexus S.U.V. moved slowly along the long, paved road under a canopy of towering, red, maple trees. Driving the vehicle was a clean-shaven man with short, dark hair, dressed in a navy serge suit, black wingtip shoes, and black-framed eyeglasses. He checked his appearance in the rearview mirror, pulled his lips back to check his teeth, reflecting his distinctive overbite and his bulbous nose.

At the end of the shaded boulevard, the man saw Judge Maxwell Caulder's comfortable home. *The house has the cozy ambiance of upper middle-class domestic tranquility,* he thought. The man stopped the Lexus in front of the house. He turned the car engine off, got out, straightened and buttoned his suit jacket, and reached for his briefcase.

He strolled up the bluestone sidewalk, climbed the cobblestone steps, and immediately noticed the wireless video-doorbell-intercom system next to the twin, mahogany-beveled glass door. He pushed the button.

"Yes?" a pleasant female voice asked.

"I have an appointment with Judge Caulder at ten this morning," the man said agreeably.

"And what is your name sir?"

"Reardan Gomez."

"Just a moment please."

As he waited, the man looked the house and grounds over more closely. Through the leaded, beveled glass doors, the man watched a tall, thin, attractive woman dressed in a maid's uniform walking across the spacious marble foyer. She opened the door and smiled.

"Judge Caulder will see you now, Mr. Gomez," she said, and she stepped aside to allow him to enter. She closed the door behind him and he followed the clean-smelling woman, meticulously cataloging everything he saw.

She knocked on a heavy, carved door and a man's stern voice said, "Come in!"

The woman opened the door and Gomez walked into a sunless room paneled with exotic ebony hardwood and lined with bookcases. A seating arrangement consisted of two camel-colored leather wing-chairs separated by a marble-capped end table and a Tiffany lamp, all set neatly on a wool Oriental rug in front of an inactive stone fireplace.

Seated like a president behind a hand-carved, mahogany desk with a maroon leather top, Judge Caulder turned the Tiffany desk lamp higher and looked up at his visitor.

"Bring us some coffee, Isabelle," Judge Caulder said sharply.

"Yes, sir," she answered, and she closed the door softly.

"This is a beautiful room," Gomez said.

"I like it. Sit down, Mr. Gomez."

"If it's all the same to you, Judge Caulder, I prefer to stand."

"Suits me. I'm accustomed to people standing when they appear before me."

There was a soft knock on the door and Isabelle entered, carrying a silver coffee service.

"You may serve my coffee, Isabelle, but Gomez here prefers to stand," Judge Caulder said coldly.

Isabelle poured coffee into two cups and she politely placed Judge Caulder's coffee cup and saucer on the left side of his desk in front of him.

Gomez declined her kind offer.

"You do your job so delicately," Gomez said to Isabelle.

"Thank you, sir," Isabelle said, and she looked up at him, fully noticing his face, which was his intention.

"Leave us!" Judge Caulder ordered Isabelle.

Humiliation stained Isabelle's face and she quietly left the room.

"I was told by your assistant that you wanted to see me today concerning some property I own on Paradise Island," Judge Caulder said bluntly.

"Tidewater Manor is one of the most beautiful compounds I have ever seen," Gomez said. "It is a 15-thousand square-foot mansion, situated on ten acres of well-tended lawns and decorated with Red-twig Dogwood trees, fragrant Mimosa trees, white oaks, Mock orange shrubbery, Bluebeard arboretum, and Forsythia hedges. There are eight bedrooms, 12 bathrooms, a winter and a summer kitchen, an indoor swimming pool with a panjea Jacuzzi, a massage area, a workout room, a theater room with a 30-foot screen, a formal and informal dining room, and an enclosed hothouse."

"You sound like one of those ridiculous real-estate promotional advertisements."

"That is no doubt true," Gomez said, moving closer to the judge's desk.

"State your case, Gomez. I'm a busy man."

"I too am a busy man, Judge Caulder."

"Be that as it may, are you interested in purchasing my property on Paradise Island? That question requires a yes or no answer," Judge Caulder said impatiently.

"In that case, my answer is… No," Gomez said.

Judge Caulder stood to his feet, his face purple with rage.

"This meeting is over!" he shouted.

Gomez dragged an armchair over and placed it in front of Judge Caulder's desk and coolly sat down. Looking quite comfortable in his surroundings, Gomez said calmly, "Your son, Clayton, has been kidnapped."

Judge Caulder held Gomez's cold gaze with an equally frigid stare of his own.

"You're full of shit," he said through clenched teeth. "Now, you get out of my house before I call the police!"

"It must be quite a challenge to sustain your extravagant lifestyle on a sitting judge's yearly salary."

"Who the hell are you?!" he shouted.

"Today, my name is Reardan Gomez. Tomorrow, it will be some other name that I use."

Judge Caulder reached for the telephone on his desk and he quickly dialed a number.

Gomez took out his cellphone and he turned the screen toward Judge Caulder.

"Does this young man look familiar?" he asked quietly.

Judge Caulder saw a picture of Clayton tied to a chair with a blindfold across his eyes.

"Maramount Police Station," a voice on the phone said. "How may I direct your call?"

"Aren't you going to answer her, Judge?" Gomez asked fiendishly.

Judge Caulder slowly replaced the telephone on the base. He sat down in his chair and folded his hands on the desk in front of him.

With a vicious leer, he said, "I am not going to pay you a ransom for my son."

"When I came into this house, I didn't see anything that represents the family who lives here. There are no family pictures, none of your son, Clayton. I see no display of Clayton's many football trophies. And absent from your desk is a smiling picture of your wife, Rose.

"I am not at all surprised that you would refuse to pay money to free your son. Clayton has caused a lot of trouble for you over the years, hasn't he, Judge Caulder?"

"I will not discuss my son with you."

"Then I will discuss Clayton with you. Two years ago, Clayton beat Johnny Bradford so badly, he put out his eye. Concerned about the repercussions of such a cruel act, to rid yourself of Clayton, you sent him away to that despicable military camp in New Guinea. Translated, I believe, it was called 'Alter the behavior of violent boys.' But those savages at the camp did not alter Clayton's demeanor. In fact, his experience there made him much worse. I expect any young man's rage would explode if he was forced to hold his piss and march for hours in the blazing sun, or be shot at with air-guns like those they use on cattle, or be made to stand naked in the rain with a bucket on his head while his fellow prisoners ran by him and pounded the bucket with heavy metal rods."

"As I said, I will not discuss my son with you, Gomez," Judge Caulder said acidly.

"As you wish," Gomez said. "The truth is, I am not here to demand a ransom for Clayton. Clayton will pay for his own mistakes. I am here to offer you a choice. I will show you a way to make amends for your many transgressions. Including, being such a poor father to your son."

"GET OUT OF MY HOUSE!" Judge Caulder roared, and he jumped to his feet and came threateningly at Gomez.

Gomez reached into his briefcase and he pulled out a small object.

"Before you do something you will live to regret, insert this into your computer and watch what it contains," Gomez said, and he handed a zip drive to the judge.

Judge Caulder grabbed the zip drive and walked angrily back to his desk. He placed the instrument into his computer and watched as his disgusting hidden life was factually exposed.

20 minutes later, the judge pulled the zip drive out of the computer and closed the lid on his laptop. He then tossed the zip drive at Gomez.

Gomez tossed it back. "Keep it," he said. "I have many copies."

"What do you want?" Judge Caulder asked, his voice considerably less commanding.

"Do you want to discuss a ransom now?" Gomez asked smugly.

The judge said nothing.

"Sexual exploitation of children is a serious crime, as you well know," Gomez said. "So is extortion, money laundering, insider trading, drug trafficking, and tax evasion."

Judge Caulder's nostrils flared, his eyes narrowed, and his gaze at Gomez intensified.

"Currently, you have unclaimed money totaling 22-million dollars in banks in the Bahamas, Hong Kong, Bahrain, and Singapore. You and your entourage are structuring your deposits into smaller amounts so the authorities do not become suspicious. As you well know, in the United States, the amount of money one deposits into any account cannot exceed $10,000 without that transaction being reported to the government."

"What...do...you...want?" Judge Caulder seethed.

"What do I want, you asked? Using your P.I.N. code, Personal Identification Number, you will be given a B.I.C., Bank Identifier Code, and an I.B.A.N., an International Bank Account Number, and using SWIFT, the Society for Worldwide Interbank Financial Telecommunications, you will transfer all the money you currently have in offshore accounts to a numbered account in Zurich, Switzerland. You will sell your houses, your furniture, Rose's jewelry, and your expensive vehicles. You are then to donate all of the money those items redeemed and give the cash to a charity concerned with helping battered women and exploited children."

Gomez noticed a malevolent thought flash in Judge Caulder's eye.

"Did you think I had forgotten about your federal pensions?" Gomez asked.

Judge Caulder's pulse increased and he struggled to breathe.

"F.E.R.S., aka the Federal Employees Retirement System, and T.S.P., aka the Thrift Savings Plan. You will combine those two pensions, take a lump sum settlement, and donate the money to food shelters and the homeless."

"That will never happen!" Judge Caulder said, and he picked up his computer and threw it at Gomez.

Gomez jumped out of his chair and narrowly dodged being hit.

"It will happen, Judge Caulder, or you will spend the rest of your life in prison! And I hear the convicts are particularly fond of child molesters."

Gomez picked up his briefcase and pulled out a cellphone.

"I am leaving this untraceable cellphone with you," he said, and he laid the phone on the desk in front of Judge Caulder. "I will know if you have completed the money transfers. I will closely monitor the remaining items you are to attend to."

"Have you considered the people who are involved in this enterprise with me?" Judge Caulder asked.

"You mean Terrance Mills, the banker, and Barbara Reynolds, the social worker, and Officers John Tardy and Joseph Embers, and Dr. Clare Powers? Yes, we are aware."

Judge Caulder lowered his large head and laid it in his hands. "How do you expect Rose and me to support ourselves?" he asked miserably.

"In honor of all the needy senior citizens who came to court and stood before you pleading for justice, but found none, you and your wife will learn how it feels to survive solely on social security."

Gomez walked toward the door. He turned and looked once again at the room and at the defeated man seated behind the desk.

"This is a nice house," Gomez said, and he opened the door and closed it behind him.

# Thirty-Two

Naked, starved, and freezing, Ben huddled in the corner of his thickly dark cell as Clayton's shrieking screams were transmitted over the blaring speaker. For days now, they hadn't eased up on Clayton. Ben often heard Clayton begging his captors, whimpering and then his piercing wails for mercy. He shuddered when he heard the sounds of rushing water, the sharp bite and sizzle of electricity, and a loud snap that sounded like a bone being crushed. The mercenaries hadn't yet come to his cell and taken him to their torture chamber, but he lived in constant fear of their arrival.

Without warning, the room went deadly silent.

"Ben Atler," a frightening voice with a strange inflection called. "We are coming for you."

"Nooooooo!" Ben cried out, and he shivered in his corner like a rat caught in a hole.

Every two minutes for the next several days, the voice warned Ben of their imminent arrival. "Ben Atler. We are coming for you."

Ben's cell door finally opened, and a bright light focused on him as he sat in the corner, muttering to himself, terrified of the sudden silence.

"Come forward, Prisoner!" an irate voice ordered.

Ben fell sideways and lay shivering in a fetal position.

"Get up, you filthy sack of shit!" the voice demanded, but Ben was so paralyzed with fear, he couldn't stand.

Three men came into the cell and they roughly hauled a much-slimmer Ben to his bleeding feet. With excessive force, they dragged him out of the cell, down a long concrete corridor and into a brightly lit room filled with instruments of torture. Whimpering, Ben wet himself when his eyesight adjusted just enough to see Clayton's battered body hanging on a metal rack. He looked dead, but Ben saw his shallow breathing.

As the men strapped Ben to a steel chair, Ben saw Clayton's once-black hair had turned as white as snow, his left eye socket was sunken and empty, and his right leg looked broken. He was missing several teeth, and on his left hand, two fingers were gone.

Ben wailed and struggled to pull away from his captors, but a sharp punch to his temple quietened him down.

"Ben Atler," the strange voice called.

One of the guards grabbed Ben's head and forced him to look up. He saw a shadowy figure standing in the skybox above him.

"Can you hear me, Ben Atler?" the voice asked.

"Yes," Ben said softly. A guard punched Ben in the stomach and told him to speak louder. "Yes!" Ben said, but his voice sounded strangled.

"Do you see your friend, Clayton Caulder?" the voice demanded. Ben turned his head slowly and looked at Clayton. "Yes, I see him," Ben said, his voice trembling.

"Are you Clayton's best friend?"

Ben was afraid to admit the truth, fearing his fate might be as bad as Clayton's.

"I've known him for a long time," Ben said.

"That was not the question, Dumbass," a burly guard said, and he kicked Ben's bare shin with his steel-toe boot.

Ben wailed and pulled his legs in under the chair.

"Is that still your answer?" the voice asked.

"Yes, I'm Clayton's best friend," Ben said, defeated.

"Were you with him the night he brutally killed Sandreen Gavel?"

"Yes, I was with him."

"Did you try to stop him from murdering her?"

"Yes, I tried. But Clayton has a mind of his own," Ben said. Ben wasn't sure his former statement was true any longer. Now when Ben looked at Clayton, he saw nothing reminiscent of his best friend.

"I didn't do anything to Sandreen!" Ben wailed.

"Perhaps not. But you weren't strong enough to stop your friend from harming Sandreen."

"Please, please, don't hurt me!" Ben wailed.

"Have we hurt you yet?" the voice asked almost soothingly.

"I'm sorry for what happened to Sandreen," Ben pleaded. "And if I had my life to live over again, I would never have anything to do with Clayton Caulder!"

"Are you saying this to avoid punishment?"

"Yes! But it is also the truth!"

"Take that miserable piece of shit down from the rack," the voice ordered.

Two guards walked over and they unfastened the chains that held Clayton to the rack. When his body dropped to the ground, the guards picked him up and dragged him over to a steel chair next to a wooden table. The guards propped him up on the chair and stepped away.

Clayton's head slowly turned toward Ben and he stared dully at him with his one eye. Ben saw no recognition whatsoever in Clayton's gaze.

"Proceed," the voice instructed.

A guard laid a pistol on the table in front of Clayton.

Ben looked around in alarm. Did they mean for Clayton to shoot him, he thought desperately.

"Clayton Caulder," the voice called. Clayton slowly raised his wobbly head and looked in the direction of the skybox.

"I now give you two choices. You may take the gun and end your own life. Or, you will spend the rest of your natural life here."

Clayton seemed unable to make any decisions. For several minutes, everyone in the room watched silently. Slowly, Clayton reached for the pistol, he raised the gun to his temple and pulled the trigger.

Ben shuttered and screamed. But when he looked at Clayton, nothing had happened.

Clayton still held the gun against his temple and he fired it again, and again, and again. But nothing happened. He kept firing the gun until a guard reached over and took the gun away from him.

"Ben!" the voice said.

"Yes, sir," Ben said and his eyes flew to the skybox.

"If we let you go, you are never to speak about anything that happened here. Is that perfectly clear?"

"Yes, sir. Thank you, sir."

Thinking his promise of silence had won him a pardon, Ben felt relieved. But his elation quickly withered when the voice said, "There is one last thing that must be done."

"What's that, sir?"

"Let's call it an insurance policy of sorts to make sure you keep your promise of silence."

Ben started to shake. "Please, don't hurt me. I give you my word. I will never talk about this!"

A guard wheeled over a table that held a battery and two jumper cables. As the guard approached Ben, Ben started to wail. Two guards stood on either side of Ben and they held him down as the guard attached the jumper cables to a sensitive part of Ben's naked body. The guard flipped a switch and a fiery jolt of electricity ripped through Ben's body. Another blazing jolt and Ben fainted.

"Take them home," the voice said, and the shadowy figure exited the skybox.

# Thirty-Three

Isabelle stood at the sink, washing dishes. She stiffened when she saw Clem walk past the kitchen window as he mowed the lawn. He wore his weeklong wardrobe, a faded and torn plaid shirt, threadbare baggy jeans, muddy boots, and that filthy Chicago Cubs ball hat.

Watching him plow through her flower garden with his ancient lawnmower, Isabelle's internal fury exploded into a homicidal hunger.

"Did Daddy mow over your flowers again, Momma?" Abby asked as she selected a bright, red crayon for her homework assignment.

"Yes, dear, he did," Isabelle said through clenched teeth.

"Why does Daddy do that, Momma?"

"You would have to ask him that question, sweetheart."

"Abby, Eden, Rick, Abby, Eden, Rick," Abby said, paying close attention not to color out of the lines. "All our names have four letters in them. Why is that, Momma?"

Isabelle smiled. Her beautiful youngest child's curiosity pleased her. Her persistent chatter, however, often wore on Isabelle's fragile nerves.

Isabelle closed the curtain to block her view of Clem.

"Did you do that on purpose, Momma?"

"Did I do what on purpose, Abby?"

"Did you name all of us with four letters, or did Daddy?"

Isabelle heard the lawnmower stop and her stomach clinched.

"Your Daddy named all of you children," Isabelle said, emptying the dishwater.

"How come he named all of us with just four letters, Momma?"

In an unguarded moment, Isabelle said angrily, "Because, Abby, your daddy only knows four letter words that contain one syllable."

Clem opened the kitchen door and kicked his boots against the door frame, throwing mud and grass all over the entrance floor. He went to the refrigerator and got a cold beer. As he passed Isabelle on his way to the living room, he roughly pinched her cheek with his dirty fingers.

Clem grabbed the T.V. remote, threw himself down on the sofa, and laid his booted feet over the armrest. While he gulped his beer, he watched baseball on television.

"Are you nearly finished with your flower book, Abby?" Isabelle asked as she peeled potatoes.

"No, Momma. I just started on it today."

"When is your assignment due?"

"Tomorrow morning," Abby said sheepishly.

"Oh, Abby!" Isabelle said, wiping her hands on a clean towel. She looked at the papers with the colorless flower pictures that Abby had scattered across the table and she said, "This could take you a week to complete."

Abby hung her head.

"Well, I guess I will have to help you with this," Isabelle said. "After dinner, we will work together until we get you caught up."

Abby jumped out of her chair and she hugged her mother. "You are the best Momma in the whole wide world!" she said.

Isabelle smiled and smoothed her daughter's wild blonde hair. She adored her precocious last child. And Abby was the last child Isabelle would ever have.

Over the years, Isabelle tried to insulate her children from Clem's brutality and his rudeness. Unfortunately, Rick had inherited a number of Clem's ugly traits. She still held out hope that Rick would become the good person she knew he was capable of being.

"Where's Dad?!" Rick shouted as he burst into the kitchen.

Clem woke up with a frown on his creased face. "In here," he grumbled.

Rick ran into the living room. "There's a dude up at the station who wants to talk to you!"

"Who is he?" Clem asked, rubbing the sleep from his eyes.

"Here's his card," Rick said, and he handed Clem a fancy, embossed, black business card with a border of glass stones.

Clem handed it back. "I ain't got my glasses on. Read it to me."

"It says, 'Armand Everstrong, C.E.O. Black Crown Oil Company, Veracruz, Mexico.' And there's a telephone number here. Dad, do you think those stones on the card are real diamonds?"

Clem sat up. He reached in his torn shirt pocket and pulled out a cheap pair of readers. He looked the card over front and back and he rubbed his calloused finger over the stones.

"Nah, Rick, them ain't diamonds. But it's a nice card."

Rick felt certain his dad wouldn't know a diamond if he saw one.

Eavesdropping on their conversation, Isabelle timidly spoke up, "What would a man from Veracruz, Mexico, want to see you about, Clem?"

Every word spoken by Isabelle inflamed Clem. He took offense even when none was intended. He hauled himself off the couch and headed toward her. Isabelle shrunk and backed away.

Rick intercepted his father by saying, "The guy's waiting for you at the station, Dad."

Clem's glare at Isabelle declared he would not forget her perceived snub.

Clem threw the business card on the coffee table. He grabbed his filthy ball hat, put it on his head, and pulled it down to ride on his large ears. He and Rick left the house.

Isabelle picked up the card and looked at the stones. She counted 65 stones on the border, and atop the arches of the crown were four pink stones, similarly sized to those on the border. She slipped the card in her pocket, hoping to have enough money hidden from Clem to have three cheap pairs of earrings made, one for herself, one for Eden, and one for Abby. But that would have to wait. Judge Caulder had put his house on the market a week ago. She hadn't told Clem yet. She feared his reaction when he learned she was now unemployed.

The telephone on the kitchen wall rang and Abby jumped up to get it.

"Hello," she said.

"Hello, Abby! It's Eden."

"Momma, its Eden!" Abby said, jumping up and down.

Isabelle rushed over to the telephone and held the receiver so Abby could hear too.

"Eden, darling! It's so good to hear your voice!"

"It's wonderful to hear yours and Abby's too. How are you both?"

"Me and Momma are just fine, Eden," Abby said and she giggled. "Where are you?"

"I'm in Hong Kong, Abby."

"Where's Hong Kong?" Abby asked. "Do they have kids there? What kind of food do those people that live there eat? Do they have dogs? I like dogs. 'Course, I like cats too. But cats scratch and dogs don't. Well, sometimes, they do."

"We'll discuss all that later, Abby," her mother said gently, knowing her time to speak with Eden was very limited.

Abby stuck her lip out, but her mother's soothing petting eased Abby's agitation.

"How have you been, sweetheart?" Isabelle asked.

"School's hectic. But the country here is so beautiful. I wish you and Abby could see it."

"Are the people on the ship nice to you?"

"Yes, Mother, they are."

"I'm so glad to hear that."

"I just wanted to call and tell you I am fine and to hear how all of you are doing. But I can't talk much longer."

"Take all the time you need," Isabelle heard a young man say in the background.

"Is someone there with you, Eden?"

"Yes, Mother. He's my friend, Alan Honnecut. It's his phone I'm using."

"Well, tell your friend thank you from Abby and me for letting you call home."

"My mother says thank you, Alan, for letting me call home."

"Tell her she is most welcome," Alan said.

Eden relayed Alan's comment.

"Despite Alan's generosity, I'm not going to run up anymore overseas minutes on his phone. I love you both so much! Goodbye for now."

"Goodbye, Eden," Isabelle and Abby said in chorus. "We love you too!"

Feeling light as air, Isabelle hung up the phone.

"Eden sounds happy, doesn't she, Momma?" Abby asked.

"Yes, darling, she does," Isabelle said, silently attributing Eden's happiness to Alan Honnecut, whoever he was.

# Thirty-Four

As Clem and Rick came around the side of the gas station, they saw a handsome, well-dressed man standing next to a gleaming, black, stretch limousine. In his manicured hands, the man carried a hand-tooled leather briefcase. His driver was seated behind the wheel, waiting patiently for his employer to conclude his work.

Clem sauntered over to where the man waited. "Whatta ya want?" he asked rudely.

The man pulled out a fancy, jeweled business card and held it out to Clem.

"Good afternoon, Mr. Owens," he said with a heavy accent. "My name is Armand Everstrong, and I represent Black Crown Oil Company."

"I already got one of them cards. Are them real diamonds on that card?" Rick asked eagerly.

Seeing Rick's greedy anticipation, Everstrong said, "I am sorry to say they are not diamonds."

"Do I need to stay for this, Dad?" Rick asked flatly.

"No, Rick. Go ahead and close down for the day."

"It was a pleasure to meet you," Everstrong said.

"Yeah, same to you," Rick said and he walked away.

Mr. Armstrong smiled and put his card back in his briefcase. "I have an important matter to discuss with you, Mr. Owens. May we go inside and use your office?"

Clem laughed in the man's face. "My office, you say? Look at this place. You really think we got an office in there?" he asked, sweeping his arm toward the crumbling gas station.

"Perhaps we might conduct our business in your home behind the station?" Everstrong asked pleasantly.

Clem bristled. "Wait a minute here. How do you know I live back there?" he asked, throwing his thumb over his left shoulder.

"I have a copy of your deed in my briefcase. In fact, that is why I am here today," Everstrong said politely.

"What the hell? You got no business having a copy of my deed."

"Actually, your deed is a matter of public record."

"That may be true. But why would a fancy dude like you want a copy of my deed?"

"I am here today to discover if you might be interested in selling your combined properties to Black Crown Oil Company."

"You're kidding, right?"

"On the contrary, sir, my employer is very interested in purchasing your business and your home," Everstrong said, and he recognized the dollar signs flashing in Clem's eyes.

Clem's shoulders rolled back and he said smugly, "Depends on how much money you're talking about."

Everstrong handed Clem a document. "This is the current market value of both your properties. On the bottom line is my employer's bid. As you can see, we are being very generous."

Clem was shocked to see the amount of the purchase price tripled the appraisal figure he had attained just one month ago for a loan he had taken out on the properties.

"Is this amount right?" Clem asked, astonished.

"Yes, that is our offer."

"What do you want with a rundown gas station and a broken-down old house?"

"My employer did not divulge his plans to me."

"If I decide to do this, when would you want possession?"

"As soon as possible."

"You mean, like today?!" Clem said incredulously.

"Well, I do have the documents with me. But I strongly suggest you take the papers to an attorney of your choice and have him look the agreement over."

"Let me see them papers," Clem said greedily.

"I caution you, Mr. Owens, the document you will sign is legal and binding. In all good faith, I feel I must insist you obtain proper legal counsel before signing the agreement."

"Are you saying I can't read?" Clem asked hotly.

"Not at all, sir."

"Then give me them papers!"

"As you wish," Everstrong said, and he opened his briefcase and brought out a neatly folded document.

Clem skimmed through the ample document.

"Where do I sign?" he asked.

"Again, I suggest you see an attorney before signing."

"Give me the pen!"

"If you insist on doing this today, we must locate a notary public. And we will need witnesses to agree to our signatures."

"There's a notary at the Maramount State Bank," Clem said. The bank had used the notary when Clem had signed for his loan.

"They'll probably be able to dig us up some witnesses too."

"If it pleases you, we can go together in my car," Everstrong said.

Clem's eyes lit up. "I never rode in one of them there limos. Guess I better get used to this good life, huh?"

Everstrong opened the door of the limousine and Clem ducked his head and started inside. Rick yelled, "Where you going, Dad?"

"I'm going to go buy me one of them Escalades that I've been wanting forever!" Clem said, and he got in the limousine and they drove away.

At Maramount State Bank, Clem signed his name on the document with a flourish. The notary, Mary Sturgeon, signed after Clem and Everstrong. The witnesses were Lawrence Emerson, the bank president, and Dale Bond, the executive vice president.

The stretch limousine and the smell of foreign money brought out the executives like vultures to a kill.

Everstrong excused himself and walked away to make a quick phone call. When he returned, he said, "I have just spoken to my employer and the money for this purchase has been sent through wire transfer to your personal bank account, Mr. Owens."

Gina Garrison, a young bank teller, brought Lawrence Emerson a slip of paper.

"Here is your deposit slip, Clem," Emerson said.

Clem looked at the deposit slip and he nearly leaped for joy. In his hand, he held proof of more money than he would earn in the rest of his lifetime.

"It has been very nice doing business with you, Mr. Owens," Everstrong said, and he held out his hand.

Clem shook the man's hand. Everstrong then shook hands with Lawrence Emerson, who spent the next few minutes touting his business acumen, and Dale Bond, who nearly bowed at the waist with adoration.

"May I drop you off somewhere, Mr. Owens?" Everstrong asked.

"You sure can. Hobermeier Cadillac, here I come!"

# Thirty-Five

After driving around town all afternoon to show off his brand-new, diamond-white Escalade to his envious friends, Clem carefully and slowly backed the vehicle alongside the gas station, across the lawn, and parked in front of the house.

Clem got out of the vehicle and walked around it with his chest stuck out like a bloated king.

The screen door slammed open and Rick exclaimed, "Great-looking delivery wagon you got there!"

"You're not hauling any of those old car parts in this like you did the old truck."

"Just kidding, Dad. Say, how did you ever come up with enough dough to afford this?"

"I sold the gas station and the house today," Clem said proudly.

The smile melted off Rick's face. "You did what?!"

"I sold this old place lock, stock, and barrel!"

"But…how are we going to make a living now?" Rick asked anxiously. "And where are all of us going to live?"

"I was about to ask those two questions myself," Isabelle said sadly, standing on the stoop by the front door.

"I don't intend to 'make a living' anymore," Clem said arrogantly. "And as for a place to live, we'll rent an apartment somewhere. I'm through with mowing and painting and fixing up."

"Will there be enough money left over for Eden and Abby to go to college?" Isabelle asked.

Isabelle could see Clem's temper flare.

"Forget college. Let them girls get married, like you did," he said smartly.

"Rick, ask your father where he thinks you will find work now," Isabelle challenged.

Rick looked at his dad. "Yeah, Dad. Where will I work?"

"Rick, you're a smart boy. You'll do okay," Clem said, and he playfully socked Rick's beefy shoulder.

"I lost my job this week with Judge Caulder," Isabelle said flatly.

Clem looked startled. He hadn't counted on that.

"You'll get another job," he said, and his gaze at her narrowed threateningly.

Isabelle turned around and she went back inside the house.

"Rick, would you like to take this beauty for a drive around the block?" Clem asked, placating.

"No, thanks," Rick said flatly. He pulled his long hair back and ponytailed it with a rubber band. "I'm going over to Gina's," he said and walked away.

Like a thundercloud, Clem entered the house. He walked over to Isabelle who was sitting at the kitchen table, reading the want ads in the newspaper. Clem grabbed the newspaper, crumpled it in his hands, and threw it in her face.

"Rick's pissed off at me because of what you said. Are you happy now?" Clem asked, his enraged face inches from Isabelle's.

"Do you really care whether I am happy?" Isabelle asked indifferently.

Clem wanted to knock her across the room, but her coldness puzzled him.

"What were you looking in the newspaper for?" he asked, his teeth clenched.

"For a job. And for an apartment."

"You look for a job. I'll find all of us an apartment."

"I don't get a say in where we will live?"

"Are you trying to make me madder than I already am?" he asked, moving his unshaven face so close to hers, she could smell his normal stench.

"Me? Make you mad? I wouldn't have to try too hard to accomplish that now, would I, Clem?"

Clem grabbed her by the forearm and threw her across the room. "Smart off again, wiseass," he said, and he walked over and kicked her thigh.

Isabelle sat unaffected on the floor. Clem backed away, knowing if he attacked her again, he wouldn't stop until he'd beaten her to death.

Isabelle raised her gaze slowly and she looked at Clem.

"I want a divorce," she said softly.

Clem laughed so loud, Isabelle had to put her hands over her ears.

"You're crazy, woman! You and them two girls got nowhere to go. And Rick sure as hell ain't gonna leave me."

"Don't be too sure," Isabelle said, and she smiled wickedly.

Clem backed down. This bolder Isabelle he didn't know.

"I'll go find us an apartment right now. You get our stuff packed up. But don't bring any of that junk your grandma left you to the new place."

Isabelle sat on the floor, looking balefully at him.

"I heard you, and so did everyone else on the block."

"You better watch your smart mouth."

"You think I'm smart?" Isabelle asked, and she laughed at him.

Clem doubled up his fist and lunged at her. But Isabelle moved like a gazelle and avoided his punch. She ran over to the knife drawer, pulled out a long, serrated blade, and swung it at him.

Bewildered, Clem stood looking at her for a silent moment. Then, he laughed.

"Nice try," he said, and he headed out the door.

# Three Weeks Later

Isabelle, Abby, Rick, and Clem were uncomfortably situated in the two-bedroom apartment that Clem had rented for them. The apartment was in a housing complex located next to the railroad tracks on Logan Street and across the boulevard from the Hillside Slaughterhouse.

The challenges imposed by living with four people in such cramped quarters proved enormous. There was a constant stampede of people needing to use the one tiny bathroom. Only three people at a time could eat in the small kitchen. The living room held a small sofa, a chair that was missing its legs, and the T.V. set on a pressed wood stand.

The bedrooms accommodated only one bed and a small dresser. When they moved out of the house, Rick, Isabelle, and Abby were forced to sacrifice items they cherished. Clem threw most of Eden's belongings in the trash. Isabelle was able to smuggle a few of Eden's things in with hers. Clem kept everything he owned.

Isabelle reluctantly forfeited all the lovely china and handmade quilts that she inherited from her grandmother to a young couple who had moved in down the road from the gas station. Rick moved his expensive stereo system over to Gina's place, since he would now have to sleep on the sofa. Abby tearfully gave Sunshine, her beloved stuffed animal, and her paper-doll collection to her friend, Krissie.

The dirty Escalade sat curbside on the street in front of the apartment building where Clem spent most of his day sacked out on the sofa in the living room. Isabelle bumped shoulders with Rick as she headed into the cramped kitchen.

"Did you put your dirty clothes in the basket in the hallway?" Isabelle asked her son.

"Yes, Mom, I did," Rick said disagreeably.

"I'm sorry, Rick," Isabelle said, understanding her son's angst at having to live in such tight quarters.

"It's not your fault. You know, I never thought I could hate anything as much as I do that Escalade," he said bitterly.

"It's not the vehicle you hate, Rick. It's the greed and the hardship that came with it."

"I wish we were back home and we still had the gas station."

"I thought I would never say this, but I wish we were back there too."

The telephone rang and Isabelle answered it. The man on the other end identified himself. Isabelle recognized Harry Bartell's voice. She had recently applied with Mr. Bartell to work as a clerk at his jewelry store.

"Hello, Mrs. Owens," he said. "I have some very good news for you. I wonder if you would mind stopping by my shop sometime today."

Isabelle's heart fluttered. She hoped his intention was to offer her a job. It would mean so much to her not to have to earn her money on her knees.

"I can be there at one o'clock this afternoon, sir," she said.

"That will be fine. See you then."

"Who was that?" Clem asked sleepily from the sofa.

"Judge Caulder," Isabelle lied. "Maybe he changed his mind and he wants me to come back to work for him."

Isabelle went into the bedroom and changed into her nicest dress. She applied a little makeup, brushed her hair, stepped into her best high-heel shoes, and headed out the backdoor.

Clem heard the backdoor creak open and he yelled, "You better be home in time to cook supper. And it better not be meatloaf!"

At five o'clock that evening, Isabelle walked into the apartment. She wore a lovely new dress and fancy high-heel shoes. She was carrying a designer handbag. In her newly pierced ears dangled tiny diamond earrings. By the look of her beautifully manicured hands and updo, it was clear she'd just come from the beauty parlor.

Clem raised up and he looked at his wife. "What the hell have you done?" he screeched.

"I spent the last of your money," she said, and she laughed until tears streamed down her face.

Clem bolted off the sofa and grabbed her by her forearms. "If you did, I'll kill you!"

Isabelle shook his hands off of her. "The look on your face is priceless!"

Clem rushed into the bedroom and he checked the strongbox where he kept what remained of the money he had from the sale. The lock didn't look like it had been tampered with, but he took the key out of his pocket and he opened the box and counted the remaining $75,000. Relief swept over him like a flood. When he went back into the living room, he saw Isabelle packing a battered suitcase with her few remaining personal items. She took the suitcase into Abby and Eden's room and she packed up their things next to hers.

"Where the hell do you think you're going?" Clem asked, and he picked up the suitcase and emptied the contents on the floor.

"I filed for divorce today, Clem. I'm leaving you and I hope I never see you again," Isabelle said, and she stepped over the pile of clothing and headed for the door.

"And just where do you think you're going?"

"To Judge Caulder's former house. Two hours ago, I accepted a job with the man who just bought the house. He's asked me to live there and act as caretaker for the estate. He said the girls and Rick, if he chooses, may also live there."

"You're full of shit!" Clem said incredulously.

"We'll see about that."

"Who is this guy?"

"He's a real estate mogul who lives abroad. Sometimes lives change in the twinkling of an eye. And I believe your due may have arrived today, Clem."

"What the hell are you yammering about now?"

"When I walked across the street toward this cesspool a moment ago, I was approached by two well-dressed men who presented badges from the E.P.A. They asked if I knew you. I told them, at the moment, you and I were related. They said they had some business to discuss with you. You know what the E.P.A. is, don't you, Clem?"

"What is it, dammit?"

"It's the Environmental Protection Agency. I asked the men what they wanted. They said there was a clause in the agreement you signed with Black Crown Oil that says you take all legal and financial responsibility for removing the underground gas tanks at the gas station."

"That could cost a fortune!" Clem said.

"I expect the money you have in your lockbox will just about pay for it. Goodbye, Clem," she said.

Abby scuttled out of her room, "Momma, you're beautiful!"

"Come on, Abby," Isabelle said, and she took her daughter's hand and walked out the door.

In the ancient elevator, Isabelle touched the diamond earrings in her ears. She had identical pairs made for Eden and Abby in her purse. When Isabelle had gone to the jewelry store earlier that day, Mr. Murray mentioned he had a customer in the store who was looking for a housekeeper. Murray said he knew she had cleaned for the Caulders, so he suggested to the man he might like to speak to her. Isabelle was very impressed with the tall, good-looking man with the kind voice. They spoke privately for an hour. When Isabelle left the store, she had a signed contract that stated how much she would earn, which far exceeded Isabelle's wildest dreams, gave her a permanent new home for both herself and her children, and paid for a college education for Eden and Abby.

When Isabelle asked who her kind benefactor was, the well-dressed man simply stated, "An equalizer." Not knowing what that meant, Isabelle asked no further questions.

Isabelle clutched her purse close to her body and she audibly thanked the good Lord for freeing her from Clem and for providing her with a life she would never have allowed herself to hope for. She also said a silent prayer for her new benefactor.

# Epilogue

A long, black limousine with darkened windows stopped next to the curb at busy Maramount Airport. Jax and Eden were seated inside.

"Thank you, Jax, for everything," Eden said.

"You're welcome, Eden. Will you continue your studies, or will you return home?"

"Thanks to you, home has a whole new meaning now. But I intend to continue my studies. I hope I do well enough to be accepted at an accredited college." Eden searched Jax's unexpressive face.

"What happened to Clayton and Ben?"

His dark gaze held hers. "Do you really want to know?"

"I don't think I do. I promise I will never tell anyone about you. Or about what happened. Is Jax Greeley your real name?"

"Does it matter what my name is?"

"I guess not. I hope, if I am ever in trouble again, you will show up and rescue me."

"I have something for you, Eden." Jax said, and he reached into his briefcase and brought out an envelope and handed it to her.

"What's this?" she asked.

"Open it."

Eden tore open the envelope, and as she read the enclosed letter, her eyes got big and filled with tears.

"Am I reading this correctly?" she asked.

"What does it say?" Jax asked slyly.

Eden swallowed around the lump in her throat. "It says I have an all-expenses paid scholarship for four years at the University of Illinois." Tears ran down her flushed cheeks. "Oh, Jax. Thank you so much!"

Jax handed Eden a piece of folded paper. "About rescuing you again, if you are ever in serious trouble, call this number."

Eden hugged Jax and she kissed his cheek. "You are my knight in shining armor," she said.

"Have a good life, Eden," Jax said, and he opened the backdoor of the limousine and got out. He walked forward and tapped on the driver's window. "See that this young lady gets home safely," he said.

\* \* \* \* \*

Jax sat impatiently in the cockpit of his sleek black jet while two small planes ahead of him prepared to take off. He needlessly rechecked his Before Takeoff Checklist, making sure his flight controls were correct, the auxiliary fuel pump was off, the instruments and radios were set, the directional gyro was set, and the altimeter was set.

Most men with Jax's wealth would hire a personal pilot. But Jax thrived on being in control.

"Tower to Sky Eagle, you may takeoff," the female air-traffic controller said seductively.

"Thank you, Tower," Jax said, and he revved the engines, sped down the runway, and pulled back on the throttle. He glanced down one last time at the city of Maramount.

His cellphone buzzed and he saw a familiar oversees phone number.

"Hi, Erik," Jax said.

"Are you on your way home?"

"I am. I just left Maramount. I'm flying nonstop, so I should be home in about 12 hours."

"Did everything go as you planned?"

"Everything went perfectly."

"Glad to hear it."

"Do you have any news for me?" Jax asked.

"I assume you're asking about Mai Ling?"

"I am."

"It took some doing, but I finally found her."

"And did she agree to do as I asked?"

"She did, but there is one condition."

255

Jax laughed. "I expected there would be. So, what does she want?"

"Mai Ling wants the same monetary arrangement you made with Sandreen."

Jax expected Sandreen's former roommate at the brothel to be difficult.

"I said I thought you would agree to her demands. But she would have to prove herself first," Erik said.

"Did she have the plastic surgery?"

"She did."

"I hope you used gentle persuasion."

"The promise of wealth was all the enticing she needed."

Jax laughed. "I'm certainly glad you're on my side, old friend!"

"You haven't asked me the most important question."

"You're right. I haven't. Was the surgery a success?"

"Let me put it this way. The woman who walked out of the private hospital in Zurich yesterday looks, speaks, and smells exactly like Sandreen."

Jax felt his pants tighten across his crotch.

"Would you like to speak to her?" Erik asked.

"In a minute. I have a job for you."

"Okay."

"Do you remember John Trevor?"

"Yes, I remember him."

"Dig through his past. I want to know every person he's screwed, both sexually and financially."

"Will do."

"Now put Mai Ling on the phone."

"Hello, darling," Mai Ling said.

Jax pictured Sandreen's slim waist, her rounded breasts, and her pouty butt.

"I'm anxious to see you," he said.

"I promise you, Jax darling, this will be a night for you to remember."

"I'm counting on it," Jax said, and his jet streaked across the sky toward Shanghai.

CPSIA information can be obtained
at www.ICGtesting.com
Printed in the USA
BVHW020849030223
R14605000001B/R146050PG657534BVX00006B/1